A
Letter
in the
Wall

A
LETTER
in the
WALL

A Novel

Eileen Brill

Published by SparkPress, a BookSparks imprint,
A division of SparkPoint Studio, LLC
Phoenix, Arizona, USA, 85007
www.gosparkpress.com

Published 2022
Printed in the United States of America
Print ISBN: 978-1-68463-133-9
E-ISBN: 978-1-68463-134-6

Library of Congress Control Number: 2021923637

Book design by Stacey Aaronson

In memory of my mother, Shelia Eskin

1

June 7, 1971

Oklahoma

JOAN SAT AT THE DESK IN HER DIMLY LIT APARTMENT AS THE last vestiges of summer daylight faded away. She reached into the drawer for her Mont Blanc pen, lifted the receiver from the telephone, and rested it on the desk. She did not want any disruptions as she wrote, though no one typically called her at this late hour anyway. Lifting her lit cigarette from the ashtray, she straightened her posture and wound her neck in circles to ease the tightness before sitting back in her chair to collect her thoughts. For several minutes she stared out the window at nothing in particular; then, resolute, she took a last drag on the cigarette, jammed it into the ashtray, and began writing:

To: Sheriff Maghan, Midwest City Police Department
Midwest City, Oklahoma

And anyone else who cares, she thought.

> *I am writing you because I fear, as I tried to*
> *explain this morning in the parking lot at Diamond*
> *Ranch, that I may not live to see tomorrow. I have been*
> *threatened by my former business partner, Chuck*
> *Galloway, a man with whom I believed I was entering*

*into a legitimate business relationship over a year ago,
only to find out he is a liar, a cheat, a predator, and an
all-around evil human being. So I want the truth out
there. If I die, I want the person responsible for my
death to be identified, arrested, taken into custody,
tried, and put in prison for the rest of his life. Without
the information I'm providing you here, I doubt there
would be any justice; too many folks protect each other
around here. I can't quite figure out why or how
Galloway has the good reputation he's got, given what
I'd heard about him in Little Rock and what he has put
me through here in Oklahoma, but if I live, and as long
as I live, I will fight him with every bone, muscle, and
cell in my body to get what I rightly deserve.*

*Chuck will say a lot of horrible things about me, but
he's lying to cover his own hide. Do not believe this
man or give him even one ounce of respect. He deserves
none.*

She stopped writing and stared at her pen, a gift from her
grandmother for Christmas in 1930. *Such a finely crafted instrument,* she thought. That was the world she came from, not here.
She continued writing.

*Here's the whole story, start to finish (in case this
is the end).*

Joan wished she hadn't left her typewriter back in Little Rock. It
was so much more time-consuming to organize her thoughts
and put them all down coherently in longhand.

At just before ten thirty, she signed the letter and sat back to
reflect on all she had written. She moved one hand around in an
orbit from the wrist, flexing her fingers in and out, and then did

the same with the other hand. She was feeling the achy stiffness of the beginnings of arthritis. She thought about her high school days, some thirty-plus years ago, when she would write reports longhand. She never quite saw the point of that kind of effort.

Joan removed another cigarette from the pack, noticing it was the last. She was tense with ambivalence and reverted to the shameful insecurity of second-guessing her judgment that had dogged her younger days. *Does this make sense? Am I insane?* As she lit the cigarette, she reconsidered why she had initially felt it would be a good idea to mail the letter, now wondering if her fear tonight was nothing more than paranoia and she would wake up tomorrow morning and head straight over to the sheriff to have that discussion he promised her.

"No, no, no, no, no!" she said out loud. "Mail this, dammit!" She recognized there was no downside beyond redundancy in sending the letter to the sheriff; it would just reinforce what she'd tell him the next day, providing she survived the night. Anyway, it was good that she got it all down in writing. She took a long drag of the cigarette and sat back in her desk chair, scanning her living room. Near the front door were her barn boots, crusted with mud and strands of hay, the ones she wore when she needed to put in some face time at the Diamond Ranch Sale Barn, typically on days when Chuck was not there. She rarely cooked in her galley kitchen and never sat at the small, round table situated next to it. Instead, she'd pop in for lunch at Freida's Country Diner or grab a sandwich at the local deli and eat it in her car while transporting horses. She might pick up barbecue on the road, buying enough for several people, and bring it to the Barn to feed whoever might be there on any given evening. When she ate dinner at home, it was takeout, and often while making phone calls to her kids or watching *Mannix* or *The Carol Burnett Show* or, her newest favorite, *The Mary Tyler Moore*

Show. Her apartment was not for entertaining; it was her office, her command central away from Chuck and the staff at the Sale Barn, and somewhere she could rest her mind and body most nights in preparation for each new day.

The apartment itself was fine, nothing special, certainly not the kind of home she was used to living in, but at the time she'd signed the lease, she had meant it to be temporary, two years max, just to get the business up and running.

What the hell was I thinking? Running a business with such a lowly, uncouth, and despicable person? I don't need him, never did.

A breeze blew in from the window over her desk. It was warm, but she shuddered nonetheless, as if this town were giving her a final warning. She knew what people said about her: that she was high-strung, overreactive. The sheriff himself had called her "pugnacious," saying the word with a chuckle as if she were supposed to see the humor as well. She knew he was not referring to some sort of fighter's instinct but, rather, that she was pushy and unrelenting in an unreasonable way. Still, she took that as a badge of honor given her tendency to dive into and embrace conflict rather than avoid it. She knew how to get what she wanted, only because she had learned to stop caring what people thought. In reality, Joan felt she was outgoing, friendly, and generous, even to folks she barely knew. She had charisma. So what if she knew how to use it?

She jammed the cigarette, only half-smoked, into an ashtray, opened a drawer in her desk, and reached inside for a large manila envelope. She put the letter, all twelve pages, into the envelope and sealed it with Scotch tape, affixing more postage than she knew it could possibly require; it was better—safer—to put it in the mailbox than to risk walking to the police station at this late hour. What would she say to the officers anyway? "Here's my story in case I am killed." They would just take the letter and say something patronizing like, "Go back to your apartment, Mrs. Dumann. Take a nice, long bath and go to bed." They certainly would not provide her with any protection for the night.

Stepping out into the musty night air, Joan could smell what this town just outside of Oklahoma City was made of: a juxtaposition of dirt roads (it had been nicknamed "Mudwest City" in its early days); paved residential streets and interstate highways running out of its center; horse manure; neatly planned homes on a former prairie; a shopping center with one of everything you need: a movie theatre, shoe store, dry goods place, furniture emporium, hamburger joint, and on and on. It had been the nation's "model planned city" when it was developed in the 1940s. *City?* Joan mused to herself. *Some city.*

Like everywhere else in the country these days, people were chatting about the Vietnam War, hippies, Kent State, Armstrong on the moon, Woodstock, the Manson murders. But what folks here cared about—*truly* cared about more than anything—were land, family, and God. In that order. Land was sacred out here. It defined a person, formed one's identity, and people's lives depended not only on what they grew and raised on that land but also how solidly they could hold onto their acreage and successfully keep it out of the hands of anyone who wasn't kin. Joan had grown up outside of Philadelphia and raised her own family in Pennsylvania, Arizona, and New Jersey, always valuing the freedom she had to move, buy, sell, change, add, downsize, or replace. Land, or rather the dwelling that sat upon it, represented to the world who she was and what she had, but Joan had little to no emotional attachment to property itself. Her family—her four children and her husband— had always been important to her of course, though at times she felt betrayed and challenged by them. And God? Well, God was something Joan could never quite accept as anything more than the default explanation for whatever people didn't understand.

She arrived at the mailbox one street over from her apartment complex. As she opened the slot, Joan noticed two figures walking toward her in the dark. They were still a half-block away, but near enough that if they wanted to reach her, they could. She thought better of dropping in the letter and spun on her heel, rushing back toward her apartment.

Once inside, Joan turned the lock on the doorknob, slid the chain lock into place, threw the envelope on her desk, and headed into the kitchen. She plunked a couple ice cubes in a glass and added one inch of Jack Daniels. Reaching into the refrigerator for a bottle of Coke, she noticed she was low on eggs, milk, and lunch meat. She topped her glass with the soda.

Leaning against the kitchen counter, Joan took a sip and relished the warmth as the fused liquids coated her throat and calmed her nerves. She stared at the envelope on the desk. Would the hours she'd just put into reconstructing a few months' worth of events be for naught, or would someone take her seriously? *I don't trust the sheriff.* She knew what she needed to do. She took one more sip of her drink, poured the rest down the drain, and made a beeline for the envelope. She sat down at her desk, grabbed her engraved, sterling silver letter opener—given to her by her late husband as one of several fiftieth birthday gifts—and quickly opened the envelope and removed the contents. She took a new envelope from the desk drawer and placed the pages into it; then she reached for her pen and began writing out a different addressee. She affixed postage and propped the envelope against her desk lamp. She would mail the letter tomorrow.

Satisfied with her decision, Joan headed into the bathroom for a shower.

The warm water running down her body provided such instantaneous relief to her tension that she momentarily considered switching to a bath in order to fully bask in the comfort. But she remembered that she was out of Calgon and made a mental note to buy more tomorrow.

Tomorrow. Her anxiety returned.

She turned off the shower and reached for her towel, wrapping it around her body as she walked into her bedroom. As she dried off, she noticed the hardback copy of Betty Freidan's *The Feminine Mystique* resting on her night table where it had sat, unread, since her eldest daughter, Barbara, had given it to her as a birthday gift months before. Barbara had recommended it strongly, believing it would resonate with her mother. *My daughter, the feminist,* Joan thought.

Joan's skin now felt sticky and uncomfortable. Crawling into bed nude, she tossed aside the bedspread and allowed the bedsheet to softly rest on her petite frame. She managed to relax, cool off, and eventually drift off to sleep.

As Joan slept, she dreamed of the bedridden woman—eyes closed, with an ashen face wet with sweat, and hair matted to her forehead. The woman's lips were whitish and dry, quivering with inaudible words that fell from them in broken pieces. Then a warm breeze blew in through the window, drying the sweat and making the woman's hair billow. Her eyelids opened slowly, as if she were coming out of a deliciously sweet slumber. Color returned to her complexion. Her ruby red lips formed into a broad, radiant smile, and her eyes were now clear and focused. The voice, melodic and rich: *Joan, my sweet little girl. Come to Mama.*

A knock on the door startled Joan from sleep. She sat up in bed and looked at her clock radio: 12:45. She'd been asleep close to an hour. She reached for her red housecoat and got up out of bed. Looking through the peephole, she recognized the two men in the hallway: Roy Herbert and Waylan Trust, her employees at the Diamond Ranch Sale Barn.

"Roy?" she called through the door.

"Yeah, it's me, Mrs. Dumann." He always called her *Mrs. Dumann*, despite the fact that she'd told him multiple times when they first met to call her Joan; she eventually stopped telling him. "Beg pardon, hope we didn't wake you. I'm here with Waylan. Do you mind if we talk to you about a few things?"

2

Ivyland, Bucks County,
Pennsylvania
June 1919

THREE-AND-A-HALF-YEAR-OLD JOAN SONDERSOHN SLOWLY
ascended the stairway of her family's summer home. She had
difficulty climbing without Mama or Dada holding her hand,
but she managed the steps one at a time, grasping each rung of
the railing as she moved upward, clutching her worn, stuffed
pony, Neigh-Neigh, in her other hand.

As she arrived at the top step, she could hear Mama's voice;
it sounded like Mama's voice, but soft, muffled. Another voice—
the lady in the white dress who had come to the front door very
early in the morning?—spoke above Mama's voice.

Joan stood in the hallway, just outside of Mama and Dada's
bedroom, looking in. The lady in the white dress now had a
piece of white material covering her face and gloves on her
hands. She wiped Mama's forehead and said, "There, there,
Jessie." Joan noticed Mama's necklace on the night table, the delicate, gold locket hanging off the side. The plant on the window
sill—Mama called it a "peace lily"—did not look as it did when
she let Joan water it, when Mama had energy and laughed about
the water spilling all over her dress. Now, the peace lily looked
much the way the locket did, as if it would topple over.

"Mama?" Joan said. Her voice sounded scratchy.

The lady in the white dress turned her head toward Joan. "Oh, sweetheart," she said through the gauze mask. "You mustn't be here now. Your mother needs to rest. Go now, okay?"

Joan could hear the lady's voice but couldn't see her lips. "A story, Mama?" Joan asked, looking toward her mother and ignoring the lady. "I want a story."

The lady stood up and walked toward Joan. She leaned out of the doorway and pulled her mask down. "Can someone please get the little girl?" she shouted toward the first floor.

Joan slipped past the lady and slowly walked toward her mother, clutching Neigh-Neigh tightly. Mama's lips trembled, and the skin on her face was shiny and wet. *Is that even Mama? She is sleeping where Mama always sleeps. Is Mama really sleeping, or is she awake?*

"Mama?" Joan whispered, her eyes filling with tears.

Just then, Joan heard someone coming up the stairs. She turned around to find a man she did not recognize; he wore big, black eyeglasses and held a big, black bag. His face was not friendly; he was scary. He stopped in the hallway and put on a white mask like the one the lady was wearing.

"Jesus," he said. He sounded angry. "Little girl, go downstairs with your father, okay?" He gently guided her into the hallway; then he turned and yelled to the first floor, "Mr. Sondersohn, your daughter is up here!"

Joan's father, Marcus, came running up the stairs. The man went into the bedroom and closed the door behind him. When Dada got to the top of the stairs, Joan thought he looked afraid. His face was scrunched up, and his mouth was wide open. He was breathing heavily. He scooped her up in his arms, kissed the top of her head.

"I want Mama. I want a story!" Joan said, now crying as she

arched her back away from her father's grasp and flailed her arms in the air in an attempt to get back to Mama.

"Your mama loves you, but she needs to rest now," her father said, squeezing her tightly. It didn't feel like the hugs Mama gave her; Joan felt trapped. He held her and carried her downstairs. "Aunt Helen will read you a story later."

"No!" Joan screamed. She twisted in his arms all the way down the stairs.

Near the front door, he put Joan down. "Go with Sonny and Mary." He opened the screen door for her to join her cousins, who were playing on the large, covered porch. The tips of willow trees on the front lawn gently touched its roof, and the wooden railing that ran across its three sides supported flower pots of petunias and zinnias. Across the narrow road from their three-acre property was a horse farm with a pond, where Joan loved to frolic with her cousins.

Joan looked at them, seven-year-old Mary Pruitt and three-year-old Sonny Pruitt, who sat cross-legged on the floor stacking wooden blocks. Mary's baby doll lay in her lap, and Sonny's teddy bear was facedown next to him. For a second, she considered joining them; it was always fun to stack the blocks, to try not to topple them as she and her cousins made tall towers or set up fences around their tiny toy farm animals. But she heard Dada's voice and turned back around. She stood just outside the screen door, squeezing Neigh-Neigh to her chest and watching as her father walked over to Aunt Helen and Uncle Fred, who sat on the living room sofa. He moved toward the wall behind them and looked at a picture of himself and Mama.

"It's hard to believe that three days ago she was a healthy, doting mother who read to her daughter. She volunteered, she cooked, laughed, danced."

Joan listened to his words, though she didn't completely

understand them. He spoke slowly and deeper than usual, as if he were tired, or maybe sad.

"This fever is going to be the death of her," her father said. Joan had heard this word *fever* many times in the last few days. Also, *flu* and a longer word she could not say or understand that ended with *enza*.

Her aunt, uncle, and father were quiet for a while. Marcus sat on an upholstered armchair with mahogany legs, its seat and back fabric of cream-and-red-colored roses and green leaves, the material fixed to the wood with brass studs. There was another matching chair next to it, and the sofa upon which Helen and Fred sat completed the set. Mama loved to sit on the sofa in the evenings, her bare feet curled up underneath her petite body, silently reading a book. Joan would crawl onto the sofa, her own book in hand, and sit beside Mama and ask for a story, shimmying close to her and listening to the rhythm of words that danced off her mother's lips. But Joan's favorite stories were the ones Mama told without any books, the ones about Sniff the bunny and Ribbons the kitten, who were best friends and shared many adventures. Often, Joan fell asleep in that very spot, hypnotized by Mama's gentle voice and the soft caress of her fingertips on Joan's arm.

As Joan watched her father, she longed for a story about Sniff and Ribbons.

Her father clasped his hands together, resting his elbows on his knees, his eyes tilted toward the floor. "I need to put Joan in your care for a little bit. Or a while," he said, without looking at them. "Please. I can't do this alone."

Aunt Helen rose and walked over to him. She put a hand on his shoulder. "You two will come live with me and Fred and the children, in the new house. We want you to, Marcus. She needs family. *You* need family."

Uncle Fred spoke. "Helen is right. The new house will be ready for move-in at the end of the summer, just before Mary starts at Abington Friends. There are bedrooms for both of you."

Marcus shook his head. "Helen, you'll have your hands full with Sonny, I couldn't ask you to. . . ."

Again, Aunt Helen placed a hand on her brother's shoulder. "How much of a problem could one more three-year-old be? Joanie and Sonny will be great playmates, just like they are here in Ivyland. It will be fine, Marcus." She patted his back.

He nodded, rubbing his eyes. Then he stood, walked toward the stairway, and disappeared to the second floor. Joan's eyes filled with water. She did not completely understand what she was hearing, but she could see that Dada was sad, just as she was. She thought perhaps he might go away. Maybe he didn't want to be her father anymore.

Aunt Helen came over, opened the screen door, and walked out onto the porch. Joan observed how the lacey edge of her yellow, high-waisted cotton dress swayed as she moved. Aunt Helen often kept a couple pieces of wrapped, hard candy in its large front pockets.

"Mary," she said, "I need you to mind Joanie, all right?"

"Yes, Mommy," Mary said.

Aunt Helen knelt down, adjusting her wire-framed glasses as she spoke to Joan. "Play with Sonny and Mary now." She wiped Joan's cheeks with both of her thumbs and cupped Joan's face with her hands. "Oh, dear. I know you can't understand all this," she said, pulling her niece into her arms.

Joan understood nothing. She didn't understand why Mama wouldn't get out of bed. She didn't understand what strangers with masks were doing with Mama. She didn't know why Dada wouldn't let her stay with Mama. She didn't feel like playing with Mary and Sonny.

But Aunt Helen took her hand and walked her over to her cousins and said, "Be a good girl." Then she reached into one of those large pockets and handed a piece of candy to each of the three children.

Joan took the candy and held it in her hand. She looked at the green cellophane wrapper, shiny and tempting. She obeyed her aunt and sat down, putting Neigh-Neigh on the floor beside her, and watched Sonny and Mary stack the blocks. Joan felt her bottom lip quiver as she watched her cousins laughing, enjoying themselves.

Then, for a reason she did not understand, she lifted her arm and swung at the blocks with the back of her hand. The blocks tumbled over, and some went flying clear across the porch.

Mary and Sonny looked at her, mouths open, eyes wide.

"Ma-ma!" Joan screamed as hard as she could.

3

THE LARGE, BLUE GRANITE COLONIAL WAS SET BACK QUITE
a distance from the street on a three-acre plot of maple, birch,
and tall cedar trees. A side porch ran the width of the house,
with three floors of windows framed by shutters adorned with
moon cutouts. Across the street was another house, a Victorian,
and three or four more large homes were also situated on the
one-mile stretch of road.

In her third-floor bedroom, sixteen-year-old Joan stood in
front of her bed, on which lay a large suitcase and a few piles of
clothes, mainly comfortable knee-length gaucho shorts, light-
weight blouses, gauzy pants, and a couple of sun dresses. She
wore her pale-blue cotton blouse with puffed short sleeves and
her cream-colored skirt with blue polka dots. Her low-heeled
blue leather shoes completed the look to her satisfaction, which
was well earned given the two hours it had taken her to choose
among her wardrobe options. Her outfit would be comfortable
for ambling about on the fields at Camp Green Meadows for the
scavenger hunt, part of the orientation for the oldest group of
campers. Joan was uncharacteristically looking forward to the
four-week sleepaway session, which would be her final summer
at the camp in Medford, New Jersey. She wasn't sure if her need
to get away from home had to do with how stifling her family

life felt of late or more because her sophomore year at Friends Central School had not gone well, academically or socially.

Joan had mostly enjoyed school right through eighth grade, when graduation was the culmination of her years at Abington Friends School. She appreciated the relatively short ride to the campus each day with her cousins, and she felt comfortable with the other students, most of whom she had known since nursery school, which she had started just after her family moved into the house in 1920. Joan had friends with whom she would go ice skating or to Farber's Pharmacy for an ice cream soda.

The comfort and familiarity came to an end once she entered Friends Central, in ninth grade. Kids she had known for years dispersed to different Quaker high schools—mostly Germantown Friends or Friends Select—or the local public high schools such as Cheltenham or Abington.

"Please, Father. I know two girls who are going to Cheltenham. What's wrong with that?" she begged Marcus in the spring of eighth grade. "Madeline's going there. It's close by. It's a very good school, you know."

"Now, Joan, it's all settled. Mary will be graduating from FCS in two months, Sonny will be heading there next year, and so will you. It's a family tradition after all; your Aunt Helen, Uncle Fred, and I are all alums."

Why did I think for a second that he—Marcus Sondersohn, Philly's well-known and beloved sports editor and drama critic— would give in to my one request? She knew how much her father cared about tradition and reputation.

The rides to and from Friends Central were agonizingly long for Joan, and she had to endure Sonny's endless chatter about his model airplanes or baseball or his hopes for admission to Penn or Swarthmore. She found it difficult to navigate the sprawling campus, and any self-confidence she might have hoped to possess was crushed by the fact that, for some reason, she could not mesh with any of the new kids she met. By her sophomore year, she had been so deluged with comparisons of her to Mary, and not in a positive way, that she considered doing something extreme just to get expelled from the school permanently.

"Joan, your uncle wants to leave in twenty minutes!" Helen yelled from the first floor.

"O-kaayy!" shouted Joan. She piled the clothing, along with a few other items, into the suitcase, pushed it closed, and grabbed her straw sun hat. She glanced at herself in the mirror above her dresser, scowling at the face looking back at her. *My skin looks ruddy. My hair's too thin.*

Joan climbed into the front passenger seat of her Uncle Fred's Studebaker.

"Did your father ever mention," asked her uncle, "that he and I know your bunkmate Emily's father from Swarthmore? Mr. Van Kirk and your father and I go way back."

She turned her face toward the window. *Father doesn't tell me anything. And why doesn't he ever drive me to camp, anyway?*

"We all had varsity letters in baseball," he continued.

Joan rolled her eyes, still peering out the window. *It figures. Quakers excel in sports. Quakers go to elite schools run by the Society of Friends. Quakers are charitable, outwardly focused. Quakers are humble. Perfect in their imperfection.* "Is that so?" she said, flatly.

"No negativity this summer, all right? Let folks know who you are. Be a leader. It's important to be direct in life. Otherwise, you'll get left out and overlooked."

"I suppose," Joan softly replied. She wondered if she could truly make an effort for once to get to know these kids, to not see them as the enemy, the competition, the epitome of what she felt she was not. As her uncle lectured on, Joan's mind strayed from the topic of camp and fitting in. She recalled the time Marcus sternly told her that she was too old to continue to call him "Dada" and needed to address him as "Father." She was five years old.

". . . and don't let other people make decisions for you," she heard her uncle say.

That's just how it goes, she thought.

Joan frequently had the feeling that, out of convenience or perhaps indifference on the part of the adults in her family, her opinions were rarely considered when it came to how she lived her life and utilized her spare time. She was sent to the same Quaker schools her cousins attended; Marcus insisted she participate in the same school activities as her cousins—tennis, glee club, model citizens club—regardless of her level of interest or aptitude; Helen passed on most of Mary's clothing to Joan, even though money never seemed to be a problem in the household; and, most importantly, everyone seemed to expect her to behave and react and socialize and feel and think in precisely the same manner as her cousins because, after all, the three of them had grown up under the same roof with the same rules and privileges. No, she thought, she would be making her own decisions at camp.

As the car pulled up the long, winding road to the camp, Joan could see Emily in the distance, surrounded by three or four other girls and one boy. Emily was talking to the kids with her arms moving in the air, her body full of that abundant energy she always seemed to possess.

Fred pulled up alongside a horse barn where three men in their twenties were loading suitcases onto a wagon hitched to a horse. He stopped the car, and one of the men walked over to him.

"Welcome to Camp Green Meadows!" he said enthusiastically as he bent down to look into the car. "Who do we have here?"

"Joan Sondersohn," she said. "Hi, Brett." She recognized the handsome groundskeeper from last summer. All the girls had a crush on him. It was rumored that, every night after the final bell rang for lights out, around ten o'clock, Brett would skinny-dip in the lake and then allow his body to air-dry as he lay on the bank under the moonlight. Last summer, Emily told a few girls in her bunk that she believed Brett had his eye on her. Such conceit made Joan's blood boil, yet, at the same time, Joan was envious of Emily's confident nature.

Looking out the window, Joan noticed one of the shy girls from her bunk last summer. "I'm going to say hello to a friend. Thanks for the ride, Uncle Fred. See you in four weeks." She hopped out of the car without hearing his good-bye.

After settling in their cabins, the older campers headed down to the patio outside of the dining hall to enjoy some lemonade before the start of the scavenger hunt at eleven o'clock. Twenty kids, ten girls and ten boys, were paired up by drawing names from a hat, and Joan was paired with a boy named Norman Lewis, who was new to the camp.

Joan decided it was fate that she was paired with Norman. He was easy to talk to, and she found herself uncharacteristically chatty. She was far less consumed with the scavenger hunt than she was with getting to know him. Each time Norman found another piece of paper with a clue, he read the inscription out loud and then continued the search, as Joan walked by his side, talking endlessly.

"My Aunt Helen thinks Mary spends too much time yakking on the horn to her beau," Joan said, raking her fingers through her hair.

"Huh?" Norman said. "What's a *horn*?"

"Why, a telephone, silly. Everyone knows that."

"Oh," he said with a shrug. "We don't have a telephone." He looked under a carved, wooden totem and found a piece of paper with another clue.

Joan assumed every family had a telephone.

While most of the kids ran around laughing and cracking jokes about the various objects they were instructed to look for, Joan and Norman gathered information about each other. This was their own private scavenger hunt, and Joan felt relieved to not have to think of clever jokes to impress the others.

"So where do you go to school, Norman?"

"Collingswood High," he said to Joan as he unfolded a piece of paper containing the fifth clue to the hunt.

"Oh. I've never heard of it," Joan said, studying his profile. He had removed his Phillies baseball cap and shoved it into his back pocket, leaving his front tuft of hair matted to his forehead; she had the instinct to brush it away for him but held herself back.

"It's not Quaker," he said, still reading the clue. He looked around, as if trying to decipher where to search.

Joan was relieved that he wasn't a Quaker because it meant she could be anyone she wanted to be with him; they had no history, no friends in common.

He continued. "I'm only here 'cause I got a scholarship," he said as he kneeled down to tie his shoelace. He had his eyes fixed on a tree trunk just ahead. "Some rich guy pays the fee for kids whose folks can't afford it."

She knew that some kids got athletic scholarships or merit scholarships to attend college, but it had not occurred to her that anyone might get a scholarship to attend sleepaway camp. She had no idea how much Camp Green Meadows cost.

Joan confided in Norman that she did not enjoy school and

that many academic subjects confounded her; Norman said he loved school and particularly enjoyed math and social studies.

A bell rang and one of the counselors called out, "Lunchtime, everyone! Meet in the dining hall!" Norman gave Joan a polite smile and extended his arm to indicate that she should lead the way. Maybe his family did not have money, but he was not lacking in manners. She walked ahead, looking back to make sure he was following her.

Then she felt a tug at her arm. It was Emily.

"Well, hi there, Joan. Who is your friend here?" Emily smiled at Norman.

"Norman Lewis," he said, holding out his hand.

Emily took his hand. "Lovely to meet you, Norman," she said, her radiant smile and perfect, while teeth gleaming in the afternoon sun. She locked her arm in Joan's. "C'mon, Joan, let's get a good spot at the table."

Joan yanked her arm away; Emily appeared offended. Joan turned to Norman, who rubbed his neck uncomfortably and looked around. Emily grunted in annoyance and stormed off. Joan was pleased.

"There's my counselor over there," Norman said. "I'll see you 'round, Joan." He smiled politely and walked away from her.

Joan stood still as kids ran past her, laughing and playing around, en route to lunch. She bit her thumbnail and folded her arms. She did not like the abrupt good-bye.

As the days went on, Joan noticed that Norman made too many cute jokes with Emily and more than once, Joan noticed Emily sitting next to Norman, chatting and laughing and occasionally pushing his upper arm in a mock gesture of offense. Joan overheard Norman tell his bunkmate that Emily was a "firecracker."

Joan wondered if that was the type of girl Norman preferred, the kind who could make sparks and fire with her wit and charm.

She could not believe there was ever a time when she idolized Emily. Now she just thought she was a cruel human being and way too full of herself.

Still, Norman always appeared happy to see Joan and eager to engage with her. She wanted to believe that Norman's kindness to everyone said something about his character and did not take away from what she was certain the two of them shared. So what could possibly explain how mixed up she felt about him?

One night, shortly before the camp session came to a close, Joan was restless in bed. Her mind was ablaze with thoughts of Norman. What could she do to make him like her more? She sat up and looked around in the dark at the sleeping bodies of her bunkmates, most of whom she had spent little time getting to know. Everyone at camp liked Norman: the boys, the girls, the counselors, the maintenance staff. And why not? He was so good-natured, so comfortable in his own skin. Maybe the truth was that she was no more special to him than any of the other girls, and the magical feeling she'd had on that first day was just her naïve foolishness.

Or maybe Emily was the problem.

Her agitation got the better of her, and she crawled out from beneath her blanket. She reached for the flashlight under her bed, slipped into her moccasins, and put on her robe. As she tiptoed passed her two counselors' beds, she stopped to make sure they were asleep.

She opened the screen door slowly, mindful of the way the springs creaked.

The walk down the hill toward the lake seemed endless, and the camp appeared ominous at night, the tall, dark pine trees hulking shadows, their pointed tips lit only by the moon. She felt an urge to run back to her bunk and hide under her blanket, but she steeled herself and continued on her mission.

Approaching the lake, she did, indeed, see a figure swimming. The water reflected the full moon as the figure dove under and then rose to the surface. The rumors about Brett were true. Joan stood back, hiding behind a tree. She watched, her heart beating fast and strong inside her chest. After a few minutes, the swimmer made his way toward the dock and climbed up the ladder.

There he stood, facing the lake, body wet and shimmering in the moonlight. Joan gasped and giggled, covering her mouth. Her impulse was to run back to the safety of her bunk, but she was fascinated by the silhouette, his broad shoulders leading to his torso, the lines of which slanted inward to a perfect "V." Each muscle in his back was defined in the moonlight. He appeared confident, relaxed. She had never seen a naked man; Brett resembled the Greek statues she'd seen at the Philadelphia Art Museum, the ones where you could see . . . *everything*.

And yet, she was terrified. She realized she knew nothing about a man's body, how it worked, what it felt like against a woman. But she had something to prove: to herself, to Emily, to Norman. To everyone.

Brett wrapped a towel around his waist and sat on the dock, leaning back on his hands, legs stretched out straight. Then he lay back. Joan emerged from behind the tree and began walking toward the dock, slowly. She paused; her heart was pounding, and she felt for a second that she might pass out until she realized she was holding her breath. She exhaled and then inhaled deeply. All her instincts told her to turn and walk away. Then she thought about Emily, and how Emily had bragged that Brett favored her last summer. She pictured the way Emily frequently touched Norman's upper arm, holding her hand there a little too long; how he laughed at her flirty comments and winked as he teased her.

Joan knew it was here, in this moment, that she would make a bold decision.

She walked toward the dock where Brett lay with his clasped hands resting on his belly. He was so still that Joan wondered if he had fallen asleep.

"Nice night for a swim, eh?" she said, surprising herself as the words seemed to come from somewhere else.

Brett sat up sharply, reached for his undershirt, and pulled it over his head.

"Wha—who's that?" he said, standing up quickly and searching into the darkness.

Joan slowly walked toward him. "It's me, Brett. It's Joan . . . Sondersohn."

"Joan? Wha . . . what are you doing here? You should be asleep. Go on, go back now. You could get yourself in a lot of trouble," he said, tightening the towel around his waist.

She continued walking toward him. "Is the water very cold at night? You're brave to go in." She wanted to sound alluring and confident, but her voice came out broken and uneven in a kind of staccato rhythm, like someone shivering from the cold.

"Uh, yeah. I'm . . . gonna head back now. We'll both get into a heap of trouble if someone sees us out here." Brett leaned over and began gathering his clothes.

Joan stood directly in front of him. He was a good ten inches taller than her. She placed her palm against his chest. She could feel the heat from his body even with his undershirt on.

He backed up. "What are you *doing*?"

"I don't know," she said. "Is your heart beating fast? Mine is." She felt stupid having admitted this and, in an attempt to come across as more sophisticated and confident than she actually felt, she moved toward him again. His face was dark, as the moon was now behind him. She was glad she could not see his expression.

"You're a strange girl," he said, almost with a chuckle.

She took that as a compliment and began to relax. "Not as strange as you swimming naked in a lake at night," she said, feeling relieved that they were teasing each other. She relaxed.

He leaned down and kissed her. Her impulse was to push him away and run, but then the image of Emily popped into her head again, and Joan forced some courage. She stood on her tiptoes and wrapped her arms around his neck, a gesture that seemed appropriate though she had no idea what she was doing. She had never been so physically close to a boy, and when he kissed her, it did not feel the way she'd hoped it would. She remembered two years earlier when she'd overheard Mary telling a friend that her fiancé Red's kisses were "electrifying" and made her want to scream out with joy. This felt nothing like that.

Brett took Joan's hand and walked her onto the grass. He knelt down, pulling her down with him, and began kissing her again, this time more forcefully. The more he kissed her, the less interested she was in continuing. He gently eased her shoulders down to the grass and moved his leg over her body, which made her feel trapped. She pushed his leg back with her knees, shoved him away, and sat up.

"What's wrong?" he asked.

She didn't respond.

"Oh, shit, what the hell am I doing?" he sternly muttered to himself. He stood up, securing the towel around his waist. He walked back over to the dock and picked up his pants. He sidled into them, all the while talking to himself, and then threw the towel over his shoulder.

Joan stood up and secured her robe. She folded her arms across her chest.

"I could lose my job, you know that? Five years I've worked at this camp, and I could lose the job like that," he said, snapping his fingers. He walked past her and headed up the hill. She listened to him chide himself as she walked briskly behind him, trying to keep up with his long strides.

They silently approached the area where the bunks divided between the girls' and boys' sections. Brett stopped and turned around to Joan.

"You got a flashlight?"

She nodded, pulling one out of the pocket of her robe. He was kind of being nice to her, which was confusing when minutes earlier he'd been so aggressive.

"All right, then." He turned and proceeded to the grounds-keepers' cabins, just beyond the boys' bunks.

Joan opened her mouth intending to speak but realized she had nothing to say.

Brett spun around. "Listen. I don't know what the heck you were doing just now. Most guys aren't like me. Most guys would've—"

"I won't tell anyone that I saw you skinny-dipping," she said defensively.

He turned and headed toward the cabin he shared with the maintenance crew and dining hall staff. A chill overcame Joan, and she ran back to her bunk, snuck inside, threw the flashlight under her bed, and crawled under her blanket without taking off her robe. Lying on her back, she stared at the wooden beams running along the ceiling of the cabin. She heard the scurry of small feet—a mouse?—move across the beam, and she pulled her blanket up to her neck.

Thinking about what had just transpired with Brett, she cursed herself and hoped that she wouldn't feel so embarrassed and ashamed in the morning as she did at that moment. It was a reminder of everything she didn't know—including whatever she was supposed to feel about any of this. The kissing and touching, the way bodies—especially boys' bodies—do things outside of their control, it all eluded her. The only thing that offset how bad she felt was realizing that perhaps she was more attractive to boys than she had previously thought. He *wanted* to kiss her.

She fell asleep considering how she might use this to her advantage someday, maybe soon. More than ever, however, she needed reassurance from Norman.

Joan made an effort to put aside the episode with Brett and focus on Norman, the boy she really cared about and whose attention she desperately wanted. At the campfire on the last night, the two of them exchanged glances as everyone sang songs and cheered. There were fireworks over the lake, and Joan surreptitiously inched closer to Norman, studying his profile in the lights from the sky. She casually brushed her pinky finger against his hand. At first, he flinched, but when he looked at her, he relaxed and entwined his fingers in hers. As the fireworks display was ending, he quickly pulled his hand loose and created just a bit more space between them, apparently aware of the throngs of campers all around. Joan put her hand on his shoulder and whispered into his ear.

"Meet me behind the arts and crafts cabin," she said with a smile.

Norman looked blankly at her. "We're supposed to go back to our bunks. Lights out and all."

"Just a few minutes. No one will notice right away. I have something I want to give you."

Norman tipped his head to one side and appeared bewildered. He looked at her sideways and acquiesced with a shrug. "Okay."

They split up, and Joan ran to their meeting place to wait.

Within five minutes, he was there. "The guys were wondering where I was going. What's up, Joan? Why all the mystery?"

She looked into his eyes and moved in for a kiss. He gently held her back.

"Don't you want to kiss me?" she asked.

"I—uh, I mean, yeah, sure." He looked around self-consciously.

"I . . . really like you, Norman," she said almost like a question. She hoped the feeling was mutual.

He opened his mouth as if to say something, but all that came out was "Uh . . ."

Joan tried again, leaning in slowly for a kiss. He did not resist this time and, instead, placed his hands on her waist. Her heart began to beat faster with a joy she had not felt while kissing Brett, and she was filled with confidence. Then, abruptly, he stopped kissing and backed away. He nervously rubbed his palms on the sides of his pants.

"What's wrong, Norman? Don't you like this? Don't you like me?"

"Yeah, Joan. You're a real nice girl. But we gotta get back to our bunks," he said, backing up slowly toward the path. "We're gonna get in trouble if we're not back by ten thirty, you know that."

His voice was different; he seemed edgy. Joan tried to hold back tears. She wanted him to say more, to not *want* to stop kissing her.

"I'll see you tomorrow," he said, waving good-bye and heading up the path, leaving her alone. When he was several yards away, he turned around.

She looked at him, expectantly, and smiled.

"I don't understand, Joan," he said calmly, but with an air of disappointment. "Why would you *do* that?"

"Norman—"

He shook his head and turned back around to continue up the path.

Joan stood alone for several minutes trying to figure out where she went wrong. And what, exactly, did she want from Norman? What was she expecting would happen, then and there? She felt stupid and cursed herself and her curiosity. She was moving too quickly, being too impulsive, not considering his feelings. It occurred to her that not every boy would be pleased with such presumptuousness, least of all, Norman Lewis.

4

THE MINUTE JOAN ARRIVED HOME FROM CAMP, SHE DASHED UP to her bedroom, nearly knocking Helen over on the stairway, to write a letter to Norman. She reached for her personalized stationery and Mont Blanc pen, both gifts from her grandmother the previous Christmas.

She didn't hesitate because she had already composed the letter in her mind.

> *My Dear Norman,*
>
> *Did you enjoy your time at Green Meadows? I hope you did.*
>
> *I wish we had more time alone together on the last night of camp. There is so much I wanted to say to you. I am worried that I have ruined your image of me. I did not mean to be so forward, but I thought you really liked me. I want you to know that I have never behaved like that with any other boy.*
>
> *I hope you will write to me.*
>
> *Yours truly,*
>
> *Joan*

She folded the letter, placed it in the envelope unsealed, and propped it against her desk lamp to go out in the next day's mail.

But the following morning, she woke up and immediately pulled the letter from its envelope to reread what she had written. Sitting on her bed, still in her nightgown, she considered her choice of words. Now, feeling clearheaded and rested, the letter sounded wishy-washy, as if she were making apologies. She felt childish. She decided to give it more time and see if Norman would write to her as he'd promised he would on the last day when she had run over to him to say good-bye. Then again, perhaps he was just being polite, as always.

Her disappointment with the way things had ended between her and Norman grew daily until it resulted in an almost full-time ache in her belly. She couldn't stand the idea of never hearing from or seeing him again. Another week passed. She opened the letter and added a postscript:

> *I expected you would write to me. But I guess I didn't prove to be what you wanted; in other words, I am a complete failure in your mind. Please let me know if this is at all true.*
>
> *If it is untrue, I would like to ask you when you can come over to Elkins Park to visit. I hope soon.*

She folded the letter, placed it back in the envelope and addressed it. For several minutes, she held the envelope in her hand and stared at Norman's name. She looked around her room, surveying its contents: her stuffed pony, Neigh-Neigh, frayed around the ears and missing an eye, sat on a shelf next to a vase with yellow and pink tissue flowers; there was a poster on the wall of a painted image of the racehorse Man O'War, a jockey seated upon the horse's long, shiny back. Joan loved the stories of this powerful thoroughbred who had become a champion in 1919 at the tender age of two. He was considered violent and belligerent, often called a "tiger," but Joan felt he was just misunderstood. She had heard that her mother admired the horse's strength and stamina, and was ecstatic was every time he won.

Those races, apparently, had given Jessie Sondersohn great joy in the final days just before she died.

Looking at the envelope again, Joan lost the nerve to mail it. *I'm a horrible writer.* She twisted and untwisted the pen. *He'll probably read it and never want to see me again.* Her uncertainty was gnawing at her insides, so, giving in to her fears for the moment, she hid the letter in her bedroom wall, behind the plate of an electrical outlet that had come loose.

A few days before school resumed, after a month of no correspondence from Norman, Joan was sitting at the dinner table with her family, which now included Mary's husband of one year, Russell "Red" Weldon. Joan halfheartedly dragged a pat of butter across her corncob.

"So, Uncle Marcus, have you been up in the Empire State Building yet?" asked Sonny.

"No, not yet. I've probably been to New York a half dozen times since it was completed in May, but, unfortunately, I haven't had the time."

"I hear the observation deck is outstanding. You can see clear over to New Jersey," said Sonny. Then he turned to Joan. "Oh, hey, I heard your friend from Green Meadows—what's his name? Norman?"

This caught her attention. "What? What about Norman?" She sat up straight.

Sonny continued. "I heard his father worked on the construction of it." He put a forkful of green beans into his mouth.

"How . . . how do you know about Norman?" Joan asked.

"I saw Emily Van Kirk last week at the country club. She mentioned him. Said he's a great guy. Everyone liked him."

Joan looked around at her family. They had stopped eating, and all eyes were focused on her as they expectantly awaited her response.

"Who is this Norman person? Do tell," Mary said with wide eyes, fingers clasped, resting under her chin.

Joan wiped butter off her fingers. She picked up a green bean between her thumb and index finger and put it back down. "He's no one. I mean, yes, he's a friend. I guess. I don't really know him. He was new this summer. Nothing special. Not very smart. I don't know how Emily found that out about his father. I never heard Norman say very much. To anyone." She imagined how she sounded to her family with her rambling words and unflattering description of Norman. She picked up her corn and sunk her teeth into the cob, avoiding Sonny's sideways stare. Sometimes Joan felt that the only time her family paid any attention to her was when they wanted some bit of juicy information.

"Emily gave me the impression that you and Norman got along really well," he said.

"Joanie, what are you keeping from us?" Red teased.

"Nothing. I'm not keeping anything from you. Emily has it all wrong. She doesn't know what she's talking about. She's a gossip."

Helen jumped in. "It's your business and we don't need to pry," she said.

Her family continued the conversation as Joan tried to tune them out. Her stomach was a ball of nerves; she felt as if she might vomit and spew corn and green beans across the table and secretly wanted to do just that. She picked up her napkin and softly belched into it.

"Well, anyway," she blurted out. "Norman isn't even Quaker. He's . . . he's . . . I don't know, Presbyterian or something. And he's probably not going to college. He's not the type of boy who. . . ." Joan stopped talking, seeing everyone's eyes on her and feeling the weight of their silence.

"The lady doth protest too much," Mary said under her breath.

"Mary," Helen chided.

"All right, Joan," Marcus said quietly without looking at her.

"Why do you always shut me up?" she screamed. She stood up. Her chair made a loud, scraping sound on the floor.

Helen flinched. She reached her hand out to Joan. "Now Joan. We don't need to use that tone at the dinner table."

"There are a million things going on in the world. A *million* things we could talk about at dinner. Al Capone was convicted—did you know that?" Joan asked Sonny.

He nodded slowly.

"And what about the Phillies? Father, you love to talk about baseball. You and Sonny and Uncle Fred talk baseball nonstop. But now, at this meal, everyone wants to talk about Norman Lewis and Emily Van Kirk."

"Joan, I'll ask you to leave the table now. You may return once you've cooled off," Marcus said without emotion.

Joan looked at her father. *Always in control*, she thought. She stormed off, mumbling under her breath. She stopped at the landing between the first and second floors, waiting to hear if her family would comment on her behavior; they always did.

After a brief silence save for the scraping of utensils and movement of a pair of feet walking from the dining room into the kitchen, Joan heard Mary's voice. "Well, *that* hasn't happened in a while."

"She'll be fine," Marcus said. "She just needs to get back to school, have something productive to focus on."

I do need to get back to school, Joan thought. *And away from this house.*

In her bedroom, Joan lay on her bed, staring at the ceiling, seething. How could her family treat her so insensitively? She turned onto her side and looked at the outlet, its cover tilted on a slight diagonal. She pushed herself up and sat on the edge of her bed, biting her thumbnail, not taking her eyes off the outlet. She stood up and walked over to it; then she knelt down and removed the plate. Carefully reaching inside, she extracted the envelope, walked back to her bed, and sat down. She held the envelope to her heart. Frustrated, she walked back to the wall and shoved the envelope deep inside.

If only Norman's family had a telephone, she could call him, but they did not. She looked over at her robe draped over her desk chair and remembered wearing it to the lake when she'd seen Brett. Her familiar self-loathing was building up inside once more. She slammed her body down on the bed, squeezing her eyes shut and burying her head under the pillow to muffle a scream.

Then, as if a light inside her brain flicked on, she removed the pillow, sat up, and felt her entire body relax. *He's a lousy, no-good creep.* It hurt her to think of Norman this way, but it felt worse to be disgusted with herself. She imagined something awfully embarrassing happening to him at some point in the future. That calmed her mood, and she fell asleep with the fantasy that somehow she was in control.

5

December 1931

THE YOUNG MAN ENTERED THE FOYER, SHOOK SNOW OFF HIS shoulders and shoes, and scanned the room as if searching for a face he recognized among the guests at the Pruitt-Sondersohn Christmas party. Joan watched him from the entrance to the butler's pantry, where she was helping Helen and a servant load mugs for eggnog onto a tray. Joan was indifferent to her aunt's request for her attention as she watched Red make a beeline for his friend at the front door.

"Franklin, my good man, you made it," Red said, extending his arm. "You sounded tentative last week. Glad you're here."

"Hello, Red," Franklin said clutching his friend's hand and giving him a hearty pat on the back. "Wasn't sure I would be, with the holiday hours at the store. Dad's really hoping the holiday spirit moves folks to make that special purchase. It's been a tough season." He removed his coat, and Red took it from him as Mary approached.

"Franklin Oakes, how's my old chum?" she said with a smile.

"Hello there, Mary Weldon." He leaned in to give her a kiss on the cheek. "Used to that last name yet?"

Mary smiled and linked her arm in his. "Why, yes. I think it suits me just fine. Merry Christmas, Franklin. Lovely to see you. You've come here solo, I see." The three of them walked into the living room.

Joan picked up a glass of eggnog and followed them, trying to listen in on their conversation without being noticed. Mary immediately saw Joan, shimmied over to her, and grabbed Joan's arm, pulling her in.

"Joanie, you remember Franklin Oakes? I believe the two of you met at our wedding," Mary said.

"Oh, yeah. Hi," Joan said, curious if he remembered *her*. They'd barely had any interaction a year and a half ago.

"Merry Christmas, Joan. I do remember you, though I must say, I would not have recognized you. You've changed something," he said with squinted eyes. "Your hairdo perhaps? Or have you gotten taller?"

Joan felt both embarrassed and flattered.

"Taller?" Mary said with a giggle. "My little cousin here is barely knee-high to a grasshopper."

She squeezed Joan's elbow, and Joan flinched and retracted it. Why were people always pinching and squeezing her?

Red added, "She's *petite*, Mary. 'Five foot two, eyes of blue,'" he said. He stared into Joan's eyes for confirmation. "Or hazel."

At this, Joan felt her cheeks flush, and she looked at the floor. *Once again*, she thought, *they're enjoying embarrassing me.* She did, in fact, have a new hairstyle since just after school began in the fall, when she'd noticed many other girls with short, curly bobs and had begged her father to allow her to do the same. She had not gotten taller, though her breasts had become fuller, and her overall appearance was more mature as well. She wore a festive and trendy holiday dress with a faux corset that accentuated her waistline and soft, flowing short sleeves that hung from her shoulders in a feminine—but still demure—fashion. Helen had taken her and Mary to Strawbridge and Clothier in Center City several weeks earlier to select holiday dresses for each of them. It was one of the rare occasions when Joan was permitted such free rein on a decision involving fashion. At Mary's wedding, where Helen had insisted she wear something modest and appropriate for a fifteen-year-old girl—and *simple*, in keeping with Quaker tradition—Joan had felt like a homely little girl in the shapeless, dull dress. But tonight, she thought, she might possibly look sophisticated.

"Nice to see you again, Joan," Franklin said.

"Same here," Joan replied. Feeling small in the shadow of Mary's big, bright personality, as was frequently the case, Joan could not bring herself to say anything beyond that, and an awkward silence filled the air. Joan looked into Mary's eyes and then Red's, beseeching one of them to speak. Finally, she filled the void herself. "Anyway, you're right. My hair is shorter now than it was at Mary's wedding."

"Ah," said Franklin. "Well then."

Joan castigated herself. *Oh, Joan, you're so childish. Can't you come up with anything clever?* She glanced around the room for some kind of out to remove her from this uncomfortable situation. "Oh, I poured this eggnog for Father. I'll just take it on over to him. Nice to see you, Franklin."

Joan walked away from the three of them, angry with herself for her retreat. What was this urge to escape? And from what? She wanted to talk to Franklin, to make an impression on him, but his presence was imposing to her. Tonight, Franklin came across as far more mature and confident than he had been at Mary's wedding, when he was fresh out of high school and goofed off at the reception with kids from their social circle. And since camp, she'd been grappling with how to navigate the line between being too aggressive or too demure with boys. Which words and actions denoted confidence and made her seem impish and playful rather than bland and forgettable?

As she walked away, a guest stopped Joan to give her a hug

and chat. Joan nodded mindlessly at whatever the old lady was blabbering on about, but she was more focused on the conversation she was overhearing between Franklin, Red, and Mary.

"Does she always scurry away like that?" Franklin joked.

"She can be awkward, unfortunately," Mary explained. "Then again, you never quite know what you're getting with Joan. She's got a good heart. She's just . . . what's the word I'm looking for? Mercurial, I suppose."

Joan listened.

"Will you two excuse me?" Mary said. "I see some friends I'd like to say hi to. Franklin, help yourself to some eggnog."

Franklin and Red continued to chat.

Joan turned her head slightly away from the old lady in order to better hear the conversation between the guys. She kept her eyes on the old lady as she tilted toward Franklin and Red.

Joan fully turned her head away from the old lady and, as she did, Franklin looked over and caught her eye. Mortified, Joan quickly looked away from Franklin and back at the old lady, who was seemingly unaware of Joan's lack of attention.

". . . because, my dear, it's of utmost importance that the younger generation remain active in the Society of Friends. . . ."

"Would you excuse me?" Joan said, gently touching the old lady's shoulder. "I poured this eggnog for my father, and I don't see him anywhere."

She walked out of the living room, placed the eggnog on a table, and sought the refuge of the kitchen where she could safely busy herself with service to her aunt.

Later in the evening, Joan sat on the sofa, lost in thought. She wondered how Norman was spending the holiday and whether or not he ever thought about her.

"You know, if you furrow your brow like that, you'll have wrinkles before you're twenty."

Startled, Joan looked up to find Franklin standing next to her with a plate of food.

"What?" she said, touching her brow.

He sat down on the armchair perpendicular to the sofa. "You were somewhere else a second ago." He placed a napkin across his legs.

"Oh, I was just thinking about, um, school. And other things." She touched the curl that had fallen across her forehead.

"School? During the Christmas holiday you're thinking about school? You must be a very serious student," he said, taking a bite of roast beef.

She shrugged, made a soft guffaw.

"Does that mean you *don't* enjoy school?"

"I enjoy some subjects I guess. Social studies, current events."

"Two very important subjects," he said.

Joan furrowed her brow again. Was he talking down to her? He watched her and pointed to his brow, grinning. She rubbed her forehead.

"Speaking of current events, do you know who I find fascinating?" he said while digging into his sweet potatoes.

She was relieved by his ability to strike up a conversation. "Who?"

"Amelia Earhart."

"Oh, I love her!" Joan lit up for the first time that evening. "She's so brave and independent. And intelligent too."

"Brave, yes," said Sonny from a few feet away. "Though I'm not sure piloting an airplane solo is a smart idea for a lady."

Joan scowled.

Then Red joined in. "I'm just surprised my spunky Mary didn't do it first."

Mary responded enthusiastically, calling across the room. "Well, don't discount that yet, Red. Stranger things have happened."

A couple of Mary's friends broke out into uproarious laughter over her response to Red.

"I swear, my wife has the ears of a seasoned spy," Red joked.

Joan smiled but, on the inside, she was simmering with envy as Mary, yet again, displayed her knack for comic timing. People were always so tickled by Mary.

"Well, I think it's rather commendable," Franklin called out to Sonny. "Earhart is a real pioneer. You gotta give her that." He turned back to Joan and looked her in the eye. "And she's a lot braver than me."

She appreciated his nod to Earhart's bravery and the fact that he redirected his attention away from Sonny and the others. And yet his gaze unsettled her. She nervously searched her brain for something clever to say in response, but could think of nothing. "So where did you graduate high school?" she asked.

"Abington High School," he said proudly.

"Oh, I didn't realize you went to public school." Joan thought back to her conversations with her father about the possibility of her going to Cheltenham High and how he had not given the idea even the slightest consideration.

"Yes, I admit it. It's true, Joan," Franklin said, with mocking sarcasm. "My proper Quaker education ended in eighth grade. Is that a deal-breaker, then?" he said with a flirtatious smile.

"I, uh, well no. . . ." Just what did he mean by "deal breaker"? Was he positioning himself as a suitor?

"It's a fine school, and certainly much closer to my home than any of the other Quaker high schools," Franklin said. "Honestly, I think my dad was happy to not have to fork out tuition."

Joan smiled, thinking of Norman and his lack of pretension about money, and his family's lack thereof. Joan had never given much thought to the fact that her father paid tuition to send her to school. In her home, it was always a given that she and her cousins attend private Quaker schools.

"Friends Central has a rigorous academic program from what I understand. You must be a very capable student."

She rolled her eyes. "I'm not exactly bringing home good marks. My father says I need to 'focus and feel connected,'" she said imitating her father's calm yet commanding voice that rarely invited discussion.

"And you don't feel connected?"

Joan flexed one foot and stared at the tip of her shoe for a moment. She rotated her foot and pulled at the stocking around her ankle as she thought about what Franklin had asked her. It was the first time anyone had wanted her opinion about school. Her inclination was to say that everything was copacetic, that she had many good friends there and found the classes engaging and was appropriately, but not unreasonably, challenged by the academics. She had learned through the years that complaining and expressing any sort of dissatisfaction in life was met with disappointment by the very people who should be most concerned with her well-being. *But, no, I don't feel connected. Not at all.*

Joan shrugged. "It's all right, I guess." She looked over at her cousins, who were laughing and enjoying themselves with other guests. She fidgeted with the hem of her dress, glowered, and stared into her drink.

"Tough being in other people's shadows." Franklin popped a forkful of food into his mouth and grinned as he chewed.

She looked up from her drink at Franklin. She'd barely said anything, and yet he seemed to understand her. His face held no judgment. "I guess. But also, I mean, this community," she said. "Everyone knows everyone. The Friends colleges." She began ticking the names off on her fingers: "Penn, Haverford, Bryn Mawr, Swarthmore. Not colleges that would admit me, that's for certain."

"Well, I graduated high school and went right into my family's business. College isn't for everyone. Then again, I didn't have much of a choice." He popped the last maple-glazed carrot into his mouth.

Helen sat down at the piano and began playing "Deck the Halls," and guests gathered round to sing. Mary was front and center, seated on the bench next to her mother.

The star of all the school productions. Class president. Lovely, ebullient Mary, Joan thought. She looked at Franklin, who had joined in the singing. Joan sang as well, studying Franklin's face as he watched Helen at the piano. Joan had marveled at how Franklin managed to eat an entire plate of food without dropping a crumb or messing up his trousers and jacket. He had a pleasant smile. And now, he appeared so joyous and consumed with the merriment of the evening.

As the song ended, Joan saw Marcus making his way over to her and Franklin. Franklin rose to greet him, extending his hand to shake.

"Franklin Oakes, how are you?"

"Fine, Mr. Sondersohn. Haven't seen you in a long time."

"I was saddened to hear about your mother—very sorry for your loss."

"Thank you, sir."

"How is your father doing?"

"The store keeps him busy, which is a good thing."

Marcus nodded. "Tough for you and your sister as well, I imagine. She was a lovely woman, your mother."

"Thank you, sir. She was."

Joan remained seated on the sofa, watching the interaction. She sat up straight and smiled politely, her eyes wide. She felt a certain pride, as if Franklin's attention reflected positively on her and pleased her father.

"I see you've met my daughter."

"Yes, sir."

"Joan's an . . . interesting young lady," Marcus spoke as if she were not sitting right there.

Joan pursed her lips. Was this an insult or a compliment? Or a warning to Franklin?

"She certainly is," Franklin said, smiling at Joan.

"Well, then. Carry on. And Merry Christmas, Franklin." Then Marcus did something she had never seen her father do before. He winked at her. Joan was so stunned and delighted by this, she sat for a minute almost in a trance, staring at her father as he moved across the room.

"Hello in there?" Franklin said, waving his hand in front of her eyes.

"Oh, gee. Your mother passed away this year? I'm very sorry."

Franklin nodded. "This summer. I miss her terribly."

Joan wanted to know about his mother: how she died, what Franklin missed about her. "What was she like?" She wondered if the questions were too personal.

"My mother was the smartest and wittiest woman I've ever known. Loved a good joke. Kept Dad on his toes," he said with a chuckle as he scanned the room. He looked at Joan. "But her kidneys failed her. Diabetes," he said. He squeezed his lips together, as if holding back tears.

Joan felt sad for Franklin, but sadder for herself. At least he had known his mother. Her mind wandered off.

"Hello again?" he said.

"Is it crazy to miss someone you don't even remember?" Joan swore she could still hear the sound of her mother's voice and the way she laughed.

"I don't think so. Feelings are powerful. They stay with us even when memories don't."

Joan pondered Franklin's words as she watched him gather the plates and utensils. She remembered nearly nothing about her mother, yet Joan had always had a sense of her mother's love for her. Marcus did not mention Jessie very often, and Joan was afraid of asking him anything for fear of upsetting him. One thing she did know, from her Grandmother Elizabeth, was that whenever Jessie read to Joan or made up a bedtime story, it was as if no one else existed in the world but the two of them.

"I'll be back with some eggnog for us. Don't you go any-where." Franklin winked at Joan as he walked away. Joan could not believe her luck. Getting winks from two men in the same night.

She liked Franklin's self-confidence, though it was without pomposity. He was modest, yet confident. Just like Norman.

For the first time in her life, Joan felt adored and appreciated.

6

"I GUESS THIS'LL BE BAPTISM BY FIRE, JOAN," FRANKLIN SAID with a smile. "Anyway, it's not as if you need to make a sale or answer complicated questions. I'm still right here." He sat on top of his father's desk in the back office of the store one evening after closing up.

"I've only been typing up new orders and filing and such," Joan said. "You really think I can speak with customers?"

"I don't think so, I *know* so."

His confidence in her was thrilling, but she wasn't sure.

It was the summer after eleventh grade, and Joan had been working for a month at the Oakes's store on Arch Street in Center City. As his father Bill's health was declining and Franklin needed extra help, he asked Joan to take on additional responsibilities.

Franklin jumped off the desk and looked around; then he picked up a pen and piece of paper and began scribbling things down.

"What the heck are you doing, Franklin?"

"Give me a sec," he said. He grabbed a ruler and handed it to her.

"What's this for?" she asked.

"It's your telephone for now," he said with a smile. He sat back on the desk and picked up the receiver of the phone, taking care to hold down the cradle so as not to connect with an operator.

"Have you lost your marbles?" she asked him.

"I'm the customer. You're, well, you're the receptionist here at Oakes's Fine Furniture." He handed the piece of paper to her. "Bbbrrring. Bbbbrrringgg!"

"You're the telephone too?" She thought he was crazy, but she obliged him, nonetheless. This seemed like fun. "Hhhelloo?" she said, feeling awkward.

"No, read what I wrote down for you," he said enthusiastically, pointing at the paper in her hand.

She looked down, holding the ruler at her side. "Good afternoon, thank you for calling Oakes's Fine Furniture. Um . . ." She looked up at Franklin. She knew how awful she sounded. She felt lost.

He said nothing, but rolled his index finger in a motion to indicate she should continue reading.

"Um, how may I help you today?"

"Good, Joan! Now, do it again! But hold the ruler—your telephone receiver—to your ear. And, Joanie, try smiling as you speak. You'd be surprised how that changes your tone."

She cleared her throat and lifted her chin. She brought the ruler to her ear, feeling terribly foolish. She looked at the paper and smiled. "Good morning. Thank you for calling Oakes's Fine Furniture. How may I help you today?" She raised her eyebrows at Franklin, wondering how she'd done.

"Hello, this is Mr. Fuddy Duddily Doo," he began, which caused Joan to break into laughter. Franklin admonished her, whispering, "You can't laugh at the customer, Joan."

"I know, but that name," she said, still cracking up. She composed herself.

He continued. "Yes, I ordered a mahogany library desk with a leather top three months ago and I'd like to check on its status for delivery," Franklin said with a gruff voice.

"What do I say?" she asked in a whisper.

"Read the paper in your hand."

She looked down and found her place. "Certainly, Mister . . ." she looked at Franklin and tried not to laugh. "Mister Fuddy Dudd—" She broke into laugher again.

They practiced over and over for another hour, and each time Franklin would pretend to be a new customer. Eventually, he showed her how to greet customers at the door. Her job was to always direct the customer to him, never attempt to sell anything or solve a problem. She was to always make the customer feel welcome and allow Franklin to take over from there.

Though they had been dating for a year, Joan still couldn't shake her insecurities entirely; she harbored the feeling that it was only a matter of time before she disappointed Franklin in some way. She could tell early on how much he liked her, so she was careful not to risk losing him by being too forward. Perhaps if at some future point she felt he was tiring of her, she might need to reconsider that option. She couldn't let him slip away, because one added benefit of dating Franklin Oakes was the praise her father bestowed on her regarding this relationship.

Throughout the remainder of the summer, Joan's confidence grew tenfold. She learned how to make customers feel at ease and appreciated, and she quickly lost the impulse to take it personally when they were impatient or irate. Whether on the phone or in person, Joan was polite and composed. She could feel changes taking place inside herself, and she wanted more responsibility. Maybe, eventually, she could be a salesperson. Surely, Franklin had enough confidence in her to allow Joan to do that.

"You wouldn't recognize me at the store, Father," she explained to Marcus, her eyes wide with exuberance as she begged him to allow her to withdraw from school before graduating and assured him that the Oakeses would be amenable to her working at the store full-time. "I feel so confident when I'm working. It's like—" she looked around, trying to figure out how best to communicate the feeling to him. "It's like I'm not *me*. I mean, I walk into that store now, and a switch goes on inside me. The customers, they like me. And Franklin says I've really grown into the position. And I love everything about the city! Isn't Reading Terminal Market thrilling? The crowds at lunchtime, the smells of all that wonderful food. And riding the train—every evening on the way back, Franklin and I buy a *Bulletin,* and we discuss what's happening around town, everywhere really. There's so much going on in the world, I never realized how much I didn't know. For instance, did you know they're going to build a subway underneath City Hall? Right underneath it."

"Mm-hmm," Marcus said while perusing the pages of a recent issue of *Life* magazine.

"And it's going to cost more than eleven *million* dollars . . . golly, I can't imagine. And did you know that the US Secretary of Labor is a lady? A *lady!*"

"Oh?" Marcus said without looking up.

"Father?" she said, trying to connect with him. "I . . . I think I'm ready to go out in the world . . . you know, to work."

"I know you've enjoyed helping out at the Oakes's store, Joan," Marcus replied. "And I'm pleased that you're doing so well with that. Now, take that strong work ethic you've developed and put it into your classes. Earn your diploma, you'll feel proud of yourself for it. It will be an accomplishment."

"Why does it matter? My grades aren't going to get me into Swarthmore or Penn. And, anyway, why do I need to go to college at all?"

"It's not about college, Joan. It's just about . . . well, it's about sticking with something and getting that piece of paper that shows the world you're not a quitter."

She was *not* a quitter, that was the point. Why couldn't he understand that working at the store made her happy? No one judged her at Oakes's Fine Furniture. She wasn't competing with her cousins or anyone, really. In fact, Joan believed she could be quite successful there. But there was nothing more she could say to him. She knew when he was resolute, no matter how ridiculous his rationale seemed. Joan dreaded returning to school.

On the Saturday afternoon just before her family's annual Christmas party, Franklin and Joan were alone at the store, closing up for the holiday. Joan was busy sweeping the showroom floor as Franklin emerged from the back office. He walked to the front of the store, flipped the sign on the front door to "Closed" and locked up. He turned off most of the lights in the front of the store, so that the Christmas tree by the large window near the street was lit mostly by the streetlights shining in from outside.

"Joan, can you come over here for a sec? I need to ask you about something?"

She stopped sweeping, leaned the broom against the wall, and walked toward him. "My goodness, Franklin, I can hardly see where I'm walking."

"Just follow the sound of my voice," he said

"What is it? Is anything wrong?"

"Well, I have something very important to discuss with you, Joan." His face was serious.

Her heart sank, and she felt her stomach twist into a ball. "Did I mess something up today? I'm afraid I was a little distracted. I don't have anything special to wear to the party tonight. I guess I'll just wear what I wore last Christmas. It's really not all that important. . . ."

"I may have something new for you to wear," he said.

She looked at him through squinted eyes. Had he bought her a new dress for Christmas?

He took her hand. "Joan, I hope you know how I feel about you."

She watched him reach into the inside breast pocket of his suit jacket. He pulled out a small box. She understood what was happening, and she felt a mixture of shock, elation, and fear. He held the box out for her, and she slowly took it from him, looking into his eyes. He did not blink.

She hesitated, swallowed hard. She stared at the unopened box in her hands.

"What, Joan?" he asked. "What's wrong?"

Joan didn't know what was wrong, but she was grateful for the relative darkness in the store.

"Joan," Franklin said, gently lifting her chin with his index finger. "Open it." He smiled, releasing her tension.

She opened the box and could barely see the ring with the dimmed lighting, but she nevertheless gasped in delight. Her reaction surprised her.

Franklin took the box from her hands, removed the ring, and put the box back in his jacket. He took her left hand and slid the ring onto her finger.

"Joan Sondersohn, will you marry me?"

"Oh, Franklin! Yes, yes!" She jumped into his arms and kissed his face from his cheek to his chin to his forehead.

"Are you surprised?"

"Surprised? Oh, gosh, yes I am. I was afraid you were going to tell me I messed up today, that you lost a sale because of me, that an order went to the wrong customer. I don't know . . . I just didn't expect . . . *this.*" Then she giggled. "I can't even see the ring, it's so dark in here."

Franklin walked to the light switch and flicked it up before returning to Joan.

"This was my grandmother's, my dad's mother's," he said. "I hope you like it."

She held out her hand. It was a simple, small solitaire diamond set in a smooth band of gold. No embellishments, no carvings, nothing opulent or ostentatious. She was pleased and wanted nothing more.

"See, I said you'd have something new to wear tonight. No one will care which dress you have on."

Joan and Franklin walked out of the store together and headed for the train station. On the ride back to the suburbs, Joan had many questions for Franklin.

"How long had you been planning to ask for my hand in marriage?"

"Honestly, Joanie, that Christmas party at your house, the night we met and sat talking . . . I had a strong feeling. I just needed for you to grow up a little," he said, elbowing her.

"And when did you tell your father that you wanted to marry me? And did he offer your grandmother's ring, or did you ask for it?"

"He offered it. He was pleased, even relieved. With his ailing health, you know . . . well, he doesn't want me to be alone, I guess." Franklin looked across the aisle and back at Joan.

"I hope my father will be fine with . . . the engagement," Joan said, twisting the ring on her finger.

"I've already asked for and received his blessing," Franklin said, grabbing Joan's hand and kissing the top of it.

"You have? When?"

"This past summer, just before you started school. He gave

just two stipulations: that I would not propose before Christmas, and that we would hold off on the wedding until after your graduation."

Joan wondered if Marcus had known about Franklin's intentions when she'd been pressing her father to let her leave Friends Central. She frowned.

"What is that sourpuss face for?" he asked her.

She didn't want to admit to Franklin that it upset her to have the two men in her life discussing her future in her absence. Her thoughts and feelings hadn't at all figured into the decision. Still, she did not want to seem ungrateful.

She shook it off. "Oh, nothing. I'm just thinking about our wedding and what I want."

"Which is?"

As she looked out the window, passing the leafless trees that surrounded the factories and mills of Wayne Junction, she was not thinking at all about the wedding. Joan recalled her father explaining at a family dinner how, as a young writer for the *Evening Bulletin*, he would take the train from Wayne Junction to New York. The station was not far from his Germantown neighborhood. He appreciated the architectural style of the building, designed by Frank Furness, with its red tile roof and decorative medallions between arched window openings. Her father always seemed to be a storehouse of knowledge.

He touched her arm. "Joan? What kind of wedding do you want?"

She turned her head back toward Franklin. "Um, well, I think. . . ." She paused. He was asking her opinion; she appreciated that. "I want a simple, traditional Quaker wedding."

"Naturally," he said. "Perhaps at Abington Friends Meetinghouse?"

"Yes. That's good. And perhaps a small reception at my

house. Just family. My father, Aunt Helen and Uncle Fred, Sonny, Mary and Red. Granny Elizabeth." She counted on her fingers. "That's seven so far. Your father. Eight."

"My sister and her husband. A few of my high school friends. Any friends you want to include?"

She thought about this. She could not think of one person outside of her family with whom she'd ever made a strong connection, as Marcus would have put it.

"Not really. No. I don't think so." She looked down at the ring. "June. A June wedding. Oh, Franklin!"

The wedding took place one week after Joan and Sonny's high school graduation, which Joan had little interest in marking despite Sonny's encouragement that she join him at various parties. She was too excited about and focused on her forthcoming wedding day and too relieved about being done with high school to care about celebrating that hallmark.

Following the ceremony at Abington Friends Meetinghouse, the immediate family members, some extended relatives, and a few of Franklin's friends gathered at Joan's house on Timber Road. The food was set up buffet style on the dining room table, on which sat two crystal vases filled with white carnations. Fine china was stacked on the credenza off to the side, and crystal wine glasses sat in a row alongside them.

"What do you suppose the goblets are for?" Joan whispered to Franklin.

He kissed the top of her head. "I'm guessing someone's got eleven-year-old bottles of wine stashed in the basement."

Joan opened her eyes wide and smiled. She had never tasted wine before and had not even expected to get to do so at her wedding.

When all the guests were seated in the living room with their full plates of food and glasses of Marcus's bottles of 1919 Bordeaux, which he had indeed safely packed away once Prohibition took effect, Marcus stood by the piano, wine glass in hand, to toast the newlyweds.

"Joan, Franklin. Congratulations. I see great things ahead for the two of you. Build a life worthy of praise and devoid of animosity and pettiness. Franklin," he said, looking directly at his new son-in-law. "You are a man of good character and sound judgment. I know you will take care of my daughter and be a devoted and faithful husband. Joan," he continued, looking at his daughter.

She straightened in her chair.

"I believe your mother would have been very proud of you today," he said. He did not mention his own pride on this day, but Joan could see it in his upbeat demeanor. His voice was higher, his words less rigid than usual.

Joan had to suppress a whimper. There was a choking sensation in her throat. Then Franklin took her hand and kissed it, and she relaxed. *My husband!* she gushed silently.

"Here's to the newlyweds," Marcus said, raising his glass.

There was a round of, "Here, here!" and a few other toasts. Helen talked about living a life in the Quaker tradition, Mary gave a humorous, rousing toast about allowing your spouse to see you at your worst and how to forgive him for "his imperfections." Everyone laughed, as usual, at Mary's wit.

Joan relished all the attention paid to her. People told her she looked radiant, that she would make a wonderful wife, that she and Franklin were made for each other. That sounded exciting, being someone's wife. She could see the path to her future clearly and, for the first time, optimistically.

As the lease for their new apartment would not begin until

after they returned from their honeymoon, Joan and Franklin spent their wedding night apart, each of them sleeping in their own twin bed in the home they grew up in. They were leaving early the next morning for a cruise from New York to Havana, and Joan was in her bedroom packing for the trip when Mary entered the room and sat on the bed.

"Congratulations, my little cousin," she said. "Can you believe you're a wife?"

"It doesn't seem real yet."

"He's a good catch, that Franklin." Mary looked around Joan's room as if searching for something. Then she took a deep breath. "I wonder if you've got any questions," she said.

"No, I think I'm all set. Father will drive Franklin and me to Thirtieth Street Station, and—"

"No, silly." Mary laughed. "I mean, since you're a wife now, you know, and you should know some things—"

"Ohhh . . . you think I don't know what to do? You think I don't have experience with boys—men—is that right?" Joan put a hand on her hip.

Mary blinked several times, clearly caught off guard by Joan's brashness. "Well, I wouldn't really know, Joan."

"It's okay, Mary," Joan said with an air of disregard as she resumed packing. "Franklin and I have done a lot of necking, even petting, and even—"

"Okay, enough. That's enough, Joan," she said, turning her head away. "I don't need to hear any more. I was only trying to be like a—"

"A what? A mother? You're *not* my mother, Mary." Joan said this calmly, nonchalantly, as if it mattered very little to her if she offended or hurt her cousin.

"Like a *sister*. I thought perhaps I could offer you, I don't know, *sisterly* advice, from a cousin. That's all." She smoothed out her skirt. "But you've obviously got all your facts down. So I'll let you finish packing."

Joan could see that her cousin was indeed hurt. "I'm sorry, Mary. I guess I *am* a little nervous. I was lying about all that. Franklin and I, well, you know, we've kissed a bit, of course."

Mary smiled. "All I know is, that man adores you, Joan. When you're alone with him, your *husband*, when you're alone tomorrow night, just remember that. And think of how much *you* love him. It's not about"—she quickly peeked outside of Joan's bedroom door—"*intercourse*," she said in a slow whisper, a smile on her face. "It's about love. And if you don't feel all that the first night, give it time. The more you love him, the better it gets."

Joan nodded, trying to make sense of what Mary was telling her. Joan certainly knew what intercourse was, and she understood that the purpose of it was for procreation. She also knew that it was something that most boys and men wanted very much and that girls were *supposed* to reserve for their husbands. Yet, here was Mary telling her that sex was also about emotion and pleasure, and that connecting all the dots was something entirely possible and, with time, probable. Joan accepted Mary's advice as fact.

"And here's something that my mother gave me," Mary said. "Just before my wedding."

"*The Married Woman's Guide to Hygiene?*" Joan asked quizzically with a smirk. She fanned the pages of the book, already beginning to imagine the wealth of information contained inside. She perused the table of contents. "Contraception," she said. "That's . . . to prevent pregnancy?"

"Mm-hmm. You want to have children, of course. Just not a whole fleet of them." She gently punched Joan's arm and winked. "It was written by two doctors. Gynecologists. Lots of important information and suggestions for . . ." She hesitated. "Well, just read it before your honeymoon. And be prepared when you do read it," she said as she poked her younger cousin's shoulder. "You may blush."

Joan was eager to read it. Mary changed the subject.

"Well, congrats and all that, Joan. Bon voyage!" She smiled broadly, turned, and left the room.

Joan put the last of her clothing into the suitcase. She sat down next to it and ran her finger along the worn buckle. The last time she'd used the suitcase was when she went off to Green Meadows. She thought about Norman. Enough time had passed that she could no longer feel all the strong positive and negative emotions she had had for him. They were mere thoughts now, recollections with little weight attached, though some residual shame and embarrassment remained. She pictured Brett, his naked body at night. She shivered remembering how he'd seemed almost hypnotized by her touch, how this power had initially thrilled her until it seemed she was no longer the one in control, and then she had felt overwhelmed.

Once, when she and Franklin were saying good-night last summer, he'd pulled her to him and kissed her passionately. She'd liked that sudden rush, the feeling of being physically attractive to a man. She was very curious about her new husband and the kind of lover he might be, yet also nervous and concerned about what to expect and how she should behave. She also wondered what her marriage would be like; would Franklin be like the other man in her life—her father—always telling her what she should and shouldn't do? She loved Franklin—at least, she assumed she loved him—but how would she know?

7

"I WANT TO BE ABLE TO TAKE A CRUISE *EVERY* YEAR OF MY LIFE. Maybe two or three a year, even," Joan said, arms in the air, upon waking up the first morning of their honeymoon.

"That'll require me to sell a lot of furniture, Mrs. Oakes."

"Then you'll need to get cracking when we get back to Philly." She hopped out of the bed. "Let's get dressed and go have some breakfast. I'm famished."

"Hold on, slow down. How about coming back over here and giving your husband a proper kiss, huh?"

Joan ambled over. She plopped down on the bed and wrapped her arms around Franklin's neck. "I am the happiest woman in the world!"

Feeling appreciated and attractive while at sea on an impressive ship with her new husband were enough happiness for Joan for the time being. There would be plenty of opportunity to learn how to enjoy sex with Franklin and, for now, that was not her priority.

They returned from the honeymoon and moved into their two-bedroom apartment in a brand-new building in Jenkintown, just a couple of miles from her childhood home in Elkins Park. Joan loved the town, where she had access to a movie theatre, two large department stores, a bakery, a butcher shop, a produce store, a library, a train station, and a host of other small businesses within walking distance. Her apartment building, one of a pair that were separated by a quaint alley reminiscent of a European village, gave Joan the feeling of living in an entirely different setting from where she was raised. She loved taking the train into Center City Philadelphia with Franklin, and she still hoped to become more involved with the business beyond her regular responsibilities and possibly take some classes at a local business school to acquire some clerical and accounting skills. At last, Joan could see a clearer path for her future, one in which she was not only a loyal and loving wife, but also an indispensable part of Oakes's Fine Furniture.

She was trying to not focus on her disappointment with sex. She was not sure what she'd expected and had regretted not accepting Mary's offer to discuss the subject in more detail, but she was so enthralled with everything else about her new life that she was willing to shelve her questions and concerns for the time being. Perhaps she'd approach Mary at a later date to bring up the topic again. The last thing on her mind, however, and something she and Franklin had never actually discussed at any length but that she knew on some level was expected and inevitable, was that she and Franklin would become parents.

In 1936, at the age of twenty, she gave birth to a baby girl, whom they named Barbara Joan. Almost immediately after arriving home from the hospital, Joan became overwhelmed. Her feelings of self-doubt and imperfection came back with a vengeance. She looked at her beautifully perfect baby girl and wondered why she was unable to easily calm the infant when she cried every night at midnight.

Each day seemed endless and without relief, and late nights awake with her daughter flowed into early mornings. One afternoon, when she was successful in putting Barbara down for a nap, Joan decided to forgo washing the breakfast dishes and instead lie down on the sofa. Fifteen minutes or so later, she awoke in a cold sweat from a frightening dream in which she had shoved the baby out the third-floor window. In her dream, she could hear the baby screaming as her tiny body fell through the air. When Joan opened her eyes and looked around the room, she saw Barbara's bassinette and could see two tiny, clenched fists waving through the air as Barbara cried loudly. Joan felt relieved, of course, to realize this had only been a dream. And yet, she was in no better state than she had been prior to falling off to sleep. This horrific dream continued for days, each time morphing into a slightly different version. In one variation, as the baby fell through the air, she immediately sprouted wings and flew off, leaving Joan momentarily relieved. In another, Joan heard the baby's screams, jumped up, ran three flights down the building's stairs, and burst out onto the sidewalk to find Franklin holding Barbara in his arms and singing to her sweetly. He looked up at Joan and initially smiled; then he twisted his face and cursed Joan for her ineptitude.

Bill Oakes's health continued to decline. Joan assumed that, because Franklin appeared so level-headed and rational through his father's illness, he was handling the whole ordeal relatively well. In any case, she was so attuned to her own precarious emotional state that she did not bother to ask about Franklin's feelings at all. Instead, she became more vocal about her isolation and fear.

"You're working so many hours, Franklin. Why would you want to stay away from Barbara and me even more than you have been?" Joan asked as they drank coffee one Saturday morning—she, still in her nightgown and robe, nursing Barbara; he with the evening paper from the day before spread out on the table in front of him.

"How can you ask me a question like that, Joan? You're making it seem like I'm being selfish. I'm only thinking of our future. Everything I do is for you and Barbara."

Joan looked down at Barbara, feeding contentedly at her breast. "I do know that, Franklin. I'm sorry. It's just . . . I don't know how to do this," she said, her lips beginning to quiver and her eyes welling up with tears.

"You don't know how to do what, Joan? I don't understand."

"*This*," she said, lowering her chin slightly for emphasis. "She cries at night. She cries in the daytime. If I don't hold her all the time, she cries. She stops crying when I nurse her; then she'll fall asleep and . . . it's wintertime, so I can't take her out for a stroll—not that I'd have any energy for walking anyway. My mind is fuzzy, Franklin. I'm tired and I'm sad. Sometimes I just feel like . . ." Joan began to cry.

Franklin waited. He raised his eyebrows and turned his head slightly sideways, trying to elicit clarification from Joan. "Like what, Joan? Sometimes you feel like what?"

"I can't tell you. You'll think I'm crazy."

He reached over and stroked her knee. "Not at all. Please tell me."

"Like I don't want to be a mother. Like my body doesn't belong to me. Having a baby is such a grown-up thing to do, and I don't feel like a grown-up. Sometimes, if I could, I'd like to hand Barbara off to the first experienced mother I see." She sniffed to inhale the mucus that had begun to drip from her nostrils onto Barbara's blanket. "My . . . " she pointed to her nipple. "They *hurt*, Franklin. They're *sore*."

Franklin stood up and lifted the baby from Joan's arms. He held Barbara in one arm and reached for a tissue on the counter with the other. He handed it to Joan, and she blew hard.

"Joan, I know what this is," he said decisively. "This is what they call 'baby blues.' Joe at the store told me his wife went through this with each of their four children. You're tired and a little sad because you miss not being around people. I always figured motherhood was the most natural thing for a woman, but I suppose some ladies struggle more than others."

Joan took offense to his characterization and furrowed her brow.

"I don't mean to imply you're not a good mother, Joan," he said defensively. "Listen, I remember the nurse telling us that babies who get formula sleep better. And if she sleeps better, so will you. So perhaps...."

"Stop nursing her?" Joan asked.

"Just a suggestion. Maybe not just yet, but maybe in a month or two?"

Joan's mouth fell open. "I'd be a failure if I did that. I'd be a *horrible* mother! The pediatrician and the nurses in the hospital told all the new mothers that we need to nurse our babies. The Mother and Baby League says it's a new mother's duty so the baby won't get infections or diarrhea." She looked down at Barbara and started to weep again. "And," she said, sniffling. "The doctor told me my body will get back to *normal* faster."

"You just need a couple of girlfriends to come over here and cheer you up. Or maybe tomorrow morning Aunt Helen can come by and spend some time with you. Or Mary. Maybe you can go up there one day. How does that sound?"

Joan blew her nose again and wiped her eyes with her hands. "Aunt Helen is so involved with the Friends Volunteer organization, I don't think she is home much. And Mary has two little ones of her own to keep her occupied up in Newtown. And girlfriends? Who are my girlfriends? I'm alone here, Franklin. And sometimes you don't make it home until well after dinnertime."

As her voiced became more agitated, her bottom lip quivered, and she began to cry again. Barbara stirred in Franklin's arms. He tried to soothe the baby by cooing to her, but she seemed to sense her mother's anxiety and began to wail. Franklin bounced Barbara in his arms and moved from side to side. Joan could tell he was struggling to keep the baby calm, but she did not volunteer to relieve him.

"It's a temporary situation," he said, "to get through this rough time."

"I feel so much pressure all the time, Franklin."

"You think running a business isn't filled with daily pressure?"

Joan was silent. She watched him move around the kitchen with Barbara. Then, looking off to the side, she said, "I think you prefer running the store to spending time with an exhausted wife and a tiny infant."

"Oh, come on, Joan," he said. "Look, the store has been around for a hundred years, and I want to make sure it survives a hundred more."

She could not acknowledge what he'd said because she felt helpless.

Franklin sighed. "The store is our future, Barbara's future, and her children's future."

Still, Joan had nothing to say. The conversation was painful. She missed the store as one might miss an old friend.

After several minutes, Franklin brightened up. "Let me call Dr. Goodall. Perhaps he can make a visit and offer some advice. Like baby formula to help Barbara sleep—or something to help you sleep, or—"

Franklin's words were cut off by the doorbell. He handed Barbara back to Joan and went to answer the door. Just before he opened it, he tightened his robe and ran his fingers through his hair.

It was Annabelle Somerton, their neighbor on the opposite side of the hallway, a widow in her mid-fifties with no children.

"Hello, Annabelle, I'm sorry if Barbara's crying woke you up just now. Joan is a little late getting her out for her morning walk."

"Not at all, Franklin. I didn't even know she was crying—I never hear that sweet angel make a peep. These thick, plaster walls." she said, patting the door frame. "No, I actually wanted to let you know that I'm leaving tomorrow morning with my pastor and some other congregants for a month-long retreat at our sister congregation in Chicago. I didn't want you to worry that something dreadful happened if you didn't see me."

"Chicago? I've heard it's a marvelous city. Never been," Franklin said.

Hearing Annabelle's voice, and seeing that Barbara had finished nursing, Joan lifted the baby to burp her as she walked out from the kitchen.

"Hello, Annabelle. Did I hear you say you are traveling to Chicago?" Joan asked, her eyes now dry but red and puffy.

"Yes, ma'am. Our train leaves Thirtieth Street bright and early tomorrow morning."

Joan felt a wave of sadness and regret overcome her. She imagined telling Annabelle she wanted—*needed*—to get on the train and head to Chicago as well.

"Annabelle, sorry, we're being rude," Franklin said, motioning for her to come in. "Please have a seat. Would you like some coffee? It's still hot."

"Yes, come in, for goodness' sake," Joan added, feeling her mood improve slightly with Annabelle's presence. "I even have some cinnamon buns from Murray's Bakery. I'll warm them up."

"If you're certain I'm not intruding. I feel terrible bothering you so early on a Saturday morning."

"Not at all. I actually need to get dressed for work. Saturdays have picked up at the store this month. But I'm quite certain that my lovely bride would enjoy some female companionship, wouldn't you, Joan?"

"Sure," Joan said with relief. "If you don't have a million other things to do before your trip." Barbara began to stir again.

"Well," Annabelle said, glancing down at Barbara. "I suppose I could spend a little time with that sweet angel." And, looking kindly into Joan's red and swollen eyes, she added, "And her sweet mother."

Joan felt a pang in her heart, the likes of which she'd not felt before. It was as if the mother she'd never known and always longed for had been transported to her in the form of this warm and friendly neighbor. She did not know Annabelle well, and their contact was limited to quick morning hellos in the hall and one or two brief visits when Annabelle had brought food: a fresh apple pie when they moved in, a casserole when Barbara was born. But in this moment, she deeply appreciated her.

Franklin entered the kitchen, freshly showered and wearing a button-down shirt, tie, and trousers. He gave Barbara, who was now in Annabelle's arms, a soft stroke on her cheek, and he squeezed Joan's shoulder.

He smiled at Annabelle. "Look how tranquil Barbara is in your arms. You've succeeded where I failed."

Annabelle lightly bounced Barbara in her arms.

"Anyway, you ladies enjoy your chat," he said as he put on his jacket. "And, Annabelle, enjoy your travels in Chicago."

Joan took a sip of coffee, looking on as this other, older woman held her baby. It was the first opportunity Joan had ever had to study Annabelle's features up close and for an extended period. She noted Annabelle's frizzy hair, dark brown and with many gray strands, pulled back into a low, thick bun, and the soft appearance of her skin, which showed no signs of age. Her plump, smooth cheeks, roundish face and saucer-shaped, warm, brown eyes were pleasing to the eye, and her full frame and bosom gave Annabelle a maternal quality that made Joan want to rush in for a hug.

As Annabelle cooed to the baby, Joan felt, for the first time since bringing Barbara home from the hospital two months earlier, a true appreciation for her child. She observed Barbara's tiny fingers curling around Annabelle's pinky and the way the baby looked intently into Annabelle's eyes, and at last a switch inside Joan's head flipped on with an epiphany. It dawned on her that it was her loneliness that was causing her to feel so resentful toward her husband and baby.

"I do love babies," Annabelle said, looking down at Barbara. "Always enjoyed holding my nieces and nephews when they were little." She looked back up at Joan and smiled. "I'm certain if my Harris hadn't passed away so young, we would've had a couple of our own."

Joan nodded with empathy, recalling how Annabelle had told her that her husband had died in the flu epidemic one year after their marriage.

"After Harris . . . I mean, did you ever . . . want to . . ." Joan hesitated, unable to say the words.

"Remarry?"

Joan nodded, now embarrassed and feeling inappropriate.

"When Harris died . . . it was so incredibly fast . . . he fell ill within a matter of hours and passed the next day. I remember you said it was the same with your mother. So awful. When Harris was gone, I was numb. He was my world. We'd been together since grade school."

"Did you have family nearby? Friends?"

Annabelle nodded. "A large family, in fact. And, of course, Harris and I had many, many friends. But it was tough. Once the initial shock wore off, I wasn't the same," she said, looking down at Barbara. She watched the baby for a few seconds, saying nothing.

Joan poured each of them another cup of coffee. "What do you mean? How were you different?"

Annabelle took a deep breath and explained how Harris's death had taken away her joy and her desire to feeling any emotion beyond grief. "You know, honey, a man can put his head into his work. No matter how much he's in pain, he's got a purpose in life . . . bring home the bacon, fill the savings account, provide shelter."

Joan thought about her own father. She remembered Helen telling her once how good-humored a person Marcus had been before Jessie's death. The only time Joan saw any inkling of happiness from her father was when he talked about the theatre.

Annabelle continued, "I never really wanted to get married again once I lost Harris. But I did find a purpose in life when I began working at the church. Pastor Michael—I think he felt sorry for me—he said he needed help organizing and typing his sermons because his wife, Lillian, had awful arthritis, and her eyesight was failing." Annabelle continued to explain how much she loved working at the church and being around the parishioners.

Annabelle's words were powerful to Joan. "I know I should be over the moon with what I have," Joan said, reaching over and stroking Barbara's tiny head. "A beautiful baby girl, a good husband, a future. I just don't understand why I feel . . ." Joan hesitated, her eyes looking upward as if to find an answer somewhere in the ceiling tiles.

"This is a big job, caring for an infant."

"I just feel so . . . alone," Joan said, ashamed that she might appear to be unappreciative and spoiled; she wanted Annabelle's approval. "What I mean is, lonely."

"Is there someone, a family member, perhaps, who can help out for a few hours a week, just so you can rest a bit, maybe get out into the fresh air or get your errands done?"

"I suppose," Joan said. Her expression turned pained and forlorn. "Yes, I do have relatives, but they . . . I mean, I . . ." Joan bit her lower lip and considered how much of her insecurity she should unleash on this woman. "My family, they're all good people. *Very* good people. But they lead extremely busy lives. My father, my aunt and uncle, my brother-in-law, my cousins . . . they're all prominent fixtures at political events and with charitable causes. They have important careers. My Uncle Fred is the VP of a chemical company. He's also the chairman of the board of some historical society or another," she said with a wave of her hand. "My father is well-known in Philly and New York. On and on." She paused, looked down at her hands, and pulled at a fingernail. "Maybe that's why I sometimes feel I don't live up to their expectations. I'm not really like them."

"I don't know your faith, Joan, but you're welcome to come by the church some time. It's Presbyterian, but we are very welcoming of everyone, all denominations. And there is a young mothers' group starting up in a month or so. Maybe you'd like to give it a try?"

Joan considered the last time she had been to meeting for worship at Abington Friends—not since before Barbara was born. She made a mental note to tell Franklin she would go next Sunday. And she'd consider Annabelle's suggestion about the mothers' group as well.

Barbara let out a sonorous burp.

Annabelle said, "All right, then, little angel, your timing is perfect. My work here is done. I'll hand you off to your mama now."

Joan did not feel ready to take the baby back into her arms.

She was enjoying the conversation and relishing Annabelle's attention and empathy.

Annabelle hesitated but held onto the baby. "I . . . probably have a few more minutes to spare, and I don't mind giving you a break, dear."

"Thanks," Joan said. "I don't want to hold you up, though."

Annabelle waved a dismissive hand. "I'm glad we finally had a chance to get to know each other, Joan. You and Franklin have been here for two years now, and this is the first time I think we've had a real conversation. I guess you spent more time away from your apartment before this little angel came along," she said, gazing down at Barbara.

Joan pressed her lips together and nodded slightly in recognition that her days as an employee at the store were over.

"Oh—I almost forgot. Would you mind if I left my key with you while I'm away?" Annabelle asked. She explained that her nephew Paul Anderson, who had just lost his job as a cook in Hartford, would be staying at her apartment while she was away. "He's going to try to find work here."

"Oh, I don't mind at all," Joan said.

Annabelle glanced at her watch. "Ho-boy, it's actually later than I realized. Now I *will* hand this angel over to you." As she stood up, she reached into a pocket and pulled out her key, placing it on the table.

Joan walked Annabelle to the door. "Enjoy Chicago. I hope to make it there one day."

Annabelle smiled. "I hope you do."

Joan closed the door, walked over to the bassinette, and placed Barbara inside. The baby began cooing softly; she was content and calm. This time, when Joan shed a tear, it was one of joy and relief, and she reassured herself, *You are a good mother.*

The following morning, as Joan and Franklin were getting

dressed for meeting for worship, she mentioned her conversation with Annabelle regarding Paul Anderson.

"So I'd like to invite him for dinner one evening, and I want to make sure you can commit to being home for that," Joan said as she buttoned her blouse.

Franklin gave a soft sigh. "As long as I have someone to cover late at the store, I can be home on time. Can I ask why this is so important to you? I didn't think you cared very much about entertaining."

Joan bristled at his characterization of her. "Aren't I permitted to evolve, Franklin? Anyway, he's new in town and it's a nice gesture, don't you think?" It was true that Joan wanted to be helpful and gracious toward Annabelle's nephew, but more importantly she wanted to connect more deeply to *Annabelle*. In Joan's mind, reaching out to Annabelle's nephew would be a good opportunity to make that happen.

Joan was distracted during meeting for worship, thinking only of what she might make Paul Anderson for dinner. She didn't feel there was anything she cooked particularly well, so she decided that this would be a good time to try one of Helen's recipes. And she could also pick up a pie from Murray's Bakery. She felt satisfied with her plan.

That evening after she put Barbara to bed, Joan grabbed a box of recipes Aunt Helen had written out for her before her wedding. She sat down at the kitchen table and began sifting through the index cards. She came across a recipe for Thanksgiving stuffing and was deluged with childhood memories of helping her aunt chop celery and mushrooms and measure out teaspoons of various dried spices to add to the breadcrumbs, pecans, and onions. She recalled feeling that she was part of a "tribe" of women, that she was being inducted into some sort of familial club that would set a course for her life. When everyone returned to their normal lives, however, she had been transported from a clan with collective goals and values back to her world of alienation—they in their worlds, she in hers.

She flipped the cards forward hoping to find a recipe for pot roast, and there it was, written in her aunt's elegantly clear handwriting. It didn't look too complicated, though all the vegetable chopping would be time-consuming. She estimated she could do the prep work during Barbara's morning nap, stick the whole thing in the oven in the afternoon, and baste every so often until dinnertime.

Though she was exhausted from her continued broken sleep, the process of planning for a dinner guest put some structure into her days and invigorated her. As she washed the breakfast dishes, she imagined buying fresh flowers for the dining table and finally using the pale-blue tablecloth with the eyelet edges given to her as a wedding gift by Mary and Red. She wondered if she could fit into any of her nice dresses since she was still carrying some extra weight from her pregnancy. It was as if the prospect of meeting and entertaining a new person was all she needed to reset her mental state. Her mind was moving in so many directions that she could barely keep one idea in her brain before the next took hold.

Barbara let out a wail, breaking Joan's racing thoughts. "Coming, your royal highness," she said, once again reminded that her time was not her own. "I haven't forgotten about you."

8

WHEN HER DOORBELL RANG AT ELEVEN THE NEXT MORNING, Joan assumed it was Aunt Helen and Mary, who had said they would stop by before heading to one of their many meetings together. Mary would be bringing her two children, John and James, ages four and one, and Joan was looking forward to the company, even if it meant enduring Mary's endless list of self-sacrificing endeavors.

"Door's open!" Joan called out as she changed Barbara's diaper.

There was a knock on the door in response.

"Hold on a minute!" She rushed to finish diapering the baby and, scooping her up, walked toward the door. She opened it quickly and, to her surprise, she found a tall, blond, young man standing on the other side.

"Oh," she said, startled. She had a feeling this was Paul Anderson, but she did not want to assume. "Can I help you?" she asked, smoothing down her hair.

"Joan Oakes? Paul Anderson," the visitor said, pointing to himself. His voice, gentle and smooth, made his tall, broad frame seem less imposing.

"Oh, my goodness, yes. Hello."

Paul looked down at Barbara. "I'm so sorry, you've got your hands full. I've obviously come by at an inconvenient time."

"No, not at all. Let me give you Annabelle's key. Please come in." She stepped aside so he could enter. "Would you like a cup of coffee?" she asked as she opened the credenza drawer to get the key. "My aunt and my cousin Mary are on their way over for a visit. You're welcome to join us for coffee. Have you had breakfast? Or lunch even?"

"Um, well, no, not yet," he said, taking the key from her. "Thanks, I appreciate the offer. I'm pretty exhausted from traveling. I think I may just shower and have a nap."

She nodded. "My husband Franklin and I would love for you to join us for dinner one night this week. Are you available?"

"Well, actually, Joan, will you allow me to make dinner for you and your husband? It would be my pleasure and it's what I do, and I do it well, if I say so myself."

Joan smiled at his confidence. "My, what an offer. All right." She took a minute to consider. "Thursday? Will that work for you? I'll double-check with Franklin, but that should be fine with him."

"Yes, that's perfect. Six-thirty, okay? Pleasure to meet you, Joan." He glanced down at the baby. "And this little one is . . . ?"

Mesmerized by Paul's piercing blue eyes, Joan had practically forgotten that she was holding her baby. "Barbara," she said, turning the infant toward Paul so that he could get a better look.

"She's a beauty," he said, smiling and leaning into the baby. "Well, so long."

"So long, Paul. Nice to meet you."

Joan backed up and closed the door, and as she did, she could hear her aunt and cousin walking up the stairs to her apartment, and the sing-song voice of her four-year-old nephew. Still, Joan closed the door to compose herself.

Joan put Barbara in the bassinette and walked toward the mirror hanging over the credenza by the dining room table. She felt relieved that her hair was neatly pulled back so that she didn't look frazzled and unkempt, yet not too matronly either.

She wished she'd worn lipstick or that she'd chosen a more colorful dress, but how could she have known that Paul Anderson would show up at her door at that particular moment?

There was a knock at the door, and Joan opened it, letting in Helen, Mary, and the boys.

"Well, hello there, Mr. John Weldon. You're getting bigger by the minute, aren't you?" she said to the toddler. "Hi, Aunt Helen," she said, kissing her aunt on the cheek. "Hi, Mary. And hello, little James."

"Who was that tall young man we saw entering the apartment across the hall?" Helen asked as she removed her thick, wool winter coat.

"Huh?" Joan feigned a complete lack of awareness and interest. "Um, oh, maybe you saw my neighbor Annabelle's nephew." She immediately turned to retrieve Barbara from the bassinette.

"Well if he's not married, he could be in about a minute," Mary joked, grabbing John's hat from his head as he ran past her.

Joan managed a disinterested chuckle and changed the subject. "Who would like a cinnamon bun?" she asked Paul and James, who were hand-in-hand, marching around the living room singing and laughing.

Mary threw the boys' coats, hats, and mittens on the sofa; then she corralled them into the kitchen, and the five of them sat at the table. Helen took Barbara from Joan's arms.

"I've barely seen this one since she was born," Helen remarked.

And whose fault is that? Joan wondered. "You've been extraordinarily busy, Aunt Helen," Joan said, pouring coffee for her aunt and cousin. "How many activities are you involved in these days?"

Mary jumped in. "Too many to count. She teaches English to two new immigrants from South America; she helped organize the opening of a recreational center and two daycare centers downtown—"

Helen broke in, "So many women are in the workforce now, what are they supposed to do with their youngest children? Thank goodness for Roosevelt and the WPA," she said, taking a sip of her coffee.

"Oh, that's the Workers Progress Administration, right? I started to read about it last week, but then Barbara woke up from a nap," Joan said.

"Now that Mayor Wilson is in office, Philadelphia can finally take advantage of Roosevelt's New Deal money," Helen said.

Joan had felt the lack of her awareness of the world outside her little apartment ever since she'd stopped working at the store. She wondered if perhaps she could return to it someday.

"I rarely have time to read the newspaper lately," Joan said, "and when I do have a spare moment, I'd rather listen to the radio while I straighten up or even just take a nap."

"Cut yourself a little slack, Joanie," Mary said, slicing a cinnamon bun into small pieces for her boys. "Being a new mother is challenging. I was lucky to have Mom's help when Johnnie was born. By the time James came along, well . . ." Mary turned to Helen.

"I would have helped out then as well had you and Red not moved up to Bucks County," said Helen. "That was much too far for me to manage on a regular basis."

Mary kissed her mother's cheek. "You're a darling, Mom. I wouldn't trade you for your weight in gold."

As Joan watched the interaction between the two women, she felt the familiar emotional void and the envy she'd grown up with in the house on Timber Road. Barbara let out a small whimper, and Joan reached over to stroke the baby's hair—more to feed her own longing for connection than to pacify the child.

"Anyway, Joan, if you need a little extra help, I'm sure Mom could lend a hand once in a while, right?" Mary said, turning to Helen and rubbing her mother's shoulder.

Helen seemed taken aback. "Oh, ah, yes, yes, naturally. Joan, all you have to do is ask. After all, I *am* Barbara's great auntie," she said, looking down at the baby and gently rocking her.

Joan had always had the feeling that her aunt felt sorry for her and tended to do things for her out of an abundance of pity rather than a strong affinity for her niece. But this time, Joan decided to take the bold step of actually asking for a favor.

"Well, then, Great Auntie Helen," Joan said. "By any chance, would you be available Thursday evening? Franklin and I have been invited to dinner."

"How lovely!" Mary exclaimed. "Where, may I ask?"

Always so nosy. "A neighbor. Here in this building, actually."

"Hmm," Helen said, tapping her lip with her index finger. "I'd love to be able to help, but I have a community outreach committee meeting that evening at Abington Friends."

"I understand," Joan said. "That's fine, Aunt Helen. Franklin and I will manage." Joan was relieved to not have to explain anything further to them about where she was going on Thursday night.

The boys gobbled up their cinnamon bun pieces and sipped warm milk, Johnnie from a glass and James from a bottle. Joan marveled at how well-behaved and good-natured they were, and how calm and confident her cousin was in her role as a mother. She observed the mutual admiration between Mary and Helen, and the way Helen spoke to Mary's sons with such affection and adoration. Joan wanted that—all of it—adoration, acceptance, support, confidence. The very things that a good mother provides for a daughter, the same things that Franklin had initially showered her with in the first few years that she'd known him.

She felt that support somehow falling away, as if the more he learned about her, the less he admired and was enamored with her.

When Helen, Mary, and the boys were getting ready to leave, Joan walked them to the door with Barbara in her arms. Barbara began to cry, just a few soft sounds at first, and Joan felt a sense of dread at the thought of, once again, being alone in the apartment with a demanding infant.

She looked at her watch. Their visit had only been forty-five minutes. "Are you sure you wouldn't like to stay for a little longer?" She smiled, though she worried it came across as a desperate plea rather than positive encouragement.

Helen hedged a bit and looked at Mary, who replied with a cheerful tone, "This has been so nice, Joanie. It's been too long since the three of us have had any time together. We really needed to catch up, and I'm so happy we did," she said, putting a jacket on her older son.

Mary is always good at making even a rejection sound sweet, Joan thought.

Mary continued, "Sorry to just pop in and pop out but I just have so much to do this afternoon, and Mom has agreed to mind the boys at her house so I can head into town."

"Oh. I see," Joan said. She felt not only let down but also resentful that Mary had the option of discarding her children for an afternoon of freedom and independence. Joan forced a more authentic smile and tried to sound upbeat as she bounced her baby, who was now wailing a bit more forcefully.

Helen gave Joan a kiss on the cheek. "So long, dear. Say, why don't you ask that nice neighbor of yours—what's her name again, Marabelle?—if she can stay with Barbara on Thursday evening. It would be a shame for you to have to miss a dinner out because you don't have a babysitter."

"That's a good idea. Thanks, Aunt Helen, I'll do that," she said, without bothering to correct the name error or say anything about Annabelle being out of town. It was pointless.

"Bye-bye, Joanie," said Mary, kissing Joan's cheek and carefully hugging her and Barbara as if they were one unit. "Take care of that little one. Sounds like she's ready for lunch."

Just after they started down the hall and before Joan had closed the door, Mary turned back. "Maybe you ought to hire someone to help out a few hours a week, Joan. You know, to give yourself a little break."

"Maybe I will," Joan said.

And with that, Helen, Mary, Johnnie, and James were gone.

Joan doubted she would follow through to find some help with the baby. Who could she call? How would she arrange that? And, for that matter, she doubted Franklin would be amenable to spending the extra money on the "extravagance." She put the idea out of her head.

9

FRANKLIN AGREED TO BE HOME FOR DINNER THAT THURSDAY, though he grumbled about having to ask the assistant manager to help with paperwork, and he said was not entirely comfortable with the idea of allowing Paul to cook for them.

"It's so roundabout, it doesn't seem worth all the fuss," he said to Joan when he arrived home Thursday evening.

Joan ignored his comment and focused on her choice of earrings. She had ruminated all day about what she would wear. She wanted to look stylish and sophisticated, but with an air of casual effortlessness. She also didn't want it to appear to Franklin that she was trying too hard, and why *was* she trying so hard?

"When's the babysitter arriving?" Franklin asked.

Joan was in front of the bathroom mirror, applying lipstick. "I haven't arranged for a babysitter," she said.

"What? Joan, we discussed this on Tuesday night. Didn't you say you were going to contact Helen?"

"Well, yes, and I did. But she isn't available tonight. And anyway, I didn't think it would be a problem. I've already fed her. We can bring over the basket."

"Honestly, Joan, I don't know what you were thinking."

Joan was embarrassed that she hadn't given more thought to the logistics of having a tiny baby in tow, but she didn't want Franklin to view her as incompetent, so she brushed off his concern and tried to sound sure of herself. "She'll probably fall asleep over there." She smiled and finished applying her lipstick;

then she walked into the kitchen to retrieve a chocolate cake she had bought from the bakery to take to dinner.

When Paul opened the door to Annabelle's apartment, the powerful aroma of something meaty and garlicky made Joan acutely aware of her hunger.

"Welcome," Paul said, stepping aside to let the couple enter. He wiped his hands on his white, full-length apron, which he wore over a button-down collared shirt with the sleeves rolled up. He peered into the basket. "Another guest, I see," he said with a smile.

"Yes, I'm sorry, Paul," Joan said. "We had a bit of trouble finding a babysitter."

"She's more than welcome here." He looked at Franklin, who stood holding the basket with both hands. "Good to meet you, Franklin. I'd shake your hand, but . . ."

Franklin set the basket down on the floor and the two men shook hands. "Nice to meet you as well," he said.

"Please, make yourselves comfortable." He directed them toward the sofa.

"This is such a lovely apartment," Joan said, handing the cake to Paul, who took it with an appreciative nod. She took note of the paintings, lamps, chairs, area rugs, and china cabinet, far more elegant furniture than she had expected. She wondered if Annabelle had bought most of it after Harris died.

"Admittedly, it's a bit strange for me to be entertaining in my aunt's home, but she encouraged me to treat it as my own, so . . ."

"Something smells delicious," Franklin said as he relocated the basket on the floor near the sofa.

"Beef bourguignon, my specialty," Paul said.

"Beef bourguignon!" Franklin exclaimed. "I don't know the last time we had *that*," he said, looking directly at Joan.

Feeling criticized, Joan pursed her lips and glared at Franklin. Then she relaxed her face and smiled, smoothing out her skirt. "You asked me to be conservative with our money, dear." She sat on the sofa and looked up at Paul. "With a new baby, money is a bit tight at the moment," she said, casually waving her hand in the air.

Paul nodded. "Well, then I hope this is truly a treat for you two."

"If the taste is anything like the aroma, I'm sure it'll be the meal of our lives," Joan said.

Paul clapped his hands. "Dinner will be ready in fifteen minutes. But first, may I offer either of you a martini?"

"A martini! My goodness, you've gone all out. Well, since you're offering," Franklin said, rubbing his neck. "It was a frustrating day at the store. I could use something to take the edge off." He took a seat next to Joan.

"Joan?" Paul asked.

"No, thank you, Paul." She very much wanted to try a martini, but she worried that the alcohol might get into her milk and make Barbara tipsy. She didn't know if this were even possible, but she felt her safest bet was to refrain altogether.

Paul handed Franklin the drink and sat down across from the couple.

"Ten more minutes on the timer, and then we can move to the table." He raised his glass, "Cheers!"

"Cheers!" said Franklin. He took a sip and winced slightly.

"Have I made it too dry for you, Franklin? I'd be happy to add something—"

"Oh, no, not at all, Paul. It's . . . perfect," he said.

Joan assumed he was lying, trying to impress Paul. She knew his experience with hard liquor was limited to the moonshine whiskey he'd once shared with a high school buddy, and which Franklin told her tasted like rubbing alcohol.

"Annabelle used to tell me stories about the speakeasies around here," Paul said. "I always found that humorous: this pious, law-abiding woman knowing where to get bootleg booze. Not that she was ever a drinker, mind you."

"My cousin Sonny claims there was a speakeasy down the street from our house," Joan said. Franklin looked at her quizzically, and she returned his gaze with conviction. She looked at Paul. "Supposedly, there was something shady going on," she said, narrowing her eyes.

"So, Franklin, you mentioned a store. What line of business are you in?" Paul asked.

Franklin took another sip, and Joan could see he was trying very hard to enjoy his drink. "Furniture. My family owns Oakes's Fine Furniture on Ninth and Arch."

The timer rang, and Paul sprang up to tend to the food. "Please excuse me."

"Can I help you?" Joan asked him.

Paul indicated that he was fine. "Why don't the two of you take a seat at the table, and I'll bring everything in. I have some great news I want to share with you."

Joan noticed that Barbara was falling asleep, so she whispered to Franklin to leave the basket in place. They stood up and walked to the table, where Paul was setting a large plate of green beans down next to a plate of bread sliced thick.

Franklin pulled a chair out for Joan and sat down next to her. She gave him a small smile, but he looked annoyed and took another sip of the martini.

Paul walked back into the kitchen and reemerged carrying a large ceramic bowl. Franklin sat up straight, his expression quickly changing to one of pleasant anticipation. Paul set the bowl by his place at the head of the table and took his seat.

"I'm not a particularly religious man, but I am in my aunt's home, and she's been so gracious to me. So I'll keep it simple: Thank you, Lord, for good food and new friends. Amen."

"Amen," said Franklin.

"Amen," said Joan. "Paul, you said you have some good news?"

"Yes, indeed," he said, spooning the beef bourguignon onto a plate for Joan. The carrots, potatoes, onions, mushrooms, and noodles glistened in the savory juice. "I've been offered a position at the Bellevue-Stratford as a sous-chef in their kitchen."

"Congratulations," said Joan.

"I'd heard the hotel was struggling," said Franklin.

"What business isn't, in this economy? I think the Republican National Convention this year turned things around for the hotel and restaurant, really brought a lot of money in," Paul said as he filled Franklin's plate.

"I suppose if they're hiring it's a good sign," Joan said, in an attempt to counter Franklin's negativity.

Paul nodded. "And I've found housing at the YMCA in Center City. It's temporary until I can find a room or apartment, but I'll be able to save several paychecks in the meantime." He handed Joan her plate and began to fill Franklin's as well.

"It's amazing you were able to secure a job in such a short period of time," Franklin said. "There are men pounding the pavement for months on end just trying to find some work—any work—to feed their families."

"I realize that," said Paul. "Honestly, I think the fact that I'm unmarried and without any children was a selling point. I can work endless shifts with no commitment to a family."

Joan took a bite of the meat and quickly grabbed her napkin before the juicy bit could drip down her chin. "Paul, this is absolutely fantastic!"

"It is," agreed Franklin. "You must give Joan the recipe."

"Tell us how you became a cook," she said.

"Well, when I was sixteen, my father passed away, and—"

Just then, the radiator creaked loudly and emitted a hiss of steam. Barbara, startled, let out a wail. Joan shot up out of her chair and rushed over to the basket. She lifted Barbara and tried to console her, but the child kept crying.

"There, there, my little sweetheart," Joan said, swaying back and forth and bouncing in an attempt to mollify her daughter. She was embarrassed as she looked over and saw Paul's stunned face.

"Is she okay?" he asked.

"She'll settle down in a minute," Joan said. She noticed Franklin rub his temples.

Barbara quieted within a few minutes, but as soon as Joan put her back into the basket, she began to cry out again.

Franklin stood up and walked over to Joan. "Maybe you should take her back to the apartment and nurse her," he said softly. "She'll fall back to sleep."

"And what do I do after that?" she said, frustrated. She walked back to the table with Barbara and sat down. "It's fine. I can hold her while I eat. That is, if you don't mind," she added to Paul.

"No, of course not," he said.

Franklin took his seat. Joan could feel his annoyance. She took a deep breath, smiled, and resumed the conversation. "Sorry, Paul, please continue," she said, with her eyes on her daughter.

He went on to describe how he had worked as a short-order cook to help his mother make ends meet following his father's death, and how much he loved the fast-paced environment of a restaurant kitchen. His last job, in Hartford, had been in a French restaurant, where he had learned the art of haute cuisine under the guidance of a master chef. He said he hoped to travel to Paris someday and possibly take culinary classes.

Joan was fascinated with everything about him: his maturity

as a teenager; his confidence as a young man; his knowledge of food and how he rattled off words like *caramelize*, *flambé*, and *bouquet garni*; his independence and sense of adventure. She envied how much he loved what he did for a living. He was responsible only for himself.

She managed to finish everything on her plate despite holding a three-month old in her left arm for the entire meal. It was not the most relaxing dinner she had ever had, but it might have been the most delicious.

"Shall I put on a pot of coffee, and we can enjoy your cake?" Paul asked.

Barbara began to stir in Joan's arms. "She's getting a bit fidgety, I'm afraid. Franklin, would you mind holding her for a bit?"

Franklin took Barbara and kissed her head. She became fussy in his arms. Paul began to clear the table, and Joan stood up to help him. She was more than happy to clean up, especially if it meant she could have a break from holding Barbara. But Paul brushed her away politely, so she sat back down. When Paul was in the kitchen, Franklin leaned into Joan.

"I think we should say our good-byes," he whispered, looking down at Barbara. "This is no longer enjoyable."

Paul returned, and Joan awkwardly apologized and explained that it was Barbara's difficult hour when she tended to become colicky and cranky.

Franklin stood up. "Thanks for your hospitality, Paul," he said, reaching out his hand. "And for the delicious meal. You're quite talented."

"Yes, Paul. This was such a treat. I'm sorry we're leaving so abruptly," Joan said. She was seething inside and felt it was not imperative they leave. But she didn't want to upset Franklin, who seemed exhausted from a long day of work, a heavy meal, and two martinis.

Back in their apartment, Franklin chided Joan. "This was not a good idea from the start," he said. "We have a three-month-old baby. How can we expect to socialize right now?"

Joan had never seen Franklin so negative and critical of her. She wondered how Paul would describe the evening to Annabelle. Joan realized Franklin had been right all along; she hadn't thought out the logistics of being someone's dinner guest while taking care of an infant. How did she even think she could have managed to host a dinner herself? She needed to focus, for now, on her role as mother and wife, and to put aside her own need for fun and social diversions. As to her relationship with Annabelle, well, Joan intended to pick up where they'd left it before Chicago. Though Joan found Paul intriguing, it was Annabelle whom Joan wanted to have in her life, and anyway, Paul would be gone once Annabelle returned.

After nursing Barbara, Joan lifted the baby against her shoulder and patted her back a few times, which elicited several small belches. She put Barbara in her crib, stroked her warm back, and silently hoped for a good night's sleep.

10

ON WEEKNIGHTS WHEN FRANKLIN WORKED LATE, USUALLY once or twice a week, Joan would invite Annabelle to join her for dinner. If Annabelle was not working late at the church or too tired and did not have other plans, she would accept Joan's invitation. Annabelle would play with Barbara while Joan finished preparing the dinner, and then the two women would sit at the kitchen table for an hour or so of topical, or sometimes emotional, discussion.

Joan could seamlessly talk to Annabelle, who did not appear to judge her or feel uncomfortable listening to personal details of her life. She appreciated the open-ended questions Annabelle would ask, as well as the perspective Annabelle provided based on her own life experience, though Joan refrained from challenging assertions Annabelle made regarding faith and God's plans. Joan did not understand why it was so important to believe in God. Mostly, she thought people talked about belief in God merely to fit in and not cause trouble. It was inconceivable to Joan that, if there really were a God, he would let horrible people get away with so much.

Joan had seen Paul on several occasions since the night he prepared dinner for her and Franklin at Annabelle's. Two Sundays a month, he would visit Annabelle and cook for her, always arriving around four thirty. On one particular Sunday in May, when Annabelle learned that Franklin was out of town, she invited Joan to join them for dinner. Joan thoroughly enjoyed herself that evening and felt more relaxed and upbeat than she had in months. She hoped to be included in more of Paul's Sunday dinners at Annabelle's, with or without Franklin.

When summer arrived, Joan assumed that she, Franklin, and Barbara would take a week's vacation to Ocean City or Cape May, but Franklin was overwhelmed with orders at the store and explained that a vacation would need to wait until the end of August. She spent the hot days taking Barbara out for early morning strolls and then retreating to the apartment, where she would plop herself in front of the fan and sip ice-cold lemonade. As Barbara napped, Joan found herself thinking about Paul every day. Something about him and the way he elevated her mood made her think of Norman Lewis, to whom she had not given even a passing thought for several years. Both Norman and Paul possessed a calm, cool self-confidence, and both were humble yet upbeat. Or it may have been Paul's eyes, the same piercing blue that Norman possessed, that looked deeply into her own and unsettled her in an exciting way, creating a kind of longing she could not make sense of. What did she want? Was something missing inside her, and could Paul help her find it? He seemed so open, not rigid or judgmental, yet his carefree affect and aloofness made it difficult for Joan to know if he shared her feelings.

On a Saturday morning in October, one of the rare ones when Franklin was not working, he and Joan sat in the kitchen drinking coffee. Barbara was asleep. There was a knock at their door, and Joan popped up to answer it.

"I bet it's Annabelle," Joan said, eager to see her friend who had been busy all week. To her surprise, it was Paul at the door.

"Paul!" she exclaimed. "Please, come in." She stepped aside and motioned for him to enter the apartment.

His face looked serious, as if he were in shock.

Franklin emerged from the kitchen. "Hello, Paul. To what do we owe the honor of your visit?" Franklin's tone sounded far less enthusiastic than Joan's.

"Has something happened to Annabelle?" Joan began to panic.

"She's. . . ." He seemed to be searching for words. "Gone. Aunt Annabelle . . . died."

Joan gasped and covered her mouth.

"Why don't you have a seat, Paul," said Franklin. "I'll get you a glass of water."

Paul sat down on the very edge of the sofa. Joan sat in a chair across from him.

She noticed Paul's trembling hands and, impulsively, she reached out to touch the top of his forearm. As she did, Franklin emerged from the kitchen. Realizing how inappropriate this must have looked to Franklin, Joan withdrew her hand quickly.

Franklin handed Paul the water and sat down in a chair next to his wife.

"What happened?" Joan asked, trying to be tactful and sensitive, yet eager to know the details.

"She was working late last night at the church, organizing the pastor's notes for Sunday's sermon, and apparently she collapsed in the office. His wife, Lillian, had come in with a cup of tea for Annabelle and found her on the floor, face down."

"Heart attack?" asked Franklin.

Paul shrugged. "Or possibly a stroke. She may have been on the floor for a while before Lillian found her. Lillian telephoned Michael at home, and he immediately called Abington Hospital, and an ambulance came, but they were too late." He took a sip of water.

"Paul, I'm . . . so sorry," Franklin said.

"How did you find out?" Joan asked. "When?"

Paul began to sob silently. "I'm sorry," he said. "I'm in shock, I suppose." He pinched the bridge of his nose.

Joan lifted her hand, almost instinctively, to reach out for him again, but then she brought it back down to her lap.

"It's okay," she said. "Take your time." Joan could feel her throat constricting.

"Pastor Michael tried to call me late last night, but I was working. He finally reached me at seven o'clock this morning." He lifted the glass of water. "She was always my favorite relative. She treated me like a son. And since I arrived in Philly, she's been so kind to me." He put the water down without taking a sip.

Joan wiped tears from her eyes as she thought about the dinners and long conversations she had shared with Annabelle; those would never happen again. "She really cared about you, Paul."

Paul reached into his breast pocket for a handkerchief. "Michael is preparing a special sermon dedicated to her for tomorrow's service," he said, wiping his nose with the handkerchief. "He's choosing a passage from Corinthians. He told me that was her favorite."

There was silence among the three of them. Franklin pressed the fingertips of his two hands together and looked uncomfortably at his shoes. Joan eyed Paul carefully and with fascination, focusing on his wet eyelashes and swollen lids. She had never seen a man cry or even discuss feelings—and with people he hardly knew, at that. It made her wonder what depth of emotions her father had felt or expressed when her mother died. She could not imagine him crying.

"She'll be laid to rest in the church's cemetery, right next to Uncle Harris." Paul was quiet for several seconds. "She used to say she didn't fear death, and she looked forward to joining Harris in heaven when that day came."

"I don't know what to say except we are both so sorry," Joan said. "She was a special person with such a big heart. I never heard her say anything bad about anyone." Joan struggled to keep her composure, but all she could focus on was her own loss. *What will I do without my Annabelle?*

"I need to find clothing, something for her to wear—she had it all written in her directives," Paul said, taking an envelope out of his inside breast pocket, "Everything right down to the brooch and earrings. But perhaps, Joan, I mean, if you wouldn't mind. . . ."

"Not at all," Joan said. "Give it to me, and I'll gather everything. I understand, this is better taken care of by another woman." Joan surprised herself at how confident and in control she felt, considering the fact that she had just lost her best friend.

"When is the funeral?" asked Franklin.

"Wednesday morning," said Paul.

"Is . . . is there anything else I—*we*—can do, Paul?" Joan asked. "Would you like some coffee? Have you eaten breakfast?"

"Thanks, but I need to get going. I'm working later today." He took a sip of water and stood up.

Franklin stood up as well. "So very sorry about Annabelle. We will hold you and your family in the light," Franklin said, reciting a Quaker expression. The two men shook hands.

Paul nodded his head slowly, as if processing the words, as he exited the apartment.

Franklin ran his fingers through his hair. "I'm already exhausted, and it's not even noon. I sure hope the guy's going to be okay."

"Of course, he will!" Joan exclaimed, her voice filled with both outrage and her own dose of concern for Paul. "He's just trying to process what happened. Can you imagine? He really cared for her. She was like a mother to him. And—" Joan paused, suddenly wanting to take back what she had said and the way in which she'd said it. *She was like a mother to me!* she wanted to scream. She looked at her watch. "Barbara will probably be awake soon."

Barbara cried out from her crib, and Joan headed into the bedroom to retrieve the baby, who had pulled herself up to a standing position, holding onto the sidebar. When she saw Joan, she smiled and softly said, "Mama," to which Joan replied, "Yes, Barbie. Mama is here. Come on, let's get a bottle."

She lifted her daughter, kissed the child's forehead, and headed into the kitchen. As she put Barbara into her high chair, she reflected on the first real conversation she'd had with Annabelle nine months earlier, when Annabelle had said that working at the church helped to ease her grief over Harris and gave her life meaning. *What will ease my grief?*

After feeding Barbara some mashed banana, Joan lifted her out of the high chair and went into the bedroom, where she found Franklin looking at himself in the mirror. He seemed to be inspecting his face closely. She walked over to him.

"I'm looking more and more like my dad," he said, running a finger over his forehead. "I'm too young to be feeling so old."

She didn't respond. She had her own emotions to contend with. "Can you hold her for a minute?" she asked Franklin.

He took his daughter in his arms, walked to the bed, and sat on the edge while Barbara drank from her bottle.

Joan grabbed a dress from her closet and held it against her body as she looked in the mirror."Do you know the first time I wore this dress?"

Franklin shook his head no.

"It was my first day at the store, that summer before my senior year. Remember? You told me I looked sophisticated and smart." She turned back toward the mirror. "I wonder if it still fits." She put the hanger over the top of the closet door, and stood back. "I'd like to wear it tomorrow, to meeting for worship." She headed into the bathroom to take a shower.

Under the warm water, Joan began to feel her breath become shallow. Her throat constricted again. Involuntarily, she let out a wail, followed by a flood of uncontrolled spasms of cries. She needed to retreat, but to where, and from whom? She hoped Franklin could not hear her as the water trickled from the shower head.

11

BACK INSIDE HER APARTMENT AFTER SUNDAY MEETING FOR worship, Joan opened the refrigerator and pulled out two left-over ham sandwiches for herself and Franklin. She placed them on plates on the table, along with some applesauce and mashed peas for the baby. Joan was ravenous and shaky from hunger, yet at the same time she was slightly queasy and anxious about entering Annabelle's apartment to gather what was needed for the funeral. She took a couple quick bites of her sandwich before wrapping it up and placing it back in the refrigerator.

Franklin entered the kitchen holding Barbara. "She's freshly diapered and ready for lunch," he said good-naturedly.

"Well, then, can you please feed her? I'm going over to Annabelle's apartment," Joan said, grabbing Annabelle's key, as well as the envelope Paul had given her. As she passed Franklin, she added, "There's a sandwich in the fridge for you. I'll be back soon." She headed out, focused only on the task at hand.

Joan opened Annabelle's door slowly, as if she didn't want to startle anyone who might be inside. Then, realizing that this was preposterous, she removed the key from the lock and entered Annabelle's apartment, leaving the door ajar. Glancing around, she noticed how tidy the apartment was; everything was in its place, and there was no sign that the occupant would not be returning. Joan walked toward Annabelle's bedroom with some trepidation. She wanted to be respectful, yet efficient and expeditious, and, having never been in Annabelle's bedroom before, it was possible Joan would need to dig around a bit to find what she needed.

Just before she entered the room, she opened the envelope and pulled out a hand-written, one-page letter, dated March 22, 1932, with instructions on how Annabelle wanted to be dressed for the funeral, what should accompany her body in the casket, and which music should be played. She requested to have the song "All Things Bright and Beautiful" sung at her graveside. There was a second page with typewritten lyrics to the song, and Joan's throat tightened and her eyes welled up with tears as she read the lyrics. She found it beautifully inspirational, with its references to animals and nature and the change in seasons, a simple appreciation of the miracles one sees and experiences every day. It seemed fitting that someone like Annabelle would choose this particular song for her own funeral in order to lift people's spirits rather than dwell on her passing. The sentiment was sweet in its simplicity, yet Joan did not relate to the gratitude. She wondered if that was the difference between her and Annabelle. There was so much about which Joan had always felt resentful.

On the dresser, a framed wedding photograph showed a very young Annabelle and Harris. She lifted the photo for a closer look. Annabelle had small, tight curls around her forehead, and her hair was pulled up with no flowers or veil adorning it. Harris's hair was neatly parted in the center. The figures did not look posed, as she and Franklin had been on their wedding day when the photographer commanded them this way and that. What struck her was that Annabelle and Harris each had a small, solemn smile, yet looked as if they might burst, unable to contain their joy. Annabelle's hand was placed around Harris's arm, and his face was downcast a bit toward her hand, as if he were honored to have her holding onto him. Joan returned the photo to the dresser and stood in the center of Annabelle's bedroom, looking around in fascination, realizing that there was actually so much she didn't know about the woman.

She pulled a handkerchief out of her dress pocket, wiped her eyes, and blew her nose. Then she began to get to work gathering the items on the list: a pale, yellow dress, cream-colored gloves, a heart-locket necklace, a wedding band.

After double-checking the list against what she had piled on the bed, she carefully lifted the clothing, jewelry, and personal items and walked out of Annabelle's bedroom. As she passed through the living room, she noticed a small, black notepad on the floor next to the sofa. She walked over to it and picked it up. Finding nothing printed or written on the front or back covers, she opened it and saw on the inside cover the handwritten line: "Property of Paul T. Anderson, The Bellevue-Stratford," along with a phone number.

Curious about what Paul used it for, she was tempted to flip to the first page, but stopped herself. This was neither the time nor place, and, anyway, she'd been away from her own apartment long enough. She held the notepad to her chest and took a long, slow breath, closing her eyes. She did not believe in God, but she could believe in fate, and finding this notepad seemed closer to fate than anything she'd ever experienced. *What to do?* She must return it to him, mustn't she? She opened her eyes and knew that she needed to see him, alone and soon. This would give her an excuse to do just that. She walked out of the apartment, gently closing the door and locking it as she whispered, "Good-bye, Annabelle."

That night, as she lay in bed trying to fall asleep, Joan could only think about what could be written on the small pages of Paul's notepad. Her father kept a small, thin, black notepad in his breast pocket for taking notes during plays, but that was what his profession required. Did Paul's notepad contain to-do lists, phone numbers, and recipes, or perhaps more personal information—his musings about people, poetry for his female conquests, or his darkest secrets? She couldn't imagine any man she knew putting down such confidential information for anyone to accidentally find. But Paul was different from any other man she knew. Was anything written about her? She glanced over at Franklin, who was fast asleep. Joan slowly pushed the blanket off her body and eased herself out of bed, trying not to disturb him.

She'd hidden the notepad in her underwear drawer, all the way toward the back and under her brassieres and slips. Slowly and quietly, she opened the drawer and reached for it. She grabbed her robe and made her way out of the bedroom, momentarily looking back at Franklin. He was a heavy sleeper; there was no need to worry.

As she sat at the kitchen table, she examined the notepad. It was worn around the edges, with stains the color of coffee on the inside beige backing. She held the notepad to her nose and sniffed, but it had no special scent.

She wanted to respect his privacy, but with the weight of her curiosity winning the ethical battle, Joan decided to just read the first page, telling herself it was in the interest of getting close to him. She opened the notepad and read the handwritten date on the first page: January 13, 1937. Below that was a to-do list of some sort. She skipped a few pages and found a recipe, a quote: *Patience is not in the waiting but in the attitude.* How was it that Paul, Annabelle, and so many other people she knew were so filled with positivity, and why did it elude her? She sifted through cryptic references and mundane notes. Nothing exciting or particularly revealing.

Every couple of pages there was a new date entry. She looked into space, trying to recall the date that she and Franklin had dined with Paul. It was several months earlier, wintertime, when they'd eaten together. February? She couldn't even consult her calendar on the wall to see what she'd written because at the end of each month she'd rip off the page and throw it away.

She did remember that it was the day Amelia Earhart announced her plan to circumnavigate the globe, because Joan had heard the report on the radio that morning.

She sifted through the pages of the notepad until she got to February dates. There it was; under February 11, 1937, she saw her name and Franklin's:

Cooked tonight for new friends, Joan and Franklin Oakes. Beef Bourg. Nice couple, new baby. Strained marriage? He is likeable, tense tho. She has a lovely smile, she's delicate. Anxious.

That was it. He mentioned his job offer at the Bellevue-Stratford, another to-do list, things he needed to buy, a phone number. Joan read the words again: *lovely smile.*

"What are you doing awake at this hour?" Franklin was standing in front of her in his robe.

Joan practically flew off the chair. She quickly closed the notepad, put it on her lap, and sat up straight. "Franklin, you startled me."

"Are you okay? Was Barb up again?"

"No, no, she's fine," she said, standing up and shoving the notepad into the pocket of her robe. "I couldn't sleep."

"What's that you were looking at?" he asked.

"Oh . . . it's just a notepad. My to-do lists, you know. Phone numbers and such: the butcher shop, the diaper service. Nothing exciting."

Franklin was quiet for a minute. She felt him observing her.

"Well, I, for one, am going back to bed," she said. "Unless you'd like me to heat up some milk for you? Help get you back to sleep?"

"No, thanks. I'll head back to bed in a minute as well."

Joan walked past Franklin. She tried to remain calm. She was glad she had thought quickly enough to be able to respond to his questioning, though she wondered how long he had been standing there as she read Paul's notepad. Back in the bedroom, she could hear Franklin in the kitchen, opening a cabinet and turning on the faucet. She quickly returned the notepad to the back of her underwear drawer.

12

GRACE PRESBYTERIAN CHURCH OF JENKINTOWN WAS FULL ON the day of Annabelle's funeral. Lillian played the organ as mourners took their seats in the pews and chatted, quietly awaiting Pastor Michael. Annabelle's closed casket—a simple, pine coffin with six brass handles and a brass cross on the top—was covered with a white pall. There was one bouquet of flowers—daylilies and lilacs—at the foot of the casket, and in front of the flowers was a framed photograph of Annabelle, apparently taken at Christmastime.

Joan and Franklin were seated in the third row from the front; Joan explained to Franklin that Annabelle was like family to her.

Pastor Michael, tall and lanky with thick silver hair, took his place at the podium as Lillian stopped playing. "Good morning, all. The brilliant sunshine this morning belies the sadness of the occasion, for we have gathered here to mourn the loss of one of God's most faithful of His flock. . . ."

Joan looked around her. She saw people of all ages: elderly couples, families with young children, teenagers. Some of those assembled looked like they were well-to-do: men dressed in fine wool suits and women wearing pearls; others came from more modest means or looked altogether indigent, in threadbare coats and scuffed, worn shoes. Joan had been unaware of the scope of Annabelle's influence on people of every ilk.

Pastor Michael continued. ". . . and the simple, white pall

atop her casket symbolizes the baptism and reminds us that, in the eyes of God, we are all equal."

There is that of God in all of us, Joan frequently heard Aunt Helen say. The Quaker custom of silent meeting, in which congregants gather in the meetinghouse and quietly sit, "awaiting" God's inspiration or guidance to move them to speak, always seemed to baffle Joan, though she could appreciate the sentiment and egalitarianism of this manner of worship. And as much as she knew that being of service to others and the world at large was an important tenet of being Quaker, she never quite felt moved to do charitable work like Helen and Mary, and because of this, Joan sometimes felt inadequate. At times, she even felt downright disdainful of her cousin's do-good perfection and selflessness.

The pastor continued to speak about Annabelle's lifelong commitment to the church, to those in need, to spreading a message of love, tolerance, compassion, and self-sacrifice. He mentioned her recent establishment of a children's daycare group for mothers entering the workforce "as our country continues to struggle with an economic depression." At this, Joan nodded with regret. Annabelle had tried several times to get Joan to come to the group.

At the end of the service, as the pallbearers walked slowly down the aisle with Annabelle's casket, Joan watched Paul pass by, his eyes glazed and his brow furrowed. At that moment, the sun streaming in from the stained-glass windows above cast an amber glow across his face, illuminating the blue in his eyes. It struck her for the first time how much he resembled a young Gary Cooper, both in stature and facial features. She gasped softly, involuntarily, and put her hand to her mouth, afraid that Franklin had noticed her reaction. And just then, the floodgates of her tears opened up, and she simultaneously felt the losses of her mother, of Annabelle, and of a life she'd thought she had just a couple years earlier, before motherhood, before marriage, and before life became complicated. Before she desperately wanted this other man.

As the mourners sifted out of the church, Franklin kissed Joan's forehead. "Helen will bring Barbara back at two thirty. I need to head to the store."

Joan nodded. "I'll see you tonight."

Outside the church, people slowly made their way to the cemetery. Near the gravesite, Joan saw Pastor Michael standing close to the coffin, Lillian by his side holding Paul's arm. Joan positioned herself across from the three of them. Once everyone was gathered, Michael said a few words; then the coffin was lowered into the ground. Paul kept his eyes on the casket as it slowly disappeared below their feet.

As mourners left the cemetery, Joan walked toward Paul, who was standing alone in front of Harris's gravestone.

"I think Pastor Michael really captured the essence of Annabelle in his sermon, don't you agree?" she asked him.

"Mm-hmm, yes. He did," Paul said.

Joan looked around. She saw the pastor and Lillian speaking with a couple of parishioners. She tucked a piece of hair behind her ear and cleared her throat.

"Listen, Paul," she said. "Would you . . . like to come over for a cup of coffee? Maybe we could chat about Annabelle, or. . . ."

"Thank you, Joan. That's kind of you, but I really should head back into the city," he said. "I've got to be at the restaurant at five."

Joan looked off to the side, as if searching for something. She turned back to him. "Paul, please. I . . . just feel so alone. You and I have lost someone very special to us. I mean, I know she was not my blood relative, but I loved her." She looked at Paul for some connection.

"I know you did, Joan. She was very fond of you as well. But I need to be on that trolley . . ."

"You can't be expected to go to work while you're in mourning, can you?"

"I might feel better if I'm busy. Anyway, isn't Franklin here?" Paul looked around.

"No, he needed to get to the store." Then her face lit up. "Oh, I found your little notepad in Annabelle's apartment." She tried to sound as if this had not been on her mind for days. "I imagine you want that, don't you? I promise not to hold you up too long," she said. "Just one cup of coffee, some conversation?" She smiled.

"I was wondering where I'd left that," he said. He looked at the entrance to the church. "I suppose I could pop in for a bit," he said.

Joan nodded and smiled again.

"Let me go say so long to Lillian and Michael. You go on ahead, and I'll be over in a few minutes."

Inside her apartment, Joan threw her autumn coat on a chair and rushed to put on a pot of coffee. She removed some cheese Danish from the refrigerator and set it on a plate on the kitchen table. Minutes later, there was a knock at the door. As she walked through the living room, she stopped to momentarily look at her face in the mirror. She puffed her hair with her hand, walked to the door, and opened it.

"C'mon in," she said. "Let me take your jacket."

"Where's Barbara today?" he asked flatly as he looked around.

"Oh, she's at my Aunt Helen's house for a few hours. Come on into the kitchen. I've got some fresh coffee and Danish."

As she took out coffee cups and plates, Paul leaned against the counter next to her.

"It doesn't feel real," Paul said.

"It'll take time," Joan said as she set the coffee cups and plates on the table. She removed two Danishes from the box and put them on the plates.

Paul nodded, but he seemed to be lost in thought.

The pot finished percolating, and the aroma of freshly brewed coffee filled the air. Joan moved to face Paul. She began to tremble. She opened her mouth to speak but hesitated.

"What is it?" Paul asked.

"It's strange," she said, looking up into his eyes.

"What's strange?"

"This . . . is the first time you and I have ever been alone. Without Annabelle."

"Yes. Or Franklin," Paul said, as if to remind her that she was a married woman.

She stepped closer to him. Her hands were shaking.

He looked down and took both of her hands in his own. "My God, what's going on, Joan? You're . . ."

Then without thinking, without saying anything, Joan wrapped her arms around his torso.

"Oh, Paul," she said.

"Joan, I . . ." He gently moved her off his frame.

"Please, don't say anything, all right? Just hold me."

He relaxed his arms and hugged her. Joan wondered if perhaps he needed this as well, to be connected in their grief over Annabelle. Who else did he have, anyway? A flood of emotions, driven by her primary desire *to be needed*, overcame her.

They did not speak, but stood embracing for several minutes. Then, taking Paul's hand, she walked him into the living room. Silently, they sat on the sofa.

"I think about you all the time, Paul," she said, feeling light-headed and shaky.

He stared at her, though she wasn't sure he had processed what she said. She leaned into him slowly, cautiously; he did not back off as she kissed his cheek and then his lips. He momentarily pulled back and stared at her; then he cupped both his hands around her face and resumed kissing her, this time in a frenzied manner. She emptied her mind of thoughts and words, of to-do lists and schedules and other people's needs. She was overcome with physical sensations she had never felt so strongly before, and she was unaware and unconcerned with repercussions in the next minute, hour, month.

Paul unbuttoned Joan's blouse and then his own shirt. Within minutes, they were naked on her sofa, grabbing, moving, kissing. No words between them, no slow exploration of each other's body, no tenderness. Joan accepted this because she felt unexpectedly empowered and emboldened by his response to her advances. All that mattered, all she could comprehend and choose to process in this moment, were Paul's desire and acceptance and the intoxicating power she felt.

It was over in minutes. As quickly as Paul's desire had surfaced, so did it seemingly retreat. He sat up and began dressing. Suddenly feeling modest and shameful, Joan rushed to put her blouse back on, mindlessly neglecting to put on her bra. She pulled on her underpants and then her slip.

Paul looked at his watch. "I should go. I'm . . . I'm sorry. I shouldn't have let this—"

"I don't regret it," she said, grabbing hold of his hand. "We have a connection, don't we?"

Paul looked at her hand, tightly gripping his own. "Uh, well, yes, I suppose we do. This is a very sad time. I'm . . . not myself." He lifted his arm to release her grip, moved away and began buttoning his shirt. He put his tie around his neck and adjusted it, all without saying a word.

Joan began putting stray pieces of her hair back into place. She reached down to the floor and picked up a bobby pin that had fallen out of her hair, and she pushed it back in. She noticed her bra on the floor and felt horribly embarrassed that she'd forgotten to put it on. She kicked it under the coffee table surreptitiously. She felt the urge to cry. Or slap him.

Paul sat, hands clasped together loosely and elbows resting on his knees, and looked down at the floor. Then he sat up straight. "Jesus Christ," he said, shaking his head from side to side.

"Paul?"

"Look, Joan," he said with a resolute tone. "I don't believe in heaven, I'm not sure I even believe in God for that matter. But if there is a heaven, Annabelle is looking down on us. She knows we are grieving for her, and she is forgiving us, and wanting you and me to continue our lives, to live as she lived her life, with regard for those who are in need—"

"Yes, yes, I couldn't agree more."

He stood up and looked down at Joan. She smiled up at him, believing they were of one mind.

He continued. His hands were expressive, his tone was positive, encouraging. "She would want us to . . . carry on . . . living our lives . . . our *separate* lives. For your sake and mine. For Franklin's sake. For Barbara's." He gave her a small, close-lipped smile.

Joan felt chastised, as if Paul believed he had to remind her that she was a wife and a mother. He was already pulling away after they had submitted to each other's desire. Her eyes filled with tears. Then the familiar feeling of abandonment surfaced.

She shot up from the sofa. "Are you trying to convince *me* of all this? Or *yourself?*" she hissed at him. She felt agitated. "I'm not a fool, Paul." Joan reached into a credenza drawer and handed him his notepad.

He put his jacket on and looked at his watch again. "We didn't have the coffee and Danish," he said, almost as an apology.

Joan sneered. *What an idiotic thing to say.*

"I'm sorry. Joan, can you forgive me? I feel like I've taken advantage of you."

She inhaled deeply and softened her tone. "When can I see you again?"

He held her hand with both of his. "Joan, you're a lovely woman. I've enjoyed getting to know you these past few months, and perhaps if we'd met several years ago . . ."

She pushed him away. Paul sighed.

"Good-bye, Paul," she said, and headed into her bedroom to shower and change. As she closed the door to her bedroom, she saw Paul tuck the notepad into his inside jacket pocket and let himself out.

13

SHORTLY AFTER ANNABELLE'S FUNERAL, JOAN BEGAN TAKING
Barbara to the church for childcare a couple hours each week.
She had become involved in the church's charitable endeavors in
an effort to distract herself from constant thoughts of Paul and
what had transpired. She had not heard from or seen him since
the day of the funeral, and her daily ruminations about him were
making her tense and anxious.

Every Tuesday morning after Franklin left for work, Joan
got herself and Barbara dressed and headed out for their morning stroll; then they went to the church on the way back. She'd
leave Barbara with the volunteers in the basement, go upstairs,
and situate herself at Annabelle's desk, making phone calls to
solicit donations for the church's food pantry and coordinating
with volunteers. These tasks gave Joan a sense of productivity
and usefulness, and she liked that the work did not take too
much time away from her daughter and her responsibilities at
home.

Lillian approached her in the church pantry one Tuesday as
Joan was taking inventory, clipboard in hand.

"It's such a beautiful day today," Lillian said, "and here you
are, once again, inside the church lending a hand instead of
walking through the park, enjoying the sunshine with your little
girl. And this isn't even your congregation. You have been a god-
send."

"Oh, Lillian, I enjoy this, and I suppose it's something I've been lacking in my life for a while now." She crossed her arms around the clipboard and pulled it to her chest. "I do love my daughter, of course. But I think about my cousin Mary, and my Aunt Helen—they are such role models for me in how much time they give to charity, and I . . . well, I guess I figured it's time I stepped up. Also . . ." she added, hesitating.

Lillian smiled and raised an inquisitive eyebrow.

"It sounds silly," Joan said, "but it makes me feel . . . I don't know, closer to Annabelle somehow."

"It doesn't sound silly. And Michael and I appreciate your time and energy." She paused. "May I ask, do you belong to a church, Joan?"

Joan told her that she had been raised as a Quaker, but that she had not been very consistent in attending meeting for worship, particularly since Barbara was born.

"I see," Lillian said. "Well, you are always welcome to attend one of our services."

Joan smiled. "I'm curious what will happen with Annabelle's position. Are you looking to hire someone to replace her? Not that anyone could truly replace her."

"Yes, Michael and I do need to discuss this. Do you have someone in mind?"

Joan stood straight, eyes wide open. She nodded eagerly. "I thought you might consider . . . me."

"That seems like it would be quite a lot for a young mother to tackle." She looked off to the side, as if mulling it around in her head. "But I wouldn't want to rule it out. You've shown such interest in the church, and we love having you around. Let me bring it up with Michael tonight. I'm sure he will want to talk with you and get an idea of your skills and experience, and how much you'd care to commit to a permanent position. You know, all the important details that relate to the job."

"Of course," Joan said, squeezing the clipboard tightly to maintain composure. She felt like she might burst with joy. Lillian had not completely shot down the idea.

Two days later, Joan sat in the pastor's office as Lillian explained how Annabelle had been a part of the church since she was a child in the Sunday School, years before Michael was the pastor. She mentioned Annabelle and Harris's wedding at the church, Harris's funeral.

"In other words, Annabelle grew up here. She was devoted to this church."

"This is all very important for someone who works so closely with me," said Michael.

Joan nodded. "I know she was very connected to the church. And . . ." Joan hesitated, as if weighing how much she was willing to put on the line. "I've been giving it a lot of thought recently. I had begun to feel very close to Annabelle. She was, well . . . you know, my own mother, she passed when I was quite young. I never knew her, and . . ." Joan struggled to find adequate words and began to think she was blabbering on about nothing relevant to their discussion. She immediately felt embarrassed by what she had revealed and wasn't sure how to connect it back to Lillian's original point. "I suppose what I'm trying to say—not very well—is that I want this church in my life. I think I'd even like to raise my daughter Presbyterian." Joan could not believe the words that had just fallen out of her mouth. She had not acknowledged these feelings even to herself, and, in a way, they frightened her. She'd never cared about God or religion and did not enjoy being told how to think or what to believe. Yet, at the same time, she felt liberated, as if she had, for the first time in her life, made an important decision for herself, independent of anyone else's expectations.

Michael suggested that Joan talk to Franklin about the posi-

112 | *Eileen Brill*

tion and expressed concern that it could be a source of friction if Franklin was not amenable to the idea. He added that he was also considering one or two congregants for the job. "And if I can be completely honest with you . . ." he began.

"Absolutely, yes."

"Well, forgive me for prying, but I assume that you and Franklin will want to give Barbara a little brother or sister at some point. I don't know how you could possibly manage all that and a full-time job."

The last thing Joan was thinking about was having another child, but she could not think of an adequate response. She decided it was best to not make excuses or push too hard. "I understand your concerns, Pastor. And I assure you, if I am to work in this church, it will be with my full commitment and my husband's approval. I will talk with Franklin tonight."

After leaving Michael's office, she headed down to the basement of the church to retrieve Barbara. She began to feel sick to her stomach as her mind became inundated with images of people in her life, past and present. She paused in the stairwell and leaned against the wall to calm herself. First, there was little Barbara, with her wide brown eyes, dark, curly hair, and infectious giggle. *Am I running away from my daughter, my precious little girl?* She could imagine Franklin's expression of bewilderment and concern, wondering why motherhood and marriage were not enough fulfillment and challenge for her, and he would suggest she become more involved with the American Friends Service Committee. Then Joan's mind raced to her aunt and her cousin Mary. She could see their faces, smiling, patient, yet somehow judging her and her choices. *I will never be like them, as much as I try. Their bond has always been strong, and, try as I may have my entire life, I've never been able to penetrate it.* Then she saw her father's face, imagined the burden he'd felt in raising a motherless daughter, his disappointment in her lack of academic accomplishment, coupled with the fact that she was a lifelong reminder of his young wife who had been taken from him too early. The only time Joan had seen Marcus truly proud of her and hopeful for her future was on her wedding day. *This will confirm everything he already, no doubt, thinks of me: that I'm a failure. A disengaged Quaker, an inattentive wife, a flawed mother.* Then there was Annabelle. Joan could see Annabelle smiling at her appreciatively, supportively, without judgment or expectations or negativity.

She thought of Paul. Again.

Then in a haze of memory combined with fabrication, as always, Joan had a flash of her mother's face. It was not the beautiful image in the picture at the summer house in Ivyland, the photograph taken on her parents' wedding day in 1913. Nor was it the face or disposition described to Joan on a few occasions by Aunt Helen, in which Helen went on and on about Jessie's apple-red cheeks and dark-brown, curly hair. No, the image that flooded Joan's mind at this moment was that of her mother on her deathbed, the young woman's face wet and white, her hair matted to her forehead. Standing in the stairwell at the church, Joan wanted nothing more than to rush to her daughter, sweep her up into her arms, hold her tightly, and kiss her forehead as she promised to never, ever leave her.

A wave of emotion—or something—overcame Joan, beginning in her stomach and moving up through her esophagus. The air became stale, and she felt light-headed. She steadied herself with the handrail, but before she could descend the stairs to the restroom, she was vomiting her breakfast all over the steps. She reached into her purse for a handkerchief and began wiping the steps. She felt better almost immediately, but she knew she had to grab her daughter and head straight back home.

14

JOAN COULD NOT FIND THE RIGHT TIME TO INITIATE WITH
Franklin the subject of working at the church, and she had to
admit to herself that perhaps she was intentionally procrastinat-
ing. She avoided the church for a few days in order to clear her
head.

One afternoon, she and Barbara went to Timber Road for
lunch at Helen's invitation. Joan's Grandmother Elizabeth,
whose health was failing, had moved into the house, and Helen
felt it would be good for Elizabeth to see Joan and Barbara. Marcus had taken the day off to prepare for a weeklong trip to New
York, so he offered to pick Joan and Barbara up and bring them
back to the house.

During the car ride, her father was uncharacteristically
buoyant and talkative. Joan could always see a change in his demeanor when he was getting ready to see and review a new
show, and this trip was particularly exciting for him as he'd be
reviewing several shows in one week.

"So, which plays are you reviewing?" she asked.

"Tomorrow is a two o'clock matinee, *A Doll's House*. It's a
play by Henrick Ibsen. Rather weighty subject matter, especially
when it debuted in Denmark in eighteen . . . let me think . . .
1879, I believe it was."

Joan was used to her father spouting out facts about the
shows he was seeing. He was a veritable storehouse of knowledge on theatrical performances. "I'm curious," she said. "What
do you mean by 'weighty'?"

"Well, broadly, it deals with a plethora of human emotions like shame, passion, frustration, lust. And it involves betrayal. More specifically, though, it's about a woman who is, shall we say, disillusioned with her existence. She has so much—a loving husband, children, a beautiful home—and yet, for some reason, she wants more."

Joan was quiet for the last five minutes before they arrived at the house. She considered the word *betrayal,* and then *shame, passion, disillusionment,* and she cringed. She stared out of the car window to distract herself.

As they walked through the front door of the house, the Pruitts' live-in housemaid from Ireland, Ellen McGrugan, greeted them.

"Hello, Mrs. Oakes. Lovely to see you again." Ellen smiled broadly, revealing deep dimples on both cheeks, and gave what appeared to be a small curtsy. Her curly auburn hair was pulled back into a tight braid that ran down her back. "And look at that wee one in your arms," she said, tapping Barbara lightly on her nose.

Barbara giggled and held her stuffed bear out for Ellen to see.

"Would you like to come tell me all about your little bear?" Ellen looked at Joan for approval, and Joan nodded, appreciating the break from her active baby. She handed Barbara over to Ellen, who headed for the kitchen, bouncing Barbara gently on her hip as she walked.

Joan could hear the voices of her grandmother and Helen coming from the second floor. It sounded as if they were arguing.

Joan entered the kitchen, where Ellen had propped Barbara on the countertop and was speaking softly to the child.

"Is everything all right with Granny?" Joan asked. "Aunt Helen tells me Elizabeth has gotten a bit ornery."

"Ah, no, Miss Elizabeth doesn't give me any trouble," Ellen replied. "She's startin' to forget this 'n' that, is all. And she doesn't always feel much like eatin'. She asked Mrs. Pruitt to help her get ready today. I guess she was needin' the attention of her daughter."

Joan nodded, feeling the familiar pang. "Is your mother back in Ireland?"

Ellen combed her fingers through the delicate curls on Barbara's forehead. "Ah, well, yes, in a manner of speaking. Ma is buried at St. Catherine's cemetery in County Kerry."

"Oh, I'm sorry, I hadn't realized—"

"Influenza. I was just a wee babe, never knew her."

Joan wondered if Ellen shared the same longing for the mother she never knew. Did she ever feel lonely and disconnected from others, as if some vital piece of herself were missing? Ellen looked to be about Joan's age, perhaps a year or two younger, and had they been of equal social standing, perhaps they would be friends.

Ellen scooped Barbara into her arms and, smiling, turned to Joan. "So I suppose you and I are kindred spirits."

Joan was surprised Ellen knew about Jessie. The two women quietly looked at each other for a moment, the silence indicating some sort of kinship between them.

Joan finally spoke. "Well, I think I'll go upstairs and say hello to my grandmother."

When Joan reached her grandmother's bedroom, Helen was fastening the buttons on the back of Elizabeth's dress. Joan noticed her grandmother's backbone, the way it protruded, each section of her spine taut against her skin.

"Heavens to Betsy, you're a sight for sore eyes!" Elizabeth greeted Joan with a hoarse but uncharacteristically animated voice.

As Joan leaned in for a hug, Elizabeth extended her arms to

hold Joan back. The older woman's eyes became gleaming crescents, and her high cheekbones pushed against the crinkles in the corners of each eye. She scanned Joan's face with delight and confusion. Joan couldn't remember a time when her grandmother, normally not such a demonstrative person, had been so loving and affectionate toward her.

"Oh, Jessie, I haven't seen you for so long, my dear." Elizabeth pulled Joan in and squeezed her tightly.

Helen slowly shook her head from side to side, and Joan felt her enthusiasm fade.

"Mother," Helen said gently, "this is Joan, your granddaughter."

Elizabeth stood back and took another look at Joan. "No," Elizabeth said calmly and somewhat condescendingly. "You are mistaken, Helen. This is Jessie Sondersohn, my son's beautiful wife. I love what you've done with your hair, Jessie. It's sophisticated."

"Th . . . thank you," Joan said, unsure of how to respond and whether she needed to play along.

"I hope you've brought little Joanie today. How is that shy little sprite?"

Joan tried to hold back tears. She knew that Elizabeth was beginning to forget where she'd placed items and would become confused mid-sentence as she was speaking to someone, but *this* was not something for which Joan was prepared. She looked at Helen and gestured toward Elizabeth. Helen closed her eyes and, again, softly shook her head from side to side as if to say, "Just let this go."

"Well, don't you look lovely in your dress," Joan said, trying her best to be positive. "Aunt Helen, let me help Granny finish getting ready for lunch. You can go downstairs and say hello to Barbara."

Helen hesitated but then seemed to reconsider. "Sure. I need to check in on Ellen as well. Hopefully, lunch is ready." She kissed Elizabeth's cheek and turned to leave the bedroom.

Joan focused on Elizabeth's gray tresses. "Can we put your hair up into a bun, then?"

"Oh, yes, thank you, sweetheart." Elizabeth spun around. She stared into Joan's eyes for a second. "You *aren't* Jessie, then?"

Joan shook her head.

Elizabeth took her granddaughter's hand, engulfed it in both of hers, and kissed it lightly. Joan noticed the blue, protruding veins in her grandmother's hands.

"Now, dear, if you'll put up my hair," Elizabeth said.

Joan reached for a couple of bobby pins, twisted Elizabeth's hair to the top of her head, and secured it in two places.

When she was finished, she extended her arm for her grandmother, and the two women walked downstairs. As much as Joan found her grandmother's confusion to be unsettling, a part of her also enjoyed the uncharacteristic warmth the old woman was exuding. This was a rare treat for Joan.

At the bottom of the stairs, Joan could hear Barbara squealing with joy. As they approached the living room, they found Marcus lifting the baby up and down in the air, high above his head. This was the first time Joan had observed her father interacting with Barbara, or any child, in such a playful manner.

Elizabeth looked at Joan. "So this little one is not Joanie?"

Joan shook her head.

"Oh," Elizabeth said with a confused sigh.

Joan walked her grandmother toward the side porch, where Ellen and Helen were putting the last of the food on the table. She returned to the living room and found Marcus still engaged with Barbara. This moment felt as if it had been pulled from someone else's life, or, more specifically, as if time had rewound by fifteen years to an earlier time in her own life. She had distinct memories of her father's playfulness and affection during summers spent in Ivyland. Perhaps all he needed was the company of a young child—his grandchild—to pull his lighthearted-ness to the surface.

Joan's eyes fell upon a small, framed photo on the mantle. From a distance, she did not recognize the woman in the picture, so she moved closer until the likeness became clear. "I never realized how much I resemble her."

"Mm," he said, nodding.

Joan studied Jessie's features: the large, deep-brown eyes, the round face with a mild cleft in the chin, the dark-brown curls that framed her face. "Her lips look so dark in this photograph," she said. "Was she wearing lipstick?" She touched her own lips, on which she'd not put any color that morning.

"Not at all. Your mother didn't wear makeup, not even on holidays. Just a natural beauty." Marcus spoke as if he were narrating a radio show.

Joan proceeded cautiously. "Do you still think about her?" The question was uncharted territory for her. She bit her bottom lip, awaiting her father's response. He took so long to reply that she doubted the wisdom of having asked the question.

Marcus put Barbara down on a large, upholstered chair, but she immediately attempted to get down. He lifted the baby and handed her to Joan. He smoothed out his trousers and straightened his tie, fixating on the knot and not looking in Joan's direction.

"She's always there, I suppose. Always in my thoughts in one fashion or another," he said, his voice slowly creeping back to his usual formal cadence and guarded tone. Then he added, "Her visage lives on in you." With his antiquated choice of words, Joan caught an air of accusation and resentment, as if looking at his daughter conjured old emotions he'd chosen not to face. She felt an onslaught of feelings: sorrow, elation, love, and guilt, all of which left her stunned, unable to say anything empathetic or relevant in response.

Helen called everyone in for lunch, and the moment of connection was lost.

In the car ride back to her apartment, Joan held a sleeping Barbara in her arms. Marcus was mostly quiet, though he whistled a bit as he drove along.

"It upsets me to see Granny Elizabeth . . . *that way*," Joan said.

"She's getting old. We all grow old." He paused and added, "If we are fortunate."

Joan understood the implication, yet she was struck by how her father's statement lacked any emotion. "Ellen told me her mother died of flu. In Ireland."

"Oh?" Marcus replied.

Joan stared out the window. It was always challenging to have any sort of meaningful conversation with her father, especially when emotions were involved. Marcus rarely made eye contact with her, hadn't hugged her in years. He wasn't uncaring or unkind, but she had trouble connecting with him. It was as if he were someone else's father.

She changed the subject as they neared her apartment. "I was wondering. . . ." she began as she gathered her purse and the bag of Barbara's things.

Marcus turned off the car. "Hold on. Let me help you." He jumped out of the car and walked around to Joan's side, opened her door, and reached for Barbara.

When they entered her apartment, Joan took Barbara from her father's arms. The baby did not wake up, so Joan put her in her crib and headed back to the living room, where Marcus was inspecting photographs on the side table.

"You don't have a photograph of your mother. I'll give you the one on our mantle. You should have it."

"I'd like that, thank you."

"Now, before I head back, what is it that you were wondering?" Marcus asked as he dusted nothing in particular off his trousers.

"Oh, yes," she said, pleased that he had followed up. "Well, I feel sort of silly for asking . . ."

Marcus raised his eyebrows.

"Dad, would you . . . I mean, may I . . ." Joan stumbled, feeling unsure of herself. Then something powerful and unfamiliar came over her, and she decided to be forthright in her intentions. "I'd like to go to New York to see the show with you."

Marcus looked at her blankly for several seconds, apparently trying to process what she'd said.

She moved in closer to him. "I can ask Aunt Helen to stay with Barbara. Or perhaps Ellen would be able to help."

"I suppose that would be fine," Marcus said. He added, with a raised index finger, "Understand, Joan, I'm at work during performances. I take notes; I focus. No chit-chat, no casual conversation. And then I typically go to a quiet place right after a show —a coffee shop or hotel lobby—where I compile my thoughts before I forget everything. I just want you to know that I may not be the most enjoyable company . . ."

Joan calmly cut him off. "I understand. I do. I won't bother you, I promise."

"All right, then. When I get home, I'll place a call to my secretary. She'll know if there are extra tickets available. In the meantime, why don't you ring up Helen and see how she might be able to lend a hand with Barbara."

"Sure, I'll do that right away," Joan said.

"Well then," he said. "Good-night." He opened the door to exit.

"And, Father?"

Marcus turned around.

"I enjoyed watching you play with Barbara today. That means a lot to me, for her to spend time with her grandfather."

Marcus pursed his lips into a small smile and nodded.

15

WHEN JOAN PROPOSED THE IDEA OF GOING TO THE PLAY TO Franklin that night, he was immediately negative and dismissive.

"It's a lot of organization and logistics with very little lead time," Franklin said. "It's a bad idea, Joan, simply a bad idea," he said, mixing a martini.

Joan felt as if she were hearing her father talk. Franklin was treating her like a child.

Franklin took a swig of the martini and continued, "And what about Barbara? If she stays with Helen, how will she get home? And at what time? I'm sorry, but we cannot have our daughter's schedule disrupted like this. I wish this could work out for you. Maybe your father can get tickets to one of the weekend shows, and I might be able to—"

Joan was prepared. "I have a lovely plan, Franklin," she said, again touching his forearm.

Franklin raised his eyebrows, angled his head.

"Barbara is going to spend the night on Timber Road with her great-aunt and great-uncle, and her great-grandmother Elizabeth, and Ellen McGrugan." Joan crossed her arms and stood back, satisfied she had made her case.

"Why is this so important to you, Joan?"

The two of them sat down at the kitchen table.

"I saw something in my father today, something I thought he had lost a long time ago."

"And what is that?"

"He seemed . . ." Her eyes scanned the space around her.

"Proud of me, pleased with me, the way he did when I was a little girl. I saw his soft side for my mother. And also for Barbara."

"What has a trip to New York got to do with all of that?"

She rested her forearms on the table and leaned into Franklin. "My father loves the theatre, probably more than anything else in the world. He's passionate about it, you know that."

"So now *you're* passionate about the theatre?" Franklin shook his head. "This sounds very complicated. Leaving your daughter for a day, getting all these people involved. Just so you can feel closer to your father. He's a tough nut to crack. He's your father, not your pal. And you're a married woman with your own family now, not some little girl." He finished off his martini.

Joan began to seethe. She had finally let down her guard and shared her feelings with Franklin, and now he was making her feel selfish, indulgent, and immature. "And also"—she hesitated, not wanting to sound hysterical—"I've never been to the theatre." She threw her arms in the air. "Marcus Sondersohn is considered the most influential critic in New York and Philadelphia, but his only child has never even been to a theatrical production. So, if it helps you to understand why I want to do this, just think of it as a way for your wife to become more enlightened and cultured." At that, Joan stood up, cleared Franklin's plate and martini glass, and headed to the sink. She was trying hard not to cry—not out of sadness or frustration, but because it had taken every ounce of fortitude to make her case. She was exhausted.

Franklin came up behind her as she washed the dishes and wrapped his arms around her waist. He kissed her shoulder.

She cringed and wanted to shove him forcefully backward.

"I can see that this is important to you. So go."

Joan exhaled. She turned around and gave her husband an appreciative hug. She was relieved. "Thank you," she said.

16

ON A BRISK MID-NOVEMBER MORNING, JOAN SETTLED INTO
her seat next to Marcus on the Pennsylvania Railroad's 20th
Century Limited train for New York City. She removed her
gloves, unbuttoned her coat, and watched as the passengers—
mostly men—boarded the train and took their seats. She had
positive feelings toward her father and was excited to be accom-
panying him on this day; perhaps she'd be his companion on
future trips.

After arriving at Penn Station in New York, Joan and Marcus
immediately headed to the theatre. They found their seats—
good ones in the orchestra section—and Marcus removed a
small notebook, his Cross pen, and a theatre light from his
leather bag. Joan observed this ritual she'd never before been
privy to, and she marveled at how silent and serious her father
was as he arranged himself in his little "seat office" and perused
the playbill, jotting down notes in the margins. Joan removed
her hat and gloves and lay them on her lap.

After a few minutes, the lights dimmed, and the heavy, red
velvet curtains parted, revealing a realistic living room set, complete with a fireplace, wooden bookshelves with actual books,
upholstered furniture, Oriental rugs, and a decorated Christmas
tree off to the side. An actress entered through a door, dressed in
nineteenth-century clothing and carrying a stack of gift boxes.
Joan's heart was pounding with excitement. She had to remind
herself to breathe, to take it all in slowly.

Throughout the performance, she was so riveted by the story that she was unaware of and undisturbed by Marcus's occasional note-taking or the light from the small flashlight that was clipped to his note pad.

When the play ended, the cast held hands and took a collective bow as most of the audience, including Joan, rose to their feet. Marcus remained in his seat, scratching down more notes. After a couple of minutes, he tucked the pen into its pocket in the leather bag and returned his notepad to the bag as well.

"How about a bite to eat and some coffee before I put you on the train back to Philly?"

"It was so much different from what I'd expected," said Joan, slicing her iceberg wedge at a café one block from Penn Station.

"Go on," he said, taking a bite of his croque monsieur, the hot, melted cheese hanging from his mouth—an uncharacteristically sloppy, yet amusing, visual of her father that Joan found endearing.

She searched for the right words to describe how she felt. It wasn't so much that she wanted to impress her father with an insightful analysis of the story; it was more that she genuinely was still processing everything, to the point where she was feeling myriad emotions and far fewer cohesive thoughts. "I don't know, but I think I sort of understand Nora."

Marcus nodded. "You mean, you relate to her?"

"Well . . ." She pondered this some more, careful not to present herself in a negative light. "I suppose so." Joan looked down and pushed her fork into a tomato section.

"I certainly hope *you* haven't forged *my* signature on anything," Marcus said playfully, knowing full well that Joan was not referring to the main character's controversial and illegal action, which the dialogue referred to at several points throughout the story.

"This woman, Nora, she's a mother and a wife—like me. And these things are important—they are—and tending to one's family is very meaningful. But in this story, Nora couldn't do everything she wanted to do to tend to her family. She wasn't completely . . ." Joan searched for the words.

"Independent?" Marcus offered, always jumping in with the appropriate word.

"Yes—independent—that's part of it. I didn't know other women felt this way." She immediately looked at Marcus to gauge his reaction. Was she revealing too much? He did not react. "And she forged her father's name to get the loan, but that was to help her sick husband . . . what was his name? Torvald?"

Marcus nodded.

"So it was illegal, yes, but she had good intentions." Joan was growing agitated. She noticed she had balled her hand into a fist and then relaxed it. "And for her husband to call her 'dishonest and immoral' . . . to say she wasn't a fit mother, well . . ." She grasped her teacup with two hands to feel the warmth and calm herself. She was embarrassed at her blatant indignance, as if it were a telescope into her mind that would sour her father's opinion of her.

"I would agree," Marcus said. "She had good intentions; she wasn't a bad person. Humans are complex, multi-dimensional. Few of us are all good or all bad. Her husband was harsh with her, it's true. In the end, they were disillusioned with one another, and their roles in the marriage became blurred—which is why yesterday I referred to this subject matter as 'weighty.'" He took a final bite of his sandwich.

Typically, Joan detested when her father would pontificate, as if he only wanted to hear his own voice. But now she felt enthralled with his validation of her commentary, and it emboldened her to continue.

"And," she said, "I think Nora felt unfulfilled being a wife and mother; it doesn't mean she didn't love her children. She was frustrated. She was such a vibrant woman, which, on the one hand, Torvald seemed to appreciate. You could tell that he loved her. But, on the other hand, he sort of made fun of her, and he wanted to control her too." Joan watched her father's expression change from one of genuine interest to one of concern. "I'm not suggesting that Franklin makes fun of or controls me," she said, defensively.

"I certainly hope not," he said, raising his arm to get the waiter's attention as he mouthed the word *check*. "On the contrary, Joan, you're in a position in life where there is very little you need to worry about, and you have access to things that most people, especially these days, couldn't even dream of. You can wake up in the morning and put your daughter in her carriage and walk five minutes up the street to Strawbridge's or Wanamaker's and buy yourself a silk scarf. If you decide that Saturday night you want a Delmonico steak, you can stop in at the butcher shop and select two for yourself and Franklin. You can take in a movie at the York Road Theatre on a Wednesday afternoon. You are fortunate that your husband's family owns a successful business and, someday, it will be his alone."

Up until that point, Joan felt that her father had been speaking to her as an adult for the very first time in her life, and it had made her want to share more with him. Now she was just a spoiled child in his eyes. She wanted to tell Marcus how much she missed working at Oakes's. How the train rides to and from the city had been as exciting as the job itself, when she and Franklin would read the newspaper or discuss current events or strategize about bringing in customers. She wanted to tell her father that she was not the same little girl he used to know.

But now she doubted that her father would be able to acknowledge any of that. He would always see her as unrealistic, negative, spoiled, whiny.

"Listen," he said, wiping the corners of his mouth and taking the check from the waiter. "There is a woman at the paper who was recently hired to clean the kitchen and restrooms. About your age, married. Two small children, I believe. Sweet girl, Julia is her name. Anyway, her husband lost his job. He drove a delivery truck in Camden for six years and showed up one morning to find out it was his last day. And the saddest part of this story is, that was two years ago." He glanced over the bill and put the check down on the table as he fished for his wallet. He put three one-dollar bills on the table. "His mother moved in with the family to help take care of the children so that he can look for work—*any* work—every day."

Joan listened intently, nodding empathetically, yet she felt her father was somehow minimizing her own dissatisfaction.

"And, Joan, this scenario is common these days. I know you're already aware of that; I don't mean to lecture you. We are so very fortunate. People's lives change in a heartbeat."

"You're right," she said. He did not understand her. He had dismissed her feelings yet again.

Marcus looked at his watch. "Five forty-five," he said. "Let's head to Penn Station and get you to your train."

At the station, there was a great flurry of activity, which thrilled Joan and made her want to stay longer.

"Thank you so much for this opportunity, Father. I will never forget this."

As Joan's train was announced, she impulsively leaned in to hug her father, who simply patted her back in return.

Despite her father's inability to validate her feelings, Joan felt a sort of peace of mind that comes with understanding oneself. She would go see the pastor and Lillian the following day.

17

"I MAY BE THE SPIRITUAL LEADER OF THIS CHURCH, BUT
Annabelle truly managed everything here. Isn't that right, Lillian?" Pastor Michael said, as he, Lillian, and Joan sat in his office one morning after Joan dropped Barbara off in the basement child care center.

"Absolutely," Lillian said. She explained how the scope of Annabelle's responsibility had grown from filing and ordering supplies to eventually assuming most of Lillian's workload.

"With all that responsibility, she could have run her own company, don't you think?"

Lillian and Michael looked at Joan quizzically.

"Well, I've certainly met women who would be capable of running a business, yes," said Lillian. "At any rate, are you prepared to spend six to seven hours a day, five days a week at a job? And at what cost?"

Joan was silent. In truth, she had not thought about the time commitment.

"Consider how this job could affect your home life, your household responsibilities, your ability to do your errands— your grocery shopping, for example. And, in essence, during your working hours, you would not be spending any time with Barbara. Keep in mind, this is not a short-term stint; Michael and I want someone who will be dedicated to the work we do here and who will feel like part of our family."

Michael chimed in, "There are married women, mothers

even, who work full-time these days out of necessity, and I'm sure it can be terribly trying on home life."

"Don't misunderstand us, Joan," Lillian added. "We have both been extremely appreciative of the hours you've given us these last few weeks . . . the phone calls, the food inventories. We rely on volunteers to keep our good work moving along—"

"And you could certainly continue to volunteer, even if you weren't actually doing Annabelle's job," added the pastor.

Joan sank down into her seat.

Then her internal voice, the one that so frequently would berate her, sabotage her good intentions, or otherwise make her doubt herself, was silenced by a louder one that told her to consider Annabelle, who seemed to believe in her, and Nora, from *A Doll's House*, who said that a woman has duties to herself that are just as important as being a wife and mother.

Joan straightened her posture. "I want you to know that I've given this careful consideration over the last few weeks. I've thought about Annabelle, and the two of you, and the wonderful volunteers in day care. I believe, in time, I could do anything you need me to do. I can type, and I am organized, and I am good on the telephone. In fact, when I worked at my husband's store, I greeted customers every day and even answered the phone." She paused. "I enjoyed it. I was . . . *good* at it."

She paused to take a breath and compose herself.

"I love my daughter and want to be the best mother I can possibly be. I grew up without a mother. But Barbara has me, and she will always know I love her. Is it such a bad thing to have her mix with other children?" She moved her eyes from the pastor to Lillian and back. "I don't think that she will suffer at all when her mother is one floor above her for a few hours a day."

Lillian and Michael looked at each other; then he spoke. "You're certainly confident, Joan."

Joan was flattered and surprised by Michael's comment; she'd never heard anyone describe her as *confident*. For that matter, she had never felt confident. Where was this coming from?

"You have given us some powerful food for thought, Joan, and trust me when I say we will take what you have said seriously."

"Thank you, Pastor," Joan said.

"One other thing," he said. "I assume Franklin is fine with your working at the church?"

"Michael and I wouldn't want to disrupt the harmony in your family," Lillian added.

Joan wasn't sure if what she and Franklin had was harmony; it wasn't the kind of harmony she could see in the relationship between Pastor Michael and Lillian. They seemed to be in agreement about everything, and they spoke in perfect congruence, as if each one's words complemented the other's.

"Franklin is fine with . . . all of it."

"Wonderful! We'd love to finally meet him. Please, bring him around this weekend." Michael said.

"I will. Thank you, Pastor," Joan said.

Joan stood up, and Lillian walked with her out toward the stairs to the basement. Lillian touched Joan's arm.

"I wanted to tell you, Joan," she said, "that Annabelle thought very highly of you."

Joan raised her eyebrows. "She did?"

"Yes. She spoke of you often."

"I thought the world of Annabelle. I wish I could've spent more time with her. We had a strong connection from the start."

Lillian smiled and touched Joan's arm before heading back toward the office.

Joan smiled as well. She felt proud of herself, and that was an unfamiliar feeling.

18

JOAN VACILLATED BETWEEN EBULLIENCE AT THE POSSIBILITY of working at the church and anxiety that she would be passed over for the position. At home, she found it impossible to focus on cooking dinner or playing with Barbara or making a grocery list; she had a much larger matter on her mind.

Before she could tell Franklin about her intentions, there was someone else she needed to speak with, and she realized that the only contact number she had for Paul was at the restaurant. She knew that he had a phone line installed in his apartment, so she called Lillian in the hopes that she could provide Joan with that number.

"I have some old photos of Annabelle's that he may want," she told Lillian, lying with surprising ease.

Joan called Paul Sunday morning, when she knew he'd be at home and when Franklin was at meeting for worship.

"Please. I need to see you. It's important, Paul."

"I really can't, I'm sorry. I've got a hectic schedule this week. Double shifts on Thursday and Friday."

"We could meet somewhere. I could take the train in and come to your apartment if that's easier," she suggested.

"No," he replied. "Can't you tell me what this is about, Joan?"

"I'd rather not say over the line."

"You're going to need to give me some inkling."

"Please trust me, Paul. It's important that I see you."

"That wouldn't be a good idea. I think we both know that."

She was silent.

"Joan?"

"Yes, I'm here," she said.

He sighed. "Listen, I need to meet a friend in fifteen minutes, so perhaps it would be best if we just—"

"Paul. I'm . . . *expecting.*"

He did not respond.

"Paul, are you there?"

"What? Yes."

"I'm pregnant. Have you forgotten? After the funer—"

"Of course I haven't forgotten." She heard him curse under his breath. "Are you . . . are you implying this is . . . *my* child?"

"Yes. I'm certain of it. Franklin and I, well, we haven't had relations in a very long time. Probably six months. So he will certainly figure out this is not his child." Her stomach tensed as she waited for him to say something.

"Have you seen your doctor? How do you know—"

"I've been pregnant before. I know. A woman knows. But, no, I haven't yet been to my doctor. I wanted to talk to you first."

"Oh, for Chrissake, Joan." His cool, calm tone belied his words.

Joan held the telephone receiver in one hand and steadied herself on the back of a kitchen chair with her other hand. She was caught off guard by his less-than-empathetic response. She herself was not exactly pleased about her predicament, but she had expected him to be more comforting in his choice of words. She'd hoped he would put her mind at ease.

"You're being very harsh," she said.

Silence.

"Paul?"

"Christ, Joan, I wasn't prepared for all this."

The nerve! "And I was?" She could hear the shrillness in her tone, and it embarrassed her. She took a deep breath and calmed herself. She realized Paul required more information, and she needed to sound rational, mature. "You should know that things haven't been going well for Franklin and me for a while. The store keeps him terribly busy. He doesn't need me. I'm not the same little girl I was when he met me, and I know it bothers him." As the words came out, she became more agitated with her predicament. "He doesn't understand that I want to be more than just a wife and a mother." Her cadence was as rapid as her thoughts, and she could feel herself once again losing composure.

"Please. Be rational. Talk to him, work this out. Franklin is a good man. Isn't that what you Quakers do? Listen and reason and find inner light?"

She scoffed at the notion. "Yes, Franklin is a good man, a *very* good man, which is why he *will not* stand for this," she said, placing her hand on her still-small belly.

She could hear Paul sigh and mumble something unintelligible.

She needed a different approach. She softened her tone. "I know there is something special between you and me. I'm certain of it. And I think you understand who I really am."

She heard him sigh yet again, which she interpreted as resignation. She knew Paul would do the right thing. That was the kind of man he was.

When Franklin arrived home that evening, he was in an unusually good mood. "Babs, my pretty little petunia," he said, lifting his daughter in the air. "Have you and Mama had a good day?"

Barbara giggled. Franklin held her tightly and nuzzled her neck, giving her little kisses and making her laugh more heartily.

He walked over to Joan, who was making dinner, and gave her a kiss on her cheek.

"Six orders today for those large, walnut, raised-panel roll-top desks. You know the one?"

Joan nodded. She knew the entire inventory of Oakes's Fine Furniture.

"And we received an order for a dozen five-drawer, tall filing cabinets," he said.

"A dozen all from the same customer?" Joan asked, flatly.

"Yes, from Pennsylvania Hospital. Their obstetrics department continues to expand, and we are the beneficiaries of their growth." Franklin walked over to the credenza where he kept the liquor and he began mixing himself a martini. "I don't know, Joan. I feel like the economy is improving. Things are looking up."

Franklin hummed and bounced about as he mixed his drink. Joan observed her husband's elation and energy. It concerned her that there was a correlation between how his day went and how many martinis he consumed. Since Franklin was upbeat from the recent order, Joan assumed tonight he would stop at one.

"Come have some dinner, Franklin. I've fixed meat loaf," she said dryly.

Franklin finished his second slice of meat loaf and proceeded to polish off the creamed spinach. He reached for another roll and butter.

"Joan, your cooking has been out of this world!"

Joan looked down. *So what*? she thought. She could not bend her lips into a smile. She had a sour taste in the back of her throat.

"And I'm so proud of you," he added. "Honestly," he said, his tone becoming serious. "I was rather worried right after Barbara came along. You seemed so forlorn and shaken. But you've embraced motherhood and home life, and it's just wonderful." He was beaming.

He has no idea how I'm feeling. Joan looked up. "Are you happy, Franklin?"

"Me?" Franklin asked as he sipped the last of his second martini.

"Yes. Are you happy?"

"Am I happy? I have no reason not to be happy, do I? I have a lovely wife who has turned into a fine cook. A beautiful daughter," he said as he tousled Barbara's hair. "And now that the store is getting more corporate business, well, I'd say I'm A-OK. Oh, and it seems Dad is actually going to hand me the baton this fall and maybe—"

"I'm not, Franklin."

"Hmm, what's that?"

"I'm not happy."

"Aw, listen to me going on and on about the store. I'm sorry, Joan. I know you miss being a part of all that. Why don't you come downtown tomorrow? We can have lunch, or maybe dinner. Perhaps Ellen or my mother can watch Barbara for a few hours, and we'll have some fun together, like we used to."

"No, I mean, with us. Franklin, I . . ." she said, searching for words.

He cocked his head. "Is this about not taking a vacation this summer? I know how much you enjoyed our honeymoon cruise, and maybe at some point in the future we'll take another cruise, but a vacation is not in the cards at the moment, sweetheart, you know that. When Barbara is a little older and we're completely out of this economic slump, well, I think we can make it happen. You've been very patient with me. We both need a getaway."

Joan stared at her plate. She'd barely eaten. It was painful to watch him go on and on about a vacation when that was the furthest thought on her mind. She and Franklin no longer knew each other, if they ever did. She didn't want him to be nice.

Franklin frowned. "What is going on, Joan?"

"It's not about a cruise, Franklin. I don't do . . . *anything.*"

"Well, I wouldn't say you don't do anything. You went to New York a couple weeks ago. You enjoyed that, didn't you? And your volunteer work at the church, I know you love that."

"Pastor Michael offered me Annabelle's position at the church," she said, testing him. "It would be about six hours a day, Monday through Friday. Barbara could go to day care in the basement of the church. She loves it there, she really does. And . . ." Joan paused as she watched Franklin's face harden.

"No," Franklin said sternly but calmly. "No, Joan. Not a good idea . . ."

". . . and it's a paid position, Franklin." She softened her tone. "And good experience for me."

"Joan. Please," Franklin said, rubbing his temples.

". . . and it wouldn't affect my ability to grocery shop or prepare dinner. And I really like the pastor and Lillian, they are such kind people and they do wonderful work at Grace. They'd love to meet you, and . . ." She knew she was pushing him, trying to get him angry.

"Stop!" Franklin yelled, startling Barbara, who let out a piercing scream.

"Franklin," Joan said in a hushed tone indicating shock at his rage. She lifted Barbara's face to her own and kissed the baby's cheek. While Franklin's ire was the reaction she'd been seeking, she had never before witnessed *this* level of intensity from him; he'd never even raised his voice in her presence. She was used to being the one raising the pitch of a conversation. Was this the alcohol?

He took a deep breath and let it out slowly. "Do you have *any* idea what *my* life is like at the moment? Do you, Joan?"

She could tell he was still upset, but his volume had lowered. She stood up, holding Barbara, almost to protect herself from . . . what?

"I have tried to keep you immune to the pressure I've been under these last several months," he said. "You've had your own struggles, and I just wanted our home life to be calm and happy. But I'm a nervous wreck. My dad—he's in bad shape, you know that. Every morning I wake up wondering if this is the day he'll go."

Joan bounced Barbara on her hip and listened. Seconds earlier, his volatile reaction to the idea of her working had eased the way for her to tell him about Paul. Now she just felt bad for Franklin.

"And business—good lord—I don't need to tell you how strained things have been. But it's looking up. So I need you to be patient and strong, just a little while longer. As I've been. I'll do my job, you do yours, and together we will get through all this."

He moved in closer to her and softly placed his hand on her upper arm. She could smell the gin—or was it vermouth?—on his breath. It made her tense up, not because the odor was repulsive, but because it felt, oddly, like a harbinger of things to come. She pulled back from his touch.

"I've already accepted the position, Franklin." She knew this was a lie, and on some level, she wanted to recharge his anger. It would make it easier for her to play the victim.

He raised his martini glass but saw he had already finished his drink. "What?"

"And there's something else I need to tell you."

19

June 1939

JOAN TOOK A SEAT AT THE END OF ONE OF THE BENCHES IN the meetinghouse and reserved the space to her right, next to the aisle. To her left, three-year-old Barbara, dressed in a pale pink dress with matching hair bow and wearing patent leather Mary Janes, sat holding her doll and nibbling on a biscuit. Joan held one-year-old Bobby on her lap. She looked toward the rear of the meetinghouse, hoping he would come. It was the one thing she'd asked of him when they'd spoken on the telephone a week after he'd left for work and not returned: "Please don't disgrace me."

She saw Marcus seated two rows up, next to Helen and Fred.

Joan sat in silence with the other worshippers, as Quaker tradition dictated. Eventually, there was some stirring in the benches, and then Frederick "Sonny" Pruitt and his bride-to-be, Leah, entered the room and walked down one of the aisles together, she holding a small, simple bouquet of white roses and sweet peas. They walked to the front of the room and took their seats, facing the worshippers.

As Friends' meetings were not overseen by clergy, a member of Abington Friends Meeting stood up and faced the worshippers.

"Friends," he began in a solemn and reverent manner. "This evening, we will bear witness to the union of Leah Easton and

Frederick Pruitt, Junior. We recognize that marriage is a binding relationship entered into in the presence of God and of witnessing Friends." He then turned to the couple, who rose to their feet, faced each other, and joined hands.

Sonny spoke first. "In the presence of God and these our friends, I take thee Leah to be my wife, promising with divine assistance to be unto thee a loving and faithful husband so long as we both shall live." He smiled at Leah, and she lowered her head momentarily to compose herself. Then she promised the same as his wife.

Joan considered those vows, the words setting forth an expectation of equality, of partnership, of support, the very same vows she and Franklin had recited to each other just five years earlier. Her father had seemed exceptionally proud that day. Five years, and so much tumult.

Sonny then placed a gold band around Leah's ring finger, and the couple took their seats.

Joan wiped a tear from her eye and took a long, slow breath to keep herself from sobbing uncontrollably.

After Sonny and Leah each signed the marriage certificate, it was read aloud, and the meeting continued with silent worship.

Growing up, Joan had never been able to quiet her mind during meetings for worship. Her thoughts would inevitably drift to her insecurities: she was not witty, brilliant, or beautiful; she did not excel at games, sports, music, or the arts; she could not engage in clever conversation; she was not academically remarkable; she had a few school friends, but she was not popular—not by a long shot. Most importantly, she could not shake feelings of envy as she compared herself to her cousins and anyone else who seemed to possess all she did not. She would sit, waiting for God to inspire her to speak up with something meaningful and relevant, watching as other students stood to express gratitude or insight or just to comment on something happening in the world. Why was it always so difficult for her to calm her mind and embrace meeting for worship for what it was meant to be, namely, an opportunity to share through prayer, meditation, or spoken messages?

And now, at her cousin's wedding, Joan reflected on the trajectory of events that had occurred in her life over the last two years: her affair with Paul, which led to her second pregnancy; Franklin's shock and anger when she told him she was pregnant with Paul's child, and how Franklin packed a bag and left their apartment that evening, saying nothing as he walked out; the following morning, he filed for a divorce.

"If it were just the affair, I could've moved beyond it and forgiven you," he wrote her in a letter weeks after she revealed her transgression. "But I cannot stay married to you and raise another man's child, not when that man is able-bodied and employed and living in Philadelphia. Further, I've given the matter of our apartment a great deal of thought, and I will continue to pay the rent until our divorce is finalized. Understand, I am doing this only because I feel it is in Barbara's best interest for now." Joan was relieved and grateful for his kindness, yet at the same time she felt overwhelming shame, realizing that Franklin had done nothing to deserve this humiliation.

What countered her negative feelings during that time was the fact that Pastor Michael had offered the position to Joan, and she had begun working in the church immediately after Franklin moved out. She imagined being married to Paul, working at the church, and building a new life, on her terms. She kept the information about her infidelity, pregnancy, and pending divorce a secret from Lillian and Michael for as long as she could. But she knew it was only a matter of time.

"Forgive me for prying, Joan, but why haven't you told me that you and Franklin are expecting?" Lillian asked one day as the two of them were stocking the church pantry.

Joan had been caught off guard.

"You don't think I noticed that growing belly and swelling bosom?" Lillian said with a wink.

Joan took a deep breath. She reached for a glass of water on her desk. She took a long, slow sip and swallowed. "Lillian, there is something I need to tell you, and . . ."

"What is it, Joan?"

Joan explained that she and Franklin were going through a divorce, that it would probably be finalized at the beginning of the new year. Lillian nodded her head slowly, eyes narrowed and focused intently on Joan. She patted her own cheek with her hand and made a soft *tsk-tsk* sound as she gently touched Joan's arm.

Joan did not mention that the baby was not Franklin's.

"I'm so very sorry for what you're going through," Lillian said. "Why didn't you tell me earlier? You accepted this position saying that Franklin was in complete agreement and that it would not cause a problem. I certainly hope that working here was not the catalyst for your marital breakdown."

Lillian's empathy made Joan dizzy. Her breathing became shallow, and she thought she might faint. She reached for the glass of water and took another long sip. When she put the glass back down on the desk, Lillian moved in close and gave Joan a hug.

"Michael and I are here for you, dear. Whatever you need. There, there." She patted Joan's back.

The floodgates opened, and Joan began wailing, weeping on Lillian's shoulder. In minutes, Lillian's blouse was damp with Joan's tears.

Joan wanted to be able to move forward with her life. She

would explain everything to Lillian after the divorce was finalized, believing that Lillian would be accepting and charitable in her reaction.

But once Joan received notice of her divorce, in February of 1938, she immediately ran into a legal stumbling block for her plan to marry Paul, as well as an emotional blow when she told Lillian the truth about how she'd gotten pregnant and what she intended to do.

Lillian stared at Joan for several minutes without saying anything. Her face was blank; Joan could not read her. Finally, Lillian sat back in her chair. She clasped her hands together and placed them under her chin, eyes cast downward. Her brow was knitted, and she did not look pleased.

"I'm disappointed. I can't lie," she said without looking at Joan. "Disappointed in you, in Paul. This is just shocking." Her tone was somber, soft, but her words cut Joan painfully. She looked at Joan. "And Paul is willing to marry you?"

"Yes." *Of course, he is. Why wouldn't he be?* Joan thought. The question was insulting.

Lillian became very businesslike. "What I can tell you, based on Michael's experience with another parishioner, is that Pennsylvania has among the harshest divorce laws in the country. There are very specific rules about"—she looked uncomfortable—"*adultery.*"

"Meaning what?" asked Joan, blowing her nose into a handkerchief.

"I recall Michael telling me that a spouse guilty of adultery cannot marry the individual with whom the adultery was committed as long as the former spouse is still living."

Joan panicked. She had no idea that marrying Paul immediately after her divorce from Franklin would be an issue. She asked Lillian if Michael could offer help in any way.

"However, if you were to move to another state, set up a permanent domicile, and get married there, then your union would be legal and recognized even within Pennsylvania, as long as your legal address was elsewhere. Mind you, Joan, I'm just the wife of a minister, not a lawyer. You may want to consult with one for this."

Joan looked down at her hands. "He will never agree to move, I'm certain of that. He has a good job at the Bellevue-Stratford." She began to sob again.

"There is another option," Lillian said. "I'm not even sure Michael knows about this. I happened to read an article about a couple in Pittsburgh who traveled to Florida, where they were married quickly by a justice of the peace, no questions asked. They didn't even need to provide proof of a domicile in the state."

Joan stopped crying. She blew her nose again. "Florida?" She was disappointed. "I . . . we have to travel to Florida just to get married?"

"Oh, for goodness' sake, Joan. How did you let this happen? And with Annabelle's *nephew*, even?" Lillian shook her head from side to side.

"Will you forgive me? Will Pastor Michael?"

"We are not the ones from whom you need forgiveness."

Paul and Joan's seventy-two-hour getaway, with Barbara in tow, included travel both ways on the Seaboard Rail line between Philadelphia and the northernmost point of Florida. When they returned, Lillian tactfully, yet clearly uncomfortably, let Joan know that the position in the church had been given to a parishioner, a woman Annabelle's age whom they had known for ten years.

"It's not just the indiscretion," Lillian explained. "I am deeply hurt because at no point did you confide in me the degree of dissatisfaction you'd been experiencing in your marriage to Franklin. Michael and I trusted you and wanted to embrace you as family. He could have counseled you, helped you navigate the waters of this indiscretion, and find a way to mend your relationship with Franklin. This is what he does."

That was the last time Joan set foot in Grace Presbyterian Church.

Now, sitting in the Friends meetinghouse at her cousin's wedding, she knew her marriage to Paul was based on wishful thinking that he would come to love her; that he would be a good father and devoted husband because, after all, from the time she met him, he seemed like the most genuine and moral person she knew, next to Annabelle; that his passion for life and sensitive nature would make him a passionate and sensitive partner. To Joan's dismay, Paul turned out to be just as weak and selfish as everyone else, including herself. She felt the oppressive weight of her bad decisions. Or perhaps she was a victim—over and over and over again—her lot in life.

In the meetinghouse, the silent worship continued. Occasionally, the quiet observance was broken by a sneeze or cough, or a child's high-pitched voice, or someone standing up to wish the couple a lifetime of health and happiness. One worshipper stood and said that she had been disturbed by news reports she'd read about hostility and violence toward Jews in Germany, and she felt grateful to live in a country where religious differences are tolerated.

Struggling to keep her active baby boy from disturbing the silence, Joan wanted to stand up and scream, *My husband has left me and my two children, and I am alone.* Instead, she bounced Bobby on her knee and kept an eye on the wall clock.

After close to forty minutes, the meeting was broken when Fred, Sr., turned to shake the hand of his brother-in-law. Then all the worshippers followed suit, shaking hands with one another.

Husbandless, and with Bobby on her hip and Barbara clutching her mother's hand, Joan headed outside for the dinner reception to which she had been invited, but at which she did not entirely feel welcome or comfortable.

Later that night, after being dropped off by a family friend at her rowhome in West Philadelphia, Joan tucked the children into bed. She was grateful that they were too young to observe and absorb the stress and bitterness that had been building between her and Paul, yet she worried what would happen if he didn't return. It was certainly a possibility; he had left for work one day, and she had not seen him since. He had given no indication when or if he was coming back. She imagined Bobby growing up without a father, always wondering why the man had dropped out of his life and longing for a replacement father figure. Would he become derelict? Weren't boys without fathers certain to always struggle with an inability to earn a livelihood and raise a family?

In her bedroom, Joan forcefully kicked off her high heels. She pounded the mattress with her fist; then she ran toward the closet and began pulling Paul's trousers and shirts from their hangers and throwing them about the room. She stopped, panting and sweaty, just as she heard the lock on the front door turn and the door creak open. As she went to the top of the stairs, she saw Paul enter and crane his neck toward the kitchen.

"You bastard!" she hissed through her teeth as she walked down the steps.

"Joan—"

"How could you *do* that to me?" She walked toward him, speaking with her lips taut against her teeth. "You promised you'd come. When we spoke on the telephone, you swore to me."

Paul mumbled. "Not sure why you wanted to go . . ." His voice trailed off.

"What? Speak up, Paul." She moved closer to him, hands on her hips.

"Joan, calm down. I couldn't. I just couldn't."

"My father was ashamed—I could tell," she said.

Paul moved past Joan toward the dining room and made a beeline for the scotch before she could keep him from it.

"Oh, no you don't!"

Paul swung around, eyes narrowed and upper lip curled into a snarl. "And exactly when was the last time you spoke to your father? Huh, Joan?"

Joan was silenced. She folded her arms and turned away from him.

"What's that?" he said, mockingly cupping his hand around his ear. "Oh, that's right. You haven't spoken to Marcus since you gave him the blessed news that you conceived a child with a man who wasn't your husband." He spoke quietly but with a stern sarcasm that shut Joan down. "You wanted me to be the mediator, right? Break the ice for you? Or maybe you just wanted to start something. Right there, in the reception hall at your cousin's wedding. Just start something with everyone who has wronged you." He poured the scotch and took a sip.

Joan whipped back around and sneered at him. "You're a jerk!" She headed back upstairs. In the bathroom, she wet her toothbrush, exhaled, and looked at herself in the mirror. She was furious and wanted to hold on to the anger so that she would not cry. *Anger is powerful; sadness is pathetic.*

As Joan was brushing her teeth, Paul entered the bedroom. She quickly spit out the toothpaste, wiped her mouth, and walked over to him, calmer now. He held a glass of scotch in his hand and leaned back against the bureau, swirling the ice in the drink and looking around the room at his clothing strewn about. He placed his drink on top of the bureau and began picking things up off the floor.

"Why didn't you come?" she asked with a weak and scratchy voice.

Paul stood with a button-down shirt draped over his arm. "I've met your father exactly *one* time. And that wasn't the most comfortable encounter. I just . . . couldn't face your whole family."

"I didn't think it was possible for my father to be even more disappointed in me than he already was." She looked at Paul. "He came over to me and said hello. He was civil. And he asked where my husband was. Didn't say your name, but he did ask where you were. And he couldn't even look at Bobby, his own grandson. Can you imagine?"

Paul looked down and put one hand in the pocket of his trousers, lightly jiggling some spare change.

Joan continued. "And you know what? I couldn't answer. I opened my mouth and nothing came out. Fortunately, Barbara started whining and Father swooped her up and took her over to Mary's kids. I was never so relieved to have my child whine for attention." She played with her wedding band. "The one thing my father felt I had done right with my life was marry Franklin, and I failed miserably at that." She dropped her head into her palms.

Paul massaged his jaw. "I don't owe you anything," he said, almost in a whisper.

Joan whipped her head back up. "What did you say?"

Paul braced himself, stood up straight. "I said I don't owe you anything. I don't owe you or your family a single thing. All that strained silence and polite tension among them and their ilk."

Joan could not believe his audacity. She'd never before heard Paul speak so bitterly about other people, much less her own family. Still, she had been noticing a change in his personality for months.

"You always say how your father is a prominent man in Philadelphia," he continued. "Your aunt and uncle—the entire family—their standing in the community is everything. Well, I don't give a damn about any of that. And why should I? What have they done for us?"

Joan was disgusted with his entitlement. Even she didn't believe her family owed her anything at this point.

"I am so tired," he said, his words coming out slowly. "It's not even about them. Your moods change on a dime. I don't know what you want from me." He paused. "*You* don't even know what you want from me. You're impossible to please."

"My moods change, that's right. You know why? Because I have two toddlers at home. That's exhausting. I have nothing else, Paul, *nothing*! I lost Annabelle. I *loved* her. I know she was your aunt and you adored her, but she was like a mother to me."

Paul raised a pointed finger and opened his mouth, and then stopped.

She went on, "And I don't have the church and Lillian and Pastor Michael anymore. They liked me and thought I was competent." She began to cry. "Why do I lose people?"

Paul reached out and touched her arm.

"The last vacation I took was my honeymoon cruise with Franklin. I don't even have that apartment I loved—"

"Now hold on a sec. It was your decision to move away from—"

"No, the lease was in Franklin's name, you know that. He was paying the rent. You and I wouldn't have been able to afford it."

Paul sat on the edge of the bed. He was quiet. He nodded his head.

"And now I don't even have my family. My aunt and uncle, Sonny, Mary, my dad. I'm such a *failure*." She sat on the bed next to him and pulled at a thread on the quilt.

"Forgive me for pointing this out," Paul said as he massaged his temples. "But you've said before that you never felt like you were really a part of your family. On several occasions, Joan, you mentioned feeling like they never wanted you. The 'black sheep' of the family, isn't that right?"

"Why are you being cruel?"

"I think you're trying to make this about me. As if I've done something to you, as if I've destroyed your life."

"Well, if the shoe fits," she said.

"You and I made a huge mistake"—he looked at Joan cautiously—"that afternoon. We weren't thinking clearly. A moment of weakness—"

"Stop!" Joan screamed. "I don't want to go down that miserable path again."

"But I did the right thing. I felt awful, just awful because obviously you didn't get yourself into that situation on your own, and I knew I had to make it right. Jesus, I think I actually convinced myself that I had *done* something to you, against your will. But, Joan, I had no interest in . . ." He stopped. "Anyway, I kept hearing Annabelle's voice in my head, something she'd always say: 'A fallible man makes mistakes; a responsible man makes amends.'"

Joan recalled Annabelle saying that as well. Her throat tightened as she considered her friend's tolerance for people's weaknesses. Would Annabelle accept her without judgment if she were still alive? Joan pushed those thoughts away.

"You know, Joan, a lot of men would have just deserted you from the start. I could've been like that, could've just run away, left town when you said you were pregnant. Or I could have denied it altogether, said the baby wasn't mine."

"Did you love me?" she asked, staring at the ceiling.

"What?"

She smiled weakly. "Is that why you did the right thing? Did you love me? *Do* you love me?"

"Joan, I can't do this now. I only came back here to—"

"Do you love me, Paul?"

He was silent.

"Paul?"

"I just came back to gather my things."

"You can't just leave me again. What about Bobby? He's your son, after all."

Paul exhaled hard. "I should have told you . . ." he began.

She sat up straight, concerned with what he was about to say.

"The day I left, when I went to work and didn't come back home, it was because I got fired."

"Fired? You never said anything." *Was he ashamed?* "You said you were doing double shifts, that you were staying with friends in the city." Joan was in shock.

"Initially, I was able to pick up odd jobs in the city, at all hours of the day and night. But there's no work here, not for me anyway."

"You lied to me. You should have told me—"

"I'm heading south, to Florida. There's work there, new resorts. I'll contact you once I figure it all out." He reached into his back pocket for his wallet and pulled out a wad of money. "Here. Take this for now, until I can get you more."

She did not want to take it from him; it felt like a payoff. But she did not have a choice; she had expenses—the house, utilities, food. Franklin contributed to the care of Barbara, but that money did not pay the rent or electric bill, and if Joan could not make ends meet, Franklin surely would take Barbara away from her, which he'd wanted to do from the start. She snatched the money out of Paul's hand.

"You should talk to your dad. Tell him . . . I don't know," he said, looking into the air, as if for an excuse. "Tell him Paul is a heck of a guy who's just down on his luck. Or tell him I'm a heel, a real son of a bitch who deserted his wife and kid. It doesn't matter, either way. He can help you out, I'm sure of that. He owes you something." He scooped up the rest of his clothing from the floor and gathered more from a drawer. He grabbed a small suitcase from the closet. Joan watched him move about their bedroom in silence. She followed him as he headed downstairs.

At the front door she tamped down her rage, closed her eyes, and counted silently to three in order to calm her voice. She touched his arm and softly spoke. "Paul, this isn't who you are. You're not the kind of man who leaves his wife and his little boy. What would Annabelle say?"

He angled his head. "You think you know me. You don't, and neither did she."

Joan was terribly hurt and confused.

"I can't give you . . ." he said, shaking his head side to side, ". . . whatever it is you need, Joan. You had a good man in Franklin.

You should have made that work, but you're just . . ." He stopped.

"I'm just what?" She wasn't sure she really wanted to know what he thought.

". . . content in your misery." He turned and headed off.

Joan watched him walk away, stunned by his cruel honesty and the ease with which he seemed to dole it out. She knew she had made mistakes, but did she deserve this? She balled her hand into a fist and was about to strike the door when she considered her two sleeping children, who, miraculously, had not been awakened by their voices. She closed the front door, rubbed her eyes, and looked around her house. She needed to sleep, but first she needed to calm her mind, so she poured some scotch into a glass and downed it all in one gulp, making a face as she did. Then she went upstairs to take a warm bath and consider her next plan of action.

In the tub, as the scotch worked its magic on her head and the warm water soothed her body, she considered all that she had been through in her twenty-four years. Two failed marriages. Had she ever loved Franklin? He was a good man, a faithful husband. He loved her, but he didn't understand her, and he tried to control her. She thought she could be happy with Paul. She thought he would be more accepting of her desire to be more than just a wife and mother. What had gone wrong?

Content in my misery? Does he think I like this? Does he think I enjoy the fact that I never seem to have any control of my own life? "Why did I ever want him?" she said out loud. She picked up a bar of soap and worked lather into her hands.

Then she had an epiphany. She let the soap fall into the water.

It occurred to Joan that she had never actually *wanted* Paul. She had wanted to *be* Paul: independent, strong, unafraid of being alone, responsible to no one.

"In charge of *my destiny*," she softly told herself.

The calming effect of the scotch and the bath were wearing off. She was angry.

The next morning, as she unpinned Bobby's soiled diaper, she looked at his blond cowlick, perpetually growing against the grain of his hairline. With his blue eyes and thick, blond hair, no one could doubt that he was Paul's son and not Franklin's. Joan looked up at the wall and the small, framed painting of a blue sailboat heading into the horizon. She felt a heaviness in every breath she took.

Barbara appeared in the bedroom doorway. "Mommy, I'm hungry!" she cried.

"I'm going to put a fresh diaper on your brother, Barb. And then I'm going to make you some scrambled eggs and toast. And *then* we are going to get dressed and take a trolley ride downtown to see Grandpa Marcus at the newspaper. Won't that be fun?" Joan tried to sound upbeat but heard her flat affect.

Barbara squealed with delight and turned and ran toward the kitchen, clapping her hands and yelling "Tuh-wollee! Tuh-wollee!" Bobby squealed as well, imitating his sister. Joan's eyes filled with tears.

She looked again at the boat sailing into the horizon. As she squinted, she could see, for the first time, a tiny man aboard the boat. How could she not have noticed the man on the boat any of the countless times she'd changed her son's diaper? It was clear the boat had sailed, taking the man far away. Joan knew it would not take much time for Paul to be permanently erased from her children's memories. It would be better that way, she reasoned.

She lifted Bobby into her arms and headed into the kitchen. She was about to begin the next chapter of her life, which would require that she eat crow and appeal to her father's sense of empathy and decency in order to ease her burden, at least temporarily, of being alone with two children.

20

THE CHECK FOR SIX MONTHS' WORTH OF RENT THAT HER
father had handed her in stony silence had already been used up,
and it had only been four months since Paul left. She had received a money order from him on one occasion; it came in an
envelope with a return address of Juniper, Florida, and a note
inside that read: "I'm sorry, this is the best I can do." She used
that to cover the current month's rent.

With Bobby on her hip and Barbara at the kitchen table
drawing with crayons, Joan picked up the telephone and dialed
the number of her landlord, Kyle Dumann. She hoped he would
be understanding, and she was trying to have "high hopes with
low expectations," as Annabelle had always advised in these situ-
ations. Joan knew very little about him, yet from the time they
secured the lease on the house, Joan thought his name sounded
familiar.

"Dumann Paving and Flooring. This is Janice speaking. How
may I help you?"

"Oh, hello," Joan said, caught off guard. She didn't realize
that she was calling a business. "Is Mr. Dumann available?"

"Well, honey, there are three Mr. Dumanns here. Would that
be Richard Senior, Richard Junior, or Kyle Dumann?"

Joan asked for Kyle Dumann, explaining that she was his
tenant. After a brief hold, he picked up the line.

"Hello, Kyle Dumann here."

His voice was soft and pleasant, not at all what Joan had expected, and he sounded rather young to her, like a twelve-year-old answering the phone in his father's office.

"Hello, Mr. Dumann. This is Mrs. Anderson, your tenant."

"I'm sorry, Mrs. Anderson. Can you tell me which address? I have several houses I rent out, and I can't place your name off the top of my head."

Several houses? Joan thought. He was not at all what she had imagined. She had assumed that Kyle Dumann was an older gentleman, possibly in his seventies, who'd raised a family in this house and relocated when his children moved on and his wife died. She had no idea where she'd gotten that idea, but Paul had always been the one to send the rent checks.

"In West Philadelphia? On Clark Street?"

"Oh, of course. Yes. Sure. What can I do for you, then? Is there a problem?"

Joan had steeled herself for a difficult conversation with a gruff and impatient individual, but her landlord's gentle tone caught her by surprise. She wanted to break down, to let it all out, to tell him that her husband had abandoned her and her two young children, and she had to put aside her self-respect in order to ask for help from her father, whose respect for her had already fallen pretty low.

"There's no problem with the house. I . . . this is difficult for me to say, Mr. Dumann. I may be late in getting next month's rent to you, and, quite honestly, I may need to break my lease early. You see, my husband, he . . ." Joan began to cry. Not real tears, she was well past that. She felt neither sorry for herself nor entitled to any pity, yet she knew she could no longer depend on anyone else to solve her problems; she was alone and would find a way to manage by surviving on her wits.

"Mrs. Anderson? Has something happened to your husband?" Kyle's voice cracked as he said the word *husband*.

Joan pretended to blow her nose. "I apologize, Mr. Dumann. I don't mean to bring you into my personal problems." She turned her back to Barbara, who was having a conversation with her Raggedy Ann doll, and lowered her voice. "My husband lost his job and unfortunately he had to leave Philadelphia to find work. I don't exactly know where he is. Oh, this is much more embarrassing than I thought it would be." Bobby was playing with the telephone cord and began giggling. She tried to quiet him.

"How old is your child?" he asked.

"Bobby's one and a half. And I have a three-year-old, Barbara."

"I don't know what to say, Mrs. Anderson. This must be difficult for you." He paused. "Do you have relatives in the area?"

"My aunt and uncle," Joan said, intentionally not mentioning her father, nor where her aunt and uncle lived, for fear that Kyle would draw conclusions about their financial means and how much assistance they were able to provide her. "However, things are a bit"—she searched for a tactful word—"strained, with them at the moment. But I am looking for employment, so . . ." She let her story sit with him.

"Not that I am putting any pressure on you to vacate the house immediately. I just want to make sure you and your children have somewhere to go . . . when you're ready."

Joan could sense an awkwardness in Kyle's voice, yet his empathy seemed genuine. This was proving to be far easier than she had imagined. She heard another voice in the background and Kyle's muffled voice in reply; he apparently covered the receiver with his hand. Then he returned to Joan. "Excuse me for one second, Mrs. Anderson." He covered the receiver again but Joan could still make out most of what he said. "Yes, Huntingdon Valley Country Club . . . my dad and brother and I are all members, so it shouldn't be a problem." He returned to Joan. "Forgive me. Trying to set up a golf outing." Then he paused. "That was rude of me, talking golf outings while you and I were discussing your . . . hardships."

It finally clicked. That was why his name sounded familiar. Her father and uncle had been members of Huntingdon Valley Country Club since she was a child, and Kyle and Sonny had become friendly while taking golf lessons with other children. Joan could vaguely recall the blond-haired, blue-eyed, soft-spoken young man who had once offered her a piece of chewing gum after he heard her father tell her she needed to smile more and complain less.

Her mind was racing. Should she use their connection to the golf club and Sonny in her favor, or would she do better to conceal her identity and safeguard her reputation? She did not want to be, yet again, the subject of gossip in her father's social circles, where word that the former Joan Sondersohn had been deserted by her second husband would spread expeditiously. Kyle sounded so kind and compassionate, and not at all pompous or impatient with her, so she wanted to preserve his goodwill. She wondered if there was a Mrs. Kyle Dumann.

"I've already taken up too much of your time, Mr. Dumann. I assure you, I will do my best to get next month's rent to you in a timely manner. I just wanted you to be aware of my circumstances."

"I appreciate your candor and . . . again, I'm very sorry for . . . well, anyway, please keep me apprised of your situation, Mrs. Anderson, and let me know if there is anything I can do to help."

"I will. Thank you."

Joan hung up the telephone and stood in the kitchen tapping her chin, thinking, planning. Perhaps she could call Sonny to see if he still had contact with Kyle Dumann and could provide any information, but Joan hadn't seen her cousin since his wedding, where she'd hugged him and his new bride and wished them well as they'd scanned the room, ostensibly searching for her missing husband. No, Joan decided, her questions might do nothing more than arouse her cousin's suspicion. She decided to place a call to someone who might not only be helpful in gathering information but would also withhold any judgment toward her.

She picked up the telephone and dialed her aunt and uncle's number. If either of them answered, Joan would hang up and try again another day.

To Joan's relief, Ellen McGrugan answered.

"Hello, Pruitt residence," she said in that Irish lilt that Joan found so pleasing.

"Hi, Ellen. It's Joan. Are you . . . home alone today?"

"Why, yes, I'm here with your grandmother. Your aunt is visitin' your cousin Mary today. What can I help you with, Mrs. Oakes . . . er, I mean.—"

"Anderson."

"Beg pardon, Mrs. Anderson. Apologies for my lame-brain today. Didn't get much sleep last night, what with your grandmother's carryin' on. She's flippin' her days and nights, so she's been keepin' me on my toes, if you don't mind my sayin' so."

"Is she all right?"

"Well, she's sleepin' now. But in the wee hours of the night she was askin' to speak with your aunt, then your father, then her lawyer, then, oh, lord knows who else, I cannot remember. I kept tellin' her, 'Miss Elizabeth, it's the middle of the night. Go back to bed.' I finally decided to lay down with her, right there in her bed next to her. I held her hand and sung a lullaby before she nodded off to sleep, probably around six o'clock this mornin.'"

"That's awful. Does that happen often?"

"Well, yes, more and more these days, poor thing."

"I should pay her a visit, I suppose," Joan said.

"I'm sure she'd love to see you. But tell me, how is that little Barbara doin'? I haven't seen her for ages."

"Oh, she's a good girl. Helps me with Bobby. She loves her little brother all right."

"I'd love to meet that little man."

Joan changed the subject. "Ellen, I need to ask a favor of you, if you don't mind."

"Certainly."

"I'm sure you know I've been rather out of touch with Aunt Helen and Uncle Fred, as well as my father."

"Yes, it's unfortunate," Ellen said. "These family breakdowns."

Joan was annoyed. "I'm not sure I'd call it a 'breakdown' exactly. More like being cast aside by the people who are supposed to love me through thick and thin, but that's not your concern." Joan immediately regretted what she'd said, yet she wondered how much Ellen knew.

"I'm terribly sorry, Mrs. Oakes." She immediately corrected herself. "*Anderson.* Beg pardon."

"Anyway, Ellen, if you wouldn't mind, I need you to find out about someone at the country club. At Huntingdon Valley. It's a member who . . . well, at least I think, who plays golf with my father or my uncle. I'm sure they know him. And I'd like to know if this gentleman is married." Her phrasing came off as awkward and inappropriate. "That is, I would like to contact his wife, if he is married, to . . . to invite her to . . . to join my group of ladies who are organizing a . . ." Joan sighed, exasperated and feeling unprepared to justify her request. Her heart began to pound and her mouth became dry. What was she *doing*?

As if throwing her a life vest, Ellen said, "Give me the gentleman's name. I'll find out what you need to know."

Joan was relieved, and somewhat surprised at Ellen's willingness to abet Joan's investigation. "Thank you, Ellen. This will be tremendously helpful for . . . this club I'm organizing."

"Certainly!" Ellen said, with the enthusiasm of someone who had not been awake all night with an elderly woman with cognitive deficits. "May I ask, how are you farin'?"

So Ellen knew. Marcus was not as tight-lipped as he portrayed himself to be.

"I'd be lying if I said I'm fine. But what can you do? Life goes on."

"Bit of a scoundrel, if you ask me, leaving a wife and his son. I mean, little Barbara, at least she's got her daddy nearby, and I know he sees her when he can. But that little boy . . . well, he's gonna need a father."

Joan was both aghast at Ellen's bluntness and relieved by the compassion she was showing. "Well, maybe I'm the scoundrel."

"Shh! Don't say such a thing. Don't let anyone make you feel bad for your decisions. We both lost our mothers to the flu when we were wee babes, so I understand how it feels to carry that loss, that . . . missin' piece of yourself. Believe me, we're kindred spirits in more ways than I care to share."

Joan listened to Ellen's cryptic words and decided that no further explanation was necessary; the message was loud and clear: Ellen was an ally, perhaps her only one.

21

IT HAD BEEN FOUR MONTHS SINCE ELLEN INFORMED JOAN THAT Kyle was not, and had never been, married; four months since Joan called Kyle to request that he come by the house one evening, after she'd put Bobby and Barbara to bed, to discuss some "personal concerns."

Four months earlier, when Kyle arrived at her house one evening after work, after her unusual request for a face-to-face meeting, she greeted him at the door with a broad smile and freshly applied lipstick. She extended her arm to shake his hand, making sure her grip was firm and professional, not loose and soft. She asked him to have a seat in the living room, where she had put out a fresh pot of coffee and pastries on doily-covered china. The radio played softly in the corner behind the sofa. He entered the living room and took a seat on the sofa, scanning the room; she assumed he was assessing the condition of his property, but Joan took care of her home and was confident that he saw nothing unsettling. She sat down next to him, reaching for a coffee cup. As she filled his cup, she began to recount their shared history at the country club. Kyle appeared to be surprised yet delighted, and he immediately remembered Joan once she told him her maiden name and who her cousin was. They reminisced about the club, the golf tournaments, families they both knew. She told him about Sonny's wedding and professional status. Kyle told her he'd graduated from Franklin and Marshall with an engineering degree two years earlier and was working as a draftsman at his father's company. Joan described her children, whom she'd already put to bed, and gushed with pride about how well-behaved and bright they were; she talked about her love for travel and adventure, and her hope that she would be able to provide her children with the same opportunities, and more, that she had enjoyed in her childhood. Her eyes filled with tears. "I want the best for my children, and I fear for their future in my current situation."

She reached for a napkin and dabbed the corners of her eyes. Then she sat up straight and looked Kyle in the eyes with as much confidence as she could muster, explaining how, due to a few lapses in judgment and "an abundance of trust in others," she had strayed from her "refined and privileged roots and social structure" and she now intended to steer her life toward the one she was meant to live.

"I am risking my pride and self-esteem by being completely honest with you, Kyle," she said as she looked down and smoothed her skirt. "And I don't want you to find me improperly candid about my intentions, but . . ." She looked away from him and toward the photograph of Jessie that sat on the side table next to the sofa. For a moment she said nothing and just studied her mother's lips, hair, and porcelain skin. *So much like mine*, she thought.

"But what, Joan? Is there something I can do?"

She turned back toward Kyle and studied his face and stature as he sat there, wide-eyed and eager, with a long, thin, boyish face, blond close-cropped hair, and broad shoulders that balanced his tall, rail-thin body. Joan looked him squarely in the eye. "I hope you won't laugh or think I'm crazy. I have this feeling deep in my core," she said, tapping her heart with all five fingers, "that you and I were destined to meet again as adults. After all these years. I don't believe it's just a random series of events that have brought us to this point." She watched for his reaction. She couldn't tell if he appeared to be stunned, offended, or slowly accepting her suggestion and coming to the same conclusion. "Do you?"

He blinked. "Do I . . . what?"

"Do you believe this is all random? Do you believe in fate, Kyle?" She touched his forearm.

"I . . . well, I don't know."

She held his gaze. This was no time to second-guess herself, as she had so many times in her life. If she was going to pursue this man, she needed to do so with full convictions about her motives. Joan moved her body slightly forward, in an almost imperceptive motion, so that it would leave just the slightest doubt in his mind as to her intention, and the next decision would be his alone.

He leaned in as the radio played Glenn Miller's "Moonlight Serenade." Joan touched his chest and gently held him back for a moment.

"Kyle, if you've got a sweetheart, tell me now."

But as Kyle leaned in toward her again, Joan closed her eyes and waited for his kiss, slow at first, and then with a ferocity that suggested that Mr. Kyle Dumann was fully receptive to any further suggestions on her part.

"Have you asked for a divorce, then?" Ellen asked Joan on the telephone one afternoon when no one was home in the Pruitt household and Ellen could speak freely.

Ah, those Irish with their sweet and gentle lilts, thought Joan. *Everything sounds so much more polite when it's asked with that accent.*

"That's not how it works. It's not so easy to end a marriage, especially in Pennsylvania," Joan explained to Ellen on the telephone.

"But the man left you with two little children—"

"I'd have to claim he abandoned us. I'd have to prove it, and he will just say he went to find employment and that he sent some checks when he was able." Joan was frustrated with the discussion. "Anyhow, by law it has to be at least two years. He's been gone for seven months, and I don't even know where to find him."

"But if he kne...." Ellen began.

"If he knew," Joan said, "what has been going on in my life since he left town, then I believe he would file for divorce."

"So would it be the worst thing in the world to . . . let him know?"

"And be known as an adulterer once again? I can't bear any more disapproval from my father. He already thinks I'm a disgrace, I'm sure of that."

"Beg pardon, Mrs. Anderson, but if things are goin' as you say they are with your new gentleman, well, don't you want to, you know, move on an' make a new life with him?"

Joan weighed how much more she wanted to confide in Ellen. She was indebted to her for the information she had gathered so stealthily and for the kindness she'd shown her, but their relationship had the potential to sabotage Ellen's position with the Pruitts. And because Joan generally felt that no one can truly be trusted when livelihoods or reputations are at stake, she knew her covert relationship with Kyle could be blown if Ellen sought retribution.

Joan decided to reign in her disclosures. "Let's just say I've been down that road before, and the legal system doesn't make it easy to 'move on and make a new life.'"

"I'm sorry," Ellen said.

"I appreciate everything you've done for me. I don't quite understand why you've been so understanding and kind, and I'd like to return the favor in some way."

"We're kindred spirits, I've told you this many times before. You know you can trust me with your secrets, just the way one might hide valuables deep inside a plaster wall." Joan heard a noise in the background that sounded like an opening door. "Agh," Ellen said, making her guttural Gaelic sound. "I need to go now. So long." She abruptly hung up the phone.

Joan hung up the phone as well. She thought about Ellen. *Perhaps if she and I weren't in such different stations in life, we could be friends.* She looked at the clock on the wall: two o'clock, time for a walk to the playground with Barbara and Bobby. Joan would see the usual group of young mothers there, women in whom she had little interest and with whom she felt she had nothing in common. They were stagnant in their lives as far as she was concerned, and Joan had grander ideas for what she wanted in her own life. As she passed through the dining room, she paused in front of a mirror. The afternoon sun was shining brightly from the kitchen right through the tiny dining room and onto the side of her face. She touched her lips and wound a curly strand of hair around her finger. *Twenty-four years old*, she thought. So much was still possible.

22

AS HE WAS STILL LIVING WITH HIS PARENTS IN THE ELKINS Park house he'd grown up in, Kyle would only see Joan at her home on Clark Street after dark, when Barbara and Bobby were asleep and the neighbors would be less likely to notice a strange man entering. She relished this time with Kyle, when she had his full attention and could talk endlessly about her hopes for their future and how she envisioned life as Mrs. Kyle Dumann. She'd ask him about his family's company, the manufacturing process, his professional goals, the employees, the corporate structure, all the while trying to feed his ambition with her own.

"You're quite charming, you know that?" he would often say to her.

And she would always reply, "Yes, and you are enamored of me, aren't you?"

Yet Joan was growing tired of this illicit arrangement and was impatient to bring her relationship with Kyle into daylight. She wasn't entirely sure how to locate Paul when the time came to serve him with the divorce papers, but she decided she would let the lawyers figure that out. An old family friend of Kyle's had some influence with a judge in Philadelphia who could expedite her divorce on the grounds of desertion. She felt certain that strings were frequently pulled for wealthy and well-known individuals seeking to end a marriage without calling to attention an affair.

What Joan did not know was that Paul was already several steps ahead of her in the process and that someone had called

Kyle Dumann's office to inquire about renting the house on Clark Street, according to Janice the receptionist.

"Janice has what's known as *loose lips*," Kyle told Joan. "She gave the guy a lot of information she shouldn't have, saying that the house was still occupied by the landlord's girlfriend and her two children. Janice also apparently thinks you are a widow."

Joan was infuriated. "She should be fired. How dare she discuss such personal details with a stranger who's calling about renting a property."

Not long after that, Joan was served with papers accusing her of adultery with Kyle Dumann and suing her for divorce. Janice the receptionist was terminated.

"Paul dropped out of touch just long enough to wreak havoc on my life, yet not long enough so I could file for divorce on my own terms." Joan said to Ellen during one of their weekly telephone conversations.

"It's just awful how difficult it is to end a bad marriage," Ellen replied.

"And now my family, their friends, everyone, will know why Paul and I are divorcing," she said.

"You misjudged Paul's character, that's all," Ellen said.

Joan already knew the protocol. She knew that Pennsylvania would not allow her to marry the man with whom she was unfaithful, but this time she did not need to travel as far south as Florida.

Her divorce was finalized in May of 1940, just after Kyle registered for the draft. In July of 1940, she and Kyle were married at the Second Presbyterian Church in Petersburg, Virginia. His brother Richard was there, as was his father. No other family members or friends were told about the wedding. Kyle's mother refused to attend, telling Kyle she loved him and hoped "that woman" could make him happy.

That night, in their brand-new, two-story brick colonial house, they conceived their first child together.

23

JOAN SAT AT THE KITCHEN TABLE, ATTEMPTING TO GET ONE-year-old Gwen to eat a spoonful of Cream of Wheat; the child refused and stubbornly moved her head away from the food. Three-year-old Lisa sat at the table as well, a half-eaten bowl of cereal in front of her, finishing a glass of milk. Bobby and Barbara sat on the kitchen floor as Barbara showed her brother how to play jacks.

Joan sat back in her chair, frustrated. "Fine, Gwen. Don't eat your breakfast," she said in a lethargic tone. She looked around the room. The kitchen was a mess, with a sink filled with dirty dishes, the countertops covered with pots and pans that hadn't been washed. She knew she should make an effort to straighten up, but she felt no compulsion to do so.

The side-door off of the kitchen opened up and Ellen walked in.

"Holy Mother of Jesus, hasn't the diaper service been here?" Ellen asked, placing a paper bag of groceries on the countertop. "There's a stench like the devil's washroom in here!"

"I think they rang the doorbell yesterday afternoon. I guess I forgot to put the bag out on the front step," Joan said, mustering just enough energy to get the words out but lacking the strength to make eye contact with Ellen.

Ellen picked up the cotton laundry bag filled with the dirty diapers and put it on the side porch. Back in the kitchen, she knelt down beside Barbara and Bobby.

"Jacks? I might have to challenge you some time to a game!"

"Yes! Now?" asked Barbara.

"No, no. You two need to get dressed and ready for school. Do ya need help, Bobby?"

He nodded yes. Ellen turned to Barbara.

"Can you get yourself dressed and help your brother to do the same?"

"Yes! I! Can!" Barbara said enthusiastically.

"Off you go, then!" Ellen unpacked the groceries, putting eggs and bacon next to the stove. "I'm glad you called me this mornin'. I could hear it in your voice, you're not feelin' well, are ya?"

Joan attempted to feed Gwen again. "Not really. I just feel so tired. Ever since Kyle went on active duty, I can't seem to catch up on sleep."

"I understand. He's far away somewhere in the Pacific—"

"—Okinawa," Joan said.

"Yes, Okinawa. And you're here with these four little rascals," she said, smiling and winking at Lisa. "You've got your hands full."

"When he was at Camp Perry, it wasn't as bad," Joan said as she mindlessly twirled Gwen's spoon in the bowl. "I could talk to him once a week. Twice a week I'd get a letter. He even came home a few times during that period. But it's like he's on an entirely different planet now. I looked at an atlas. . .he's on the other side of the world, for god's sake! Anything could happen, and then I'd be alone, a widow with four young children."

Lisa wiped her mouth with the sleeve of her nightgown, then hopped off her chair and ran over to Ellen. She hugged Ellen's leg. Ellen leaned over to kiss Lisa's head.

"Listen, I will walk the children to school after breakfast," she said as she beat eggs in a bowl. "It's cold, but dry. And maybe you'd like to join us? Put the young ones in strollers and we'll enjoy the mornin' air?"

"Not today. I'm not feeling up to it. I think I need to crawl back in bed." Then, looking at Ellen for the first time, "Would you be able to stay here for a few hours? Maybe just to tend to Lisa and Gwen until they have their afternoon naps? I just feel so tired."

Ellen nodded. She turned back toward the stovetop and poured the egg batter onto a cast iron pan.

"You do remember that your father, aunt and uncle are moving to Ivyland in April, don'cha?," she asked, her back facing Joan.

Joan looked up. "Ivyland? They're moving?"

"Yes, Joan. I told you this two weeks ago," Ellen said as she scrambled the eggs in the pan. Shortly after Joan married Kyle, she had begun calling Joan by her first name after Joan explained 'You do not work for me, we are about the same age, and I've confided in you so much that it no longer feels comfortable to hear you call me Mrs. *Anything*.'

Ellen scraped the eggs from the pan and transferred them to a plate. She gently pushed Lisa away from the stove, then placed several strips of bacon on the pan. "The house went on the market the first of the year, you know that."

Joan tried to remember the conversation. She had a vague recollection of Ellen mentioning the move but could not fathom why it did not register.

Gwen was attempting to wriggle out of her high chair. Lisa pulled on the belt of Joan's robe, causing it to open up.

"Lisa! Stop that!" Joan screamed. Lisa wailed, which made Gwen break into tears.

Ellen turned off the flame under the pan, quickly transferred the bacon onto a plate, and lifted Lisa onto her hip. "Ssshhh, my little lady. It's okay." She walked over toward the stove and grabbed a slab of bacon. Waving it in the air to cool it, she said softly, "Would you like a crispy piece of bacon?" She bit off the end, then handed it to Lisa, who ran her tongue across it, then licked her lips. She put it in her mouth and bit off a piece. Ellen put Lisa back in her chair and handed her the full strip of bacon.

Barbara and Bobby came into the kitchen, fully clothed and smiling with pride. Ellen pointed to the chairs. "Sit," she said to Barbara and Bobby. She loaded plates with eggs and bacon, then served the two of them.

"See, my baby brother is ready for school and so am I!" Barbara said.

Joan attempted to console Gwen, who was still whimpering, by holding a spoon of Cream of Wheat in front of her mouth, but, yet again, Gwen shoved the spoon away.

"For Christ's sake," Joan said in full surrender. "I'm too tired for this," she said under her breath while looking at Gwen. She stood up and paced around the kitchen, feeling agitated.

"Have a seat and eat something," Ellen said.

Joan sat back down. She watched as Ellen set up the coffee percolator. Ellen put eggs and a strip of bacon onto a plate and placed it on the table, in front of Joan.

"Let it cool a bit," Ellen said. She sat down and reached for the bowl of Cream of Wheat and put a spoonful in her mouth.

"Mmmm. . .this is good!" Ellen said. Gwen suddenly was interested in eating.

"You can't imagine what it's like," Joan said as she bit the end of the bacon.

"No, I can't," Ellen said. "You've got a little army here. Maybe that's why you've apparently had no time to buy groceries?"

Joan stabbed at the eggs with her fork.

Ellen continued. "And that is why I'm offering to help you out, maybe just a couple mornings every week, to ease your burden a bit. Your Aunt Helen doesn't need me much for these next couple of months."

Joan didn't think Helen needed Ellen much at all in the years since Elizabeth died, though it was a big house to manage.

"I'll certainly assist them with the packin'," she continued. "But I'm sure she won't mind if I lend a hand where it's truly needed for now."

Joan looked at Ellen. "You would do that?"

Ellen nodded. "With pleasure!"

Joan was stunned. She knew Ellen's kindness was genuine, and yet it was overwhelming. She lay her face in her hands. Ellen touched her shoulder.

"It's all gonna be alright. Just a little mountain to climb for a bit of time."

The aroma of the percolating coffee filled the air, temporarily pulling Joan out of her foggy misery. She sniffed the coffee and wiped her eyes.

"I love the smell of coffee," she said softly. "It always makes me hopeful."

"Then let us have a cup, yeah?"

Ellen jumped up and grabbed a cup. Once the urn was full, she poured a cup and set it in front of Joan. Bobby and Barbara were finishing their breakfast.

"Okay, then, little ones. Let us head to school, yeah? Kiss your ma so long!"

They each gave Joan a kiss on the cheek and happily headed toward the front door, grabbing their hats, mittens and scarves along the way.

"Maybe tomorrow you'll join us for the walk?" Ellen asked Joan.

Joan smiled weakly.

"Why don'cha call the diaper service this mornin'. I'm sure they can come out again."

And with that, Ellen and the children were out the door. Joan looked around at the mess in her kitchen. The pungent odor of dirty diapers had been replaced with the smell of bacon fat and melted butter, along with freshly-brewed coffee. She took a sip of the coffee, then sat back in her chair. She looked at her two little girls who were happily munching on bacon. The room was quiet, and Joan felt a sense of relief wash over her, thanks to Ellen.

Where did her confidence come from, this independent, young woman from Ireland who, by all accounts, was alone in the world? Ellen was accommodating, but in a manner beyond what one would expect from a servant. She had an abundance of benevolence.

Joan decided that she'd shower and get dressed when Ellen returned from walking the children to school. Perhaps she would even compose a letter to Kyle. She took another sip of coffee, then stood up and got to work cleaning the kitchen.

Two months later, with Ellen spending three mornings a week at the Dumanns', Joan's mood had improved to the point where she no longer fixated on the idea of Kyle dying.

"Your father's not doin' well, you know that, don'cha?" Ellen asked Joan one morning after the two women had walked Bobby and Barbara to school.

"I know," Joan said, sounding regretful. "His heart. You've mentioned it." She wanted to put it out of her mind.

Marcus had been diagnosed with congestive heart failure, making even a simple walk around the block a challenge for him.

"Might you, then, perhaps want to come by the house with me one day? Maybe even bring the children?"

"For what reason? He doesn't want to see me. Or any of us."

"Don't be so sure. You're still his daughter. And your children are still his grandchildren."

"He has never quite warmed to the idea that Bobby, Lisa and Gwen are his grandchildren," Joan said, reaching over to Gwen and brushing long locks of the child's delicate hair off her forehead.

"Nevertheless, they *are* his grandchildren. The whole lot of 'em! He'll be movin' up to Ivyland next month and it'll be that much harder to see him after that. Ach, Joan—he really should see them—and you—while he's still able to . . . ." Her voice trailed off.

"He'll just make me feel. . .inadequate. I'm a failure to him."

Ellen cleared her throat and folded her hands on the table. "I understand what you're feelin', I think. I understand the shame, the humiliation. I felt rejected by my father, too. He sort of . . . he cast me aside, as if he didn't love me."

Joan gave Ellen her full attention. "What happened?" She was brimming with interest.

"Once a month, ever since I came to this country at seventeen, I been sendin' money back home."

Joan listened intently.

"To my sister Maureen and her husband."

Joan didn't understand. Lisa crawled into Joan's lap. Joan kissed her on the top of her head without taking her eyes off of Ellen.

"They're carin' for my daughter." Ellen paused. "Bethany."

Joan brought her hand to her chest. "You've never mentioned. . .how old is she?"

"Ten," Ellen said.

Joan was astonished. How could Ellen have kept this secret for so long?

"But you have to understand," Ellen said casually. "I don't

really feel she's mine. I haven't seen her since she was six months old."

Joan was in disbelief. "The father?"

"Agh," Ellen said with a dismissive, backhanded wave. "Caleb McMenniman. He was four years older than me. His Da' had a small dairy farm in County Kerry where I lived. I worked there for a year, milkin' cows, helpin' in the kitchen, mendin' things. His Ma was gone like mine."

"Were you in school?"

"School? Yeah, I attended school, but things were tough, money was tight everywhere in Ireland. My own Da' was ill. Emphysema. And our house was in terrible disrepair, oh, it was awful," she said, shaking her head.

Lisa turned around on Joan's lap and began to play with the hair around her mother's face. Joan gently swatted her daughter's hand away.

"C'mon over here, Lisa," Ellen said with outstretched arms. "Give your mommy a break, yeah?"

Lisa happily jumped out of Joan's lap and into Ellen's.

"Alright, then," Ellen said.

Joan couldn't believe what she was hearing. "What happened? Why did you leave Ireland?"

"My family, we were dirt-poor." She went on to explain that she was the youngest of eight children, and that her mother passed away when Ellen was still a baby. One by one her siblings left home to find work.

"By the time I was a teenager, most of them were scattered across Ireland and England, and all but one of them were married."

Joan listened, barely blinking.

"Two of my brothers were day laborers, one in Dublin and one in Liverpool. My sisters Amelia and Dolores worked in the home of a wealthy family in the English countryside." She smiled. "I was gonna follow them. I was excited, ya know?" She looked off to the side. Then back at Joan. "Lucy and Arnie worked in factories. That left me and Maureen. She's two years older than me." Ellen smiled. "She married her sweetheart and they had a beautiful baby boy."

"They live with your father?"

"They did, 'til he passed seven years ago." Ellen's face became grim.

"Seven years ago? You never said anything, never told anyone?"

Ellen shook her head.

"You didn't want to go back for his funeral?"

"That would've been a lot of money and time." She played with a curl on Lisa's head. "You know what I'm sorry about? I never wrote to him after I left home. I was hurt, and so angry."

"I'm guessing he was not pleased about the pregnancy."

Ellen shook her head from side to side. "Jesus, Joseph an' Mary, no," she said.

"Did Caleb ever find out about the baby?"

"Nah! He and I barely knew each other. He left town right after the night we conceived Bethany. Maureen and I didn't even tell my Da' until I had to go to hospital. You couldn't even tell I was pregnant until practically the week before I gave birth."

She continued the story, telling Joan how disgraced her father was when she returned from the hospital, that he couldn't bear to look at her or the baby. He was becoming more and more ill. "Then, one day, when Bethany was just a couple months, he said, 'You need to leave this house. This baby here, she's Maureen's and Douglass'. They can take care of her."

"So, you came to the U.S. Why didn't you join your sisters at that country estate? Work closer to home?"

"I don't know, I can't explain it now. I guess I was young. I made bad decisions," she said as she removed Lisa from her lap. "At the time, I didn't want to see my Da or hear about him or feel any more pain than I was feelin'." She rested her elbows on the table. "My father lost the love of his life when Ma died. He raised eight children as best he could, then he got sick, so Maureen moved back in to help care for him. I don't think he was angry with *me*. I think he was just angry. Still, I suppose I did let him down." A wide smile spread across her face. "He had such hope for me, ya know? He got to know me better than the others because they were all gone. But we had time together, time to talk." She looked down. "I know he was hurt that I didn't tell him about the baby until I was headin' off to hospital. I was scared. And he was probably scared for me."

"Oh, this story burns me up!" Joan said with clenched teeth. "You didn't make that baby on your own!"

"Of course not," she said. "That's not the point, though, Joan. All these years later, and I'm fine. Bethany is wonderful! She's better off there with Maureen and Douglass. Their son Stuart is like a big brother to her. No, the point is, I always told myself I'd write to Da', tell him I loved him, I didn't mean to hurt him." Her chin began to quiver. "I even thought I'd make it back there for a visit before. . .," her voice trailed off and she wiped both eyes. "Maureen told me he'd been askin' for me, wonderin' if I'd be comin' back." Ellen broke down. Lisa noticed and wrapped her little arms around Ellen's lap.

Joan watched and began to cry as well.

Ellen blew her nose on a napkin, then sat up straight. "You're fortunate that your father lives so close by. For now, anyway."

Joan stood up and lifted Gwen, who had begun to whimper, out of her high chair. She walked around the kitchen, bouncing the child on her hip to soothe her and trying to calm her own mind as well. Joan's thoughts were racing. Her stomach churned from the two cups of coffee she'd drank, or perhaps from the topic of conversation, and she thought she might vomit.

"I'm sure you can make a long list of everything you dislike about your father," Ellen said. "I was like that, too. It sometimes feels easier to be angry than to be sad. Once I started forgivin' my Da, the sadness came crashin' through and I started hurtin' again. By then, it was too late."

Joan pressed her lips to Gwen's head, then inhaled deeply to take in the sweet smell of her daughter's hair.

"Your father, he has his own pain, I'm sure. And I *know* you love him," Ellen said.

Joan remembered how he handed her money after Paul left her. At the time, her father's cold silence cut her to the core, made her feel shameful and inadequate, and she took the money in anger despite the fact that the money was her very objective for visiting him that day. She was basically using him, willing to tolerate however he treated her because she needed his help.

She stood at the window, still holding Gwen, and recalled the trip she and Marcus took to New York. She could picture his face that day as they sat in the café discussing the play. She had his full attention as they ate and chatted. He looked her in the eye, listened and reacted to what she had said. It was one moment in her life when she felt he might actually like her.

"You need to tell your dad you love him, you're sorry if you've disappointed and hurt him. If you can't say the words, then write 'em down, put 'em in a letter. Your father, he's a writer. He appreciates the written word."

"I don't know," Joan said.

"No harm will come of it. I only wish I'd done the same."

Joan was torn, yet pulled by the weight of Ellen's encouragement. She imagined that the kind of regret Ellen experienced, knowing she had lost an opportunity, could possibly be harder to endure than rejection from a failed outreach.

That night, just before she crawled into bed, Joan sat at her desk and picked up her Mont Blanc pen. She looked around the room, then out the window. Snow was gently falling. It helped her relax, concentrate.

> *Dear Father,*
>
> *I cannot express how sad I am to know that you are ill. You were always the picture of health, with limitless energy, always busy with this or that. I've always admired that in you. It must be difficult to feel as you do, unable to move about as you're used to, getting winded easily.*

She stopped again to read what she had written, concerned that the letter was beginning on too much of a negative note. She decided not to overthink it, and continued:

> *I would very much like to see you. I could even bring the children over if you would enjoy that. But, most of all Dad, I want you to know that I love you. I have always looked up to you and admired your intelligence, talent and humor. I know I have disappointed you in many ways, and I'm sorry. It was never my intention to do so.*
>
> *Hopefully, in some small way, I have made you proud.*

Joan's eyes became teary, not over sadness, but regret. All the letters in the world would not undo years of bad decisions and missed opportunities. She pulled on the end of her nightgown sleeve and dabbed her eyes. There was no point in hoping she made her father proud; she was quite sure she had not. She grabbed a fresh piece of stationary and rewrote the letter, this time omitting the last sentence and replacing it with:

> *I will telephone Aunt Helen to find out when might be a suitable day to visit. I will know from her response whether or not you would like to see me.*
> *Always,*
> *Your Joan*

She folded the letter and tucked it into an envelope, then addressed it to Marcus Sondersohn and propped it against her desk lamp with the intention of sending it out in the next day's mail..

24

OVER THE COURSE OF THE WAR, JOAN'S LETTERS TO KYLE morphed from a series of platitudes about her well-being intended to disguise her fear, desperation, and hopelessness—with brief, emotionless reports of the children's daily activities—to expressions of gratitude over Ellen's support and graciousness, and cheery odes to Kyle as a spouse and father. In the last letter, she indicated that she wanted to reciprocate Ellen's kindness, and she cryptically suggested she had an idea of how to do that.

"I look forward to hearing all about your plan, my sweet," Kyle had written back. "In just three weeks I will be back home with you and the kids."

"I've been thinking," Joan said to Ellen as they walked back from morning drop-off at Barbara and Bobby's school one late-September day, Ellen pushing Gwen in a stroller and Lisa holding Joan's hand. It had been five months since Ellen moved in with the Dumanns, which Ellen eventually admitted had been Aunt Helen's suggestion. "It might be a good idea for you to take a trip back to Ireland."

"Ireland? Whatever for?" asked Ellen.

"For your daughter. For Bethany," Joan said, looking straight ahead.

Ellen did not immediately respond. She picked up Gwen's doll, which had fallen from the stroller. She pointed to a cracked robin's egg on the sidewalk and explained to Lisa what it was and what may have happened to the bird.

Joan did not press the issue, but later that day, she visited her travel agent and purchased a round-trip ticket, with open-ended dates, on a transatlantic ocean liner bound for England and Ireland. Two weeks later, Joan brought up the subject again.

"Are you suggestin' that I tell Bethany I'm her mother?" Ellen said.

"Why, yes. I am. I think you will regret it for the rest of your life if you don't raise her as your own," Joan said.

Ellen furrowed her brow.

"Now, I understand it would be terribly emotional for you and Bethany at first. But, in the end, the two of you would be together, as you should." Joan smiled.

"Beg pardon, Joan, but Maureen and Douglas are doin' a fine job of raisin' Bethany. They love her just as much as they love the son they conceived." Her tone was civil.

"I'm sure they do. They are probably wonderful parents. Understand, this is not about that at all. Think of it this way: you've sacrificed ten years of income so that they wouldn't bear the full burden of another child. It's not like you just gave her up without a second thought."

"I don't mean any disrespect, Joan. But I must take issue with what you're sayin'. Number one, I do not send my full compensation each month to them, just a portion of it. And two, I don't see it as a sacrifice. I brought a life into this world and, though I don't call her my child, I do take responsibility for her well-being."

"Yes, well, she could have a much better life here in the United States. Think of what she could do and the kind of education she could have. The world's best universities and all sorts of new opportunities for women. So much at her disposal." Joan was enthusiastic and, though she could read Ellen's facial expression to see that she wasn't buying into it, she persisted, nevertheless. "The American dream."

"Bethany has two lovin' parents and a brother in Ireland. I cannot give her that."

Joan was offended. "I didn't have a sibling, and I had just one parent who I'm not sure I'd describe as *loving*. And I turned out just fine, now, didn't I?"

"I didn't mean to suggest . . ." Ellen reached out to Joan, who pulled away. Ellen exhaled slowly and silently.

The two women did not speak to one another for an entire day. At night, as Joan was emerging from Barbara and Bobby's room after a tuck-in, she saw Ellen coming out of the bathroom.

"Good-night, Joan," Ellen said sweetly. "And I'm so sorry about our row. Please forgive me." She bowed her head respectfully and headed to her bedroom.

Joan took hold of Ellen's hand gently. "You have nothing to apologize for. I'm the one who spoke out of turn. I only have the best intentions," she said in a whisper. "For you and for Bethany."

Joan pulled Ellen away from the children's bedrooms so she could speak at a normal volume. She kept a hold on Ellen's hand.

"I haven't mentioned this to you yet, but when Kyle returns next week, we are putting down a deposit on a new house. It's beautiful, Ellen. And the best part is, there are six bedrooms."

Ellen looked blankly at Joan.

Joan wiggled Ellen's arm playfully. "A bedroom for each of my children and one for you and Bethany. This is why I was so disappointed that you don't see this opportunity as I do."

Ellen angled her head quizzically. She opened her mouth as if to speak and closed it.

Joan let go of Ellen's hand. "You don't seem pleased."

"I . . . agh . . . Joan, perhaps we should speak in the mornin'. When we are both rested." She smiled feebly, but her eyes were weary. "Sleep well," she said and turned into her room.

The next morning, Joan entered the kitchen to find Gwen in her high chair as Ellen was warming milk for her bottle. Fresh coffee had been set on the table, and pancake batter was in a bowl next to the stove.

"I cannot believe my husband will be home in a week. Oh, I'm simply bursting, Ellen!" She walked over to Gwen and kissed the top of her daughter's head.

There was no mention of the night before.

Barbara and Bobby ambled into the kitchen holding hands. Joan greeted each of them with a hug and went to the refrigerator to get the orange juice, chatting frenetically about the exciting events of the summer as the war came to an end, first with the German surrender in May, followed by the Japanese in August. She turned on the radio and began dancing about the kitchen.

"They're coming home," Joan said, taking Barbara's hands and twirling her around. "All those heroic soldiers, including your daddy," she said to Bobby. "He'll be home in time to enjoy a proper Thanksgiving turkey," she said to Ellen.

Barbara and Bobby laughed as they watched their mother, but Ellen continued to assemble breakfast for everyone and largely ignored Joan.

"I'm so full of energy, I may burst! Why don't I walk Bobby and Barbara to school this morning?" Joan said to Ellen. "Would you stay behind and get the little ones dressed?"

"Certainly," Ellen said.

Joan thought that Ellen's tone seemed uncharacteristically stiff and professional, as if the camaraderie two women shared didn't exist. She assumed Ellen was still offended by the recent disagreement and decided she'd make things right when she returned, maybe even formally apologize.

When Joan arrived back home, Ellen was sitting on the living room floor, playing with the two girls. Joan walked into the kitchen and saw that the table had been cleared and wiped, and all the breakfast dishes had been washed and were drying in the rack. She heated some coffee, filled a cup, and sat down on the sofa.

"Oh, it'll be so nice to have more *space*," she said, tapping Lisa on the nose.

"Joan, I won't be goin' with you. To the new house."

"Oh, Ellen, don't be like that. You're part of the family now. We all want you, we *need* you. I need you! And Bethany will love it here, I just know it. It's not like you're kidnapping her, for god's sake. You're her mother."

"Why are you pushing this? Can you not hear yourself, Joan?" Ellen did not raise her voice. "This isn't something I want. And it's not your concern anyway. I need to ask you to stop. *Please*." Ellen choked on that last word and then composed herself.

Joan was hurt. How could Ellen not see that she was only trying to help her by encouraging a relationship between Ellen and Bethany. Why was this unclear?

"Okay. Okay, I understand," Joan said. "Maybe I've been out of line. But . . ." Joan realized she needed a different tactic. "We give each other advice, don't we? We counsel each other. Right? Remember when you told me to get in touch with my dad?"

"And *did* you?" Ellen asked calmly.

"It wasn't the right time to—"

"Not the right time to what? To tell your sick father you love him?"

Joan bit her lower lip and looked on the fireplace mantle at the photograph of Jessie, always watching, always present. She looked at Ellen. "I believe a mother and daughter should be together. I don't think that's unreasonable to expect."

"Agh, you're afraid, Joan. I can see it so clearly. You are afraid of pain. You think you cannot deal with it. You're afraid of bein' alone. You're afraid that everyone thinks you're a failure. But, most of all, you're afraid that people will tell you wha'cha don't want to hear. That you can't have something your way all the time. You challenge people who make the mistake of showin' you too much kindness." Ellen stopped suddenly. She was breathing heavily.

Joan sat back on the sofa. She held the coffee cup between her hands and stared into it. She hated the way Ellen was making her feel at this moment. She wished she could look into Ellen's eyes and say, *You are out of line, speaking to me this way.*

"Oh, my god, Joan, I . . . I'm sorry. This is not the kind of person I am." She lifted Lisa's doll from the floor and smoothed its hair. "Listen, I've been meaning to talk to you for weeks now. I'm moving to New York. My brother Joseph and his wife Louise are there now. They're expectin' their third child, and they want me to live with them for a bit. I wasn't plannin' on headin' up until Kyle returned, but I think it's best if— "

"I agree. It's time for you to go, Ellen," Joan said without looking up.

Ellen stood up. Gwen reached up for her, wiggling her tiny fingers, and Ellen bent down to lift her up. She hugged Gwen tightly. Joan could hear her whisper "I love you" in Gwen's ear. She put the child next to Joan on the sofa and knelt down to kiss Lisa. "Be good, little girl. I love you." Then, standing up and smoothing out her skirt, she looked at Joan, who kept her eyes fixed on her girls. "Please tell Barbara and Bobby that I love them."

Joan nodded solemnly and stood up, finally looking directly into Ellen's eyes. What Joan wanted to do more than ever was to grab Ellen and hug her, to thank her for being so unwaveringly supportive and nonjudgmental. That felt like the right thing to do, so what was holding her back? She was angry and hurt. Ellen was deserting her.

Ellen lifted her arms and moved in to hug Joan, but Joan merely patted Ellen's back once and moved backward.

"Again, Joan, I'm so sorry."

A taxi's horn beeped outside the front door. Ellen lifted her two suitcases, which she'd left next to the sofa. As she walked out, Lisa called for her.

Ellen did not turn around. She walked through the front door and gently closed it behind her.

25

"WHAT WILL ELLEN DO? WHERE WILL SHE GO NOW THAT
I'm back?" Kyle asked as he took the glass of scotch Joan handed
him on his second night home. He set up the checker board for a
game with Bobby, who sat on the floor on the opposite side of
the coffee table, sipping chocolate milk. "She's been in service to
others since she arrived from Ireland, always living in other people's homes."

Joan placed her glass of Jack Daniels and Coke on a coaster
and sat down next to her husband on the living room sofa. "Oh,
she's in good shape financially. No rent, no groceries. I bet she's
put away a nice little nest egg in the years she's been in this country. Anyway, she's up in New York, living with her brother and
his wife. I'm sure she'll be fine." She hoped Kyle would let it go at
that. Joan had a feeling she'd be refilling her drink at least once
more.

"I wanna play the winner!" Barbara cried out.

"Shh, Barbara," Joan said. "I just put Gwen to bed. You're
going to wake her with that loud voice."

Barbara put her fingers over her mouth in embarrassment.
She slumped down on the floor next to Bobby.

"Hi, Daddy," Lisa said, crawling into her father's lap.

"Careful, sweetie. You'll make Daddy spill his drink," Joan
said as she grabbed the scotch out of Kyle's hand. Joan was irri-
tated.

"Daddy, I can say the Plecha Fleegance," Lisa said.

Barbara broke into laughter, falling backwards. "It's the *Pledge* of *Allegiance*, dumb-dumb!"

"Barbara!" Joan scolded. "Stop making fun of your sister. She isn't in school yet, so she doesn't know what she's saying. Oh, these kids!"

Lisa began to cry and wrapped her arms around Kyle's neck. He hugged her and looked at Joan, helplessly.

"C'mere, Lisa," said Joan, extending her arms.

"Let me hear the Pledge of Allegiance, Lisa," Kyle said in his gentle voice.

"Daddy, let's play checkers!" Bobby cried.

"I plech . . ." Lisa began, looking sideways at Barbara. Barbara tried to stifle her giggle behind her hand, which caused Lisa to break into tears again.

"Oh," Joan sighed in exasperation. "You kids are gonna make your father want to go back to Okinawa, for god's sake."

"It's all right, Joan. I'll take this commotion over wartime any day." He winked at Barbara, and she smiled proudly. "I'm just happy to be with my family again," he said.

"Checkers, Daddy!" Bobby cried out.

"You kids need to keep your voices down," Joan said in a loud whisper.

"All set, Bobby. Your move first," Kyle said as his sipped his scotch.

Joan downed her Jack and Coke with two quick swigs and popped up to make another. Then she took a seat back on the sofa and watched her children. Bobby and Lisa had been clamoring for Kyle's attention from the minute he walked through the door a day earlier. Gwen was too young to feel Kyle's absence, much less say anything about it. But Gwen did ask for Ellen, "Eh-wen," and each time Joan responded, "Ellen went bye-bye."

To her husband, Joan revealed nothing. He did not know

about the argument, just a week earlier. Joan could not have explained her intentions to Kyle in a letter because he would have counseled her against helping Ellen go back to Ireland to retrieve Bethany. He would have told her it would be wrong to take a child away from the parents she has known and the country in which she was born.

Joan did not want anyone to convince her that her motivation was anything but noble.

Later that night, after the children were tucked in, Joan and Kyle sat alone in the living room with another round of drinks.

Kyle reached out his hand for Joan's. "It's so good to be back, I can't say this enough."

"It's good to have you back. I missed you so much, Kyle. Honestly, I thought I would die being here alone with the kids. I was a mess, *everything* was a mess—the house, the children's faces, my thoughts." She took a swig of her drink. "I even considered dropping the kids off at your parents' house."

Kyle's eyes flung open wide, and his jaw dropped. "That bad? Wow, I can't even imagine what Mom would have said." He shook his head and took a sip of his scotch.

"She would have said, 'If you drop them off here, you're never getting them back'—and she wouldn't have meant it in the cute grandmotherly way either. You know how your mother feels about me." She rolled her eyes.

Kyle smiled. "I'm glad you didn't do that. Thank God for Ellen, eh?"

Joan stared straight ahead. Her eyes fixed on the photo of Jessie.

"Hello in there," Kyle said. "What are you thinking about, Joan?"

"How different my life might have been if I had grown up with a mother," she said without looking at Kyle. "Perhaps I wouldn't have made all the mistakes I made. Maybe I'd be a more tolerant mother. Maybe I wouldn't be such a moody person." She thought about Ellen, and a surge of regret washed over her. It felt as if her insides were being squeezed so forcefully that her breathing became shallow.

"Are you all right, honey?" Kyle asked.

Joan exhaled; she hadn't realized she'd been holding her breath. She turned to her husband. "I'm so sorry, Kyle. None of this matters because I have no regrets where you're concerned. I don't know what I'd do without you." She moved in closer to him. He wrapped his arms around her and kissed the top of her head. "You're the only person who has ever made me feel like I matter, like I am not a total failure. Thank God you're home. Thank God the war's over." Then she pulled away from him. She needed to be decisive and clear.

He raised his eyebrows.

"I'm ready for a move. From this house. We could use something larger, for the kids."

"Larger?" Kyle said. "You've found something, haven't you?"

She nodded, lips pressed tightly together in a devious little grin. "It's beautiful, Kyle."

26

THE THREE-STORY, SIX-BEDROOM VICTORIAN HOUSE, BUILT
in 1890, was just a half a mile from Kyle's boyhood home in
Elkins Park, where his parents still lived, and a mile from Timber
Road, where no one from Joan's family still lived. It was situated
on the corner of a leafy, quiet street, with a stone wall surrounding the slightly elevated front and side lawns. The front path led
to a small, covered front porch, and there was a second, larger
covered porch on the side. The side porch, as well as the bay
window in the living room, were two of Joan's favorite features,
places she tended to go to when she needed to be alone with her
thoughts.

One month after the Dumanns settled into their new home,
Joan received a lengthy letter from Ellen.

Dear Joan,

*I hope this letter finds you and the family well. I
spoke with your Aunt Helen, and she said you've settled
into your new house. I am very happy for you.*

*As for myself, I am doing exceedingly well, I'm
pleased to say. I did make use of the ocean liner ticket
you bought me, and I spent a month in Ireland with
Maureen, Douglas, and the children. I was able to see
my other brothers and sisters and their families, and*

they all embraced me with loving arms after so many years apart. It was a blessing.

Oh, Joan, Bethany is a wonderful child. She and I got to know each other well. She is bright and sweet, and she loves horses. Perhaps you cannot understand this, but just being near her, hugging her and listening to her stories of school and friends—that was all the contentment I needed. She is happy. To her, I am Auntie El, and I feel not one bit of regret for my decision.

I love New York City! I would like to finally become a US citizen, and I have plans to get my GED.

I cannot thank you enough for paying my way to Ireland, and for everything you did for me. I regret the way things ended between us, and I pray that you are happy and fulfilled. You have a beautiful family and a husband who returned from war. God has blessed you indeed.

Always,
Ellen McGrugan

Joan folded Ellen's letter back into its envelope. She was filled with a sense of satisfaction that Ellen had followed her advice and traveled to Ireland, and that the trip had gone so well, though she held firm to her belief that Bethany would be better off with Ellen in the United States.

She opened her desk drawer and reached for the envelope containing the letter to Marcus that she had never mailed a year earlier. Her father was still alive, albeit in a weakened condition, but breathing clean country air and resting comfortably according to Helen, with whom Joan spoke every few weeks. Joan looked at the address—Timber Road—and tore open the envelope. She sat down to write out his new address in Ivyland, folded her letter into the new envelope, and decided to seize the moment and walk around the corner to the neighborhood mailbox.

As she walked, she thought about the many opportunities she'd squandered in her life by not following through on simple tasks, like putting a letter into a mailbox.

That night, when she crawled into bed and laid her head on the pillow, she felt a kind of liberation knowing that she had taken the first step toward a new beginning with her father.

She was jolted out of a dream state early the next morning by the ringing telephone.

"Hello?"

Kyle turned over under the covers.

"Uncle Fred?" Joan paused. "What . . ." She was quiet, listening to her uncle. "I see. I will." Again, she paused. "Yes. Goodbye." She returned the receiver to its handle.

Kyle sat up. "Joan? Has something happened? Your father, has he . . ."

Joan looked over toward her desk at the envelope with the Timber Road address, torn open the day before, its letter in a new envelope en route to Ivyland.

"Joan?" Kyle touched her shoulder.

"Who will read the letter?"

"Huh? Joan? What did Fred say?" Kyle got out of bed and walked around to Joan. He sat down on the bed next to her.

Joan's eyes flooded with tears. "It's true. I really am a failure." She stood up and walked over to the desk. She picked up the envelope and began to rip it over and over and over until it was nothing but confetti falling to the floor. She cried and cursed herself. She let out a wail. Kyle rushed over to her and held her.

"Marcus Sondersohn passed away in his sleep last night!"

she screamed. "He never saw my letter. He didn't know that I loved him."

Her sobs were loud and forceful enough to wake her four children who, one by one, began crying as well.

27

December 1950

"THIS WILL BE A PROPER WEDDING RECEPTION AND honeymoon," Joan whispered enthusiastically in Kyle's ear as they waited to board their flight to Miami with the children. She was fidgety with excitement, thinking about renewing her vows in front of friends and family, wearing a designer wedding gown, and celebrating the marriage that had given her the sense of stability that the previous two had not provided, either emotionally or financially.

She watched Kyle walk over to Gwen and kneel down to tie her shoelace. Then he untied it and asked her to try to tie it herself. *He's so patient with the children*, Joan thought. He pinched Gwen's cheek; then he stood up and took hold of her hand, swinging it playfully. When Bobby tapped him on the shoulder and mumbled something, Kyle turned around, and the two of them shared a laugh.

Joan often wondered how she would have managed the kids if Kyle hadn't come back from the war.

On the plane, the entire family was buzzing with excitement.

"Mom, where's the party again?" Barbara asked from across the aisle.

"Coco's. It's a restaurant right by the beach. You kids will love it. There's a band, with dancing on a veranda. You can look out at the ocean."

Joan heard Barbara explaining to Bobby the word *veranda*.

Joan and Kyle had rented a cottage in Pompano Beach for a weeklong trip during the children's Christmas break from school. Two other families from Elkins Park, as well as Kyle's brother Richard and his family, also flew down for the celebration. Unlike their original wedding date in 1940, which had been rushed and without any celebration, this occasion would be marked exactly as Joan wanted it.

Joan unfolded the newspaper she had bought at the airport and handed part of it to Kyle. An ad caught her eye. "Sixty-second anniversary of Horn and Hardart." She looked out the window and tapped on the ad. "He and I used to go there for lunch sometimes," she said.

"Who?" asked Kyle, perusing the pages of the paper. "You and your dad?"

She looked over at Barbara and whispered. "No. *Franklin.*"

Kyle looked up from his paper and raised his eyebrows.

Joan regretted what she'd said. "My point is, it's a great restaurant, a Philly institution. That's all." She looked down at the newspaper in her lap, mindlessly scanned Walter Winchell's "Gossip of the Nation" section, folded the paper, and stuffed it into the seat pocket in front of her. "Anyway, I can't read the paper; I'm too excited."

Kyle found the crossword page and handed it to her. "Try this."

She took the page from him, fished for a pen in her purse, and focused on the puzzle.

❧

"On this day, I renew my promise to be your faithful and loving wife, for better or for worse, for richer or for poorer, in sickness and in health, so long as we both shall live."

Joan and Kyle stood, facing each other, in front of their children and invited guests, under the veranda of Coco's on the Beach. Kyle reached for Joan's hands.

"On this day," he began, echoing the vows that Joan had spoken. "I renew my promise to you . . ."

She thought she saw tears in his eyes.

The brief ceremony was performed by a justice of the peace, as Joan stated that she did not want any "God-talk, prayers, or irrelevant homilies" for this ceremony, yet she did want something heartfelt and personalized.

She appreciated being able to do everything entirely her way this time around. The celebration that followed the ceremony was extravagant, with a lavish dinner, endless bottles of champagne, and an inappropriately large, three-tiered wedding cake that was devoured not only by their party of twenty, but also by the rest of the patrons at the restaurant that night. Joan wore a floor-length, lacy, white gown and decorated her hair with white baby's breath flowers. She was ebullient all night, making toasts to her husband and calling her children up to sing along with the bandleader.

"I have four beautiful children," she said into the microphone, her speech slightly slurred. She held a glass of champagne in her left hand and a cigarette in her right. "And I'd like to call the oldest one up here first. C'mon up, Barb." Joan looked out onto the dance floor and over the tables for her daughter. Her diamond bracelet—Kyle's gift to her for this occasion—shimmered under the lights of the cabana. When she got no response from Barbara, she moved on to Bobby.

Throughout the night, Joan drank champagne and danced with several different partners, including strangers. By the time the party ended close to midnight, she could barely stand.

As she and Kyle crawled into bed at two in the morning, she sidled up to her husband of ten years and whispered in his ear.

"You've given me the life I wanted."

"I would do anything for you," he said.

In the morning, Joan's head was throbbing, she had an acidic taste in the back of her throat, and her stomach was tense. And though she could barely raise her head from the pillow, she needed to get a glass of water. She removed her silk sleep mask and, looking over at Kyle, who was fast asleep, cursed out loud, threw the blanket to the side, and ambled out of bed. In the bathroom, she drank water from the sink and splashed more of it onto her face. She looked at herself in the mirror and noticed her bloodshot eyes and the circles beneath them, and, again, she cursed. It was eight thirty, and she could hear Bobby and Lisa laughing in the bedroom next door.

"Dammit," she said under her breath. She didn't want to deal with the children just yet. She was exhausted and not at all hungry, and she needed coffee and more water. She walked over to the bed and stared at Kyle, who was snoring softly and not anywhere close to waking up despite her best efforts to "inadvertently" disturb his slumber by mumbling and sighing in the bedroom as she stood near him. How could he be so comfortable and so oblivious to her agitation? Joan knew there was no logical reason for her to have such negative feelings toward her husband; he'd given her exactly what she'd asked for, sparing no expense. But she did not want to be the first parent awake after the late-night celebration and, anyway, Kyle did a much better job of entertaining the children in the morning. On weekends and holidays, Joan would sleep in until eleven and wake to find an empty house, a fresh pot of coffee, and a note from Kyle that read: "Off to the playground" or "... ball field" or "... library" or "... IHOP" or "... my parents' house." He excelled at "keeping the troops on active duty" as he called it. Barbara would say it was his way of keeping the kids "out of Mom's hair."

Joan sat on the edge of the bed trying to decide if she wanted to crawl back under the covers or take a shower. Just then, there was a knock at the bedroom door. She hesitated, reluctant to let anyone know she was up and "open for business," but after two more knocks she stood up, walked over to the door, and opened it. Seven-year-old Gwen stood in the hallway holding something up for Joan to see. It appeared to be a lovely snail shell, and when Joan held out her hand, Gwen placed a live hermit crab into Joan's palm. She screamed and dropped the crab onto the floor.

"Oh, my god, Gwen, get that thing out of the house!"

Gwen dropped to the floor to retrieve the crab, which had fallen onto the back of its shell and was struggling, legs flailing, to reorient.

"You're so mean, Mommy!" Gwen yelled. "Why are you such a meanie?" She scooped the hermit crab up and ran out. Bobby then came running toward Joan.

"What happened, Mom? What did you do?"

"What did *I* do? Your sister brought a live snail into the house." She waved her hands in the air, to shake off her disgust. "Ugh!"

Gwen yelled from the front porch. "It's not a snail. It's a hermit crab."

Eleven-year-old Lisa poked her head out from the bedroom she was sharing with Barbara.

"What's going on? Did someone get hurt?"

"Mommy thought Gwen had a snail." Bobby began laughing

hysterically. "She doesn't know the difference between a snail and a hermit crab."

Joan slammed the door and headed back to the bed, where Kyle was waking up.

"Everything okay? Are you all right?" He stretched as he sat up.

"My God, how do you sleep through such ruckus? No, I'm *not* all right. I have a splitting headache, and I'm exhausted. I can't deal with the kids right now, Kyle. You've got to get up and get them some breakfast. I need to rest."

Kyle fell back into his pillow and rubbed his eyes. "Can you give me a moment? I was in a deep sleep."

"So was I before my headache woke me up. Oh, forget it." She picked up her sleep mask and threw it at Kyle. "I'm already awake. I need water anyway." She stormed out of the bedroom.

Ten minutes later, as Joan sat at the kitchen table with Bobby and Lisa, Kyle walked in, wearing a short-sleeved, collared tennis shirt, shorts, and sneakers, his hair wet and combed back. He kissed Joan's neck and then set about making coffee.

"The shower made me feel like a new man," he said with a smile. He looked over at the kids, who were eating cereal, and at Joan, who had just a half-full glass of water in front of her. "I highly recommend it, Joan."

She grunted. She knew she should feel grateful for a week's vacation in Florida and the successful and enjoyable celebration she had orchestrated, yet she was in a sour mood.

"All I want to do today is lie in the hammock," she said.

Kyle filled the coffee pot with water. "I should have flagged you after your fifth glass of champagne."

"Mommy, you were funny last night," said Lisa as cereal and milk leaked from the corner of her mouth.

"Don't speak with your mouth full," Joan said as she rubbed her eyes.

"It was embarrassing," Bobby said, "when you sang with the band."

"I thought your mother sounded good," Kyle said. He threw two pieces of bread into the toaster. "'The Anniversary Song.' You did a perfect Dinah Shore, my dear."

Joan shook her head back and forth. She remembered taking the microphone from the lead singer and asking the pianist if he knew the song. She had a slight recollection of looking out onto the dance floor and seeing Kyle's brother Richard and his wife dancing. In the moment, she had felt like Dinah Shore. Now, she felt foolish.

28

JOAN SETTLED INTO THE HAMMOCK BEHIND THE COTTAGE later that morning, a full glass of water, a recent issue of *Life* magazine, and a pack of L&M cigarettes at her side. She had been a "social smoker" for the last two years, only allowing herself to enjoy a cigarette while drinking with friends. But she found herself smoking more these days, even when she was alone.

"Okay, honey, my brother took his kids and Bobby, Lisa, and Gwen fishing for the day," Kyle said as he zipped his tennis racquet cover. "Barbara and I are going to play a few rounds. You okay?"

"Mm," she grunted. "Have fun." She opened the pack of cigarettes, lit one, reached for the magazine, and settled back in the hammock to read.

When Kyle and Barbara returned, Joan overheard their conversation coming from the kitchen window as she was waking up from a nap.

"Why do you do whatever she tells you to do?" Barbara asked.

"It brings me joy to see Mom happy. When people are married, that's the way it should be. Anyway, she frequently has wonderful ideas. Like the party. Didn't you have fun last night?"

"Not especially."

"You didn't? How come?"

"I don't know. I just..."

Joan could hear a tennis ball being bounced on the floor. She hated when the kids bounced balls inside.

"I just wanted to be...somewhere else."

"With Franklin," he said.

Joan heard the sink running.

"Yeah. Why couldn't I stay back with him? Why wouldn't Mom let me spend my Christmas break with him?"

Hearing this infuriated Joan. She recalled Kyle noting once that Franklin and Barbara were similar in temperament; both were calm and, for the most part, upbeat. But then again, so was Kyle. Still, it made sense that Barbara wanted to be with Franklin; he had remained a part of her life since the divorce, though Joan had begun limiting how much time Franklin and Barbara spent together, much to Barbara's chagrin. Perhaps that would explain Barbara's recent rebelliousness: the normally compliant child now challenged everything Joan said and had lost interest in all the fun mother-daughter activities the two of them had always shared. Regardless, it just didn't feel right to Joan anymore to allow her daughter to spend so much time with Franklin; Barbara's family was Joan, Kyle, and the other children.

Joan reached for the glass on the little table next to her and took a sip. The water was warm.

"This was a special occasion for us, Barb. A real celebration, and it was important for the six of us to be together and have fun. You surely enjoyed being with your cousins, didn't you?"

"I see them all the time at home. Anyway, I'm gonna change into my swimsuit."

Joan eased herself out of the hammock.

Kyle emerged from the house. "You're awake," he said with a smile.

"Awake in body, not in spirit," she said. "How was tennis?"

"She's competitive. It's good to have an athletic daughter."

One more way Barbara and I are dissimilar, Joan thought.

Barbara appeared in the backyard. "Ready for the pool?" she asked Kyle.

"You bet," he said. "Why don't you head over, and I'll join you soon. I want to talk to Mommy for a while."

"Are you coming to the pool too?" Barbara asked Joan.

"I suppose I will," Joan said. She couldn't tell by Barbara's tone if her daughter actually wanted her to join them. In any case, what Joan really wanted was to go inside and lie down on the bed. "Go on, Barb. Dad and I will be there soon."

Kyle held out his hand for Joan. "Feeling any better?" he asked.

"Headache's gone. I'm tired, but I'll be good for dinner tonight," she said. "Let's get changed for the pool." The thought of dipping her toes into the cool water now seemed like the most wonderful idea.

They walked together into the house.

Inside the kitchen, Joan refilled her glass with tap water. She leaned against the counter.

"Remember when Barb was little, when she started calling you 'Daddy-Kyle'?" Joan asked.

He smiled and nodded. "And Franklin was 'Daddy-Franklin.' I'm sure it was confusing for her."

"She's crazy about you, Kyle. You *are* her father." She put the glass on the counter. "Franklin's like . . . like a beloved uncle."

He walked over to give Joan a hug. "We're a family, Joan. Always will be."

29

Spring 1953

"BUT WHY? I DON'T UNDERSTAND . . . HOW COME?" GWEN
asked, beginning to tear up. She had chocolate ice cream around
her lips.

"Yeah, why now?" Lisa asked. "I like my school and my
friends." Her eyes darted back and forth quickly between her
parents.

"I don't even understand where Arizona is," said Gwen, now
with tears streaming down her cheeks. "It's so stupid, do we have
to move?" She mixed the now-melting ice cream in the bowl in
front of her.

"Kids, calm down," Joan said. "It's not like we are doing
something horrible to you. Phoenix is beautiful, you'll see. Lots
of sunshine, no rain, and cactus grows *everywhere*. And all the
houses are pretty and new." She lit a cigarette, took a puff, and
exhaled.

"But *why*?" Lisa whined.

Joan took another puff. She was becoming agitated with the
younger girls' complaints. She faced her son. "Bobby? You're awfully quiet. What do you think?" She flicked ashes into an ashtray while rubbing his arm. He sat next to her in stony silence.

"I told you, call me 'Bob,' not 'Bobby,'" he said, looking down
at the piece of paper he had folded into a triangle "football." He

flicked it across the table. It hit Barbara in the face and fell into her ice cream. She glared at him.

"I think you'll like Phoenix," Joan said to him. "Lots of open land, mountains all around." Then, looking at the younger girls. "*Horses!* You two will love that. Imagine horseback riding every weekend."

"You've obviously made your decision, Mom," Barbara said. "That's why you and Dad went out there last month, isn't it? To look at houses?"

"Well," she said, straightening her posture defensively. "Yes. Yes, we did look at houses. And we made an offer on one in a brand-new neighborhood."

"It's very nice," Kyle said to Barbara as he entered the kitchen. "A ranch house—"

"We're going to live on a *ranch*?" asked Lisa with a high-pitched screech.

"Geez, Lisa," Bob said, covering his ears.

"No, we're not going to live on a ranch," Kyle said. "A ranch house means there is only one floor."

"So where are the bedrooms?" asked Gwen. "If there isn't another floor?"

"Oh, my god," Bob said.

Joan hit his arm this time. "Okay, everyone just *calm down!*" Joan screamed.

"Joan—" Kyle began, taking a seat next to her and putting his hand on top of hers.

"No! No, Kyle, don't try to shut me up!" She put out her cigarette as her eyes moved from child to child as she spoke. "Now, listen, kids. This move is so the company can expand into another part of the country. That's how we make money, right? By growing and getting new accounts. Dumann is up and down the East Coast, and this will be a new market with more opportunities."

She was calm now, and smiling at each child, hoping for a positive reaction from one of them. Joan always felt it was best to explain motives and decisions to her children, not only to help them understand but also to teach them about life and practical matters involving money and business.

"Listen, Mom," Barbara began. "While I'm not thrilled about the idea, it's not that big a deal for me. I mean, sure, it'll be my senior year and all, but I don't really care about high school anymore."

"I like that you're on board with this," Joan said, clapping her hands softly. Joan's goal was always to get Barbara to comply with new ideas, as she held influence with the three younger children. "Though I'm surprised to hear you say you don't care about high school. And you're such a good student."

"I mean, it's okay. But maybe I won't even finish high school. Maybe I'll go to flying school."

Joan saw Barbara wink at Lisa, who giggled in response.

Barbara continued. "Heck, now that I think of it, I don't even need to move with everyone. I can live with Daddy-Franklin. I'm sure he wouldn't mind—"

"Nooooo!" cried Lisa and Gwen simultaneously.

Joan rested her head in her hands. She had expected a lot of questions and a little resistance, but she didn't think the children would react so negatively to the news. She felt unappreciated, as usual. She'd made her meat loaf for dinner, which everyone always enjoyed, and had bought each of the children their favorite ice cream for dessert.

"Mom is right that it's good for a company to expand," Kyle said. "I don't need to get into the nuts and bolts of it, but sometimes personal sacrifices must be made because of a business objective."

"Why can't Uncle Rich move out there?" asked Bob. "He's

the company president." Bob had folded a second paper football.

"He and I discussed this, and it made more sense for me to do it," Kyle explained.

Joan lifted her head from her hands. She looked at her son. "That's not the way it works, honey. The company president makes the big decisions, but it's people like your father who actually make things happen." she said, placing a hand on Kyle's shoulder. "However, I personally feel your dad would do a wonderful job running the company." She smiled and rubbed Kyle's back. Then she looked at Barbara. "We all want you to move out there with us. We are a family. You'll finish high school out there; it's a brand-new building from what I understand."

Barbara slowly shook her head from side to side.

"And you two," Joan said to Gwen, who had stopped crying and was wiping her wet face, and Lisa, who had put her arm around her younger sister. "I know you'll enjoy living in Phoenix. You'll make lots of new friends, and you'll have new bedrooms that you can decorate, and it will be an adventure."

"May I be excused?" Bob asked, already standing.

Kyle nodded.

"Me too. I have a lot of homework," Barbara said, pushing her chair out from the table.

"When are we moving anyway?" Lisa asked.

Bob and Barbara both stopped in their tracks and turned around to face Joan.

"Now *that's* a very smart question," said Kyle.

"We are moving a week after school ends," Joan said, steeling herself for the reaction.

"What about camp?" whined Lisa. "You said I was going back after last summer."

"Mommy, you promised I could go this summer too," cried Gwen.

"And the beach at the end of the summer," Lisa chimed in. She appealed to her father, pulling on his shirt sleeve. "We aren't going to Stone Harbor like we do every August?"

Kyle rubbed Lisa's back.

"Fabulous," Bob said with soft sarcasm, and left the kitchen.

"Summer in Phoenix, Arizona?" Barbara said, looking at Kyle. "Really, Dad?"

Kyle looked at Joan. "Maybe this summer she can stay back, go to camp?"

"Mom, I was going to be a junior counselor. All summer. Please?" She sat down next to her mother.

"Franklin is here. It'll be fine," Kyle said, leaning in to Joan. "Barb can come out to Phoenix after camp ends."

Joan let out a big puff of air. On the one hand she felt defeated; she wanted her eldest child there from the start, but Joan knew that anything she might say to the contrary would only make her look like the bad guy once again. She acquiesced, nodding with her eyes closed.

When camp ended that summer, Barbara did not move to Phoenix to join her family. Instead, she moved in with Franklin and enrolled at Abington Friends School, the first Quaker institution she had ever attended, for her senior year.

The decision for Barbara to spend her senior year with Franklin and attend Abington Friends did not sit well with Joan, who had worked so hard to separate herself from that world in which her childhood family were so engrained. She imagined Barbara becoming fully immersed in the Quaker community and pulling away from Joan and Kyle. Thinking about this called to mind all Joan's feelings of inadequacy from her youth.

The move to Arizona was supposed to be a clean break to a place where Joan wasn't constantly reminded of who she had not become and the people she had disappointed. The failures. On some level, she resented that her eldest child was tied to part of what Joan was trying to escape. But, more importantly, she feared that Barbara would grow closer to Franklin and somehow learn how Joan had betrayed him as a young mother and misunderstood wife.

30

June 1956

WHEN JOAN CONFRONTED BOB ABOUT THE BOTTLE OF bourbon in his hand on a Saturday afternoon, two days after his graduation from high school, Bob threw up all over the dining room rug. Joan immediately grounded him for the weekend.

"I think he may have seen his birth certificate," Kyle said. "It was on my desk, and he got the bourbon from my office."

"Dammit, Kyle!" Joan screamed. "Why was it left out like that?" She picked up a pack of cigarettes from the kitchen counter and pulled one from the pack. She lit it and took a deep drag, blowing it out forcefully.

"You said you wanted to take care of all that immediately, now that he's eighteen, remember?"

"Of course I remember. But how could you be so careless?" She ran her fingers through her hair. She bit her nail. "Didn't you consider there was a chance one of the kids would see it?"

"Are you blaming me for this?"

"No, I'm not blaming you," she said. "Look, I initiated this whole thing; I know it was my idea. But he's going to need a social security card with the proper name on it. It's a straight-forward process and, fortunately, that lawyer friend of yours said he could push it through without Bob's involvement. But now . . ." She grunted in frustration.

Kyle nodded. "You know I'm uncomfortable with this . . ."

Joan stood with a hand on her hips, the other hand nervously flicking ashes into an ashtray. She was annoyed with Kyle. He was always so fastidious about putting every personal item in its place, to the point that it made her feel inept regarding her own organizational tendencies. He made their bed every morning; he couldn't stand clutter. Yet now, this one act of carelessness had rendered his perfect record of organization inconsequential in Joan's eyes.

"So what do we do now?" he asked.

Joan took a puff, exhaled, and smashed the cigarette hard into the ashtray. She folded her arms across her chest, looked at Kyle. "This is what is going to happen: You are going to have a talk with Bob."

"Hold on, hold on," Kyle said.

"It makes sense. It'll be a father-son conversation." She laughed, considering the irony of the statement. "You don't have to say anything, at least not until you see what, if anything, he knows. In fact, don't bring anything up, just see how he's feeling."

"Joan, I—"

"We are in this together, Kyle," she said, a finger pointed at him, her volume rising again.

It was clear to Joan that her children, and anyone who met her after she became Mrs. Kyle Dumann, assumed that Joan met and married Kyle not long after her divorce from Franklin. To the extent that Barbara and Bob had any curiosity about it, they never pressed Joan on why she and Franklin had divorced, and Lisa and Gwen were just too young to consider the timeline of events. The only time Barbara brought up anything related to the divorce was when, at age eleven, she asked Joan if people get divorced because they stop loving each other. Joan's response, before she changed the subject entirely, was simply, "Marriage isn't easy." Joan promised herself that, as long as she was alive, she would never again speak the name Paul Anderson.

31

"BOB'S BEEN WITH THE COMPANY FOR EIGHT YEARS. IT just makes sense. It's time," Kyle said to Joan as they drove to work one morning. "I can't think of anyone who's more qualified to run it at this point than him."

"I agree," she said as she lit a cigarette. "In some ways he's more prepared than we—" She corrected herself, ". . . than *you* were after your brother died. Remember how chaotic that was?" She shook her head, reflecting on her brother-in-law's sudden massive heart attack, after which Kyle realized that, in his capacity as vice-president, his focus had mostly been on sales and marketing, and that he had lost touch with the manufacturing side of the business. Joan had recommended he immediately meet with the company's top engineers, foremen, plant supervisors, and installers so they could bring him up to speed. She often wished that she could have taken over as president of Dumann Paving and Flooring after her brother-in-law passed away. In a way, she thought perhaps Kyle would have preferred that as well.

"Bob has all the angles covered: the design and manufacturing process, the marketing and sales side of the business," Kyle said.

"But . . ." she said.

"But what?"

"This doesn't mean retirement, though, right? You're fifty-one, Kyle. You've still got to stay involved in important developments and decisions about the direction of the business." *We both need to stay involved*, she thought.

"True," said Kyle. "I just need a slightly different focus, more big-picture perspective."

She took a puff of her cigarette.

"I thought you were going to quit this summer," Kyle said, eyeing her cigarette.

"Well, I was. But that was before these Virginia Slims came along," she said, inspecting the cigarette's long, sleek profile. "Now I'm enjoying smoking all over again."

"You just like their motto, 'You've come a long way, baby,'" he said with a wink.

She laughed. He was right. "But, anyhow," she said, "speaking of big-picture perspective, you realize there's a whole untapped region we could focus on."

"And where would that be?" Kyle asked.

"The Bible belt—Arkansas, Oklahoma." She broke into song, jumping about in her seat. "'Ohhhhk-lahoma, where the wind comes sweepin' down the plain!'"

Kyle laughed. "Your father is smiling in heaven."

"That musical came out the year Gwen was born, you know. My father reviewed the opening." She was proud that she remembered that tidbit of information, and sad that she had not been with him at that performance, nor at any other after *A Doll's House*. "Seriously, though," she said with a poke to his arm. "Consider the agricultural market, Kyle. I've had a couple conversations with Lisa about it. She's got connections throughout Little Rock—business leaders, politicians, farmers. I really think it would be the perfect market to roll out Steri-

Stone." She had a gut feeling about the company's newest product and knew that Kyle would give her idea consideration, as he always did.

He took the key out of the ignition and grabbed his brief-case. "Hmm. Interesting idea."

"Yep," she said as they parked in front of the entrance to Dumann Paving. She put out her cigarette in the car's ashtray. "These large farms, especially breeding operations, they could use durable brick flooring that's sanitary and maintenance-free," she said with another poke to his arm just before opening the door to their Cadillac DeVille.

"I'm not sure about expanding now, Joan." He got out of the car, dropped the keys in his pants pocket, and opened the office door for Joan.

Joan knew that Kyle had felt discouraged by the failed ex-pansion into the Southwest in 1953; closing the Arizona and New Mexico plants after just three years had hit him particularly hard. But Joan didn't regret that she pushed him to convince his brother to allow the expansion, nor did she feel guilty for relo-cating her family to Phoenix and then back to the East Coast.

"The offices out West were mismanaged, Kyle. We've talked about that. If you'd only allowed me to manage operations, we wouldn't have failed."

They entered the front door of the building into a small re-ception area with a teak-and-leather Scandinavian sofa and matching coffee table, two fake plastic floor plants on either side of the entrance, and a teak desk for a receptionist. It had been Joan's idea to make the vestibule more of a lobby, despite the fact that Dumann's salesforce tended to visit clients' place of busi-ness, rather than the other way around. After Richard's death, she'd insisted that the corporate office needed a design overhaul and had hired an interior decorator to "make the entire space feel more like a Madison Avenue advertising agency than an industrial flooring company," as Joan put it.

They walked through a door leading to Kyle's office, outside of which sat his secretary, Karen.

"Oh, look," he said. "Karen bought donuts . . . thanks Karen!" he yelled into his secretary's office. She waved and smiled, busy on the telephone.

Joan could see that Kyle was not in the mood to discuss, yet again, what had gone wrong in Arizona and New Mexico, so she changed the subject. "Are we still taking that January trip?" she asked him with a smile.

"Absolutely. Ten days in St. John. I need that more than anything." He threw his attaché onto his desk.

"Wonderful. I'll call the travel agency this morning," she said, reaching for a donut. She headed to the other side of the lobby, where she had her own small office.

She sat down at her desk and took a bite of the donut before placing it on a napkin. She fished through her Rolodex for her travel agent's number, pulled the card, and set it next to the donut. She was looking forward to going to St. John, where she could soak up some sunshine, have a massage or two, and discuss with Kyle the game plan for securing new business. She was confident about giving their son Bob the new title of president; he had matured considerably since his high school and college days, when he often drove his car recklessly and partied too hard. He'd be fine at the helm, and she fully expected to have his ear as she had always had Kyle's.

32

JOAN HUNG UP THE PHONE AFTER CALLING BOB WITH THE news and walked over to the sofa in the hospital emergency room, where she had spent the last twelve hours. Her eyes burned, and her throat was raw from crying. She sat down and looked across the room at a painting on the wall of a beach scene, complete with palm tree, ocean waves, and a seagull or two. She remembered something Kyle had said the morning before while they lay in the hotel bed, musing why anyone would hang a painting of a beach in a place that had a real beach.

They always had such fun on vacations, whether it was just the two of them, or with another couple or several couples. Kyle was so congenial, so focused on making her happy. She recalled the numerous times he'd tried to get her to take golf lessons so that they could both play on vacation, but she had no interest.

"That ship has sailed," she would say. "As a kid, I would have loved to take lessons with Sonny, but Dad would never let me, so..."

Just outside the emergency room, an ambulance siren whirred, jolting Joan from her thoughts. The double doors burst open and two medics rushed in, pushing a gurney. Joan wondered if the patient was another tourist, like Kyle, or a Virgin Islander. She was tense and needing a cigarette, but her pack was back at the hotel. She collected the paperwork given to her by the ER doctor, stood up, and walked over to a woman sitting behind a desk.

"Can I help ya, ma'am?" the woman asked with her lovely island accent.

"I've filled out this paperwork to have my husband transferred back to the States," she said, holding the papers up for the woman to see. "Do I give this to you, or someone else?"

"Has he already been admitted here?"

"Admitted? Um, well, no. He's. . . ." She looked at the papers in her hand, saw the line that said, "Time and cause of death: 8:42 a.m., myocardial infarction."

The woman raised her eyebrows.

"My husband is dead," Joan said. The words made her sick.

"I'll take those for ya. I'm so very sorry, ma'am. Do ya have anyone with ya here?"

Joan shook her head. "No. I'm alone." Her eyes filled with tears.

"Aw," she said, shaking her head from side to side and clicking her tongue in sympathy. "Can I call ya a taxi, then?"

"Thank you. I need to get back to my hotel on St. John."

"It's just a short ride from the hospital to the dock. You can get the ferry there, twenty minutes to St. John."

Joan nodded.

The woman picked up the phone, dialed, said something in a Creole dialect, and hung up.

"Your ride will be here shortly."

Joan nodded again. She tried to muster a small smile.

"Oh my, again, I'm so sorry for your loss. Dis shoulda been a happy time for ya."

On the ferry back to St. John, Joan wondered why Kyle rarely got angry, never demanded anything. On some level, Joan knew she could be difficult; she pushed the envelope with him, maybe took advantage of his easygoing nature at times. Yet, he was the one person she always was certain loved her. Why wasn't that enough for her? Her throat was so tense she felt it might burst open from her neck.

She remembered losing her temper when Kyle told her of his plan to take Bob to Pebble Beach for a golfing getaway after Bob's graduation from high school. She was angry because Kyle had not asked her to accompany him on the trip and because he'd spoken to Bob about going without consulting with her first. Was it possible she was jealous of her own son?

Joan had wanted to hold on to her anger then; she didn't know why, but it always felt like a comfortably familiar place to be. Kyle knew how to break her out of her heightened state every time. Kyle the conciliator. Kyle the pacifier. *Kyle, my rock.* She began to feel anxious at the thought of being alone. What would she do with herself now that he was gone? She was an integral part of Dumann Paving and guided Kyle when she felt it was necessary, but would her involvement in the business feel the same without him? She needed to talk to someone, but who would listen without judging her state of confusion, without assuming she was falling apart? Her mind drifted to another time . . . *kindred spirits* . . . Joan could hear that lovely Irish accent.

All alone. Maybe she *would* fall apart.

33

LISA AND JOAN SAT AT LISA'S KITCHEN TABLE ON THE second day of Joan's visit to Little Rock, two months after Kyle's death. Joan had come for a two-week visit, at Lisa and Justin's invitation, to visit her grandchildren, Lizzie and Shawn, to escape the extreme cold of the East Coast, and, hopefully, to clear her mind now that the administrative demands of and details associated with Kyle's death were mostly behind her.

Justin stood at the stove, stirring chili in a large pot and occasionally bringing the wooden spoon to his lips for a taste. Joan looked at his large belly, which fell over his thick leather belt. *Justin Hepp sure loves to eat,* she thought. He wore his sideburns on the longer side, perhaps to compensate for the lack of hair on the top of his head.

The temperature outside was warm for a Little Rock morning in March—just about seventy degrees—and the steam rising from the pot of chili added humidity to the small room.

"Justin, turn on the fan, would you? I'm actually sweating over here," Lisa said as she pushed back her thick, blond bangs. "Anyway, Mom, what do you think you'll do now that Dad's . . ." Lisa hesitated. "I mean, I know you had some involvement in the business, but I don't think Bob wants to expand for now, so . . ."

Joan focused on Lisa's upturned nose, which was exactly like Kyle's. Lisa and Gwen had inherited their father's nose and his hair, but not his height. Joan's daughters were all petite, like her.

"Mom?"

Joan raised a glass of water to her lips. She took a few small sips, put the glass down, and brushed stray crumbs from the morning's breakfast into her palm. She stood up and walked over to the garbage can to throw the crumbs away. She was craving a cigarette, but Lisa would not allow her to smoke in the house.

"Mom, are you listening to me? I feel like you're somewhere else."

Joan did not want to be grilled by Lisa, or anyone else for that matter, regarding her plan, her life, or her mindset. "Sorry, Lisa. I'm listening." She sat back down.

"Are you okay in New Jersey? I mean, you like it there, right? You've got friends. The club and all, right?"

"I'm not going back to New Jersey."

"What? Why not?" asked Lisa.

"What would I be going back for? Things are different now. My social life won't be the same without your father. There's no point in returning to that life."

"Mom, I know it's painful, but—"

"Your father and I had plans," Joan said. She grabbed two used paper napkins, crushed them in her hands, and stood up again to discard them in the trash can.

"You can't expand Dumann into this region now that he's gone."

"Perhaps not." Joan snapped her fingers and pointed an enthusiastic finger at Lisa. "I could do what you do. I'd love to train horses, especially the foals. The idea of being outside all day, in this beautiful region. Reminds me of my summers in Ivyland."

"I don't know. It's exhausting work; you're on your feet all day. You get kicked; you're in manure."

Joan gave a closed-lip smile and shook her head. "That's exactly how I've felt since your Dad passed away . . . exhausted, kicked around, stuck in shit."

Justin chuckled again.

Lisa glared at him and said, "Listen, Mom, you're in a good situation now. Financially, you're secure, especially with the life insurance payout coming to you from Dad's policy. The company's stable; you've got the regular income from that for now, and the business is in good hands with Bob, so you don't need to be muddled in the ups and downs and hassles of running a business."

That's exactly where I want to be. Now, she really craved a cigarette.

Justin put down the wooden spoon and turned down the flame under the chili. He took a seat on one of the red vinyl chairs next to Joan and brushed some crumbs off the white laminate tabletop. "Listen, Joan," he said, clasping his hands and resting them on the table. "We know it's been very trying for you since Kyle passed."

Justin looked at Lisa as if requesting permission to continue. She nodded.

"Take some time," he said. "Think about what you want. You could go anywhere, *any*where."

"Justin's right. You've always loved Florida, Mom. What about Palm Beach or Fort Lauderdale? I've got such wonderful memories of family trips to Lauderdale."

"There's an idea," Justin said, perhaps a bit too enthusiastically. "What do they say? 'When life closes one door, another gets opened'?"

"I believe it's a quote from the Bible: 'When God closes one door, he opens another,'" Lisa replied authoritatively.

Joan swirled the last of the water around in the glass. "*The Sound of Music*," Joan muttered nonchalantly, under her breath. She drank the water.

"What?" Lisa replied.

Joan took a deep sigh. "I think you're referring to a line from *The Sound of Music*."

Joan watched as Lisa and Justin looked at each other with blank expressions.

"It's not a line from the Bible," she said. Though Joan had come to love musical productions, she knew Lisa did not share her mother's or her maternal grandfather's love for the theatre. Joan wondered what her father would have thought of *The Sound of Music*. She didn't bother to mention his name: Lisa had no recollection of him.

Joan looked away from Lisa and Justin and toward the window as the sun abruptly streamed in. "I need to think everything through," she declared, smacking the table and standing up. She decided, right then and there, she would embrace a more optimistic perspective on her life. Lisa was always challenging her, always underestimating her. *Enough is enough.*

34

JOAN SAT AT LISA'S KITCHEN TABLE, A FOLDER OF PAPERS TO her left, and the *Northwest Arkansas Times* to her right, the first page fully open. She was studying a road map in front of her, which she had marked up with circles and arrows and handwritten notes around the edges.

She lowered her reading glasses onto her cheeks and reflected on the evening before, when her mind was ablaze as she washed the dinner dishes, hearing her grandchildren giggle upstairs as Lisa and Justin tucked them in. The same thought crept into her head over and over again: *They underestimate me.*

Her reverie was broken as she heard Lisa coming down the stairs. She covered the map with the newspaper and adjusted her reading glasses.

"You're up early," Lisa said.

"Yeah, I think the time zone is still messing me up," Joan said.

Lisa removed a bowl from the cabinet, turned around, and leaned against the counter. "It's only a one-hour difference."

"Mm. Well, in any case," Joan said, pretending to read the paper.

"So where'd you go last night?" Lisa asked.

"What? Oh, well, I pretty much just drove around."

"You were gone for three hours. I almost made Justin go out looking for you."

"Nonsense," Joan said. "I told you I needed to clear my head. And I wanted to go somewhere I could enjoy a smoke. Besides, I'm a big girl." She turned the page of the paper.

"You could use a touch-up."

Joan looked up from the newspaper. "Huh?"

Lisa poured corn flakes into the bowl. "Your hair," she said, pointing. "The gray is coming through."

Joan pulled at a few strands. "Oh, is it?" She had noticed it herself, but coloring her hair had not been much of a priority of late. She looked down at her hands, noticing the chipped nail polish. "I could use a manicure as well." She looked at Lisa. "Ah, well, at some point." She smiled, but she was embarrassed. Since marrying Kyle, she had been fastidious about tending to her makeup, hair, and nails, but since his death, she had been neglecting her appearance. Now Joan felt self-conscious, as if she were a teenager again.

Lisa poured milk into the bowl, walked behind Joan, and perused the front page of the newspaper over Joan's shoulder. "Jesus Christ, thirty-three thousand Americans killed in Vietnam since this damned war started. Thirty-three *thousand*!" Lisa put a spoonful of cereal in her mouth.

"Yes, I read. It's a war without end, and for no good reason," Joan said as she surreptitiously slid a piece of scratch paper filled with dollar figures, calculations, and bank account information under the newspaper.

"Don't tell that to Justin. He firmly believes we're in there to rid the world of the evil communist machine—and doing a great job of it," Lisa said with cynicism in her tone.

"Yeah, well, let him read these articles. Lots of sad stories about young men dying." Joan shook her head.

"I agree. I'm just sayin', don't get into it with Justin."

"Ten-four. I'll avoid debating the subject with him. I'll just stick to conversations about Apollo 9 and Jim Morrison's indecent exposure," Joan replied.

The two women chuckled.

"What's with the maps?" Lisa inspected them. "Northwestern Oklahoma? Arkansas?"

"Just trying to get the lay of the land, that's all."

"And all these lines and circles?" Lisa asked, pointing at the map. "Looking for buried treasure?"

Joan was silent. *Lisa is so pushy, so nosy.*

"Mom . . . where did you really go?"

"Okay, okay," Joan said. She indicated for Lisa to take a seat and looked her daughter in the eye, speaking with enthusiasm. "I may want to pursue a business opportunity out here—"

"Mom, I told you Bob doesn't want—"

"This is not about Bob. This is my own thing. I'm . . . exploring different things, investment opportunities and such."

Lisa was silent. She pushed her cereal bowl away and sat back, arms folded across her chest.

"Okay," Joan continued, "here's the deal. That guy who drives horses for you, Chuck?"

"Chuck Galloway. What about him?"

"Well, I saw him last night at that place up the road on Route 43, what is it? Bodiddly's? Bought him a beer, we chatted."

"You mean BoDean's? You went there last night? Whatever for?"

"I told you. I was restless. I drove around for a bit; then I came upon BoDean's and figured I'd have a drink, maybe listen to some jukebox music, talk to the locals."

"BoDean's is not a place I would've recommended."

Joan waved a dismissive hand at Lisa. "Anyway, Chuck has a business idea and . . ." Joan hesitated, placing her fingers against her mouth. "Listen, maybe I'm breaching his confidence here. I mean, he's your employee after all, and maybe he doesn't want you to know—"

"Mom, please, do *not* get involved with Chuck Galloway. I'm

234 | *Eileen Brill*

serious." Lisa picked up her cereal bowl and walked to the sink. She stared out of the window. Without turning to look at Joan, Lisa continued, "I don't know what Chuck lured you into, but you gotta be careful. He kind of has a reputation around here."

"Justin must not think so if he hired him," Joan said.

"Chuck does his job, keeps to himself. But he's a wheeler-dealer type. You should avoid him."

"See, this is typical of you, Lisa," Joan said, stabbing the air with her index finger. "You want to keep me in my little box, far away from you and your thrilling world of horses and ranches and the great outdoors. 'Just stay in New Jersey, Mom. Go on a cruise, move to Florida, find another husband.'" She hurriedly gathered all the papers off the table and folded the map. She was furious. She held everything close to her chest with one hand and put the other hand on her hip, mocking Lisa. "'But whatever you do, Mom, don't try to make something of yourself. Because, everyone knows, you've only ever been someone's wife or mother.' Do you have *any* idea how much your father depended on me for his business decisions?" she asked, pointing at herself for emphasis. She could feel how she was furrowing her brow, and it bothered her. Another crease in her forehead.

Lisa took a deep breath. "Jesus, Mom. Can you for once just trust me on something? Can you? I'm only looking out for you. If you want to invest in something out here . . ." Lisa looked around. "Buy a few foals, let me train them, we'll find a jockey from South America, get them on the track. You can make great money as an owner. You come out here a few times a year. Nice, right?" Lisa smiled encouragingly.

"Mm. Yeah, I suppose, but . . ."

"Now that will be fun. Kind of like a hobby, except you can make a nice chunk of change if you've got the right trainer . . . and you do." She proudly pointed to herself with her thumb.

Joan nodded. She knew she should not have opened her mouth about Chuck. Fortunately, she had not provided any information to Lisa about the nature of the business, nor had she mentioned her plan to meet with Chuck the following morning.

Joan awoke early and made breakfast for Lizzie and Shawn. She was in a good mood, humming and laughing, dancing around the kitchen as her grandchildren laughed along with her, happily eating the chocolate chip pancakes she'd made and begging her to extend her stay. It brought to mind the days when Ellen would commandeer the kitchen in the morning, the aroma of coffee and bacon grease filling the air, while the children ate breakfast or played on the floor, happy and cared for. Once Ellen was a part of it all, Joan could tolerate the early-morning commotion from her children.

Lisa sauntered into the kitchen and headed straight for the coffee urn. "Dammit," she said. "Still percolating."

"Mommy said a bad word," Joan teased, looking at her grandchildren. They giggled. "If I remember correctly, your mommy was just about your age when she said her first bad word," she said, tapping Lizzie on the nose.

"What did she say? What did she say?" Lizzie screamed out with a big smile and wide eyes.

"Oh, I couldn't *possibly* tell you what she said, now could I? If I did, I'd be repeating the bad word, and Mom-Mom doesn't say bad words, I certainly do not." She leaned back against the counter, grinning, arms folded and spoke to the children again. "Would you like Mom-Mom to drive you to school today?"

"Yes!" Lizzie shouted.

"We don't like the school bus," Shawn added. "The big kids are mean."

"It's settled then," Joan said, clearing the plates from the table. "I'm going to drive the children to school today, and then I'm going to take a little drive around town."

"Mom, listen, we need to talk, okay? Let the kids take the bus, it's fine—"

"Noooo!" Lizzie and Shawn screamed in tandem.

"Aw, Lisa, look how disappointed they are. Let them spend twenty extra minutes this morning with their grandmother."

Joan watched Lisa wrap both hands tightly around the coffee thermos, put her face into the hot steam, and inhale, eyes closed. "Fine," she said. "Go. Drive carefully. Lots of folks speed on these country roads."

"Yay!" Shawn screamed. "Thanks, Mommy."

Lisa bent over to hug and kiss each of her children.

Joan walked past her and pinched Lisa's cheek. "You're a good egg," Joan said as her grandchildren gathered their school bags from the pantry.

"I'm a *rotten* egg," Lisa said. She tugged on her mother's blouse. "So what exactly did I say? What was the bad word?"

Joan mouthed the word. *Fuck.* Lisa rolled her eyes.

"I rinsed your mouth out with soap," Joan said, recalling that Lisa was the only one of her children whose behavior was not easily controlled with threats. Consequently, she was the only child who actually ever had a bar of soap in her mouth.

"Lovely, Mom," Lisa said flatly.

Joan dropped Lizzie and Shawn in front of their school and watched them scurry inside; then she drove off to meet her future business partner at the Pit Stop Diner. She wanted to arrive before him so she could scout out the best table offering the most privacy.

Inside the diner, a waitress breezed by, balancing dirty dishes and coffee cups with both hands.

"Sit where you like, hon. Someone'll be right with ya. Can I bring ya coffee?"

"Two please." Joan perused the diner. Just half of the tables were taken, mostly with senior citizens and a couple of forty-something men with cowboy hats resting on the seats beside them. *This is so cliché*, she mused. Almost all of the patrons were smoking, which made Joan crave a cigarette as well. She reached into her purse but remembered she had thrown away her last pack in an effort to quit. She considered asking to bum one from a sweet-looking elderly woman she passed but reined herself in. *Get some will power*, she admonished herself.

Joan decided on the last booth at the far end of the diner. She chose the "power seat," the spot at the table that would allow her to see Chuck as he arrived. She commended herself on remembering that portion of the two-day business seminar that she and Kyle had attended years before, entitled Strategies That Work. The workshops were intended to give business owners the best mindset to achieve optimum results. "Negotiating for Yourself" explained how to mitigate being caught off guard and to establish dominance by finding a psychological advantage from the start through positioning.

She settled into her seat, removed a leather attaché case from her shoulder, and placed it on her lap. She looked at the initials on the side: KRD, *Kyle Randall Dumann*. When she'd grabbed his briefcase just before heading to the airport for her flight to Little Rock, it was because she figured it would be a good idea to travel with Steri-Stone brochures and marketing materials, just in case there was an opportunity to tout the product and send someone Bob's way. This morning, she had emptied the case and filled it with sample business contracts, maps, income projections, and vendor information, along with a calculator, two freshly sharpened pencils, her Mont Blanc pen, and her resumé. She felt prepared for this meeting, based on the long conversation they'd had at BoDean's, and she fully expected to dominate the conversation with her agenda items.

Casual conversation over beers at BoDean's was one thing, and Chuck was definitely in his comfort zone the night he pitched his idea to her, calling the livestock and horse auction outfit his "dream business" and saying he was just looking for the right partner. He had done at least some of his homework, noting that the $150,000 initial investment he needed was to buy the property and some equipment.

But this morning, Joan was in charge.

The waitress delivered a cup of coffee. "Waitin' on a friend?"

"Yes. My business partner," Joan said without making eye contact as she opened the case and flipped through papers to make it clear to the waitress that the man who would soon arrive and sit opposite her was not a love interest. There would be no fodder for gossip this morning; Joan would be the epitome of professionalism and polite aloofness.

She took a sip of coffee and looked out the window to the parking lot. She watched a dented blue Ford pickup pull into a space right in front, and out of it stepped Chuck Galloway, empty-handed except for a cigarette, which he immediately dropped onto the ground and crushed with his shoe. He stood by his car door for a second, removed his mud-caked Stetson, grabbed a comb from the back pocket of his jeans, and slicked his hair back off his face. He put the comb back in his pocket and reached into his other back pocket, from which he pulled a folded piece of paper. He opened the paper, looked at it, refolded it, and returned it to his pocket as he headed into the diner.

As he entered, Joan placed the briefcase on the seat beside

her and straightened in her chair. She held her arm up and waved casually to Chuck, keeping her expression serious but relaxed. As he approached her, he tipped his hat to the waitress. Joan heard him ask for a cup of coffee.

"The lady beat you to the table," the waitress said with a smile in Joan's direction, like a coconspirator.

Joan stood up and reached out to shake his hand. He clasped hers with a weak grip. She realized that they had not shaken hands when they met or parted at BoDean's. She didn't appreciate Chuck's limp handshake and decided that he must not respect her, perhaps because of her gender, but she would prove who was the stronger. She hadn't realized how diminutive he was the other night; perhaps they had not stood next to each other until now. He looked to be just about five foot six, with broad shoulders and a very thin build; he could almost be mistaken for a fifteen-year-old boy from behind.

He had told her he was forty-three and had been married once, in his twenties, for just a year and a half. Joan did not ask about that marriage, nor anything else about his personal life. She offered very little in the way of personal information to him, beyond the fact that her husband had recently died and that they had a family business back East.

Joan was satisfied that Chuck Galloway was no match for Joan Dumann, cultured world-traveler, part of the Dumann Paving and Flooring conglomerate, who had nothing to lose except several thousand dollars and the social network she'd built with Kyle during their twenty-nine-year marriage. Back in New Jersey, the Dumanns' friends, associates, and acquaintances were doctors, lawyers, local politicians, business leaders, couples from old money, couples with new money, people who belonged to elite, private places like the Stork Club in New York, where Joan and Kyle were occasional guests and where it was not unusual to catch a glimpse of someone like Grace Kelly. The Dumanns had no trouble finding companions to accompany them on trips to the Bahamas, Barbados, or the Riviera three to four times a year, and once or twice a year Joan would vacation alone with her daughters. The Dumanns' social plans and vacations often appeared on the pages of *The Paterson Evening News*. She and Kyle were ongoing benefactors of the New Jersey Symphony Orchestra, and Joan was a member of the school board of Verona. She was proud of the status she'd earned in her little world, but so much of her identity was tied to being Mrs. Kyle Dumann. That phase of her life was over, and Joan was ready to cast a net into dark waters with the hope that whatever she caught would be exactly the thing that would define who she always wanted to be.

"When you walked into BoDean's last night, I pegged you for an outsider right away." Chuck said, cutting into his stack of pancakes. "Stuck out like a sore thumb." He laughed and shook his head.

Joan took a sip of coffee, raised her eyebrows. "Am I supposed to be insulted by that? Because, I can tell you, I am not."

"See, and that's what I mean, Joan," he said, waggling his pointer finger in her direction. "You can't expect to earn people's trust, get folks to like you, if you act all—"

"All what?" she asked, scooping a banana slice and corn flakes with her spoon and allowing the milk to spill off a bit before putting the cereal into her mouth. She waited for his response as she finished her mouthful. He remained quiet. "If you were going to say something like 'high and mighty,' you need to know something about me, Chuck."

"No, ma'am, I wasn't trying to—"

"I know *people*. I know how to talk to folks of every ilk. I've traveled the world and been in countries where they don't speak English. I've had dinner with politicians. I have a sense, when I meet someone, who they are and what makes them tick." She scooped up more cereal. This was starting on a bad note.

"If you don't mind my sayin', you don't know these parts," he said, waving his arm around the diner. "And that's precisely why our partnership is gonna work so well." He popped too much pancake into his mouth and added, with muffled words, "You got your experience, I got mine."

Joan wrinkled her nose. She was disgusted that he talked with his mouth full. But she did have to agree with the statement. She finished the last of her cereal, wiped her mouth with a napkin, and pushed the bowl aside. Folding her arms and leaning forward on the table, she said, "I admit, I don't have experience in animal husbandry. I learned to ride horses as a child. But I'm eager to learn about livestock and the transactional side of all that."

Chuck pushed his plate to the side. "That's my point," he said, arms extended, palms up, fingers splayed. "That's where I come in. Growin' up on my uncle's farm, I had tons of experience with cows, hogs, horses. I'd go with him when he bought calves at auction. I even helped birth a few of 'em right there."

Joan reached for her briefcase.

"Joan," he said, taking a respectful tone. "You and I are total strangers. We're from different worlds, and I . . . I just want you to know that I respect what you're doin' here, puttin' faith in me and this dream of mine. I promise you, as your partner, I'll consider anything you have to say."

She looked at Chuck, noticing a missing button on his shirt. No one was going to sew that button back on, Joan was certain.

She smiled. "Okay, Chuck." She leaned forward, extended her arm. "Now, let's get down to business," she said.

"All righty then," Chuck said, putting a toothpick to his mouth.

Joan looked at the toothpick as she removed papers from her briefcase. She did not try to be subtle. Chuck broke the toothpick in half, threw it in an ashtray, and reached for a cigarette.

Two and a half hours and three cups of coffee later, Joan was convinced that she was making a sound judgment about Chuck and moving forward with the plan. Sure, Chuck was a little rough around the edges—her cultured and sophisticated friends back in New Jersey would be horrified to know she was entering into a partnership with such a man—but apart from his being slightly uncouth, Joan did not sense anything nefarious about him. And his knowledge was crucial at this point in time. Joan had the cash to put the idea into motion and, she felt, the business acumen and interpersonal skills to grow it into a legitimate enterprise. In time, Joan believed she would be steering the management of the Diamond Ranch Sales Barn, a horse and livestock auction house and entertainment venue, with Chuck little more than the face of the organization, her worker bee. Finally, Joan would have something of her very own. No longer would anyone underestimate her or doubt her capability. Her terms, her decisions.

35

"SO EXPLAIN TO ME AGAIN WHY YOU WANT TO BUILD A house on our property?" Justin gently asked Joan as he and Lisa walked two foals around a fenced-in ring. Joan walked by Lisa's side.

Lisa nodded, the corner of her mouth pointing up into a smirk.

Joan glared at her daughter. "I just want to be able to see my grandchildren more frequently and I need my breathing space when I'm visiting. Having Lizzie and Shawn double up in his room is all well and good while I'm here for a short visit. But it's not ideal, is it?"

"Well," Lisa said.

"I mean," Justin added.

"It'll be good for you as well," Joan explained, jogging ahead and then walking in front of them backwards, her eyes moving from Justin to Lisa and back. "Say, if Bob or Gwen visit, right? With their kids? They can stay there when I'm not visiting. Actually, anyone can. There's more space. It just makes sense. And I'm financing the whole project, so it's a win-win for you." She reached to pet one of the foals on the nose.

Lisa stopped walking. "You say it like it's a done deal!" she shouted. "I can't believe you've got the audacity to think—"

Justin stopped walking as well. "Easy, easy," he said, patting Lisa's shoulder. "Hang on, maybe your mother has a point."

"Thank you, Justin," Joan said. Justin could usually be counted on to be rational.

"Hear me out," he said to Lisa. "We certainly want her to visit. And to feel comfortable when she does. Let's just take a minute here and get a general sense of things," he said. "I'm curious, Joan. What is your intention regarding ownership of this house you wanna build?"

"You mean, whose name will be on the deed?" Joan asked.

"Exactly. You'd be making a huge investment on this project," Justin said.

"On *our* property," Lisa added with an air of indignation.

"Well," Joan said. She mulled it over for a minute as she ran her fingers through the soft mane of one of the foals. She hadn't given this any thought and wanted to be both diplomatic and protective of her rights. "How about this: We draw up a deed that says you two are the owners and I get a . . . what is it called? Like, I can live there until I die, and maybe I pay the taxes. Does that make sense?" she asked, looking only at Justin.

"I know what you're talking about," he replied. "It's a lifetime tenancy. Basically, I think, even if we sold our property, you would still, by law, have the right to live in the house. The new owners would have to abide by that, unless you relinquished that right."

Joan was lost in thought, only minimally listening to the conversation. She cared less about the legal mumbo-jumbo relating to property ownership and mostly about protecting her privacy. She looked off to the side, to a spot where she could imagine building her house. She wanted her own place where no one could meddle in her business.

"Mom?"

Joan looked at Lisa, though she was still lost in her thoughts.

"Legally, you wouldn't own the house," Justin clarified. "You couldn't sell it." He touched Joan's arm. "Are you okay with that?"

Joan snapped out of it. Her expression became upbeat. "Okay," she said, clapping her hands together. "We've got a deal. We'll have a lawyer draw up a deed and go from there." She looked at her watch. "Hoo-boy, I'm late. I told the kids I'd pick them up from school today. We can revisit this later." She ran off.

"You're spoiling them, Mom," Lisa called out.

On the way to the school, Joan thought about her plans. She believed that all Justin and Lisa needed to know, for the time being, was that she wanted a place of her own when she visited them. They did not need to know that she wanted to use the house as home base while her partner, Chuck, was in Oklahoma working out the nuts and bolts of the Sale Barn. Joan had told Chuck that she would lie low for a while, but her intention was to head up to Shawnee more frequently to manage him, and then have an apartment there once the business was up and running.

The next morning, Joan was on the phone with contractors. She flew back to New Jersey as planned, but she came right back to Little Rock in late April with a suitcase full of warm-weather clothing.

36

THROUGHOUT THE SUMMER, IN ADDITION TO SUPERVISING the construction of her house, Joan would drive her new Buick LeSabre to meet Chuck in various locations outside Little Rock and attempt to hash out the details of the business and the specifics of their partnership. Joan suggested they work with a business transactional lawyer in Oklahoma City, but Chuck was resistant to spending money on attorney fees. They also differed on how much money to put toward advertising. When these initial differences of opinion happened a little too often for Joan's comfort, she would remind him of their power dynamics regarding financing.

"Remember," she said during one of their disagreements, "that I have the financial wherewithal to fund these initial investments. Let's not kid ourselves, Chuck. That's one of the benefits of your partnership with me."

Chuck had quit his job with the Hepps, telling them, at Joan's request, only that he was planning on relocating out of state and giving a vague explanation of the reason.

In mid-June, they rode together in Chuck's truck for the five-hour drive to Shawnee so that Joan could see the land and barn for the first time. In order to keep Lisa's suspicion at bay, Joan told her she was doing an overnight trip to Dallas to visit an old Phoenix friend who was traveling on business with her husband. During the ride, which Joan initially dreaded and anticipated would feel agonizingly long seated next to Chuck, she actually began to warm up to him. She saw a softer, almost likeable side to him as he recounted growing up on his uncle's dairy farm, where he would awaken at four thirty every morning before school to milk cows. He made her laugh when he described each cow by name, insisting that each "girl" had her own personality and preferences.

"Lila was stubborn and would only let me milk her last. She wasn't a morning person," he said, smiling broadly. "Doreen, well, she had a sense of humor. Always passed gas when I reached for the teat."

"You're quite the comedian, Chuck," Joan said, wiping away tears of laughter at the absurdity of his story. "I'm guessing you were a bit of a class clown in school."

"Nah. I wasn't much of a nothin' in school. I was a quiet type. I'm not ashamed to say I didn't have many friends. Kind of a loner, you might say. But that's the way I wanted it, I guess."

Joan didn't have a lot of friends in her younger days, either. But she was not going to draw any similarities between herself and Chuck.

"Why would you choose to be a loner?" she asked.

"I always noticed how two-faced kids were. Sayin' one thing to someone's face, promisin' this and that, 'You're so great, man, we're buddies,' and all that. Then, to someone else, all you hear is, 'Aw, he's a no-good, son of a bitch.'" Chuck looked at Joan. "Pardon my language, Joan."

She waved a hand. "We're adults here." She assumed she was hearing the narrative of his teenaged years.

By the time they pulled into the driveway at the Diamond Ranch Sale Barn, Joan was relaxed and upbeat, and she was beginning to feel a renewed sense of optimism about her partner. And as they toured the property, Joan was ecstatic: the "barn," which exceeded her expectations, was actually a large, fairly new building, set up to store farm equipment and machinery for auctions in its former incarnation. Though its aluminum, fiberglass, and concrete construction was practical, it had a rustic appearance and fit in aesthetically with the two other, smaller barns.

After the tour, Joan, Chuck, and the property owner sat down to sign an agreement of sale on the main building and its surrounding land, as well as the two smaller barns, and they agreed to buy the existing name of the business as well. Joan put down the bulk of the deposit.

"So when are you planning on officially moving up here?" Joan asked Chuck as they pulled away from the Diamond Ranch Sale Barn.

"Next week, as a matter of fact," he said, striking a match for his cigarette at a red light. He offered one to Joan.

She held up her hand and shook it to decline. She had no interest in his Marlboros; she only smoked Virginia Slims, and she was still trying to quit. "Next week, huh? Where will you be living?"

"Tecumseh. Just south of Shawnee. Rentin' a room to start, from an old friend. Then we'll see."

A room? she thought. She made a mental note to look for a place nowhere near Tecumseh.

The ride back to Little Rock was filled with far less conversation than the ride to Shawnee and was certainly less animated. What they discussed involved mostly the logistics for the next couple of months and where to open a bank account for the business. Joan took notes the entire trip, mostly to give herself a task list and also to commit to paper every word out of Chuck's mouth. While she was still excited about this new venture, she began to get the sense that Chuck saw her mainly as an investor, a silent partner, in the Diamond Ranch Sale Barn. She would need to be more vested in the day-to-day operations of the company and, to that end, she would need to be a presence on site and learn all she could about transactional business.

As they neared Little Rock, Joan assembled her paperwork and stuffed it into Kyle's attaché case.

"You can drop me off at the Pit Stop Diner, if you wouldn't mind. I'll call a taxi from there to take me back to Lisa's," she said. She needed to keep up the ruse of having just flown in from Dallas.

It was nine o'clock on a Tuesday evening, so the parking lot at the diner was relatively empty. Chuck pulled into a spot around the back and put the truck into park. Joan grabbed her overnight bag from the floor and began to thank Chuck for driving, when he interrupted her.

"That's quite a nice leather bag ya got there," he said, taking a drag from his Marlboro.

"Oh, this? Yes, it . . . was my husband's," she said, running her finger across his initials. She forced a smile.

"What was his name? Your husband."

"Kyle," she said, keeping her eyes on the initials.

"Never knew a Kyle before." He took a drag of his cigarette and forcefully blew the smoke out of the window.

Joan clenched her teeth. She did not want to engage in small talk at this moment, and she especially did not want to discuss Kyle with someone like Chuck Galloway. There was nothing Chuck needed to know about her deceased husband. "It's not a name you hear every day, and Kyle was certainly rare among men." She opened the door and began easing out of the truck.

He crushed his cigarette into the ashtray. "Hey, Joan, we can try to be, you know, friends." He wiped his lips with the back of his hand. "I mean, damn, we haven't even congratulated each other or nothin'. Kinda odd for new partners, don't ya think?"

Joan sensed nervousness in his voice for the first time. He seemed vulnerable, sad.

"I suppose you're right," she said. "Well . . . congratulations to us, Chuck. We're doing this, we are actually making this happen. This was your dream, and now it's real." She knew she came across as guarded and phony, but so be it. She needed to establish boundaries from the get-go. And she was trying to make it crystal clear that she was ready to say good-night.

"Listen," he said, "we could go inside for some coffee, or even a bite to eat. Or, I mean, I don't have to let you off here. We could have a beer at BoDean's, ya know? Toast the new Diamond Ranch Sale Barn." He nodded his head slightly as if to coax Joan into accepting the idea.

Joan looked at her watch and hedged. "I don't know, Chuck. I think I'd better get back home. Lisa's going to start wondering where I am. But . . . another time, certainly." She thanked him once more for driving, and when she noticed his downcast face she attempted to project more positivity. "This is going to be great, Chuck. We'll make that toast another time." She tapped the door twice for emphasis and walked toward the front of the diner.

37

JOAN'S TWO-BEDROOM RANCH HOUSE WAS COMPLETED IN October of 1969 at a cost of $25,000, and she spent another $20,000 on improvements: hooking up the water to Lisa and Justin's line, which involved replacing some of the plumbing inside Lisa's home; installing a septic system; adding a paved driveway as well as furnishing and landscaping. Her long driveway branched directly off the street so Joan could come and go and not need to use the Hepps' driveway. Traversing the entrance to Joan's driveway from the road was an antique wrought-iron gate, the design of which matched neither the farm's Craftsman-style house and out-buildings nor the nondescript ranch house Joan had constructed, but she felt it gave her new residence a heightened sense of significance. A local real estate attorney drew up an agreement stipulating that Joan would have a lifetime claim on the house and the land immediately surrounding it, and Joan had a verbal agreement from Lisa and Justin that if they decided to sell their property, Joan would be entitled to full reimbursement of her investment.

At about the same time, Joan S. Dumann and Charles R. Galloway became co-owners of the Diamond Ranch Sale Barn. Their plan was to hold auctions of registered horses—those who were on a breed registry and would bring in higher prices than "grade" horses without registries—one Wednesday every month, and auctions of grade horses on the remaining Wednesday mornings. In addition, there would be weekly Saturday auctions for grade horses and livestock. Chuck was responsible for hiring an auctioneer to run the events, a driver to transport horses and livestock, and three barn hands for on-site maintenance—mucking out stables, supplying hay, setting up the arena for auctions, and moving the animals between trailers, stables and the arena. Joan would hire an auction coordinator to oversee the administration of the auctions and an accounting manager to track sales and procure payments. The plan for the summer months was to add Saturday night auctions with a more family-oriented, carnival-like atmosphere; for that they would hire additional summer employees as necessary to help with concessions and parking.

Joan's head reeled from the flow of new information, but it thrilled her, nonetheless. For the time being, she reluctantly agreed to allow Chuck to oversee the daily operations of the Sale Barn in his capacity as general manager, and Joan would be more of a silent partner, at least initially. She wasn't quite ready to leave Little Rock anyway.

"For now," Chuck said, with a hand on her shoulder and a condescending tone, "stay in Little Rock. I'll get things started up in Shawnee, make sure the men know what they're doin'. Then, when we have our first registered horse auction, you decide what you wanna do—stay in Little Rock or move on up here. Maybe 'tween now and then you drive up every so often, we sit down for a face-to-face, make sure we're seeing eye-to-eye on everything. Sound good?"

Joan held off asserting herself in order to see just how Chuck operated, and she needed to educate herself on the nuts and bolts of the business. She knew to pick and choose her battles, and it was important to her that Chuck miscalculate just how formidable and shrewd a business partner she could be when challenged.

Joan immediately sprang into action, getting to know the

horse and livestock breeders and farmers in and around Little Rock. She drove from ranch to ranch introducing herself and letting people know that she was the owner of the Diamond Ranch Sale Barn in Shawnee, Oklahoma, and that horses could be auctioned off on consignment beginning in April. She made no mention of her partner during these introductions.

One evening in early November, Joan sat in the kitchen of her ranch house reviewing notes about farmers she had met, the size of their operations, and any other incidental or personal information she had gathered. After an hour, she put the type-written list into a large envelope and included a handwritten note to her son.

> Hi, Bob,
> How's life? Hope all is well at work and at home.
> I've enclosed a list of farmers I've met out here. I think there is some interest in Steri-Stone, so you should follow up if possible. Let me know if you need my help.
> Give Rebecca and the kids my hugs.
> Love, Mom

As she sealed the envelope, there was a knock at the door, and Lisa peered in.

"Mom? Can we talk?"

"C'mon in. Want a cup of tea?"

"No, thanks." Lisa slowly approached her mother. "Listen, there's something I want to ask you about," she said, raking her fingers through her hair as she sat at the table opposite Joan.

"Everything OK?"

"Well, I don't know. I sincerely hope so. This guy Justin knows, a dairy farmer up in Sherwood, he says he's driving some of his livestock up to Shawnee next month for an auction."

Joan froze, but then composed herself. "Mm-hmm," she said, feigning ignorance as she licked a postage stamp.

Lisa looked serious. Joan put the envelope to the side.

"You seem bothered, Lisa. What's on your mind?" Joan folded her arms and leaned her elbows on the table, staring earnestly into Lisa's eyes.

"Well, to start, where have you been driving every day? What're you filling your days with?"

Joan looked down and busied herself with the items in front of her, stacking postage stamp booklets on top of her address book, straightening the pile of typewriter paper.

"Mom," Lisa said, forcefully holding down Joan's hand. "I know you've been driving around, introducing yourself as the owner of some business. I do know that much. Please tell me what else are you doing."

"What are you suggesting, Lisa?" she asked coldly and without making eye contact.

"Bob's running the business. You've got to let it go."

Joan sat back and folded her arms.

"I'm trying to give you the opportunity to be straight with me," Lisa said. "People talk. I need to know what's true and what's rumor."

Joan could no longer act obtuse. It was time to tell Lisa, but her silence said it all.

Lisa shook her head. "I didn't want to believe it. I just didn't want to believe you'd actually disregard my warning. I feel so *stupid*." Lisa pushed the chair back and stood up. She walked away from Joan and spun around. "And this house. You built this house on false pretenses. 'I just want to be with my grandchildren more.'"

"I did. I *do*!" Joan insisted.

"That's just going to be a by-product, a side benefit of . . .

whatever it is you're doing with Chuck Galloway." She folded her arms, glaring at her mother. "And I *knew* you didn't go to Dallas that day to visit a friend, I just *knew* it. And when Chuck told Justin he was quitting, I *knew* I should put you on the spot."

"Lisa, just calm down, okay?"

"For God's sake, tell me what you're doing up in Shawnee!" Lisa screamed.

"Let me explain. It's all going according to plan. I think you'll be pleased, really. Just . . . just please, sit down and let me tell you about it."

Lisa stood in place.

Joan laid out the details of the business. She needed to deflate Lisa's concern, to allay her fears, mostly to keep her daughter out of her hair. It infuriated Joan that her own children frequently underestimated her judgment.

Lisa said, "I didn't—I don't want you to get taken advantage of, that's all. I wish you had just been honest with me from the start."

"I tried. You shut me down. Anyway, Lisa, don't worry about me where Chuck's concerned. I can handle him. I've seen worse." In truth, Chuck was about the crudest, most uncouth person she'd ever come across, but she did not feel intimidated by him. Her superiority felt like a shield around her, giving her some kind of insightful power over him. "Rest assured, though, I will not agree to sit back and assume he knows what he's doing just because he knows livestock and can get two quarter horses to enter into coitus."

Lisa dragged her hands down her cheeks and looked at the ceiling. "Mom."

"I put up a lot of money for this business. Do you really think I'm going to allow myself to be cheated, taken advantage of?"

"Why on earth did you go into business with someone you don't know and don't seem to trust?"

"Because he presented me with a good idea, and he just needed an interested party to transform it into something profitable," Joan said. "And, hell, he seems to know quite a lot of people."

"Listen, I was glad to be rid of Chuck. Didn't think much of his character," Lisa said, looking down. She slid her hands in the back pockets of her jeans and looked up at Joan. "But Justin was always satisfied with him. And, you're right, Chuck does know a lot of people in Arkansas, Oklahoma, and Texas."

Joan stood up and walked over to the stove to turn on the gas under the tea kettle. Reservations about Chuck aside, she wanted, *needed*, to make her mark in this world, independent of her family of origin and their expectations, her ties to her late husband and his family's business, and her adult children's beliefs about who she should be and what she should do at this point in her life. Without turning to face Lisa, Joan said, "This is *my* business Lisa. It feels good to have something of my own."

Lisa inhaled deeply and slowly and exhaled. "Fine. I get it."

Joan swung around and bowed dramatically. "Thank you. Finally!"

"Oh, by the way, Bob called me," Lisa said. "He was kind of frustrated."

"Oh?" Joan was annoyed. *Why is Lisa the messenger?*

"He wants you to back off. Forget about expansions."

Joan resented Lisa for getting involved. *My children have never been in my corner.*

"Mom?"

Joan placed her hands on her hips. "There's potential here that shouldn't go by the wayside. And why doesn't Bob respect my experience and knowledge with this? He would've been fine with it if Dad were still around."

Lisa took a deep breath. "Look, it's not up to you. You have your new business. Bob is running the company. *His* company, and he has a vision for its future and prefers to start clean, I guess. You've got to let it go."

"And he can't call his mother and discuss this with me directly?" Joan asked, indignant.

"Maybe he feels bad and knows I can do a better job of getting the point across."

The tea kettle began to whistle, and Joan turned around to shut off the flame. She stood in silence for several moments, her arms stretched wide across the countertop.

"Hello in there? Anybody home?"

"I understand. I'll back off," she said without turning around. It was difficult to say these words, but she didn't need the hassle now.

Joan reached for a Brillo pad on the sink. She turned on the faucet to soak the pad with water, fixating on the sudsy froth as she squeezed the steel wool. She was stewing. After a moment, she dropped the pad into the sink and spun around to face Lisa. Now she was irate.

"You know, Lisa, your father and I provided the four of you with everything kids could possibly want: summer camp, trips to Florida, cruises, tennis lessons, ballet lessons, horseback riding lessons, new dresses for dances, college, a beautiful wedding. How many times did I take you and your sisters on cruises, just us girls, for any old reason? Getting good grades, making the tennis team, or just . . . because. And you've got yourself a pretty damned good life here," Joan said, sweeping both her hands around in the air. "You're doing your dream job, right? I mean, owning race horses, raising them on this

258 | *Eileen Brill*

lovely ranch here? Dammit, Lisa, you get to do what you want. It's my turn."

Lisa nodded.

Joan was at least relieved that her daughter was listening. "Anyway, I've made mistakes before," she said, laughing cynically. "And I'm still standing." She looked at her fingernails and picked at what remained of the chipped polish.

Lisa turned and headed toward the front door. "Good-night, Mom." She walked out, closing the door gently behind her.

Joan heard one of the horses whinnying in the barn. She lifted the typewriter off the table and stowed it in a kitchen cabinet. She straightened up the table, turned off the kitchen light, and headed to bed.

38

January 1970

JOAN AWOKE TO THE ALARM BUZZER AT FOUR FORTY-FIVE. Her plan was to shower, get dressed, and immediately hit the road for the long drive to Oklahoma. The weatherman on the eleven o'clock news had said it would be fifty-five today, certainly warmer than a winter day back in New Jersey, so she knew she'd be able to get by with a dark brown suede jacket and no gloves or hat.

She'd carefully chosen and laid out her outfit the night before; she needed to make the best first impression with her employees. She wanted to feel attractive and professional, but not too formal and certainly not too much like an outsider. It was of utmost importance to be taken seriously from the outset, to be in control. After showering and setting her hair, she put on a cream-colored, Diane Von Furstenberg scoop neck sweater and a blue silk scarf—intentionally the same blue as the color of the Oklahoma flag, and with a green pattern that mimicked the flag's olive branch—around her neck. It was another psychological trick she'd learned at the Strategies That Work seminar. This particular workshop described subtle ways to ensure people immediately like and trust you in a business environment.

She dusted her face with a little powder, put on some mascara and frost-colored eyeshadow, and headed downstairs to grab a thermos of coffee and one of Lisa's corn muffins.

When Chuck mentioned that he needed to spend the day in Fort Worth to visit his sister, Joan saw this as an opportunity to find an apartment and take care of some business. She made an appointment to see a one-bedroom unit in Midwest City, just outside of Oklahoma City. Following that, she needed to stop by the Barn and make her mark.

After a quick tour of the apartment, which still looked relatively new with freshly painted walls and clean carpeting, Joan put down a security deposit and the first and last month's rent. Though the building was modest by her standards, it was only two years old and had a central courtyard with a pool. And while she didn't envision herself lounging out there with her neighbors, she knew it would be an easy way to introduce herself and spread the word about the summer plan for Saturday night auction carnivals.

She looked at her watch: eleven forty-five. She was on schedule. She drove to Grady's Grocery and went directly to the deli counter. A girl who appeared to be no more than sixteen was behind the meat case.

"Hi there, ma'am. What can I help you with?"

"I'd like to order a tray of sandwiches and sides."

"You must be having some kind of party," the girl said.

"In a way," Joan said, eyeing the offerings in the refrigerated case.

She handed two dollars to each of the two boys who carried the food out to her car and loaded it in the back seat. They were clearly appreciative. Joan prided herself on her generosity.

Forty-five minutes later, Joan pulled into the parking lot at the Diamond Ranch Sale Barn. She noticed two Chevy pickup trucks, an old Buick Riviera and a beaten-up Mustang, all parked alongside the large barn. She got out of her car and smoothed her slacks against her legs. Leaving the food in her car, she walked over to one of the smaller barns, where she could see two men leaning against the large, open door. They were chatting and smoking, and as she neared the barn, Joan could hear more voices coming from inside. The men looked at her as she approached.

This is it, Joan. Your first impression with your employees. Make it work.

"Afternoon, gentlemen," she said with a broad smile.

"Help you, ma'am?" said the better-looking of the two men. He dropped his cigarette and stomped it out with the toe of his cowboy boot. The other man barely moved and took another drag of his cigarette, lowering his head and eying Joan's outfit.

"I'm Joan Dumann," she said, extending her hand. He shook it respectfully but seemed confused. She extended her hand to the other man, who put the cigarette on his lip and reluctantly shook her hand. "I'm Mr. Galloway's business partner," she said.

The two men looked at each other, seemingly baffled.

"Surely, you know he has a partner?"

"Well, I can't say Chuck ever mentioned it, but pleased to make your acquaintance, Mrs. Dumann," the nice-looking man said, tipping his hat. "I'm Roy Herbert; this here is Waylan Trust." Waylan nodded his head with a steely stare. "Chuck isn't here today. I think he drove down to Fort Worth to see his sister. Something we can help you with?" asked Roy.

"Yes, I was aware that he's out of town. I just wanted to come by and introduce myself, see how things are going. We're just a couple months out from the first auction, you know," she said, peering into the barn. She saw a couple of the men inside look up.

"Everything's comin' along just fine, Mrs. Dumann," said Waylan. "Chuck's got everythin' under control." His tone was filled with suspicion and condescension.

"Glad to hear it." Joan maintained a positive disposition. She was not about to allow Waylan to fluster her. "Have you gentlemen had lunch yet?" she asked. She pointed toward her car. "I've brought some food for all of you," she said, looking into the barn. "Wasn't quite sure how many people would be here today but there's plenty for seconds and even thirds. Or to take home to your families." Joan knew from what Chuck had told her that he had hired some temporary workers to help with repairs in and around the buildings. She walked between Roy and Waylan and called into the barn. "Anyone hungry, I got some sandwiches and potato salad." She turned to Waylan. "Can you help me get it out of my car, please?"

Waylan looked at Roy.

"Is no one hungry around here?" Joan asked with a smile, hands on her hips.

"Nice of you to bring lunch, ma'am," said a man emerging from inside the barn. He walked up to Joan and held out his hand. "Name's Bill Kind. I'll be one of the drivers when we're up and runnin'. For now, I'm a handyman, I suppose."

"Good to meet you, Bill. Shall we?" she said to the men. The three followed her to her car. She opened the door and handed them the two trays of sandwiches and a bag with containers of side dishes. She walked with them back to the barn. "I've not eaten lunch myself, so I think I'll join you fellows," she said.

In the barn, Joan introduced herself to six more men, all of whom were temporary workers doing repairs or running errands or moving equipment. There was a large, wooden table with several metal folding chairs. Joan noticed a few opened beer cans on the table, crushed cigarettes on the floor of the barn, and several hammers, saws, and brooms scattered about. She grabbed a rag, dusted off one of the chairs, and took a seat. The men sat down all around her and began grabbing sandwiches and opening containers. Joan had brought a package of plastic utensils and napkins with her from home.

"Oh," she said, snapping her fingers. "Almost forgot. I've got bottles of Coke in my car as well." She stood up to go to her car, and Roy stood up as well.

"I'll give you a hand there, Mrs. Dumann," he said.

As they walked to her car, Roy said, "I don't know why Chuck didn't mention he had a partner, but I hope you won't take offense at that. I don't think he meant to leave you out of anything. Probably just scramblin' like crazy, tryin' to get everything runnin'. Do you live around here?"

"I'll be moving up here soon, from Little Rock," she said as she opened her trunk. "And don't worry, Roy," she said, gently touching his forearm. "Everything's great between Chuck and me, I assure you. Most business partnerships involve one person who's the day-to-day manager, the one who everyone reports to, more like a figurehead. And then there's one who does more of the long-term strategic planning and financial management. In this case, Chuck's the former, and I'm the latter," she said. She pretended to whisper secretly to Roy. "I shouldn't admit it, but I'm a bit older than Chuck, so no surprise I have more business experience."

Roy removed a large crate filled with glass bottles of Coke.

"This'll last us a month," he said.

Joan sat with the men for almost an hour. She asked questions about Oklahoma City, Shawnee, and Midwest City. She mentioned, several times, that her family owned an industrial flooring company back East that she helped run, and the men wanted to know about Dumann Paving and life on the East Coast. One of the men noticed her scarf.

"May I ask where you bought that scarf? My wife would love it. Kinda resembles our flag, you know?" he said looking around at the guys. He turned back to Joan. "Junie, she's pure Oklahoman, born and bred."

Joan untied the scarf and removed it from her neck. "Well, then, here you go," she said, handing it to him.

"Oh, ma'am, I couldn't—"

"Nonsense, I got a hundred scarves I don't wear. Wrap it up nicely. Say 'Junie, this is from Joanie, a brand-new Oklahoman to a native-born Oklahoman,' and tell her I look forward to meeting her soon." Joan took a sip from her bottle of Coke and sat back, satisfied. The men chuckled, all except for Waylan, who took a long puff on his cigarette and eyed Joan, expressionless. She returned his stare and managed a smile, though she did feel unsettled by him. She could tell he would be difficult, a challenge, but she would not be broken by a scraggly, impertinent barn boy.

"Well, gentlemen, it has been an absolute pleasure chatting with all of you. I'll be back and forth between here and Little Rock for the next several weeks. In the meantime, you're in good hands with my partner." As she stood up, all of the men did as well. Waylan slowly rose to his feet, dropped his cigarette on the floor, and crushed it with his boot.

As she cleared her place at the table, Joan took in a chorus of appreciation from her employees. One by one, each of the men, except for Waylan, walked away from the table to resume their work, and Joan headed to her car, satisfied that she had accomplished her mission: these men liked her and probably respected her as well. There was something chilling about Waylan, but Joan reminded herself of something else she learned at the Strategies That Work seminar: a simple acronym QTIP—Quit Taking It Personally. Some people automatically distrust outsiders and often it just takes a lot of time and patience to win them over.

39

April 1970

JOAN STOOD BEHIND A LONG TABLE ON WHICH SEVERAL cartons of donuts and large urns of coffee were set up for attendees of the first registered horse auction of the Diamond Ranch Sale Barn. The line for the food went out the door, the bleachers were filling up, and the parking area was already filled to capacity, even though the Barn had only been open for a half hour.

"Here," Joan said, handing a ten-dollar bill to Roy's teenaged son. "Run down the road to the big old farmhouse and ask the couple if we can use the field immediately adjacent to their home for spillover parking."

"Wow! Sure thing, Mrs. Dumann."

"Excuse me, ma'am," said a large man in a thick, suede coat. "This all free?" he asked, waving his hand across the table.

"Yes, sir," Joan replied. She extended her hand. "Name's Joan Dumann. I'm one of the owners of the Sale Barn. Thank you for coming today. Grab a donut and some coffee. We'll be starting the first auction in about twenty minutes."

The morning was already exceeding Joan and Chuck's expectations for their first event. Regardless of whether people showed up for the free concessions or the discounted opening-day commission, both of which were Joan's ideas, or because of the name recognition of Diamond Ranch Sale Barn, there was a large crowd buzzing with excitement. Joan took it all in, scanning the faces in the bleachers and watching handlers moving horses around the ring. She had to smile. *I made all this happen.*

She'd shaken quite a few hands and introduced herself repeatedly since deciding to help man the tables with Roy's son and one of the Barn employees, but the hospitality had served its purpose for now. She needed to redirect her energy. She excused herself, giving full responsibility for the food distribution to the young Barn employee, and went to search for Chuck.

Minutes later, she found him by the PA system, talking to the auctioneer, a man by the name of Dexter Daulton.

"So I'm thinkin', let me make the first announcement, I'll welcome the crowd to the Barn, et cetera, et cetera, introduce myself, and then introduce you," Chuck said to Dexter. "You'll explain the rules of the auction, how to bid, where to pick up an auction ticket, you know, case there's actually anyone here who don't understand auctions, right?" He laughed, elbowing Dexter.

Joan cleared her throat.

"Uh, yeah, Dexter, I'd like to introduce you to Joan Dumann, my, uh . . ."

"Partner," Joan said, extending her hand to Dexter.

"Of course, yeah, my partner, here at Diamond Ranch," Chuck said, adjusting his hat and scratching his neck.

"Pleased to meet you, ma'am," Dexter said.

"Likewise, Dexter," she said. "Oh, and Chuck. How about you and I both go to the mic and introduce ourselves?"

"Yes, yes, certainly, Joan. Didn't mean to leave you out, just wasn't sure how comfortable you feel in front of crowds," he replied, placing a patronizing hand on her shoulder. Joan let it go. She was in too good a mood to let something trivial upset her.

"Excuse me," Dexter said to both of them. "I'm just gonna grab a cup of coffee and a donut before we get started. I think we got everything worked out on my end. Nice to meet you, Joan—look forward to workin' with you." He tipped his hat and walked away.

"Quite a crowd," Joan said, looking around. "We should probably close the doors soon. Not much space left in the bleachers."

Chuck nodded.

"We're good with the PA system?" she asked him.

"Yep. We tested it earlier," Chuck said.

"Okay, then." Joan noticed that almost all the men in the crowd were wearing cowboy hats of one kind or another. She suddenly wished she had thought to purchase one before the first auction, so that she could put herself on equal standing, visually, with Chuck.

The young guy working the PA system switched on a button, and music began to play through the speakers set up all around the barn.

"Ready to go?" Chuck said to Joan. He extended his arm and allowed her to walk to the center of the barn first.

She took a deep breath and was aware of her heart beating forcefully. She had to admit that she was actually nervous about this, not because crowds intimidated her but because she hadn't prepared, hadn't expected to make a statement. She walked slowly to the center, Chuck just behind her. There was a microphone on a stand. When she got to it, she saw it was set much too high for her to speak into, and she struggled with adjusting it. She was embarrassed at how awkward she felt.

Chuck moved in to help. He lifted the mic out of the stand, flicked on the switch, and spoke into it.

"Ladies and Gentlemen," he began. "My name is Chuck Galloway and this here is my partner, Mrs. Joan Dumann." He held on to the mic.

Joan waved to the crowd and smiled. But she was seething inside; she had wanted to make the first introduction.

"Welcome to the first ever registered horse auction of the Diamond Ranch Sale Barn!" he said enthusiastically. The crowd cheered and clapped. "Joan and I are thrilled to see so many faces here today, some old friends and some who, we're hopeful, will become new friends. Now, we hope you've all enjoyed some coffee and donuts, and we're gonna get started in just a minute." He paused to mouth something to Dexter, who was standing off to the side.

Joan gently took the microphone from his hands. "I've met quite a few of you this morning already," she said, "but please feel free to come over to me or my partner here at any point today, and let us know what you think. We want this auction barn to meet your needs and provide the highest level of service, whether you're looking to buy or sell." She waved, smiled again, and handed the microphone back to Chuck. She did not get much of a response from the crowd. Maybe it was her accent. Or lack thereof.

"All righty, well, it's time to introduce our auctioneer, who most of you probably know. Ladies and gentlemen, Mr. Dexter Daulton."

The crowd applauded enthusiastically. Joan headed off to the side, where a young quarter horse was waiting with a handler to walk into the ring. She chatted with the handler about the horse and gave the animal a soft scratch on the nose. Touching the animal, feeling his breath near her shoulder, smelling the manure—all this was familiar and gave her that wonderfully visceral feeling that conjured up childhood memories of Ivyland.

As Dexter was explaining the rules of bidding, Chuck approached Joan.

"Just a small piece of advice, Joan," he said quietly.

She steeled herself.

"You gotta be just a little less formal, you know what I mean?"

"Formal?" she asked. His advice was unsolicited and unwanted.

"Yeah. 'We want to provide the highest level of service,'" he said. "Sounds like something you read in a newspaper advertisement. I'm just tryin' to ease you into the way we do things around here."

"Well, I think it's important to speak to people with respect and to show that you're intelligent. What did you want me to say? 'Hey y'all. Thanks fer comin' by today. Swing on by later and let us know how we're doin', all right? Yee-haw!'" she said in a southern twang.

Chuck pursed his lips together and furrowed his brow. He looked insulted.

"I'm sorry," she said. "That was uncalled for on my part. I appreciate your advice, Chuck. Thanks." She didn't want his advice, though it was not her intention to hurt his feelings. She had lowered herself with her childish mockery.

"No hard feelings on my end, Joan," Chuck said with a smile.

The success of their first auction was electrifying to Joan, and she gained a new-found respect for her partner. She had not realized until this point the extent of Chuck's familiarity with the business of buying and selling thoroughbred horses or coordinating an auction, and she had underestimated the value of his connection to these kinds of people. She observed him throughout the morning, chatting with customers, addressing their concerns, name-dropping. He was quick with terminology that was new to her: a bucket-broke calf, polled livestock, a wether, a barrow. She made mental notes to look up these terms. Whatever negative associations people in Little Rock had with his name, in and around Shawnee, Oklahoma, folks were glad to shoot the crap with him, and she realized his value to the business.

Ten days later, on the evening of their first livestock auction, Joan observed a dramatic change in Chuck's manner.

"Listen, Joan, if you don't mind, I was wonderin' if you would take the mic tonight and do the intro announcements," he said.

"Of course, happy to," she said. "Can I ask why? You seemed very comfortable last time."

"I think it's good for people to get to know you. You're still new in these parts."

He seemed sincere, and she relished the opportunity to stand before the crowd without Chuck.

Later in the evening, he pulled her over to introduce her to a couple of the cattle farmers he knew from Arkansas, men who were expected to make some large purchases.

"Mrs. Joan Dumann," he said. "This is Lenny Watt and John Marsden. These guys have ranches that make my uncle's dairy farm look no bigger than a postage stamp."

"Pleasure," she said. Tonight, she was wearing a long, buttoned, denim skirt, embroidered cowboy boots, and her new brown, wool cowboy hat, its floral headband matching the colors of her button-down blouse. She needed to dress the part during auctions, but what would her friends back in New Jersey think of her fashion choice?

As the event came to a close and the last of the cars drove away, Joan observed Chuck from across the auction floor talking with the auction coordinator, a young man by the name of Zak Henley. It was Zak's job to keep a journal of all transactions, to record the bids and register all sales information. He would produce a sales ticket for each animal and give it to the successful bidder as proof of the transaction. Each morning after an auction, it would be Zak's responsibility to pass the journal on to Edie Holbrook, the accounting manager, who would procure payments from buyers and record payments received. But her responsibility went only as far as the activity at the auctions. The general accounting of the business—paying rent and other bills, purchasing equipment and supplies, writing paychecks— would be the responsibility of Ernest Walls, whom Joan had lured away from his accounting position at a feed store outside of Little Rock. She had liked Ernest immediately and could tell he was bright and detail-oriented.

As Joan watched Chuck and Zak chat, she knew it had been a good night based on the way Chuck affectionately slapped Zak on the back several times as Zak enthusiastically pointed to various pages in the ledger. Zak closed the ledger and handed it to Chuck, who shook Zak's hand, waved good-night to him, and headed over to Joan.

"What a night! Can you believe how many bids went out for the cows and calves? Never seen anything like it," Chuck said with the biggest smile she'd ever seen on him. He came so close that she worried he was going to lift her up, so to prevent this she turned her entire body sideways and waved toward the bleachers for emphasis.

"Quite unbelievable," she said. "I must say, Chuck, you know a lot of folks around here. All night long, I watched people come up to you, shake your hand, congratulate you. Gotta give you credit."

"Well, yeah, okay. But I'll give credit where it's due, you helped bring 'em in too." He extended his hand. She shook it, and this time, Joan felt it was the firm, respectable shake from a businessman who valued his partner. She saw him making an effort at equalizing their relationship, and she was optimistic and confident.

The following morning, Joan and Chuck met at Freida's Country Diner to review how the first auction went, prepare for the next one, and discuss long-term needs and modifications.

"Maybe we should limit the Saturday night auctions until we are more settled," Joan said, slicing into her chocolate chip pancakes. She expressed to Chuck her concerns about a business growing too fast and moving too quickly on hiring additional employees.

But Chuck was more eager. "Spend more to make more. We did better than expected, right? These registered horse sales are where the money is." Chuck lifted his coffee cup as if it were a bottle of Coke, wrapping his fingers and thumb around it and chugging the liquid.

Joan made a face.

He put the cup down and raised his arm to his mouth, about to wipe with the back of his sleeve; then he corrected himself and picked up a napkin. He told Joan he was confident that people would keep coming to the auctions, that Oklahomans wanted to keep business in Oklahoma and not go elsewhere to buy and sell horses and livestock. He talked up the social aspect of the auctions. He wanted to charge more for the auction catalogs, set higher commission rates. On and on.

Joan sensed some condescension on Chuck's part, but she had to acknowledge to herself that he seemed to understand the business. She knew what the going commission rates were for auction houses, though she realized her overall knowledge base was limited. She sat back and remained quiet. She let him talk.

After an hour or so, they agreed on the need to buy a larger horse trailer and another section of bleachers. Joan asked Chuck to price those things out, and she would ask Ernest to cut some checks.

Chuck bit off a piece of bacon. He was quiet. Then he asked, "You like that Ernest?"

"Why, sure. I hired him. He gets to work early every day, stays a full eight, nine hours, sometimes longer. Very detail-oriented. Nice guy." She looked sideways at Chuck. "Is there a reason I shouldn't like him?"

Chuck shrugged his shoulders. "Ah, no, I guess not. Just . . . just seems a little shifty, if you ask me."

"Shifty? I don't get that at all from him. In what way?"

"I don't know. But, sometimes, you just get a *feelin'* about a person. Body language an' all."

Joan watched Chuck push eggs, bacon, and home fries into his mouth in one large forkful. He picked up his napkin and wiped his mouth.

"If you see or notice anything specific, be sure to let me know." She said this to Chuck as a formality; she saw nothing in Ernest that seemed disreputable. "And since we're on the subject of employees, I just need to mention to you that I have some concerns about Waylan," she said while fishing in her purse for her Virginia Slims; she wasn't having any luck quitting. She pulled out the pack and tweezed out a cigarette with her freshly painted fingernails.

Chuck reached into the back pocket of his jeans, pulled out a lighter, flipped it open, and offered her the flame.

"Thanks," she said. She took a long puff and blew out the smoke to the side.

"Waylan? What's he up to now? Did he forget again to muck the stables last Thursday? I need to have a talk with him."

"No, that's not the problem." She leaned forward on her elbows. "He's extremely disrespectful." She eyed her cigarette. "I wouldn't ordinarily get you involved. This is the kind of thing I like to handle on my own."

"Disrespectful? Well, I don't like to hear that." His words were fine but his tone was blasé. Chuck opened a new pack of Marlboros.

"I'm not sure he takes me seriously, and I need to nip this in the bud, so to speak. I cannot, *will* not tolerate impudence. He'd better watch himself."

Chuck pushed his lower lip out and up. He nodded slowly.

Joan continued. "I'll have a talk with him and let him know specifically what I'm displeased with, but that will be it. There will be no second chances."

"Well, Joan, you gotta do what you gotta do. We have to feel like family at Diamond Ranch, right? There's gotta be trust, admiration, support, respect. From the bottom to the top."

"You're saying all the right things, but I'm having a hard time believing your sincerity." She sat back with a bended arm holding her cigarette. She had presented her case.

"Well, Joan, I'll tell you, I've known Waylan goin' on three years, and he's never struck me as a bad guy. Sure, he's a little rough around the edges. He's never been out of Oklahoma, for Chrissake!"

"Well, that's no excuse." She wiped coffee off the table and put the wet napkin on her plate.

"You know, more I think about it . . . maybe you should let me talk to him. Now, I know you've got your women's lib and all, but he's the type of guy who speaks one language: man-talk." Chuck laughed at his joke.

Joan tried to give him her best stone-faced stare.

"I'm sorry, Joan. I don't mean to offend. Just . . . just let me have a one-on-one with Waylan. I'm sure I can straighten everything out."

"Fine. I certainly don't need to waste my time. But I'll be keeping my eye on him nevertheless." Joan looked at her watch. "Oh, ten thirty. I should get going. I've got a meeting with the sound guy, the one putting in the new PA system." She took a final swig of her coffee, which had gone cold.

The waitress brought over the check, and Joan went to pick it up, but Chuck grabbed it quickly. He looked at it and put down what Joan felt was a miserly tip. Standing up, he winked at the young waitress walking by. Joan reached into her pocket and threw two extra dollars on top of Chuck's tip when he wasn't looking.

As they walked out together, Joan heard him ask for a receipt at the cash register, and she looked at him quizzically.

He pointed to his head. "Tax purposes. Business deduction, you know."

40

JOAN PARKED IN THE SMALL LOT ADJACENT TO THE SAVINGS and Loan of Midwest City. She fished in her purse for lipstick, lowered the sun visor, applied a nice, subdued mauve to her lips, and blotted the color a bit with a tissue. Then she got out of her car and made her way into the office of Mr. Weston Sacks, the bank manager with whom she and Chuck had met two weeks earlier to apply for a business loan for some large, unforeseen expenditures.

She had not expected the curveball he would throw her.

"After you and Mr. Galloway initially came into the bank," he said shortly after Joan made herself comfortable in the chair in front of his desk, "I made some phone calls down to Little Rock, got some information from TransUnion too. I don't know how to put this . . . as your business partner, Mr. Galloway is no asset to your loan application, I'm afraid." He shuffled through some papers, noting each financial demerit. "He defaulted on a personal loan in sixty-eight . . . very little in the way of savings . . . one credit card with a maximum balance . . ."

So those are the nuts and bolts of it. Joan knew Chuck did not have a sound financial record but she had not been aware of the details.

". . . that went unpaid for months." He suddenly looked up at Joan. "I probably shouldn't be sharing all that with you."

"I completely understand your concerns regarding Mr. Galloway, and I certainly would not want to enter into a relationship with SLMC without your full confidence." She paused. "However, I'm sure you've found my credit and financial situation to be solid."

She watched Sacks push aside Chuck's information and review papers with Joan's name. She gave him a minute. Then she continued.

"When my husband died two years ago, I had such a good relationship with our local bank that the manager vouched for me so that I could obtain my own Diner's Club card and Carte Blanche. My credit is impeccable."

He adjusted his reading glasses. "Yes, I do see that. And you've got a nice income from your late husband's insurance policy . . . some annuities . . . income from Dumann Paving and Flooring, profit sharing." He looked at her, lowered his reading glasses. "This is your company?" he asked.

"It is. Well it *was*. My husband was the president until he turned it over to my son, Bob. It's a family business." Joan felt uncomfortable saying all this out loud. She had gone from being an integral part of the company to feeling like persona non grata in just over two years.

"I want to help you out, Mrs. Dumann, I really do. It's just that Mr. Galloway is a bit of a . . . *liability*."

"Well, I am *not* a liability. I provided most of the financing for Diamond Ranch," she said proudly.

Sacks touched his fingertips together, nodded, and leaned in toward her, as if he were sharing a secret. "If we were talking about a personal loan for you, I'd approve it, no question."

Joan understood. She was thinking, trying to move the process along. *He needs some kind of assurance. Some kind of collateral.*

And then it hit her.

"Would you consider using my home as collateral?" she asked.

"Oh, do you own real estate here?"

"Not here. In Arkansas. Little Rock. I had a lovely ranch house built last year."

He sat back in his chair. "That certainly would help. We'd need an appraisal of the house and land immediately surrounding it. Oh, and the deed, naturally."

The deed. This was problematic. "Yes, the deed. Of course."

They spent a few more minutes discussing the timeline for processing the application and concluded with some pleasantries, after which Joan stood up and reached out her hand.

"I look forward to a mutually beneficial relationship, Mr. Sacks," she said with a confident smile.

When Joan submitted the completed loan application a week later to Weston Sacks, she included the full appraisal she had been given immediately following the completion of construction.

"Looks like everything's in order here, good, good," Mr. Sacks said. "But, I don't see the deed." He looked at her. "You can submit a photocopy, that's fine. We don't need to see the original deed."

Joan told Sacks that the deed was in her safe in Little Rock and she had no idea when she might be able to get down there. She requested that he begin the approval process, and she promised to get the deed to him as soon as she could. He agreed to get the ball rolling, saying he was confident there would not be an issue.

Two days later, as she was getting ready to head to the Barn, she received a call from the bank.

"Hello, Joan, it's Weston Sacks from SLMC. How are you this morning?"

"I'm doing quite well, Weston," she said. "Just about to head to work. I hope you're calling with some good news."

"In fact, I do have good news. We've approved your business loan. You were right: your credit is excellent; your references check out. Your home is appropriately valued to use as collateral. Now, just as soon as I have a copy of the deed in my possession, I can initiate the loan, even get the money right into your business account here."

That damned deed! "Weston, I've been so crazy with everything going on, I'd completely forgotten to mention that I had to request a correction on the deed a couple months ago. You see, there was an error, nothing serious, just a spelling error, and I've been waiting for the corrected deed to arrive. These administrative things take months. I'm sure you can appreciate my situation. But you've got the appraisal on the house and land, so you know what it's worth. I even gave you my construction costs, so you can see I financed the house. Seems like the deed is more of a formality."

"Actually, a bank cannot take as collateral property for which the owner has not been legally verified. Can you imagine what would happen if someone defaulted on a loan, and the collateralized property was not owned by the borrower?"

Joan's stomach tightened. She was losing patience and trying to think fast.

He continued. "But I understand your predicament. It's frustrating, I'm sure. If you can provide the parcel number, the bank can do a title search. We just need to confirm that you are the owner. I mean, I, personally, believe you; it has nothing to do with that."

"I understand, of course." She looked at her watch. "I'm afraid I need to run now. I'll be in touch in a day or two; will that be all right?" she asked.

"Absolutely, Joan. I'm here for you."

I'm here for you. She could take advantage of him if she chose to, she was certain. She knew how to manipulate people, especially men. She'd figured that out a long time ago. "Have a good day, Weston."

"Okay, Joan. I look forward to hearing back from you."

She hung up the phone and paced around her living room. She felt like canceling the loan application and telling Chuck they needed to forgo additional expenditures for the time being. She could tell him that his poor credit was the reason they could not get approval on the business loan. She would put the blame squarely on him, be done with this fiasco, and not have to face the uncomfortable scrutiny of Westin Sacks or, worse, Lisa's harsh judgment and anger.

She stepped into her barn boots, grabbed her purse, and headed to Diamond Ranch.

"Good news, Joan," Weston told her on the telephone in late August. "I went ahead and contacted the county for you and obtained the ownership information I needed. So you're all set, congratulations!"

"You . . . got a copy of the deed?" she asked. She was relieved, yet also confused and a tad nervous.

"Yes, got a copy, and it's on file in my office. Is that okay? I hope you don't mind that I took the liberty of following through for you. I know how busy you are, and I actually have a friend in the Registry of Deeds office, so it was no problem getting the info. And, you were right, they still hadn't corrected the spelling error, so I let them know that your last name has two Ns, not one. You should be getting the amended deed in a month or so."

Joan was dumbfounded. Somehow, the deed had erroneously

been recorded with incorrect owner information. Somewhere along the line, a lawyer or the county registrar or a lower-level administrative employee had made a terrible mistake. Thankfully, Lisa and Justin were evidently oblivious to the whereabouts of the deed. But, unless or until the Hepps began to wonder about that, Joan could push this matter to the back burner for now. Diamond Ranch had its additional financing in place.

41

Early December

JOAN SAT IN HER APARTMENT ON A CHILLY MORNING, drinking her customary mug of Sanka and picking at an Entenmann's coffee cake. Her mind was ablaze thinking about a conversation she'd had with Ernest three weeks earlier, when he had stopped by her apartment unexpectedly one Saturday morning to express concerns about Chuck.

"I can't be certain; I just have a gut feeling," he said to Joan. "I'm unable to reconcile the numbers."

He went on to describe checks made out to unknown individuals and entities since August.

Initially, each time he came across a check signed personally by Chuck and with a mysterious payee, he would ask Chuck about it. Chuck would typically brush off the inquiry and claim that he had bought used equipment, such as a commercial freezer for ice cream for the fairgrounds, directly from a seller, or paid a subcontractor to drive in a large herd of cattle from a longer distance. But when there was no physical evidence of any of these transactions, Ernest became uneasy about his interactions with Chuck. "I don't think it's my accounting, Mrs. Dumann."

"I'm sure it's not your accounting, Ernest," Joan said, taking a puff of her cigarette and touching his shoulder for reassurance. "Just the fact that you've come to me today, speaking in confidence, makes me certain that you're doing your job correctly and ethically."

"I don't want to point fingers at your business partner. But, we're talking several thousand dollars that I can't account for, missing since . . . well, since your loan was approved," he said. His face was tight with anguish. "And then there's money that went into his account alone, not split between yours and his, you know, with the right percentages and all."

Joan told Ernest she wanted to review the books with him the following Monday, when Chuck would be out of town for the day.

She pushed aside the coffee cake and took a swig of Sanka, looking out of the window toward the courtyard of the complex. In the distance, she could see the swimming pool, where months earlier excited children had played and splashed and laughed in the sun until dark, their voices coming into her apartment on the summer afternoons she'd left the barn early. She'd gotten to know the crew who mowed the lawn and did the landscaping at the complex, and the two young guys who cleaned the pool. They all liked her, she could tell. She'd given them all sorts of freebies: passes to the private auctions, movie theatre gift certificates, cases of Coke and sometimes Budweiser. She'd recruited three of the younger ones to work weekends cleaning up after the auctions, and she'd paid them generously.

Her employees liked her as well. She'd once given Roy two hundred dollars in cash, on the spot, when he had mentioned that his daughter needed orthodontia and he had no idea how he would pay for it, and had gifted Edie an expensive Yves St. Laurent dress that no longer fit her because Edie was going to a cocktail affair in Oklahoma City and had nothing to wear.

The only person who had an ax to grind with Joan and had no misgivings about showing his dislike was Waylan. From the day they met, Joan and Waylan had a mutual distrust, and she learned early on that spending time and effort to try to put him in his place was fruitless. She was quite sure Chuck had never had that talk with Waylan regarding respect and deference toward one's superior.

Throughout the late summer and fall, she had noticed how upbeat Chuck was, how respectfully he treated her. She assumed he was pleased about how well the auctions were going; she was as well. But, perhaps it was more than that. *Was he just trying to keep me at bay, to not arouse suspicion?*

The Sanka tasted bitter, so she stirred in more sugar. She thought about her grandchildren, all seven of them, and her adult children. Joan and Bob seldom spoke anymore; he always seemed preoccupied and short on patience when it came to telephone calls. His children, five and seven years old, had seen Joan frequently when they were younger and lived five miles from Joan and Kyle, but now they spent holidays with Bob's wife's parents in New York.

It had been even longer since Joan had seen Gwen's four-year-old, who'd been a baby the last time Joan spent time with her, when Kyle was still alive and everything seemed like it made sense, when Joan's life revolved around twice-yearly cruises and dinners at the club and biweekly meetings with the staff at Dumann Paving and visits from her grandchildren during holidays. She became wistful. *What am I doing here?*

She wondered if Lizzie and Shawn had enjoyed their summer. Though Lisa had come by herself to an auction back in May, she kept promising Joan she would bring the kids to one of the Saturday night auctions in June or July.

"I'm sorry Mom, but Justin and I are in the middle of all kinds of repairs on the property," Lisa had told her, "plus the construction of another stable. Shawn's got the 4H and baseball, Lizzie has Girl Scouts. It's just not feasible at the moment."

By midsummer, it had become clear to Joan that Lisa, Justin, and the kids would not be visiting any time soon.

Joan took one more swig of coffee and reached for a cigarette. She lit it, took a puff, and picked up the phone to call her eldest. She immediately felt calmer once she heard her daughter's lovely voice. "Hi, Barb, did I catch you at a bad time?"

"Oh, hey, Mom. No, it's fine. I was just paying some bills, but I can take a break for a few minutes. How's everything?"

"Super! I'm busy, for sure, but things are going well. Our summer fairground auctions were very successful. Wish you'd been able to bring the kids out. They would've loved it."

"They probably would have. I don't know where the summer went."

"It's okay. Maybe you'll make it out here for the holidays. How are the kids doing anyway? I haven't heard from the three of them for so long. No letters, nothing."

"Didn't Marie send you a thank you card for the birthday check? I swore she wrote it and put it in the mail."

"She did, yes. I hope she did something special with the money. Sweet sixteen, that's a special occasion," Joan said. "I wish I could've been there to celebrate."

"She had quite a party. Fourteen girls and ten boys in a private room at the club. I'll send you a photo once they're developed."

"I'd like that."

Joan missed Barbara, the most sensitive and, often, the most rational of her children. She was always the one with whom Joan could have hour-long conversations or watch reruns of *Twilight Zone* over a bowl of popcorn. Bob was dependable, tolerant and fair, much like Kyle, but the business had consumed him ever since he took over. Lisa was opinionated, confident, and vocal, and, though she reached out to Joan more than the others, she and Joan often disagreed on many topics, and their discussions could get heated. Gwen was a free spirit, very involved with her two small children and husband and life in Florida, not very interested in committing to family reunions, and certainly not interested in catching up with her mother.

"So have you spoken to Franklin—sorry, to your father, lately?" Joan understood, ever since Barbara headed off for her freshman year at Vassar College, that Franklin was to be referred to as Barbara's father, not Franklin, except when in the company of Kyle.

"Yes, as a matter of fact. He came out here for Marie's party. His first time in California."

Joan tried to suppress her envy. "Well, that's nice. I'm sure he enjoyed seeing his grandchildren and spending time in LA."

"Mm-hmm, I think he did. They loved seeing him too." She paused. "So you're a real career woman, Mom. Good for you! I'm . . . really proud of you."

"Thanks. But it's not like this is my first time as a working woman. I mean, yes, it's a brand-new business, a totally different field than manufacturing and sales, you know. But I really took to this. I think it was meant to be."

"Oh, yeah, sure. But, I mean, this is your own thing. It's not like you're someone's side-kick, you know. It's your stand-alone business."

"You seem like you're discounting what I did at Dumann. What I did with Dad—Kyle, I mean." Joan was becoming agitated. "Oh, for god's sake, Barb, why do we have to refer to him as *Kyle*? He was your father."

"First of all, I'm not discounting anything. I just mean . . . dammit, you know what I mean, Mom. I'm telling you I'm proud of you, I think it's fantastic what you're doing out there, and you're just looking to start something with me."

"No, no I am *not* trying to start anything. It's hurtful to me that you call Franklin your father when he wasn't involved much in your childhood."

"I cannot believe we are having an argument about this. I loved Dad! There, I called him Dad. Kyle Dumann was my dad, my daddy, my father. Are you happy? Jesus, why is every telephone call these days an argument with you about semantics?"

Joan took a deep breath. She regretted going down the path of indignation, but she couldn't stop. "When I was a young mother, I didn't have the opportunities that mothers have now. I wanted a job, not a *career* necessarily, but a job, something to break up the monotony of being at home with a baby. I've told you about the church, haven't I?"

"Many times, yes."

"It's just," Joan took a long drag of her cigarette and exhaled. "I'm doing something so huge now, so outside of where I come from, and none of my children, except for Lisa, seem interested in supporting this endeavor. And even her interest is questionable. I don't feel like any of you take me seriously. And we are all so scattered. Gwen's down in Florida, you're in LA, Bob's back in New Jersey. And, speaking of Bob, I tried to get him out here on business to install cement flooring for the animal pens. Don't you think Steri-Stone would make sense here?" Joan was out of breath. Her brain seemed to be running at a hundred miles an hour. Why was she blabbering on and on like this about something so unimportant, when what she really wanted—*needed*—to discuss, the one thing weighing on her mind, was her business partner.

"Regarding Steri-Stone, I wouldn't know. Seems like something to discuss with Bob. And why are we wasting our precious telephone time, not to mention your long-distance bill, on all that?"

"I don't know. I'm just so . . . tired. This is wearing me down."

"What is?"

"This business."

"I thought you said you're enjoying it. I'm confused."

"I am. It's thrilling. I've met so many interesting people. And I love being around the animals, the horses. It's a very lucrative business, these thoroughbreds. Lisa can tell you, they can make you a mint if you know what you're doing."

"But?"

"Oh, it's just my business partner. You know, partnerships can be tricky. Personalities, all that. I won't bother you with it now. We've already spent too much time on negative subjects. I'm sorry. I just miss you, Barbara."

"It's okay, Mom. I get it. I . . . miss you too. Maybe . . . maybe you'll come out here when things slow down there in Oklahoma. Can you take time away?"

Joan thought about it. It wasn't an impossibility. Getting out of town for five days to a week would be possible, depending on the time of year. The question was more whether or not she was comfortable leaving things in Chuck's unmonitored hands for that long, given what Ernest had told her.

But she could not explain this to her daughter. Not yet. Not until Joan knew exactly what she was talking about.

"I'll think about it," Joan said. "Give Marie, John, and Stephanie a kiss and hug from Mom-Mom. I love you, sweetheart."

"Love you too, Mom. Thanks for calling."

Joan hung up the phone and sat back on her desk chair as she absorbed the overwhelming loneliness that had rushed through her the moment she heard the voice of her eldest daughter on the line. For many years following their move back to New Jersey from Phoenix, Joan had faulted herself for wanting to move to Arizona in the first place. Joan fully believed that, had they not moved out West, her relationship with Barbara would be solid. Barbara would never have had the opportunity to get to know Franklin as well as she ultimately did; she would not have chosen to embrace Quakerism; she would not have attended an elite, liberal arts college, spending the trust fund left to her by Marcus on a post-secondary education where she earned a BA in literature; she would not have met her future husband, a West Point graduate, and moved to California, and raised a family there; but most importantly, in Joan's mind, she and Barbara would not have grown apart emotionally. And now Barbara had three well-behaved, bright, kind children who barely knew their maternal grandmother. It was one of a small handful of regrets Joan allowed herself to experience from time to time before tucking them back into her subconscious and telling herself that few people have ever truly understood or appreciated Joan Sondersohn Dumann.

42

JOAN AND ERNEST SPENT NEARLY FIVE HOURS BEHIND closed doors reviewing transactional information and accounting records. She could clearly see where Ernest's calculations fell short and, in each case, the problems came down to unexplained expenditures on checks signed by Chuck, as well as missing cash, over ten thousand dollars, from the safe in the barn.

"Now, we made some large purchases since August, including converting the little barn," Ernest said, referring to the smallest of the three buildings, which had been made into an auction site for private auctions, with theatre-style, flip-up seats and insulation. "But, every purchase, large or small, every contractor who was paid, I recorded in the ledger. It just doesn't explain the outstanding losses."

"Tell me about the evening and weekend auctions. What happens with the payments we receive outside of bank hours?" she asked.

"Checks or cash from sales, and also cash from concessions, go into the safe until the next business morning. Zak's responsible for that. Then, next business day, I, or sometimes Edie, deposit it at SLMC," he explained.

Joan felt moderately embarrassed that she didn't know this protocol. She noticed Ernest looking off to the side, as if trying to figure something out.

"What is it?" she asked him.

"Oh, probably nothing. I was just remembering there were a

few times Chuck said he was going to handle the deposit himself. And then, whenever I'd ask him for the receipt from the deposit, he'd have some excuse."

Joan wondered if Chuck was taking a larger percentage of the profits than he was allowed based on their partnership agreement.

"This was extremely helpful, Ernest," she said as she gathered the ledgers, bank statements, canceled checks, and miscellaneous notes. She could see stress on Ernest's face. "Don't worry. You've done the right thing," she said, trying to sound reassuring.

Joan spent December through March mimeographing checks and ledger entries at the library, tracking down payees in local and out-of-state telephone books, keeping records and a paper trail, making notes of her conversations with Chuck, and generally building her case against him.

The moment of truth happened unexpectedly late one evening in early April when she was at the Barn returning the small horse trailer for maintenance. Everyone had gone home, so Joan used the opportunity to poke around in the office where Ernest and Edie worked. She found two stacks of bid tickets on Edie's desk, one in a box marked "pending" and another in one marked "fulfilled"; there were random notes, handwritten by Edie, like "follow up with M. Holden re: Tues. pre-bids on calves" and "ask Zak re: full seller contact info for payments." Ernest's desk was immaculate; she opened the top drawer of a filing cabinet and found folders of alphabetized purchases: AD-VERTISING; AUDIO EQUIPMENT; BEVERAGES; CALF/CATTLE PENS; CANDY MACHINE; COFFEE URNS. She didn't know what she was searching for, and in the process of looking, she realized just how little time she typically spent in this office. On any given day, Joan was usually out and about, driving horses between ranches; passing out her business card at stores, farms, and offices; or networking to bring community leaders and local celebrities to the fairgrounds. She had become the silent partner she assumed Chuck wished her to be. She cursed herself for trusting him.

The telephone rang. As it was nine thirty at night, Joan was curious who would be calling and for what purpose.

"Diamond Ranch," she said into the receiver.

"Hello, I'm calling for Chuck Galloway," the man on the other end said.

"He just . . . stepped out. May I help you with anything?"

"Well, I haven't been successful getting through, so perhaps I've been calling the wrong number. I finally called information, they got me to this number."

"You've reached the right number but, unfortunately, he's not here at the moment. Can I relay a message to him for you?"

"I need to speak with him as soon as possible. Please have him call Malcom D'Argento, D-apostrophe A-R-G-E-N-T-O at 213-555-2324."

"Certainly, Mr. D'Argento. Two-one-three, that's a Los Angeles area code, isn't it? You're quite a ways from here. Can I ask, did you recently buy livestock or horses at one of our auctions? Or perhaps sell with us on consignment in the last several weeks?"

The man laughed. "Oh, no, no. My boss breeds top-notch thoroughbreds out here in California. He's not bringing them to the middle of the country for sale." He chuckled again. "No, he's got people coming to him from . . . well, all over the world, really."

"Is that so?" Joan was processing what he had said.

"Yes. Saudi Arabia, Venezuela, Switzerland, Japan. So now you understand who you're dealing with."

"I understand what your boss does, but you haven't explained the reason for your call, Mr. D'Argento. I'm the owner of the Diamond Ranch Sale Barn, and you've called me here in the office. So, please, tell me what specifically you need from Chuck." She was short on patience and couldn't tell if this call was something about which she should be concerned.

There was a long pause.

"Mr. D'Argento? Are you still there?"

"I'm here, yes. Just a little confused. Mr. Galloway put in an order for two Arabians. He was going to arrange for delivery last week, but we haven't heard from him. He put down quite a large deposit on these young mares."

Joan's heart was pounding as she searched for the best response. She took a deep breath and steadied herself so her rage wouldn't be apparent.

"I'll tell you what," she said. "I'll talk to Chuck when he comes in tomorrow morning. Would you mind telling me how he paid the deposit, so I can look it up? Was it in cash or a check made out to someone?"

"Let's see here," he said. Joan could hear him rifling through papers. "Ah, here we go. Mr. Galloway wired us a $250,000 cash deposit on the two colts. From, let's see . . . Savings and Loan of Midwest City, from the account of Diamond Ranch Incorporated."

The business account. "I'll . . . get this straightened out," she said. "And the colts were being transported here? To Diamond Ranch, yes?"

"Well, uh, actually, no. It says they were going to Texas. To a breeding outfit near Dallas."

Joan was silent as she tried to make sense of what she was hearing.

"Is there a problem, Mrs. . . . ?" he asked.

"Joan Dumann. No, not at all Mr. D'Argento. We've got so

many business interests going on, I just need to speak with Mr. Galloway about specifics."

"Got it. Is Mr. Galloway your partner, then?"

Joan hesitated. "No. No, he is not. Just an employee here. I'll make sure he gets back to you."

She hung up the phone and sat very still for a long time. Her head was pounding, her thoughts were muddled, and her body felt tense, but it was imperative she remain clear-headed and rational. She needed to confront Chuck. She couldn't imagine what he could possibly tell her that might convince her that he wasn't, in fact, the embodiment of exactly what Lisa had predicted. For the first time, she was beginning to regret her involvement with Chuck, as she felt everything she had worked so hard for was about to implode. *What were you thinking, Joan?*

43

April 1971

A FEW DAYS BEFORE EASTER, WHEN THE BARN WOULD SHUT down operations for a few days, Joan was on a mission. She peeked into Ernest and Edie's office and found it empty. Chuck was not at his desk either. She walked out onto the auction floor to see who might be there clearing hay or picking up trash from the previous day's auction, but it had already been cleaned and cleared. Passing back through the hallway to the offices, she came upon Zak, clipboard in hand, who stopped to talk.

"Hi, Joan. How you doin'?"

"Oh, hi, Zak. I'm good, good. How are you?"

"So any plans for Easter? Visiting family?" he asked.

Joan was not in the mood for small-talk. "Yes. I'll be back at my house in Little Rock with my daughter and her family. And you?"

"My family always has Easter brunch at my Aunt Linda's house, outside of Norman. All my cousins on my mom's side will be there. And I'll be bringing my new girlfriend for the first time."

Joan was impatient and not processing any of it. "That's nice, really nice." She pointed to Ernest and Edie's office. "Hey, do you know why they aren't in yet? It's almost eleven," she said, looking at her watch.

"Edie is under the weather. I believe she called earlier to let

Chuck know she wouldn't be in. I don't know about Ernest. He wasn't here yesterday."

"He wasn't? Has anyone heard from him?"

"Uh, well . . ." Zak looked uncomfortable.

"What is it, Zak?"

"I probably shouldn't say anything 'cause I don't know, and it's none of my business . . ."

"Zak, just say it."

"Well, I sorta heard that Ernest was fired."

"What? Fired? Where did you hear that?"

"Like I said, he wasn't here yesterday, and Waylan seems to think he was fired, that . . . Chuck fired him."

Joan felt a rush of adrenaline and thought she might throw up. Her heart began to pound, and she could feel the blood whooshing in her ears.

"That would certainly be something I'd know about, don't you think?" she asked him rhetorically. "I need to find Chuck. Have you seen him?"

"Yeah, about twenty minutes ago, I think he said something about needing something from the shed."

"Thanks, Zak," she said, and dashed off.

Standing just outside the shed, she paused to take a deep breath. Then she burst through the doors to find Chuck sitting on an upside-down bucket, pulling a wad of cash from an envelope. She did not waste time mincing words.

"It's called 'embezzlement,' Chuck," she said through tight lips and clenched teeth. "How much do you have there?"

He bolted upright and shoved the money back into the envelope. "Whoa! Hey, hang on a minute! Before you go accusin' me of anything shady you'd better have a damned good reason."

"That's cash from the safe, isn't it? What's it for, Chuck?"

"I don't like what you're implying, but since you asked, it's to buy a new scale. Remember, we talked about gettin' one of those smaller ones just for calves and piglets?"

"With cash? Why are you buying a scale with cash? And from whom?"

"I got a good price on a used one from a guy in Choctaw. No one in the office needs to see me standing around counting cash."

"How much?"

"Huh?"

"How much is the scale, Chuck?" She was breathing rapidly.

"Aw, c'mon, Joan. What's the beef you got with me? I never heard you question my purchasing activities before. Do we need to talk about somethin'?" He stood up and slowly walked toward her. He came a little too close and Joan took a step back, feeling she might need to escape.

Then she corrected her stance and stood up straight, planting her boots firmly. "Okay, okay. To start: Where is Ernest?"

Chuck sighed and reached inside his jacket for his pack of cigarettes. In silence, he removed a cigarette from the pack and offered Joan one.

She shook her head emphatically. *Christ, doesn't he know by now I don't smoke Marlboros?*

"All right, Joan," he said as he returned the pack to his jacket and removed his lighter from the back pocket of his jeans. "Let's talk." He lit the cigarette then blew out a long, slow puff of smoke. "I'm glad you asked. I was about to discuss that very situation with you. That is, before you stormed in and started makin' accusations."

"Did you fire him? Did you, Chuck?"

"Now, I told you a while ago I had my suspicions about him. He comes across as professional and polite and all that, but I never quite trusted him. This is a big operation now, we're doin' real well and I probably shoulda been more on top of the accounting and where the money's goin' and all, but—"

"Stop! You are lying through your teeth. I know about everything. The wire transfer for the pair of thoroughbreds in California; the checks made out to mysterious payees; the bank transfers to some horse-breeding operation in Texas. I haven't figured all of it out, but there's too many unexplained payments for you to not be up to something that's lining your own pockets. And *that*, Mr. Galloway, is the very definition of embezzlement."

"I honestly don't know what you're talking about, Joan, but you're goin' into hysterics, and I'm kinda worried about you. Now, I know you hired Ernest, and you like him and trust him. But you're not here day to day, and you don't really see things as they are."

"Don't patronize me. I'm here several times a week."

"Anyway, even if I did use some of our profits for myself, nothing illegal there. You and I are the owners of this business. We can take the money and use as we see fit. If I wanna take my share and invest in . . . whatever . . . that's my prerogative. And you can do the same, right?" He took another drag on his cigarette and seemed satisfied with his rationalization.

"You fired a decent, honest employee without cause, just to pin the blame on someone else. You had no justification for letting him go. Do you think I'm stupid, Chuck?"

Chuck snorted.

"What's that obnoxious guffaw supposed to mean?"

"Don't act all high and mighty. You were gonna order that cement flooring from your family business in Jersey, right? You were gonna just go ahead and order it without discussing with me. Then you and your family profit from that, plus any word-of-mouth business while the work's being done. Isn't that what they call nepotism? Not using a local company and supportin' other Oklahomans and instead bringing in your son?"

"Oh, my god, you've got to be joking. There's no comparison between that and what you've done. First of all, I don't know where you're getting your information from, but I had *one* conversation with my son about installing the product, just to get his opinion. It's not like I went ahead and placed an order. And, second, there is no other flooring anywhere else in the country like Steri-Stone. It's the perfect surface for what we talked about doing here."

Chuck snorted again. "You sound like a damned commercial."

She ignored his remark. "And you know what, Chuck? I'm not sure we can make that investment at this point anyway, not the way you've been stealing."

"I'm gonna ask you to stop throwin' around words like *embezzlement* and *stealing* if you know what's good for you."

"Are you threatening me, Chuck?"

"I'm tellin' you to cool off. Go back to Little Rock and have a nice Easter with your grandkids. Enjoy the holiday. When we all get back, you and I will hash everything out, as partners should do."

Joan knew he was not trying to sound reassuring; he wanted to control her, to intimidate her. She would not allow that. She was no longer little Joan Sondersohn, desperately needing her father's approval and given few choices of her own, nor was she young Joan Oakes, having to push hard against her husband for a simple day-trip to New York or lie to him about a job she wanted to pursue; and she certainly was not Joan Anderson, helplessly deserted by her son's father as he went on to live life on his own terms.

"You know I could sue you?" she said.

He threw his cigarette to the ground and stomped out the butt.

"Yeah? You're gonna sue me, Joan?" He moved in closer. "Would that be before or after I tell the Savings and Loan of Midwest City that the legal owners of your house in Little Rock are the Hepps?"

Joan froze. There was no way he could know that. The thought of how he may have found out was more frightening to her than the repercussions of the offense itself.

"Right, Joan? Your daughter and son-in-law have no idea that our business loan was collateralized with their house, do they? You're just a, what, a tenant or something? Makes me wonder what Lisa and Justin would say if they were to find out what you did." He rolled his head around to stretch his neck. "It's a tricky situation, Joan," he said, shaking his head. He placed his foot on top of the bucket, licked his thumb, and used it to and wipe the tip of his boot. "Frankly, I don't know how the bank didn't pick up on that. Guess you worked your magic on that Sacks guy."

Joan's mind was racing. *How the hell did I ever think I could have a business with this jerkoff after meeting him one time in a scummy bar?*

He continued. "Now, I've given it some thought, and I'm no lawyer so I can't be certain what it means legally. I guess we just want to make sure we keep makin' payments on the loan and not go into default. 'Cause that would be disastrous."

She decided to shrug off his intimidation tactics and get down to the facts. "How would you know any of this? I don't like that you were digging around like that, and I don't know why you think you're right about what you're saying."

"You must've forgotten that Justin Hepp and me, we got along nicely when I worked for him. We keep in touch, I call him

302 | Eileen Brill

from time to time, see if he ever wants to buy or sell, if he knows people who're lookin'. He calls me as well."

"Justin would contact *me* if he needed anything. He'd have no reason to go through you."

"Well, he did call me. Matter-of-fact, it was just after our loan was approved, if I remember correctly. He was inquiring for a friend about buying several grade A Holstein dairy cows. Guy was willing to pay top dollar, and Justin requested my help with the transaction." Chuck was calm now.

She sensed she was losing control of this game.

He continued. "Phone call was windin' down and I said, 'Justin would you mind if I speak to Joan about rentin' out her house to my sister? She wants to get herself and her little boy outta Fort Worth, find a nice, stable place to live.' I wanted to run it by him first, you know, 'cause the house is on his property and all."

"You were asking Justin about *my* house?"

"Why, I had no idea you'd be goin' back and forth, still livin' there. I figured you were up here for good. Anyway, Justin says, 'Well, I'm afraid Joan has a lifetime claim on the house, Chuck. She's pretty much a tenant there for life.' He tells me, 'Joan's allowed to sublet out the house or even give up her claim, but technically she still lives here.'"

Joan tried to remain steely and unaffected by Chuck's insinuation. She shook her head in disbelief.

"So then I said, 'Oh, I see. I must be mistaken then, 'cause I was under the impression she owned the house. She told me she paid to have it built an' all.' Justin just laughed and said, 'In the eyes of the law, Joan's my tenant.'"

"You're a dirty son of a bitch, Chuck, you know that?"

"Why don't we stop all this accusin' and blamin' and name callin'? It's bad for business and bad for the soul," Chuck said, patting his heart.

"I'm not going to allow you to run this business into the ground," Joan said.

"Aw, c'mon, Joan. Let's work this out. Now, listen, I admit I got real excited with the money we were makin'," he explained. "I heard about some investment opportunities, and I suppose I got a little crazy. But I never wanted to hurt the Barn and our employees. Especially you, Joan. Never meant to cause problems between you and me."

He was saying all the right words, but she wasn't buying any of it.

He promised not to say anything to anyone about the bank loan and the deed, and he said he would do whatever was necessary to pay back what he took from the business, even if it meant foregoing his share of the profits for the time being. He suggested that both he and Joan maintain a presence at the Barn every day, in the interest of establishing trust between them once again. He wanted to continue to manage the maintenance and auction crews and Zak, and Joan should hire an accounting manager to replace Ernest. "I can't have Ernest working here, now that there's bad blood between me and him," he said.

"You know what, Chuck? I know a swindler when I look him in the eye." She stared him down as best she could, feeling grateful she'd worn her cowboy boots with the higher heels.

Chuck fastened the top buttons on his coat and walked past Joan to the shed door. He opened it then faced her, his eyes just a few inches from hers. "You really don't know this business, don't understand how things work in this part of the country," he said. His face was contorted with disdain.

Chuck left the shed, and Joan exhaled. She needed to figure out a strategy to wrest control of the Barn, deal with forthcoming expenses, and get out of this financial mess.

Fortunately, she had been thinking one step ahead of

Chuck, and she had secured the partnership books that she had removed from the office safe and taken home with her as proof of Chuck's illicit use of finances and manipulation of assets. And, despite the fact that she didn't believe he was remorseful when he acknowledged his transgressions, she also had his verbal confession, something to hold against him if she needed to do so.

She needed to get her ducks in a row and force him out or bring a case against him. She believed that either of these scenarios were possible, but she needed to tread carefully in a prudent and patient manner as she had tried so hard to do all throughout her life.

44

JOAN COULD NOT GET HER THOUGHTS OUT FAST ENOUGH once she had the attention of her old friend Dick Weidnitz. She moved the telephone receiver to her other ear.

"I've made some poor decisions in my life, that's for sure, but in every case, I thought I was doing what was best for myself, so I wasn't exactly wrong. I was just ill-informed. I suppose part of that was just my naïveté and immaturity."

Dick exhaled loudly on the telephone. "Joan, can we please stay on topic, here? As I've been telling you, it's imperative that you find yourself a good lawyer out there. I'm not admitted to practice law outside the state of New Jersey. But as a friend, I'm telling you that I think you're in over your head now."

"Right, right. Sorry, didn't mean to digress. But, just so you know, I entered into this business with eyes wide open," Joan said. The last thing she wanted anyone to think was that she was easily manipulated. "But, can I ask you something, in confidence, as a friend?"

"Of course," he said.

"Let's say someone gets a loan and uses a house as collateral, to secure the loan. But, the house isn't technically theirs."

"Joan, are you asking because you're concerned that you collateralized your house fraudulently?"

"That's the thing. It's . . ." she hesitated. Was it problematic to discuss this with Weidnitz? He said she could speak with him in confidence. Regardless, she needed to know.

"What, Joan?"

"It's not my house. I mean, it's not supposed to be. Justin and Lisa are under the impression that it's their names on the deed. But it was recorded in my name." It was the first time she felt shame in connection with the loan.

"The loan you're referring to is the one you and Chuck have with SLMC?"

"Yes. What am I going to do?"

"Let's just think this thing through," he said. He explained that, from the bank's perspective, Joan owned the house. Clerical errors with deeds happen, he assured her, and often go undetected until a title search is performed when the house is being sold.

"But, I have this loan. And now . . ." She stopped herself. It was like an epiphany.

"What is it?" he asked.

"I think I've figured it out. I know what to do. Thank you, Dick."

"Joan, don't do anything foolish. Maybe you should speak with Lisa first. Or even consult a real estate attorney."

She hung up the phone and suddenly felt a burden lifted, the weight of Chuck's threat now insignificant. It occurred to Joan that she was allowing him to transform her back into that insecure little girl who had let everyone else make decisions for her, and she reminded herself that she'd learned a long time ago how to influence people, size them up, find their weaknesses.

She would call his bluff.

45

May 1971

ON THE MORNING THAT JOAN S. DUMANN AND CHUCK
Galloway signed an agreement dissolving their partnership at
the Diamond Ranch Sale Barn, Joan drove to Freida's for a cele-
bratory breakfast. She did not feel defeated; in fact, she congratulated herself at how she had been able to steer the outcome of
their unfortunate union toward a conclusion in which her reputation, legally and morally, would be preserved.

She sat at a small table near the window.

"Coffee, Mrs. Dumann?" asked the waitress. "We've got
those sticky buns you love."

"Perfect. Thanks, Jean." She reached into her purse and took
out her pack of Virginia Slims and her lighter, lit the cigarette,
took a puff, and exhaled slowly, finishing with a smoke ring. She
smiled. It was a good day, all things considered.

She reflected on her conversation with Chuck in April, right
after it dawned on her that he stood more to lose with an accusation of embezzlement than she did from Lisa finding out about
the deed mishap.

She had approached Chuck in his office one evening after
everyone had headed home. She was most concerned with en-
suring that Waylan, with his tendency to linger and eavesdrop,
had driven away in his truck.

"You don't give a damn about this business, Chuck," she said calmly, with the self-assurance of someone who had already examined a situation from all angles. "That's abundantly clear to me now. You use people, you lie, and you do whatever suits you so that you can prop yourself up, make yourself feel like a big shot." She stood leaning against the doorway to his office, her arms folded. "We were doing well, unbelievably well, in just the first few months, but I'm guessing you have never done well at anything in your life. It was probably overwhelming for you." She spoke assertively. She felt confident.

He sat back in his chair, grinning. "There's somethin' seriously wrong with you, Joan. I mean, like, you're not right in the head," he said, pointing to his temple. "Things been goin' good between us, haven't they? We straightened everything up after Christmas, right? I'm holdin' back on my share, tryin' to make it square between us. So what the hell are you thinkin'?"

She took a seat in front of his desk. "I'll tell you what I'm thinking. I'm thinking after two years of planning and working with me, you still don't respect my knowledge, experience, and insight. I'm thinking you saw me as nothing more than a big bag of money to finance something you'd never in a million years have been able to do on your own." She stared at him, nodding her head slowly. "I'm thinking we need to dissolve this partnership. We're done."

"You serious?" He sat forward in his chair.

"Dead serious. You need me, but I don't need you. Do you know how many horse deals I've brokered on my own since we started? I spend a lot of my time driving a hundred-mile radius around Shawnee, talking to people, making connections. That's probably where I screwed up. Not being here at the Barn enough. It's clear you've still got your little deals going on behind my back," she said, using air quotes to emphasize the word *deals*. "I can't lie to myself any longer. I'm tired, Chuck."

"And what makes you think I'm gonna let you outta this so easily? You know I could tell Justin about the loan collateral. I could tell Sacks—"

"Go ahead, Chuck. Tell them. Tell everyone," she said, smacking her thigh. "You're still an embezzler with bad credit. The only thing keeping you afloat is that Diamond Ranch remains in good standing with SLMC. That's where you might be okay. For now. But let me tell you something, Chuck," she said, leaning closer into his desk. "I'm secure. I've got more than enough to sustain a lengthy lawsuit and, believe me, it would be lengthy. I've got everything on paper showing what you've done. I have witnesses. What do *you* have?"

He was quiet. His upper lip curled slightly, and he looked off to the side.

She sat back and let her words linger.

He reached for his cigarettes, pulled one from the pack, and threw it across the desk.

"Goddammit, you're a fuckin' manipulative bitch, you know that, Joan?"

She smiled. "Yes I am. And it took me a long time to get here."

"So what do we have to do? To dissolve this?"

"I'll tell you exactly what we have to do," she said, handing him a typewritten description of her demands.

Joan's coffee and sticky bun arrived, and she put out her cigarette. She took a bite of the warmed-up pastry and licked the sweetness from her fingers.

As part of their dissolution, in accordance with the original partnership agreement, Joan was to get back her initial investment, plus interest, along with her additional capital contributions and money owed to her as a result of Chuck's misallocation of profits. Chuck would be the sole owner of the Barn, and Joan was released of all debt associated with the business. The balance of the bank loan was transferred to a loan in Chuck's name only, Joan's house was removed as collateral, and their partnership business account was closed. With the help of a lawyer, and before the partnership was dissolved, she was able to recoup her initial investment of $75,000, albeit in three payments, as well as a schedule of payments toward her capital contributions during their two-year partnership.

But, as far as Joan was concerned, it was not over.

46

JOAN STARED THROUGH THE PEEPHOLE AT ROY.

"Beg pardon, hope we didn't wake you. I'm here with Waylan. Do you mind if we talk to you about a few things?"

"Uh, hold on." She looked over toward her desk to make sure she hadn't left out any personal information. Her hand still ached from hours earlier when she'd written the letter to the sheriff. She lifted the manila envelope containing the letter and stared at it for a few seconds. Then she turned around and walked toward the corner of her living room. Kneeling down, she pulled back hard on a corner section of carpeting, revealing the padding underneath. She placed the envelope on top of the padding and tucked the carpeting back into place.

Joan walked back over to the door and unlocked it, keeping the chain on. "Is everything all right? Did something happen at the Barn?" she asked, peeking through the three-inch opening.

"Naw, naw, nothin's up at the Barn," Roy said. "Listen, I apologize for stopping by so late and not callin' first. We just wanna..."

Joan's eyes moved to Waylan, who was repeatedly running his fingers through his oily, thinning hair.

"... Mrs. Dumann," Roy continued. "Can we just have a few minutes of your time? Please?"

Joan exhaled. "Okay, sure. C'mon in." She moved to the side

and allowed the men to enter her apartment, leaving the door ajar. She noticed how Waylan's eyes scanned her living room, as if he were making an estimation of some kind.

Joan buttoned the top of her house coat and folded her arms across her chest. "So what's so important that you two gentlemen need to knock on my door after midnight?" Seeing them standing side by side, it suddenly struck Joan that the two men were the same height, yet Roy gave the impression of being so much taller than Waylan. She noted Waylan's perpetual five-o'clock shadow and wrinkled, squinty eyes, as if he were always sizing people up. Roy, on the other hand, was always clean-shaven, and he kept his hair close-cropped, with the exception of his extra-long side burns. Joan admired Roy's calm, soulful eyes and his cleft chin.

"I tried to call you several times earlier. The line was busy," Roy said.

Joan glanced over at the telephone, realizing she'd not replaced the receiver.

"The thing is, Mrs. Dumann," Roy continued. "Chuck don't want you messin' with the Barn since you two signed that dissolution agreement. He's irate, Mrs. Dumann. And he wants the books back, the partnership books. Said you're supposed to return them to him."

Waylan jumped in, aggressively. "He says you keep comin' by the Barn, bringin' folks, threatening him, sayin' you're gonna get your lawyer after him."

Roy reinforced Waylan's comment with a softer touch. "Like I said, he's irate, and he don't want trouble, but if it comes to that, I'm afraid he might . . ."

Joan's voice became stern. "Yes, I'm aware of Chuck's threats," she said, glancing toward her desk for the pack of cigarettes. She noticed the half-smoked, crushed one in the ashtray

and regretted wasting it. "I'm not afraid of Chuck." She said this
as much to convince herself as to persuade Roy and Waylan. The
last time she'd stopped by the Barn to ask Chuck why she hadn't
yet received any payments from him, he made no secret of his
hostility, saying that she "oughta step off before I find a good
way to make you step off."

"Chuck says it ain't your business no more," Waylan said,
pointing an accusatory finger. "An' that's why you got served this
mornin' with a restrainin' order. Chuck let us all know we got
justification to do whatever we need to do to keep you in your
place."

Joan raised her voice. "I don't think that's any of your concern. This is between me and Chuck." She was annoyed and, for
the first time, frightened by Waylan. She looked away from him.
"Roy, I don't quite understand why you two are involving yourselves in this, and besides . . ."

At that moment, someone entered the still-open door to her
apartment. It was a man Joan did not recognize, and she
watched Roy and Waylan turn around in unison as he stepped
inside.

"What do you want? Who are you?" Joan said, her voice
now uneasy. She glanced at the telephone.

"What I want," the man said, slowly and quietly as he closed
the door. "Is for you to listen very carefully to what I have to say."
As the man approached Joan, Waylan moved out of the way
while Roy subtly wedged himself in front of her.

Joan noticed the man's large hands and tense, splayed fingers, as if he were preparing to catch a fast-flying football. He
was a good five inches taller than Roy.

Joan wrapped her fingers around Roy's upper arm and
turned him back toward her. "Roy? Do you know what's going
on?" She felt Roy's bicep twitch.

Roy put his hands up and shook his head. "Mrs. Dumann, I swear, I have no idea—"

"Get out of here, all of you!" Joan shouted. "Now!" She glanced sideways at the telephone.

Waylan moved behind Joan and pressed his hand against her mouth.

"C'mon, Waylan. That's not necessary," Roy said. Then, moving closer to Joan, his palms turned up in a defensive, conciliatory gesture, he added, "I'm sorry, Mrs. Dumann. I assure you, I don't know who this man is or what he's here for."

The man moved to within inches of Joan and pulled out a pistol from inside his jacket. He cocked it and pointed at her face, speaking slowly to her. "I want you to listen very carefully. Understand?"

Joan was breathing heavily with Waylan's hand over her mouth. She nodded her head, staring at the man's lower lip, which had a fresh cut.

"So take your hand off of her mouth. Let her be," the stranger said to Waylan, who released his grip on Joan. "I'm sure she ain't gonna do anything stupid now that she's got a gun pointed at her."

Shaking, her voice quivering, Joan turned to Roy. "Listen, Roy. It's true, I've been going back to the Barn. And I know he doesn't like it, not at all . . ."

"No, he don't," said Waylan, now standing next to the man with the gun.

Without turning away from Roy, Joan continued. "Chuck stole money, misallocated funds. And since we severed our partnership, legally he has to give me back my initial investment plus interest and more. That's what we decided, it's all there in the agreement. And he was supposed to have already begun paying me, but he hasn't. So that's why I've been coming around. But then he started threatening me."

Roy listened, clearly conflicted. He was now sweating pro-fusely. "Mrs. Dumann—Joan—maybe you oughta listen to this man here who's pointin' a *gun* at you," he said, choking on his words. "Honestly, I don't know this guy. I'm as shocked and con-fused as you—"

"So what am I supposed to do? I've spent two years of my life building this business." She appealed to the man with the gun as well.

"I swear, I never seen someone flap their lips so much when they got a gun in their face," the man said, his face tightening.

"Please," Roy said to the gunman, as if requesting another minute to talk sense to Joan. Then, turning to her, he said, "Just . . . just leave. Go back to Little Rock. Better yet, go back to New Jersey. You had a nice life there, didn't you? Cruises every year, fancy country clubs. Never understood what you want with this kind of business." Roy looked at the man, who was loudly clearing his throat as if he was about to spit, and con-tinued appealing to Joan, with greater urgency. "I like you, Mrs. Dumann. You're a real nice lady, you been good to me since I met you. This isn't where you belong." He turned to the man. "C'mon, she don't deserve this."

"I can run the Barn myself," Joan said "Yes, that's what I'll do. I'll buy him out. I'll just concentrate on horses. Roy, you could help me manage it. I've been thinking about this a lot, and . . ."

The man with the gun took a step closer to Joan. "Okay, so I'm seeing this ain't gonna be easy," he said. "I'm gonna ask you both to shut the fuck up now." He lifted his arm, pointed the gun at Joan's head.

"Please, don't do this!" she screamed.

At that instant, Roy lunged forward, grabbing the gunman's wrist with one hand and the gun with the other. The gunman lifted his free arm and shoved Roy backward. Roy fell to the floor, and the gunman pointed his gun at Roy. Waylan pulled a handgun from inside his jacket and wrapped his arm around Joan's torso and arms, pointing the gun at Joan's head. She squirmed as she felt the cold muzzle of the gun touch her temple.

Joan twisted her body free, dropped to the floor, and crawled toward the door.

Waylan raised his pistol.

"No!" Roy shouted.

47

June 10, 1971

THE BOY SAT DOWN AT THE EDGE OF THE POND JUST before noon. It was warm and sunny—comfortably so—and he had this spot all to himself today. He rested his fishing pole on the ground beside him and reached into a paper bag for his sandwich. He took one bite and a swig of Coke; then he put his lunch aside and grabbed the bait box. Inside the box were a dozen or so squirming earthworms he had dug up that morning. Poking his finger through the wriggling bunch, he searched for the thickest worm he could find and skewered it on the hook he'd already tied onto his fishing line. He cast the line far out into the water and sat there, motionless, for several minutes, just looking all around and enjoying the serenity of his favorite spot in Seminole. Only he and a handful of his friends ever fished at this pond, which was on farmland just off the Old Pasture Road, an unpaved stretch off Route 31. It was entirely possible they were the only people in all of Pottawattomie County, Oklahoma, who knew there was a pond there at all.

He secured the fishing rod between his feet and reached into his lunch bag again. He took a few more bites of his sandwich and reached for the bottle of Coke propped up against his tackle box. As he did, he felt a tug at the line and, quickly bringing both hands back to the reel, he leaned back to pull in his catch.

In his haste, he knocked over the Coke bottle and it toppled into the pond with a *plunk*. He reeled in the line to find a nice, fat bass that he immediately threw back in.

With all the commotion in the water, the bottle had drifted into the middle of the pond, so he put down the rod, pulled off his T-shirt, and kicked off his sneakers so he could get into the water to retrieve it. He placed one foot and the other, gently into the cold water and waded slowly toward the center. At its deepest point the pond was just four feet, but he never liked to touch the bottom ever since his cousin teased him that people threw dead bodies into the water. He treaded over to the bottle, grabbed it, and suddenly felt something—a fish? an eel? a snake? —brush his leg. Whatever it was knocked his leg several times before he panicked and swam back to the edge. As he was climbing back onto the bank, he saw his cousin heading toward the pond, fishing pole in hand. His cousin screamed out to him.

"What the hell are you doin'? That pond is so muddy and nasty."

"C'mere," he said, tossing the bottle into his fishing box.

"What's goin' on? Why are you breathin' so hard? Somethin' spook you? A dead body, maybe?" he said with a big smile as he poked his cousin in the ribs.

"I think there really is a body in there, I'm not kidding."

"You outta your mind? I'm gonna go in."

Without hesitation, he put down his fishing pole, stripped down to his underwear and walked purposefully toward the pond. He hopped right in without flinching at the cold water.

"Where was it?" he asked, walking slowly toward the center.

"Exactly where you're walking. Where that willow branch is pointing. Yep, right there."

At five foot ten, his cousin's body was out of the water from the chest up.

"I don't feel anything. Nope, nothing. I think it was all your imagina—"

"Feel it?"

His cousin stood still and looked straight out, concentrating, trying to decipher what his foot was touching.

"It's like a cinder-block or somethin." He paused. Then his eyes grew wide and he gasped. "Jake!" He moved quickly back to the bank and hoisted himself up in one swift motion. He jumped into his clothing and the two boys ran as fast as they could, leaving their fishing rods, boxes, and lunch behind, down the dirt road and toward the Esso station to place a call to the sheriff of Midwest City.

48

BOB WAS EXHAUSTED WHEN HE ARRIVED AT WILL ROGERS
Airport in Oklahoma City close to midnight, after a change of
planes in Chicago. The trip from Philadelphia had been excruci-
ating for him as he unsuccessfully attempted to busy his mind
with paperwork and settle his nerves with scotch on both flights.
His thoughts kept drifting back to conversations with his mother,
memories of his adolescence. It had been a difficult couple of
years for him since Kyle's death, and now this.

Memories of his teenaged years in Phoenix, and even more
so in New Jersey, were tinged with episodes of Joan's unreasonable and sometimes unpleasant behavior, when she'd fly into a
rage, and Bob would hear her ranting in her bedroom to Kyle
about feeling fat or not being taken seriously. During her fits,
Bob would go to his bedroom and blast his record player; he
could always lose himself in Buddy Holly or Elvis. If his mother
went on a tirade through the house, Bob would slip out the back
door and into his 1957 Jaguar, the best Christmas gift his parents
had ever given him.

He could never figure out the dynamics of his parents'
marriage: Kyle showered Joan with unconditional love, gave in
to her every whim, appeared content. Yet, Joan was erratic,
sometimes coming across as unappreciative of the caring and
supportive husband she was fortunate to have.

The taxi dropped Bob off at the Cattle Car Motel in Midwest City. When he entered the office, a twenty-something man,
with long hair pulled back in a ponytail and a mustache and

beard in strong need of a trim, was dozing in a chair behind the front desk as the local Oklahoma City channel blared the news on a television behind him.

"*. . . National Security Advisor Henry Kissinger, in secret peace negotiations with North Vietnam, introduced a new proposal to withdraw troops from South Vietnam. . . .*"

Bob watched the broadcast for a couple seconds before clearing his throat to get the man's attention. When that didn't work, Bob tapped lightly on the bell that sat atop the counter. The man stirred from his snooze.

"Oh, hey, man, sorry. Was catching some z's there. How's it going?"

Bob studied the man, who now, fully awake, appeared several years older. "I have a reservation under the name Dumann: D-U-M—"

"Yep, we spoke on the phone yesterday. It's here, in the book," he said. Then, sideways under his breath, "Not that you really need a reservation." He chuckled at the idea. "Well, 'cept for when there's a weekend auction over in Shawnee and, wow-ee, we gotta turn people away," he said, reaching for his reservation book.

All Bob could hear was *blah-blah-blah*.

"Okay, sir, so I'll need a driver's license and a credit card or a thirty-five-dollar cash deposit for one night. Just the one night, right?"

Bob fished through his wallet. "I'm not actually sure. One night, maybe two. I can't really say. I—"

"Aw, no problem, man." Then, sideways again, under his breath, he added, "Not like there's a big convention in town."

"*. . . and in local news, the nude body of a Midwest City woman found in a pond off Route 31 in Shawnee has been identified as that of fifty-five-year-old businesswoman Joan Dumann, a partner at the Diamond Ranch Horse and Livestock Sales Barn. Mrs. Dumann,*" *who lived in the Stagecoach Apartments, Midwest City, had been shot twice in the head before her body was dumped, weighted down, in the center of the shallow pond on a farm not far from Diamond Ranch."*

As he was removing his wallet from his back pocket, Bob fixed his eyes on the television screen. He held the wallet in his hand, just above the counter. After *Joan Dumann,* the only other words he processed were *body, nude, dumped, shot, twice.* The police officer who called yesterday told him only that they had found his mother's body in a pond and that her death appeared to be by at least one gunshot wound. The news report made it sickeningly real, yet, at the same time, all the more surreal.

"Mr. Dumann, oh, man I'm so sorry. Was she your . . ?"

Bob noticed crumbs in the man's beard. Or maybe it was marijuana. "My mother. Yes."

"Really. I hope they catch and crucify the bastard who did that."

Bob silently handed his entire wallet to the clerk, who gently refused it.

"Just a credit card and your license, that's all."

"What? Oh, of course," Bob said, still dazed.

The clerk handed Bob a check-in form to fill out. "Listen, man, anything you need, let me know, okay?" He handed Bob's driver's license back to him.

Bob returned his driver's license and credit card to his wallet. He filled out the form with his name, home address, and phone number, and when he got to the bottom, he read the line: *What brings you to Midwest City? Business? Pleasure? Other?* He thought of circling "Other" and adding, *My mother was fucking murdered—that's what brings me to Midwest City.* He felt a rush of adrenaline that made him sick to his stomach.

The man handed Bob the room key. "Here you go, room one-sixteen. There's an ice machine right outside the office here.

Across the street is the liquor store: they open at nine and close at ten tonight. You can pick up some sandwiches and snacks at the service station next door."

"Thanks," Bob said, taking the key.

"The name's Derick. Anything you need, man."

Once inside the room, Bob threw his bag on the bed and sat on the edge. He removed his shoes and pants and sat still for a few minutes, looking around at the western motif of the wallpaper and the framed posters of herds of cattle and chuck wagons and cowboys; it reminded him of his teenaged years in Phoenix, where he never felt like he fit in with the other kids. That time in Phoenix was just a blip in his life, three short years, yet it was the period that held the most vivid memories of his mother's erratic moods and familial conflicts.

"He's fifteen, Joan. It's okay if he'd rather not go with us," Kyle said one November day in 1953 as the family was heading out to the Arizona State Fair.

Bob lay back on the motel bed, recalling that day and his mother's *freak out*, as he had taken to calling her episodes of seemingly unjustified rage.

"This is our first year in Phoenix, and we are going to this fair as a *family*," Joan insisted.

Bob could still see her face, twisted and full of resentment, as she spit the word *family* at Kyle. All Bob wanted was to go to the fair with the one kid he had befriended at school. Why had she been so unable to understand that?

"C'mon, Mom," Bob had pleaded. "You're just gonna make me be responsible for Gwen and Lisa the whole time so you can go off and watch the races or hand out your business cards."

At that, Joan began ranting and raving that she was "not

appreciated in this household" and all she ever wanted to do was to have a nice family outing, and Bob could see his school friend any time, and this was going to be an event they enjoyed together.

Bob had stormed out of the house that day and gone to see his friend. Joan had not spoken to him for close to a week.

After calling his wife to let her know he had arrived safely, Bob cracked open the other mini-sized scotch he'd taken from the plane. He didn't bother with ice or a cup, drinking it straight out of the tiny bottle.

He'd been upset with his mother for starting a business relationship with this Galloway guy. Lisa had told Bob negative things about their mother's partner, but when Bob tried to discuss his concerns with Joan, she had shut him down and become angry.

She had frequently been angry with him, always jumping to conclusions about his motives, all throughout his life.

She'd been angry when she caught him with the bottle of bourbon his senior year of high school. He had puked right in front of her, and she had grounded him. Just like that. He could have confronted her, then and there, about the birth certificate. He could have asked her who Paul Anderson was and what the hell happened to him. But that was irrelevant to Bob. Whatever had occurred in his mother's life in the years just before he was born was not, he was sure, out of character for the person he knew her to be. He could speculate about what happened, whether she was a victim or the perpetrator, why this was kept secret, what had caused her divorce from Franklin, and a host of other ruminations that would just lead him back to the same conclusion: Joan Dumann, his mother, was unpredictable and complicated. It was useless trying to figure her out.

He turned on the television and, within minutes, fell asleep to the sound of the white noise of the end of the programming day.

The following morning, Bob sat in a chair in an office of the Oklahoma County Sheriff's Department in Midwest City. He stared into a mug of black coffee handed to him by a young woman who looked barely older than seventeen. He had no recollection of either being offered it or of indicating he wanted coffee, but the last thing she said to him before leaving Bob alone was, "You take care, now, all right Mr. Dumann? Sheriff Maghan will be with you shortly. He's a real nice man, easy to talk to." Then she closed the office door behind her. The smell of the coffee was nauseating, so he set the mug on the desk and glanced around at the photos on the credenza under the window. There was one of a smiling man in a cowboy hat, arm draped around a petite woman who also wore a cowboy hat. There seemed to be a barn behind the couple. Another photo was of the same man, dressed in his law enforcement uniform, complete with badge and Western hat, shaking hands with an older, official-looking man in a suit who was surrounded by a small crowd of other official-looking individuals. A small, bronze statue of a bucking horse stood next to a photograph of a smiling President Richard Nixon.

The door opened and the man in the photos walked in. Bob rose abruptly to shake his hand.

"Mornin', Mr. Dumann," he said in a warm, deep voice with a slight Oklahoman drawl. He shook Bob's hand. "Burt Maghan, Oklahoma County Sheriff." He walked behind his desk and sat down, as did Bob. "Mr. Dumann, please accept my sincerest condolences."

"Thank you," Bob said.

"I sure appreciate your comin' all the way out here from New Jersey. I know my secretary spoke on the phone with your sister Lisa."

"Yes, she did."

"I know this is a horrific shock for you and your family. This must have been an agonizing few days while your mother was missin'."

Bob nodded and reached for the mug of coffee, more for something to hold onto than to drink. "We are grateful to the Midwest City Police Department for tracking . . . for finding her . . . for finding my mother." Bob thought about how the words had come out, like some sort of morbid acceptance speech from an awards ceremony.

"We will want to ask you questions, Mr. Dumann, with the goal of narrowing down the pool of suspects, motives, timelines, that sort of thing. Any information you or your family can provide us will be helpful in understanding who may have done this. No information is insignificant, so feel free to offer us anything your mother said to you at any point in time. Phone calls, letters, casual mentioning of conversations she told you about, people she knew and liked, or didn't like . . ."

Bob nodded.

"I believe it was explained to you that, as her next of kin, you, or Lisa, if she's able, will be asked to identify the body of the deceased. Are you able to do that, Mr. Dumann?"

"I can. I mean, I will. Go to the morgue, that is."

"Certainly. Thank you. Now, I'm goin' to bring in Police Chief Langstrom, of Midwest City, to sit in on the questionin', if you don't mind."

"Not at all," Bob said. He was lying. He minded very much. He did not want to be having a conversation about his mother's murder. Not with Sheriff Maghan. Not with Police Chief Langstrom. This was a fucking awful thing to be doing.

Sheriff Maghan picked up the phone and dialed four numbers. "Hey, Mimi, c'mon in, we're ready for ya. Thanks, honey."

Seconds later, a tall, red-haired man in a police uniform entered the office, along with an attractive thirty-something woman in a collared, gray dress with a small horseshoe pin above her left breast. She sat down in a chair against the wall and set a legal-sized notepad on her knee.

"Mr. Dumann, this is Chief Langstrom, and this here is Mimi Berk, my assistant. She's gonna be takin' some notes, if you don't mind."

"I'm sorry for your loss, Mr. Dumann," Chief Langstrom said. "We were all riveted by this at the precinct. I had met your mother once or twice. She was a nice lady, seemed like a decent person." He sat down and turned to the sheriff. "Senseless," he said, shaking his head.

"Yes, it's a real shame," Mimi said. "I'm so sorry."

Bob appreciated the condolences, but was already weary of hearing "I'm sorry" spoken over and over by people who had not known his mother. *Did I even know my mother?*

"Mr. Dumann," Chief Langstrom began, "when was the last time you spoke with or had any contact with your mother?"

"I guess, last Tuesday. I mean, we didn't actually talk. She spoke with my secretary. She wanted to see how business was going, how I was doing, my family, that kind of thing."

"I understand you have a family business?" asked the sheriff.

"Yes. Commercial flooring. Factories, restaurants, schools. It was my father's business, and my grandfather's before that."

"Was your mother involved in the business at all?" asked Chief Langstrom.

"She was, yes, up until my father's passing two years ago." He

328 | Eileen Brill

paused for a moment, recalling several conversations with his mother, shortly after the Barn was up and running. "She really wanted to stay involved in the family business," he said. "She didn't want to completely let go . . . she was pressuring me to come out here and take a look at their property, to give an estimate for installing flooring and such." Bob looked at the sheriff and Langstrom for some indication that this was relevant in any way.

The sheriff nodded. Langstrom did not seem that interested in this particular information. Mimi took notes.

"I told her we weren't set up to serve this market region. I explained it would be tough to get supplies and workers here," Bob said. "She seemed disappointed, so I asked how *her* business was going. You know? I found it strange that she was still so focused on Dumann." Then he looked to the side, trying to remember something specific. "She said . . . something about her partner . . . Galloway. She said, 'Things are good, very busy . . . my partner and I, we aren't exactly a match made in heaven' and when I pressed her on what she meant, she changed the subject."

"I see," said Langstrom.

"We all got the feeling . . . my sisters and I . . . that Galloway wasn't on the up-and-up," Bob said.

"I understand your mother moved out here . . . when? Two years ago, is that right?" asked Chief Langstrom.

"Well, no. She moved to Arkansas right after my dad's death."

"For what reason?" asked Chief Langstrom.

"I . . . uh, let's see," Bob exhaled. He felt foggy-headed. "I think to be near my sister and her family. Uh, maybe get involved in my sister Lisa's business." He ran his fingers through his hair. *Why did she move to Arkansas?*

"What does your sister do?" asked Maghan.

"She's a horse trainer. She and her husband own racehorses. Thoroughbreds," Bob added. "That's how my mother got involved in the horse barn here, I think."

"Can you tell us more about that, Mr. Dumann?"

"I'll tell you what I know. But you'll probably want to speak with Lisa directly." *Goddammed Galloway*, Bob thought. *It was him.*

49

after he had identified Joan's body. She knocked on the door of his motel room, and he immediately opened it.

His eyes were red and swollen. He looked pale and exhausted.

"Hey, Bob," she said, giving her brother a hug.

He indicated for her to sit in the only chair in the room. He grabbed a bottle of Scotch he had purchased at the liquor store across the street and poured some into two plastic cups.

"No, none for me," she said, waving her hands.

"Don't make me drink alone," he said with a pleading smile. He handed her the cup and sat down on the bed across from her.

"Are you okay?" she asked.

"Aw, Lis, it was awful. The most horrific thing I've ever experienced." He took a swig of his Scotch.

Lisa listened, her tears welling up.

"It was *her*, I could tell by the hair, her wedding ring, that heart-shaped mole on her neck. But . . ." He hesitated and put his head in his hand.

Lisa covered her mouth.

"Oh, Jesus fucking Christ, Lisa." He began sobbing.

Lisa moved to the bed to comfort her brother. She put an arm around him and put her forehead on his shoulder.

"Who would do that? Who would do such a thing to another person? To our mother?" he asked.

It had to have been Chuck, Lisa thought. *That goddamned son of a bitch.*

Bob wiped his eyes with his sleeve. He stood up and walked to the bathroom, splashed his face with water, and dried it. "I gotta get outta here."

Lisa and Bob drove to Freida's Country Diner. Neither of them was particularly hungry, so they ordered coffee and sat talking.

"You're seeing the police chief in the morning?" Bob asked.

Lisa nodded. "I got a room at the motel. I'll tell him what I know about Chuck, but Mom never really discussed him with me. When she told me they were breaking up the partnership, she alluded to things he was supposed to be doing and wasn't. Payments, something. But when I pressed her—whenever I would press her—she would kind of shut down."

"Same with me," Bob said. "I eventually got so frustrated with her. She'd call and sometimes make it seem like things were great. Then she'd get all quiet and kind of seem like she wanted to talk, and when I asked what was going on, she'd gloss over it." He paused, looking down. Then he looked at his sister, cautiously. "Mom could be . . . difficult. You know?"

Lisa nodded. "Yeah. She wanted what she wanted, I guess." She looked out the window and back at Bob. "Do you remember the pool debacle? In Verona?"

"Do I? Oh, my god, Mom was on a mission," he said with a chuckle.

"I think I was, what, sixteen? I remember every night at dinner she'd rant about wanting a pool. What was the issue?" she asked.

Bob lightened up. "The borough didn't allow swimming pools for some reason." He sipped his coffee. "Mom's lawyer, Dick Weidnitz—remember him?"

"Yes."

Bob and Lisa smiled at each other and, in unison, said, "Weid-nitz don't take no shits." They both broke into laughter.

"That guy fought tooth and nail for her," Bob said. "But there were restrictions on water usage and so on."

Lisa shook her head and sipped her coffee.

A waitress came by. "Changed your minds? It's getting on dinner time. We've got some meat loaf, hot outta the oven," she said.

Lisa and Bob looked at each other. Neither had eaten all day. They nodded.

Bob suddenly realized he was famished. "Remember Mom's meat loaf?"

Lisa nodded. "So good."

"Anyway," Bob continued. "The township eventually told her she could have her pool if she drilled her own well on her property to supply the water."

"They probably figured she'd relent," Lisa said.

"Probably. They didn't know who they were dealing with."

"God, did she *ever* back down from a fight?" Lisa asked rhetorically.

"She eventually did," Bob said. "She probably didn't even want the pool at that point. Dad was so patient with her."

Lisa agreed.

They were silent for several minutes. The waitress returned with their food.

"Meat loaf, gravy on the side, green beans, and mashed potatoes," she said. "Can I get you something else to drink besides coffee? Coca-Cola maybe?"

Bob and Lisa each nodded. The waitress walked away.

Lisa cut into her meat loaf and ate a small bite. "How did we end up in Verona anyway? After Phoenix?" Lisa asked.

Bob placed a napkin on his lap and picked up a fork. He quickly gobbled three forkfuls of meat loaf, took a swig of Coke and replied as he wiped his mouth. "What I'd heard is, after they closed Arizona and New Mexico, Mom drew a twenty-five-mile circle around New York City and picked a town. Totally random. Dad said her only demand was a nice house on a hill, with a view. That was it."

"On a hill?" Lisa asked.

Bob nodded, shrugged. "No idea. That was our mother."

Lisa laughed. It felt good to laugh, but it felt awfully wrong to laugh. She cut another piece of meat loaf, lifted it with her fork, and stared at it. A heavy, sick feeling overcame her as her thoughts returned to the harsh reality of what she was doing in Midwest City. After a few minutes of silence, she spoke. "I remember this conversation we had," she said, putting down her fork with the uneaten piece of meat loaf. "Must've been about a month after her house was completed. I asked her about Chuck —I figured out that something was going on. I confronted her."

Bob nodded.

"She seemed so . . . I don't know. Like she was this little kid who wanted to be a grown-up. Like she had something to prove." Lisa ran her fork across the mashed potatoes. "She was resolute about what she was getting into. And . . ." She looked at Bob and stopped herself.

"And what?" he asked.

She hesitated. Then, "She really wanted to keep her hands in the company. In Dumann. She was resentful that you didn't want her involved anymore."

Bob protested. "I needed to make changes, and I—"

Lisa shook her head. "I'm not saying you did anything wrong, Bob. Mom could be tough to work with. She and Dad had some kind of, what do they call it? Kismet? They were *supposed* to be together. Fate. He could handle her, siphon off the good stuff. No one else was able to do that."

"Symbiosis. That's what they had," Bob said.

"But, I remember that night so clearly. When I walked out of her house, the air was dry and crisp, and the sky was so black. So many stars," Lisa said, looking out and visualizing the night. "I stood there, looking into Mom's kitchen. I could see her moving around like a tiny little ant. Then the light went out. I wanted to give her the benefit of the doubt, maybe she knew what she was doing. But, I also had this feeling of doom, you know? Like she was making a really bad decision." She looked at Bob for confirmation.

He nodded.

She continued. "I used to think that all Mom ever did was busy herself with luncheons and fundraisers and vacations. I figured Dad gave her a desk in the office just to inflate her ego."

"We all thought that," Bob said. "Maybe he did. I really don't know how involved she was, but she definitely had influence."

"Do you think she liked being a mother, raising kids?" Lisa asked. "Because it often seemed like she found the whole family thing a nuisance."

Bob shrugged, shook his head. "Honestly? I think a lot of the time it just overwhelmed her." He took a sip of Coke. "You were probably too young to remember Ellen."

"The Irish girl? Barb mentioned her once or twice, but I have no memory of her," Lisa said. "She lived with us for a short period when Dad was in Okinawa, right? That's about all I know. Was she a friend? Did she work for Mom?"

"Good question," Bob said. "I was pretty young myself—seven, maybe eight. But I have this memory of all of us in the kitchen . . . you, me, Barb, and Gwen. And Mom and Ellen. There was music and commotion, but, you know, in a good way, and I can picture Mom dancing around."

"I can't imagine that Mom would've been happy with Dad so far away," Lisa said.

"Exactly. Which would explain why Ellen was there."

"I wonder what happened to her. Did she and Mom keep in touch?" Lisa asked.

"Who knows."

Lisa took a mouthful of potatoes and became lost in thought. Feelings of regret and guilt surfaced. She pushed her plate to the side. "I felt so angry, betrayed, when I found out she was working with Chuck and then driving around Little Rock, *my* town, telling strangers what she was doing. And keeping it all from me."

"You were right to be upset. Look where we are now," Bob said.

"But, I don't want to badmouth her," she said. She began to cry. "All summer, she was asking me to bring the kids to an auction. I gave her so many excuses. Why didn't I just do it, come to Oklahoma, bring Shawn and Lizzie and make her happy?" Lisa put her face in her hands and sobbed. She picked up her napkin and blew her nose.

Bob understood the guilt Lisa felt; he felt it as well. If he had just indulged his mother's desire for inclusion at Dumann Paving, perhaps she might've dropped the whole idea of the auction barn. If he had let her know from the start, just after Kyle's death, that she still had a desk in the office, she might never have moved to Oklahoma.

"And you know," Lisa said. "There was some screw-up with the house she built. I have no idea how it happened, but her name was on the deed, not mine and Justin's."

Bob raised his eyebrows.

"Right after she and Chuck separated, she told me about the deed. Came clean. She was even crying, said she took advantage of the error and got their business loan by collateralizing the house."

"Jesus Christ," Bob said. "That's ... *bad*."

"It is, I know. I was furious. *Furious!* She said she wanted to make it right. I mean, she'd been paying the property taxes anyway, and all the utilities. She paid for construction, for god's sake." Lisa picked up her roll and took a bite. "She said she was selling the house to us for one dollar, and she'd continue to pay taxes on it if..." Lisa threw down the roll and cried.

Bob pushed his empty plate aside and waited.

Lisa wiped her eyes, blew her nose again, and looked at Bob. "... if I'd let her continue to live there." She sobbed. Through her tears, she added, "Can you imagine? She actually thought I might not allow her to stay."

They finished their meals in silence.

50

Late August 1971

THE MOURNERS, WHO INCLUDED JOAN'S IMMEDIATE family, most of the seventy-five Philadelphia-based employees from Dumann Paving and Flooring and friends from Elkins Park and Verona, stood around the gravesite. Pastor Donald Lewis from Grace Presbyterian Church in Jenkintown spoke quietly with Bob, who stood holding his younger daughter in his arms. Bob's wife, Rebecca, was by his side holding their older daughter's hand.

"So just your sister Barbara will come up to speak, is that right?" the pastor asked Bob.

"Ah . . . yes, that's right," he said, turning to look at the gathering crowd around him. He felt slightly ashamed that he didn't want to speak to the mourners. Or that he was unable to.

Gwen placed a bouquet of flowers on Kyle's headstone. "Love you, Daddy. Always," she whispered. She put a second bouquet by her mother's headstone, which was carved and ready to be set in its reserved spot long before Joan's body arrived at Stonewood Cemetery, near Trenton.

"Love you too, Mom," Gwen said. She looked at the casket that sat on large bands of heavy canvas, hovering above the freshly dug hole in the ground. She walked back to stand next to her husband.

The family did not place an obituary in any newspaper, but

word of Joan's murder made its way to the East Coast. It was big news throughout Oklahoma, where details of questioning, arrests, and anticipated trial dates were included in articles on the front pages of the *Oklahoma Times* and newspapers throughout Arkansas and Texas. The *Courier-Post, Philadelphia Inquirer,* and *Evening Bulletin* picked up the news but only reported on it once.

"Are we ready, then?" asked the pastor.

Bob checked with his siblings and nodded.

"On this sunny August morning, which is already quite humid," the pastor began, "we are reminded of nature's contradictions. On the one hand, the sun warms our bodies and our souls, brings us joy, entices us to come outdoors, enjoy fresh air, ride a bike." He looked at Lisa. "Or, in some cases, a horse," he added with a soft smile.

Lisa took Justin's hand.

"Parents frequently tell their children to get out in the sunshine. Don't stay inside on a sunny day like this." He looked at Barbara's oldest child, Marie. "Right?" he asked her. She nodded sheepishly. "And yet, the sun can do damage, for sure. Its heat can be oppressive, forcing us to retreat indoors. It can burn our skin, make us shield our eyes. Those same parents who tell their children to go outside on a sunny day will also caution against too much sun." This time, he looked at Barbara's youngest child, ten-year-old Stephanie. "Wear a hat, don't get too much sun, you'll burn," he said in a fatherly manner. Stephanie giggled.

"He's nice-looking," Lisa whispered to Barbara. "I like him."

Barbara smiled. She'd heard so many of her mother's stories about volunteering at the church, about a brief job there, about the pastor and his wife, Lillian, that Barbara felt it was somehow appropriate to bring this church back to Joan again. She knew her mother had regrets for some reason in connection with Grace Church, though Barbara never understood what they were. When Barbara called the church and explained the nature of her request, the pastor was accommodating and sympathetic. Barbara offered to make a generous donation to Grace in Joan's memory.

"It's important to know when to embrace the sun and when to retreat," he said, pausing to connect with as many mourners as possible. He fixed his eyes on Mary, off to the side, who stood holding Red's arm. Next to her were John and James, who did not remember Joan, and their wives, who'd never met Joan. Mary's two youngest children had also never met Joan. Mary brushed away a tear.

The pastor continued. "How do we know when something is helpful or harmful? Sometimes we heed the warning of those who love us. Sometimes, we can just feel it, we get a sense that we are in a situation that doesn't feel comfortable or safe, and we can either retreat or ask for help to move forward." He paused again to look around. "Joan set out on a journey following Kyle's death. She wanted to make a new life for herself, to be independent, to do something exciting. For whatever reasons—and none of us will ever truly know what they are—Joan chose to live this new life her own way, on her own terms, without heeding the concerns of those who loved her."

He looked at Franklin, standing next to Barbara, her arm locked in his. Franklin recalled Joan's dismay as a new mother, her sadness and frustrations. He couldn't understand it back then; she seemingly had everything. It was a different time.

"Joan Sondersohn Dumann was a generous, witty, outgoing, fun-loving, and, yes, complicated woman," the pastor said. "We do not blame her for her own demise; she was a victim of a cold-hearted individual. Likewise, we cannot blame ourselves."

He looked at Lisa. Lisa *did* blame herself. Tears stained her cheeks. Gwen handed her a tissue.

"Yes, she was complicated. But let's remind ourselves why we loved her," he said, speaking so personally it was hard to believe he had never met her. "She gave her four children a wonderful home life, with trips and summer camp. She made sure they were safe, that they knew they were loved. They grew into strong, kind, and successful adults, people you want to emulate." He looked at each of them. "Your mother did a good job," he said, nodding and smiling. "Now, I would like to ask Barbara Oakes Wilson to come read something she has prepared."

He held out his arm, and Barbara walked toward him. She took out a folded piece of paper from her purse. Before unfolding it, she blew her nose. She looked at Franklin, who smiled at her encouragingly.

"I live in California, so my mother and I would talk on the phone every few weeks to keep in touch. During one of our conversations earlier in the year, she told me that one of the maintenance guys who worked at her apartment complex called her 'Silver Girl.' Not in a disrespectful way. He was very fond of her." She looked at her siblings. "A lot of people liked Mom. She could be very charismatic and funny."

Gwen smiled and nodded.

Barbara continued. "I asked her why he called her that, and Mom explained that she had mentioned to this guy that she liked the song 'Bridge Over Troubled Water' by Simon and Garfunkel."

Bob saw the pastor close his eyes, smile, nod.

"She said she loved the song because it felt like her anthem, particularly the lines, 'Sail on, silvergirl / Sail on by / Your time has come to shine / All your dreams are on their way.'"

Barbara choked on the last word and tried to hold back sobs. She attempted to speak but couldn't. Her husband rushed to her side and placed both hands on her shoulders. He held her for a minute. Lisa and Gwen, along with other mourners, cried as well.

Barbara nodded, blew her nose again. She mumbled something to her husband, took a deep breath, and continued. "She said the song was like Dad talking to her, encouraging her." Barbara took another deep breath, blew out slowly. She was calmer now. "She told me that the maintenance guy remarked that she wasn't yet a 'Silver Girl' and Mom said, 'Kiddo, you have no idea what a bottle of hair dye can do.'" Barbara broke into laughter through her tears, and several people in the crowd laughed as well. "That was Mom," she said with a smile. Then she looked at the casket. "I hope all your dreams are on their way. Rest in peace, Mom." Barbara's husband held her arm as they walked back to the group.

Pastor Lewis returned to his spot before the mourners. "That was a moving and beautiful story, Barbara. Now, I'm told that Joan was not a particularly religious person. She didn't belong to a church. She questioned God's existence. And that's okay," he said reassuringly. "But since she loved popular music, I don't think I'll ruffle any feathers if I recite Ecclesiastes 3:1–15, which was also made popular in a rock music version by the Byrds, of whom I'm personally a fan," he said with a smile. He began. "There is a time for everything, and a season for every purpose under the heavens. A time to be born and a time to die..."

Bob squeezed his eyes together. His bottom lip tightened. He put his daughter down, raised his hand to his face, and began to cry.

Mary recalled the last time she'd seen her cousin. It was thirty-two years ago, at Sonny's wedding. Joan was alone, with her two small children, and Mary had hugged her, engaged in some small-talk with her. She'd invited Joan to come up to Bucks County for lunch with Barbara and Bob. She remembered Joan looking pleased, almost thankful and relieved. Mary had been sincere about the invitation; Red was less enthralled with the idea when she mentioned it to him. "After what she did to Franklin?" was his response.

Mary had fond memories of Joan during their long, lazy summer days at Ivyland. She recalled a time before the family sold the house, when she was ten and Joan was six, and she taught Joan how to play jacks on the kitchen floor. It was a rainy day, there wasn't much else to do. *We must've played all afternoon*, Mary thought, picturing Joan's delight at learning something new. *And she was good at it.*

Following the service, the mourners gathered at Bob's spacious house in Holmdel, New Jersey, for lunch and remembrances about Joan. Cars were parked one after another on his leafy street and down around the block as well.

In the living room, Barbara walked over to Bob, who was filling a glass with Scotch as caterers set out dessert trays and coffee.

"Quite a crowd," Barbara said, looking around the room.

"It's touching people want to pay their respects." He took a sip of his drink and looked around. "Did Franklin not come back with you?"

"No. I think he didn't want to . . . you know . . ."

"Have to explain to people who he was?"

"Exactly," she said.

"It was nice of him to attend the funeral. Considering," he said while taking another sip and carefully eyeing his sister.

Barbara nodded. "He still loved her, even after all this time. Can you believe it?"

"He loves *you*," Bob said. "Don't you think that's why he was there? For you?"

She reached for a bottle of white wine and filled a glass. "Yes, of course. But, I mean . . ." she said. Then she stopped herself.

"What?" he asked.

"Why are we talking about all that now? On this day? It just seems, I don't know, disrespectful."

"We all loved Mom. But that was part of who she was, her history, her choices. For whatever reasons." He swirled the ice around in his glass. "Do you ever wonder . . . ?"

"What?" she asked.

"I mean, the divorce. The affair. Why did Mom . . . you know—"

"You're wondering why she cheated on Franklin?" Barbara asked, feeling annoyed. "I swear, Bob, does it really matter? She was very young. Maybe she was depressed." She sipped her wine.

"Did it upset you when I told you about finding my birth certificate?" he asked.

She looked around the room and back at Bob. "Maybe a little. I was a new mother myself, so I was going through so many emotions. So, yeah, I guess it was unsettling. It made me feel really bad for Franklin. And a little bad for you, too, to think that you'd been keeping that secret to yourself since high school."

An older couple approached Bob and Barbara.

"Hello, I don't know if you remember us," the woman said to Bob. "Milt and Linda Gross? From Verona?"

"Of course," said Bob. "I played football with your son, um . . ."

"Arthur," Milt said. "We are so very sorry about your mother. She was a delightful person. We took a cruise with your parents one year, had a fabulous time. Remember?" he asked his wife.

"Do I!" She looked at Bob. "Your mother was hysterical. Got up on the stage with the band, started singing 'Que Sera Sera.'"

"She was quite good, as I remember," said Milt.

They smiled at Barbara.

"Hi, I'm Barbara, Joan's oldest daughter," she said, extending her hand toward Linda. "I was already out of the house by the time my family moved to Verona; that's probably why we've never met."

"Nice to meet you," Linda said. "Has anyone told you how much you resemble her? At least . . . the way she looked twenty-some years ago." She looked at Milt.

"Regrettably, we lost touch with your parents," he said.

Barbara attempted to smile.

"Anyway, so tragic, the whole thing," Linda said, with honest sympathy in her tone.

"Have there been any leads?" Milt asked. "I mean, arrests?"

Bob and Barbara were uncomfortably quiet.

Linda elbowed her husband.

Bob broke the silence. "Thanks so much for reaching out." He placed his hand on Linda's arm. "Listen, go ahead and get yourselves some food," said Bob enthusiastically. "There's plenty of it."

After the couple walked away, Bob took another sip of Scotch. "It's true, you know," he said, still looking at the people eating lunch, whispering to each other about why anyone would want Joan Dumann dead.

"What's true?" asked Barbara.

He looked at his sister. "You are her spitting image. And me? I look nothing like her. So I guess I must be the spitting image of . . . Paul Anderson, that son of a bitch."

"He did you a favor. Kyle was the best father you could ask for," she said, gently taking the glass from Bob's hand. "I think you might want to hold off on this. No one wants to pay their respects to a drunk."

He gave his sister a fake punch. "I need some air," he said and headed to the backyard.

Barbara began to make her way toward the kitchen when she was stopped by a couple she did not recognize. The woman touched Barbara's arm gently.

"Hello, Barbara," she said with a smile. "I'm sure you don't remember me. I'm your mother's cousin, Mary. I guess that makes me your first cousin once removed." Mary was nervous. "Or, I don't know, I've never understood those *removed* designations."

Barbara remembered Mary in name only. "Of course. Hello, Mary."

Both women felt awkward. Then Mary leaned in to hug Barbara.

"I'm sorry. I truly am," Mary whispered into Barbara's ear. She moved back a little and rubbed Barbara's arm softly. "God, you were just a little girl the last time I saw you."

Barbara noticed how red Mary's eyes were.

Red held out his hand to Barbara. "I'm Russell. So sorry for your loss, Barbara. I mean, this was a loss for all of us."

Barbara nodded politely.

Mary's eyes scanned Barbara's face. "You look so much like her," she said, wistfully.

"People have told me that."

"Barbara," she began. She wanted to be tactful, but honest. She knew Joan's children were in pain, and she had her own feelings of loss and regret. "I want you to know that I always cared about Joan. Growing up, you know, we were four years apart, so I was often in my own world. But she was a sweet little girl. Shy, awkward."

346 | *Eileen Brill*

Barbara was curious. She wanted more.

"I do remember happy times, laughing with her. Especially at Ivyland, you know, the family had a summer house, and your mother was different up there. Carefree, unrestricted. As a child should be."

Pastor Lewis approached Barbara, Mary, and Red. Barbara made introductions.

"It was a lovely sermon, Pastor," Mary said.

"Thank you, Mary." He turned to Barbara. "I wanted to tell you and your siblings that my father actually knew your mother when they were kids."

Barbara was surprised. "Really? We haven't heard from any of her childhood friends."

The pastor nodded. "Yes, well, Dad read the article in the paper, and he recognized her maiden name. He mentioned the story to me, and he said, 'Don, I knew this woman. This is so sad,' and I told him that your family asked me to do the service. It was quite a coincidence."

"Who is your father? Mary asked."

"Norman Lewis," he replied. "He went to camp with your mother."

"Oh, that must've been Camp Green Meadows," Mary said.

"Yes, that's it!" said the pastor, pointing toward Mary. He looked at Barbara. "Dad spoke of your mother fondly. I believe he referred to her as 'a lovely, confident young woman.'"

Mary and Red exchanged subtle glances. Neither would have thought to characterize young Joan as confident. Regardless, when Mary turned her head, what she saw on Barbara's face was the same broad smile she could remember seeing on her young cousin, many, many years ago.

"Yes," Mary said. "She sure was . . . lovely and confident. That was my little cousin."

51

WHEN DEAN RANDALL ENTERED JOAN DUMANN'S apartment three months after her murder, a chill ran down his spine. He did not want to be the one to have to gather the last of her possessions, insignificant items that had not been claimed by her daughter, donated, or thrown away, but since he'd drawn the shortest straw among the other guys in the maintenance crew, today was his lucky day. The superintendent also asked Dean to try to pull up the carpeting, if possible, so that the guys from the carpet company could just do the installation and not be troubled by the gruesome scene of a bloodied apartment. Folks had finally stopped gossiping about the murder; maybe the reputation of the Stagecoach Apartments could be restored.

The venetian blinds were drawn, giving the living room a dark, ominous sadness. Dean opened them, and bright sunshine immediately spilled in, changing the blood stains from a grayish hue to deep mauve, almost black. He was prepared for the dried blood, caked into the carpet, because he'd seen it each time he stood just outside her apartment watching the cops collect evidence in the first few days after she was killed. Everyone did that: lurked around, peeking inside to see the murder scene, whether from some macabre fascination or to help figure out what happened and who might be guilty. He'd also seen the blood spots that trailed outside to the parking lot on the carpet in the hallway of her building. The superintendent had pulled up that portion immediately after the cops were finished with their work.

The living room was empty except for a bookshelf. He had come prepared to throw trash into plastic bags and maybe box up a few things, but he had not expected to see any large items like furniture. In the kitchen he found a frying pan that appeared to be new, and a 1971 calendar on the wall. He opened each drawer and cabinet, finding nothing. The refrigerator had been disconnected. He pulled the calendar off the wall and picked up the frying pan. A dead plant sat on the window sill; he tossed them all into the plastic bag. He peered into the bedroom; it was empty. On the bathroom vanity were some cosmetics, a roll of toilet paper, a pack of matches. He added them all to the bag. He walked back into the living room and scanned the floor, looking for the easiest place to begin ripping up the carpet.

He headed toward one corner of the room and knelt down, reaching his fingers into where the floor met the two walls. The rug was loose and easy to pull back, and as he yanked it further, he saw a large, manila envelope resting on top of the padding. He grabbed the envelope and inspected the handwritten New York address of a Miss Ellen McGrugan, along with Joan's return address. Plenty of stamps already affixed. *Who the hell missed this during the investigation?* he wondered. Such a shame Joan hadn't gotten to mail it. He put it on the floor by the front door, propping it against the wall, reached into his back pocket for a carpet knife, and resumed the work of removing the carpeting.

Thirty minutes later, the large sections of carpet rolled and bound with rope, he stood by the front door, sweat pouring down his face and neck. He took one last glance around the apartment. He had liked Joan; she was funny, outgoing, and confident. And generous. She did nice things for people just for the hell of it, like when she gave him tickets to a two-day rock music festival in the Arbuckle Mountains.

For weeks since Joan's murder, Dean had followed every news article in the *Oklahoma Times*. It made no sense to him that not one of Joan's neighbors had heard or witnessed anything that could help the case. One neighbor across the hall said he heard two loud bangs, as if heavy books or other objects had fallen to the floor. The neighbor also heard a woman's muffled voice saying, "Don't do this," and it sounded to him like some sort of lover's quarrel. Chuck Galloway had been questioned by the DA in the weeks following her death but had pled the Fifth. And now, months after her body had been recovered from the pond, her murder case was finally coming to trial. Two guys, employees at Diamond Ranch, were being tried for her murder. There was talk of a third suspect who had not been publicly identified.

Dean opened the door to leave and bent down to grab the large envelope on the floor. He stared at it for a minute, considering the best course of action. He decided to throw it in the mailbox before lunch. What the hell.

"So long, Silver Girl," he said as he closed the door.

52

October 1971

DESPITE THE "INSUFFICIENT POSTAGE" STAMP ON THE large manila envelope, it nevertheless arrived at its destination, albeit probably much later than it should have. Ellen recognized the return address; Joan had sent her a birthday card in April, along with a brief mention of the business, "My horse and live-stock auction outfit is up and running."

It was early on a Saturday evening, one of the few in which Ellen did not have plans with friends, family, or colleagues from Ranstead High School where she had been the nurse for the last ten years. She took a seat at the dining room table in her home, the second floor of the Staten Island duplex owned by her brother Joseph and his wife, Louise. She stared at the large envelope, trying to guess what it might contain; Ellen and Joan had never exchanged anything more than birthday greet-ings or Christmas cards in the last twenty-five years. She didn't know if the contents would involve something wonderful or unfortunate. Using a butter knife, she sliced open one end of the envelope, peered inside, and pulled out the papers, looking again inside the envelope for photos. None. Unfolding the pa-pers, she recognized Joan's handwriting immediately, and when she saw the salutation, her stomach tightened. She put the letter down and went in the kitchen to pour herself a glass of wine before reading whatever was written to Sheriff Maghan of the Midwest City Police Department.

Filling a glass from an open bottle of cabernet sauvignon, Ellen recalled the last time the two women had seen each other, at Marcus's funeral.

"I've missed you," Joan had said to Ellen as the two women embraced in the meetinghouse following the service. "You left so abruptly—I had hoped it wasn't me."

Ellen held her friend tightly as Joan broke down with uncontrollable sobs, to which Ellen fully related.

Sitting back down at the table, Ellen took a sip of wine and lifted the first page of Joan's letter. As she read the description of Chuck Galloway, it dawned on her that Joan had never mentioned a business partner, though not much detail about anything was ever included in the cards Joan and Ellen sent to each other. Upon reading the words *I may not live to see daylight tomorrow*, Ellen froze. She took another sip of wine and held onto the glass, keeping it close to her lips, as she steeled herself for what was to come. The description of Chuck did not bode well for what was written on the remaining pages. Joan described meeting Chuck for the first time in Little Rock and her initial instincts about him. She talked about money, providing exact dollar figures that she invested in the business and the amount of the loan from the bank in Midwest City. She mentioned threats made to her by Chuck and one of his underlings, who was also her employee, someone named Waylan Trust, and she provided dates and locations of various hostile interactions between herself and her partner. She said she'd once overheard Waylan say he would commit arson for Chuck if the business was failing.

She gave the name of a lawyer in New Jersey, Dick Weidnitz, who was counseling her, as a friend, as to what information she needed to gather to protect herself, legally, financially, and otherwise, against Chuck. She also mentioned that Mr. Weidnitz had drawn up her will and estate plan, which he had on file. She listed contact information and names of two former employees, Ernest Walls, who had been falsely accused of theft and fired by Chuck, and Edie Holbrook, who had quit her job immediately after learning the partnership was being dissolved. Joan was certain both Ernest and Edie would be willing to testify against Chuck, if necessary. She provided other names and phone numbers: Malcom D'Argento, who had been unable to collect the balance on two colts purchased by Chuck; Weston Sacks, the manager at the Savings and Loan of Midwest City; a man who owned a horse-breeding ranch in Dallas, of which Chuck apparently owned a small share; Roy Herbert, the head handler at auctions.

Ellen read six pages and counted those remaining; she was halfway through the letter and entirely through her glass of wine. She felt buzzed from the cabernet, but it had not eased her tension. She skipped to the last page:

> *Since you said we could meet in the morning to discuss my concerns, I will be in your office bright and early. Hopefully, by the time you receive this letter, you and I will have already had a long conversation and discussed everything I've written and then my fears will finally be taken seriously. I can't bear to think of the other scenario in which you are learning all this for the first time. Regretfully, that would only mean one thing.*
> *Sincerely,*
> *Joan S. Dumann*

Ellen was nauseated. Joan's words read like some kind of suspenseful murder mystery, and she had to wonder if perhaps

Joan had, in fact, lost her marbles. Why would Joan have mailed this complicated and alarming letter to Ellen and not the sheriff, and with no note attached by way of explanation? Who in her right mind would stay in a place where she felt unsafe, unsupported, and alone, when she had options?

After living among the Sondersohn/Pruitt clan for several years, Ellen certainly was privy to myriad conversations about Joan and her supposed histrionics, her tendency to create problems where there were none, yet Ellen had always believed that Joan was misunderstood. Ellen's frequent reference to Joan about their being kindred spirits had been heartfelt and genuine back then. But time, distance, and her own life experience and maturity had given Ellen a new perspective on many people from her younger years, so perhaps she was unable back then to fully grasp the implications of what may have been Joan's fragile psychological state.

Ellen recalled the birthday card Joan sent her in April, which had included a photo of Joan smiling, arms extended in a victory pose, in front of a large, painted sign that read "Diamond Ranch Sale Barn, Auctions Wednesdays and Saturdays." Behind her was a large horse trailer parked in front of a barn. On the back of the photo, Joan had written "Joan the Horse Broker! September 1970." Ellen thought it seemed like an odd business venture for a woman in her fifties—and from Joan's background—to embark on, but, regardless, this was not the photo of a woman under duress or in danger. It occurred to Ellen that she no longer knew Joan or the kind of person she had become over the course of twenty-five years. Joan could push people's buttons; it was what had ultimately caused a rift between the two of them. But would that lead someone to commit murder?

Throughout Joan's moves from Pennsylvania to Phoenix to New Jersey to Little Rock and, finally, to Oklahoma, they had shared photographs—Joan of her children as they grew, and her grandchildren, and the myriad trips she took, and the houses she lived in; Ellen of her naturalization certificate, GED diploma, nursing certificate, and trips to Coney Island and Asbury Park—along with simple messages like, "Enjoy the holidays with your family," or "Hope your birthday is relaxing and fun." But neither woman made promises they would not keep or extended invitations on which they would not follow through. Their relationship, however it had been defined so long ago, was part of another time, and each woman understood this and asked for nothing more than to know that the other was alive and well. But what Ellen had just read did not provide that reassurance. She walked over to the telephone and dialed "0."

"Yes, hello, Operator. I'm tryin' to reach someone in Oklahoma," she said, her Irish accent less pronounced than it had been thirty years ago. She glanced over at the return address on Joan's Envelope. "Ah, Midwest City. Outside of Oklahoma City, I believe. Joan Dumann, D U M A N N."

After a few moments, the operator gave Ellen a number and told her she would be connected. Ellen took down the number and had the impulse to hang up and call the next day when she might feel less anxious and better prepared for . . . whatever. She wasn't sure she was ready to have a conversation with Joan, in the event she even answered.

After four rings, there was a click and a recorded message: "I'm sorry. The number you have dialed is no longer in service. Thank you."

Ellen hung up. She picked up the receiver, looked at the number she'd written down, and proceeded to dial it. There was a chance the operator had connected her to the wrong number.

"I'm sorry. The number you have dialed is no longer in service. Thank you."

Ellen felt a sudden tightness in her stomach, and nausea quickly set in. She reassured herself that there were infinite explanations, none of which had anything to do with Joan losing her life: she'd moved, she'd had her number changed to an unlisted one, her line had been cut off by the telephone company for nonpayment; perhaps there was even another Joan Dumann in Midwest City whose line had been disconnected.

She sat down and considered her options. She could try to call one of Joan's children. Since she did not know the girls' married names, she decided to try Bob. She knew he still lived in New Jersey, but where?

"Hello, Operator," she said. "I need the telephone number of a Robert Dumann. That's D U M A N N. No, I'm sorry, I don't know which town."

Ellen waited, playing nervously with the telephone cord. *Haven't seen Bob since Marcus's funeral . . . when was that? Nineteen fifty . . .* "Yes, Operator. Thank you."

The operator connected her. Three rings and a click.

"Hello?"

"Yes, hello. Ah, my name is Ellen McGrugan and, ah, I am calling for Bob Dumann. Have I reached the right number?" She could hear her voice quivering.

"Yes," Rebecca said. "This is his wife. Can I help you?"

Ellen explained that she was an old family friend, someone who knew Bob when he was a little boy. She apologized for calling out of the blue, and said she received a cryptic letter from Joan, with whom she'd had very little contact over the years. She wanted to make sure Joan was okay.

"A letter? From Joan?"

"Yes. It was rather . . . disturbin'," Ellen said.

Rebecca paused. "I . . . think I should take your number and have Bob call you back. He should be home in about an hour."

"Certainly," Ellen said. "But, I, agh . . . this is a strange and awkward question, but . . . oh, I'm just going to say it. Can you please, I'm sorry, would you mind tellin' me . . . is Joan . . . *alive?*" Her voice cracked. She knew this was direct. She needed to know. There was no way around it.

"I'm . . . sorry . . . I'm sorry to say, there was a terribly tragedy."

Ellen tensed up. She prepared herself for the words. She knew it was coming, the very thing she feared.

Rebecca stayed on the phone with Ellen and told her about the murder and the rather brief trial, after which the jury of nine men and three women had acquitted Waylan Trust and Roy Herbert of murder following just five hours of deliberation.

"Unfortunately, the state didn't manage to build a very strong case against the defendants. Key pieces of evidence couldn't be located, and the defense attorneys . . . well, they just poked holes in every witness's testimony," Rebecca said.

She explained there had apparently been a third man in Joan's apartment the night she was murdered, but neither Roy nor Waylan knew him.

"Roy was knocked unconscious and woke up several hours later, alone. Didn't remember much. But he said there was definitely a third guy who was pointing a gun at Joan's head."

"I am in shock," Ellen said. "I'd like to share this letter with the family, you know, because it seems it was the last thing she ever wrote. And, frankly, there's a lot in here," she said, shaking the letter in her hand. "There's information which, I would think, the prosecutin' attorney or the DA or the police, I don't know, might want to investigate. That is, unless it's too late?" Ellen looked down at the letter. "She says her partner, this Galloway guy, threatened her. Told her to watch her back. Said there were people who had axes to grind with her." Ellen shivered.

"Give me your number, Ellen. I'll make sure Bob calls you. He will want to talk to you, I'm sure of it."

A copy of Joan's letter arrived in the DA's office three days after the conclusion of the trial. The partnership books, along with a copy of Joan's last will and testament, of which Dick Weidnitz had the original, were located in Joan's ranch house inside a hidden safe, the location of which she described in her letter. Also in the safe were receipts, canceled checks, and Ernest's notes on the many fabricated vendors.

The DA found compelling evidence in Joan's letter of Chuck's shady business dealings and unethical practices, and possibly even proof that Chuck had embezzled funds from Diamond Ranch. Such information might've helped build a case for why Chuck would have wanted Joan dead. Yet the DA could not find a direct link to tie Chuck to the murder, and so the State of Oklahoma did not open up a new case once the verdict had been rendered in the case against Trust and Herbert.

53

September 1973

LISA HAD LEARNED THAT THE *OKLAHOMA TIMES* WAS DOING a follow-up article on Diamond Ranch two years after Joan's murder, so she called a staff reporter she had met during the trial.

"My family is not finished with this," she said to the reporter. "We want to tell our side of the story, our mother's side. Galloway may not have been charged with her murder. He may not have killed her or had anything directly to do with her death. We may never know for sure either way. But he needs to be held accountable for how he treated her, the utter disrespect he showed her. His unethical practices." Lisa sent the reporter a copy of Joan's letter.

What began as a local story about the Sale Barn and Chuck's meteoric rise in the community eventually became, after weeks of investigations by three staff writers, an all-out exposé of a group spreading throughout Oklahoma City and Fort Worth, known as the "Lower Heartland Gang" or "LowHeart Gang."

And now, Chuck was facing ten to twenty years in prison on racketeering charges related to bribery for kickbacks to the group.

"He's a despicable human being, especially compared with how authentic and generous your mother was," Rebecca commented to Bob one evening over dinner. "Can you believe what she did for Ellen?"

No one, including Ellen herself, had any inkling of the extent of Joan's appreciation of Ellen's past kindness.

"I'm in her will?"

"Yes. If you can believe it, her estate only recently finished probate, because, as you can imagine, there was so much to sort out. But, yes, she indicated that she wanted to leave Miss Ellen McGrugan the sum of five thousand dollars."

Ellen was in shock. "F... five thou—?" She sat at her desk in the nurse's office at Ranstead High School on the first day of classes, holding the receiver, staring at the poster on the wall with the words "Infections aren't fun... for *Any*one!"

Dick Weidnitz spoke again. "Miss McGrugan? Are you there?"

"Yes, I am, sorry. I guess I'm just a bit... mystified. She and I hadn't seen each other for over twenty-five years. Why would she leave me anything?"

"I can't answer that. I only know what her will stipulates. Anyway, you'll need to come to my office in Morristown, New Jersey. Are you able to do that?"

"Yes, of course."

Ellen hung up the phone and sat back in her chair, reflecting. Joan had closed the door on their friendship long ago. The casual and occasional cards back and forth had seemed to satisfy Joan's need for contact, and she never asked for more. Then the letter. So mysteriously sent, as if it had been a spontaneous, and a final, gesture. Yet her inclusion of Ellen in the will... well, that had obviously taken some forethought.

Such an enigma, Ellen mused.

Arriving home after work, Ellen sifted through her mail and perused the recent issue of *Ms.* magazine. She read the cover

("Yes! We Do Have Women Astronauts!") and began skimming the article about an astronaut named Mary Funk, who, along with twelve other women who passed NASA's rigorous testing program in 1961, had been cast aside by the agency when it canceled all further testing of female astronaut candidates.

Ellen looked up from the magazine, recalling a time when Joan mentioned that Amelia Earhart had been her childhood heroine.

Ellen tossed the magazine aside and grabbed a pen and some scratch paper. She began jotting down some figures. She opened her desk drawer and pulled out a calculator and began ticking away. She sat back in the chair, stunned. Then she perked up, reached for the telephone and called her brother.

"Joe? It's me. Yes, everything is fine. Listen, you know that cute little property by the water? The one with the retail space in front? Yes, that one. It's been on the market for over a year now. Joe, I . . . think I'd like to buy it. I mean, I'm *able* to buy it. I'll explain tonight."

She hung up the phone and looked around her office. She loved being the school nurse, loved the students, the teachers. It was a rewarding career. She was proud of where she'd taken her life, considering her modest beginnings in this country, and how her career choice had led to a financially secure and independent life.

But she'd had the idea for the last three years: a new direction, something that would be hers alone. And Joan, with her abundant generosity, was the conduit who could make it happen. "We're kindred spirits," Ellen remembered telling Joan many times in the beginning of their relationship. As time went on, Ellen knew this wasn't entirely accurate, but it felt right when she said it, and she had genuinely meant it at the time. Like Joan, Ellen understood the pain, as a young woman, of feeling judged, alone, and vulnerable, of wanting to control your own life, make your own choices. Of always longing for the mother you never knew.

Six months later, the tiny bar/cafe was up and running. Ellen had moved out of her brother and sister-in-law's house and into the second floor of the property on which she'd been able to put a down payment with Joan's gift. Her brother had hand-painted the wooden sign next to the front window, and the name on the sign always piqued people's curiosity and led to many conversations between Ellen and her patrons. They would ask her to tell them the origins of the name of the bar: Kindred Spirits. Ellen would explain that, in her younger years, she'd had a dear friend who was fashionable, funny, generous, engaging, ambitious, and strong-willed. And that Ellen and her friend found in each other a kindred spirit, *a meaningful connection*, if only for a brief time in their lives.

That was all her patrons needed to know about Joan.

54

THE ELECTRICIAN CROUCHED ON THE FLOOR OF ONE OF THE
bedrooms in the blue granite colonial house. Reaching into the
hole he'd just cut in the wall for an additional outlet, he had to
shove his arm in practically to his armpit to feel for the wires. As
his fingers searched, they brushed past a piece of paper wedged
in the wall and, as he pulled the wiring out, the paper came out
as well. It was an envelope—rather tattered and torn around the
edges—with an address written in long-hand to someone in
Collingswood, New Jersey. He read the name of the addressee:
Norman Lewis. He turned on his flashlight to peer inside the
wall—for what? Dollar bills? Jewels? Photographs? Skeletal remains? Something else that would make this the day he had a
good story to tell?

Deciding that the envelope and its letter inside were not of
any interest or value to him, he put it aside for the fifth, and
most recent, owner of the house, Grace Jasner.

"He's still alive," Grace said to her husband and three sons later
that night as she sat down at the table for dinner.

"Who?" her husband Rob asked, placing the vegetable
bourguignon on a trivet in front of her.

She leaned forward to take in the aroma. "The guy on the envelope, Norman Lewis. I googled him," she said, plunging the serving spoon into the savory dish.

"Mom was on the internet all day," her eldest, Ben, said as he ripped off a chunk of crusty bread. "She's obsessed with this Joan person." He rolled his eyes and popped the bread into his mouth.

"Joan and her family were the first residents of this beautiful house," Grace said.

"So, what, you're going to contact this Norman guy?" Ben asked.

She nodded enthusiastically. "Joan never mailed the letter. Maybe Norman would appreciate reading it after . . . however many years it's been."

"How old is he anyway? Do you even know?"

"Yes, I do," she said, satisfied with her day of research. "They were the same age. Both born in 1915." She winked at Matt.

Matt calculated using his fingers. "Ninety-two? That's older than Grandma and Grandpa."

"I'm not sure it's a good idea to contact him, Grace," Rob said as he took his seat next to his wife. "You don't know his physical or mental state. He could be very fragile. Seeing the letter could be very upsetting."

"Give me some credit, Rob," she said. "I'm not out to give an old man heart failure. I just . . . wonder if there's a love story here."

"Or an unrequited love story," said Rob.

"How did you find him, Mom?" Ben asked. "How do you know he's alive, that it's the right Norman Lewis? Sounds like a common name to me."

Grace tapped her head and squinted her eyes. "Your mother is a good investigator, Benjamin."

"A great investigator," Rob said. "And a talented writer as well." He reached for her glass and took a sip of her wine.

Grace passed the salad bowl to Rob. "It's really sad," she said to him. "I didn't find much about Joan other than the fact that she was murdered. I'm so curious about her and what her life was like. And the *letter*." She put a forkful of the bourguignon into her mouth. "Oh, my god, Rob, this is delicious! My mom used to make beef bourguignon once in a while when I was a kid. It's such an old-fashioned dish," she said, wiping her mouth. "But *this*, this is outstanding."

"Glad you like it," Rob said.

"I'm going to delve into Joan Sondersohn," she said. "There's a story here, I bet. I'll dig around, see what I can find."

"You know, Mom, not everyone's life is so remarkable. You might find out she was just, like, a nobody," Ben said. "Then what kind of story will you have?"

Grace sipped her wine. "You know something, Ben? I sometimes think the most interesting stories are about people who are rather unremarkable on the surface, but you dig a little and find a story. You connect the dots. Cause and effect. A letter never mailed. A murder. The butterfly effect," she said, her eyes wide and intensely focused on her son.

"What's the butterfly effect?" asked Matt.

"Mom's saying that Joan's life might have taken a different course if she had mailed the letter," Rob explained. "The universe would have shifted from that one decision."

"That's crazy," said Matt.

"Not really," said Grace. "We're all products of our decisions." She looked at each of her sons and her husband, and smiled.

THE END

Author's Note

A Letter in the Wall is a work of fiction, but the inspiration for the story came from a letter found in a bedroom wall of my house in 2007. I immediately began researching the name on the personalized stationery and quickly learned a lot about the real Joan's family, but not much about Joan herself. What I did find out, and what was overwhelmingly the most prominent piece of information about her on the internet, was that she had been murdered in 1971. Thus began my journey to know Joan and learn how and why she ended up in Oklahoma. My initial goal was to try to piece together a biography of this woman, who had been raised in the Quaker tradition but who seemed to have strayed far from her ancestral and geographic roots.

The internet is a miracle of our time, a storehouse of information that, when used effectively and critically, can shed light on who a person, long-deceased, *may* have been. Websites such as Ancestry.com can supply a wealth of information in the form of public records, and from these sources I learned of the real Joan's multiple marriages, divorces, the births of her children, the death of her mother and other family members, and her various addresses.

But public records from the past, I discovered, are often unreliable, with multiple and conflicting dates, misspelling of names, and barely legible handwriting serving as the only method of record-keeping.

And even when complete and accurate information can be found, it cannot provide the *why*, the juicy meat of a person's life that reflects decisions, conflicts, challenges, hardships, and longings—all the drama of being human and existing among other humans in a world that is, more often than not, out of our control.

So I took what scant information I could piece together about my letter-writer and began to imagine the person she had been, from her early childhood up until her death. She became real to me, to the point where I knew what brought her joy, what motivated her, what frightened her, and what confounded her. I crafted a story about someone named Joan, so that she could exist somewhere, forever.

Perhaps the truth would make an even more compelling story because, as Mark Twain famously said, "Truth is stranger than fiction, but it is because fiction is obliged to stick to possibilities; truth isn't." I wanted to explore the possibilities through a fictionalized story. I wanted to make sense of my character.

As with Grace in the last chapter, I wondered how Joan's life might have turned out differently had she mailed that letter to the boy from camp. The actual letter I found in the wall of my house was rather cryptic and gave no indication of how she knew the boy nor what their relationship had been. There was limited information on him as well, so I imagined how these two teenagers, one from Pennsylvania and one from New Jersey, might have met each other in the 1930s and what in Joan's mind could have prompted her to write, but never mail, a letter to the boy. As I considered the emotional and situational complexities that could have fostered Joan's ambivalence, I began to get a picture of who this girl might have been, and my imagination took over from there.

1. In the first three chapters, we see Joan at different points in her life: in her mid-fifties, as a three-year-old, and as a teenager. What similarities and differences in her personality are apparent in the various stages of her life?

2. What family dynamics do you observe during the dinner conversation after Joan comes home from camp? Why do you think is Joan so reticent to engage with them?

3. Joan's challenges in being a new mother are compounded by her loneliness and post-partum depression—experiences that the medical community (and husbands!) have historically tended to minimize. How might today's resources and information have changed things for Joan, both in the short term and the long term?

4. What need does Paul fill for Joan immediately following Annabelle's death? What do you think she hopes to accomplish by seducing him?

5. What is the relevance of Joan's observation of her cognitively declining grandmother? What effect do you think that experience has on Joan?

6. After Joan goes to New York with her father, she suddenly has "peace of mind" despite feeling invalidated by Marcus. Where does this feeling of resolution and peace come from, and how does the experience embolden her to move forward in seeking the church position?

7. What changes does Joan experience after the loss of each of her husbands? How do these losses help her to evolve and better understand herself?

8. What similarities are there between Anabelle and Ellen in terms of the roles they play in Joan's life and what they each teach her about herself?

9. Why do you think Kyle is so accepting of Joan and willing to endure her erratic moods and demands? Can you speculate what role she may have filled for him?

10. How might Joan's life have turned out different if she had been given an actual job title at Dumann Paving? Would she have been capable of running the company after Kyle's death?

11. Why do you think Joan chooses to stay in Little Rock after Kyle's death? What is the allure of partnering with Chuck?

12. What evolution do you see from young Joan to the woman she becomes at the end of her life? Which of her external struggles are still prevalent today? What resources are available to young women now that may not have been available to her as a young woman?

13. Is Joan a sympathetic character? Can you relate to her challenges, ambitions and frustrations?

Acknowledgments

Thank you to Brooke Warner, Lauren Wise, Jennifer Caven, Laura Matthews and the rest of the staff at SparkPress for your superb work.

My heartfelt appreciation to Anne Dubuisson, my developmental editor, whose enthusiasm made me feel like mine was the only manuscript she was reading, and to Rachel Kobin, founder and director of the Philadelphia Writers Workshop, whose feedback and support helped me kick-start the direction of the book in its early stages. I am grateful to the archivist at Friends' Central School, who allowed me to sift through old yearbooks and files.

Thanks to my dear friends who served as beta readers and cheerleaders, providing honest and constructive feedback on the manuscript: Allison Boise, Julie Cohen, Carol Meranus, Mindi Roeser, Nancy Schnee, Scott Schnee, Mirjam Seeger, Susan Weinberg, and Susan Wisch.

Last but not least, thank you to my beloved Eli (MT^2), my most avid cheerleader, and Jared and Aaron for your love, enthusiasm and support.

About the Author

EILEEN GRACE BRILL was born and raised in Philadelphia. She graduated from Carnegie Mellon University with a BS in Economics and spent several years writing professionally for the hotel, restaurant, and commercial real estate industries. She stepped out of the corporate world to raise her two sons, and for the last several years she has been a sign language interpreter and a painter.

Eileen lives outside of Philadelphia with her husband, Eli, and their two mutts, Athena and Gaia.

A Letter in the Wall is her first novel.

CPSIA information can be obtained
at www.ICGtesting.com
Printed in the USA
BVHW070715171221
623984BV00002B/10

2 370001 604018